To Mom,
"Merry Christmas 2003".
All our
Ian, Jane, & ....mom
and Sister.

X X X X .

The Evergreen Tea House

HONG KONG STORIES
CONNECTIONS — STORIES OF EAST ASIA
LOST RIVER AND OTHER STORIES

The Evergreen Tea House

by

David T. K. Wong

Muse Publishing Limited

First published in 2003
by Muse Publishing Limited
26 Mill Road Salisbury SP2 7RZ UK

Printed in Hong Kong by Paramount Printing Co. Ltd

© David T. K. Wong, 2003

David T. K Wong is hereby identified as the author of this
work in accordance with section 77 of the Copyright,
Design and Patents Act 1988

A CIP record of this book
is available from the British Library

ISBN 0-9546102-0-2

To my sons
For things left unsaid

Chronology of chapters

Catching snakes

1

School was out for the summer. The colony was smothered by a damp, sapping heat, a harbinger of the more severe ordeal to come in August. The sky was cloudless and empty, except for two kites circling in search of prey. Below the city spread like a thick, discoloured garland of concrete around Victoria Harbour. Here and there, on both sides of the harbour, small squatter settlements erupted like eczema on the indifferent faces of distant hills.

Chu Wing-seng, walking behind Little Ho, took off his horn-rimmed spectacles with his right hand and wiped his brow with the short sleeve of his white shirt. He did so without breaking stride with his Patrol Leader. His shirt was already sticking to his body and the long khaki trousers, the thick cotton socks and the sturdy shoes recommended by his leader were adding to his discomfort. His left hand was clamped around a four-foot walking staff.

The haversack on his back seemed increasingly burdensome, though it contained only a bottle of mineral water, a packet of Jacobs' tea biscuits, a first-aid kit and a white cotton face towel. His mother had packed them in the belief that he would be practising some woodman's craft for a Boy Scout proficiency badge. If she had known he was out to hunt venomous snakes, she would have been deeply distressed, both for exposing himself to danger and for going against one of the Buddhist notions she held inviolate.

His mother believed life to be sacred, even if it were that of a mosquito or a fly. An insect might be the reincarnation of an unfortunate person, she explained. Doing harm in one existence attracted retribution in the next. It was therefore always essential for a person to accumulate merit by living well and doing good deeds.

Chu Wing-seng found some of his mother's ideas irrational. If nobody took a life, how could there be meat and fowl to eat? Not everyone could be a vegetarian like her. Besides, why shouldn't harmful pests such as lice and gnats be eliminated? DDT had been invented for that purpose.

If his mother had meant to broaden his mind, she should dwell on more practical matters, he reflected, as he gazed upon the city. There, on the waterfront, in the heart of the business district, stood his father's new and gleaming Gold Star Plaza. It dominated the cityscape like a symbol of victory because it was the first building in the colony to be constructed after the war that had risen to twelve storeys. One day it would be his. Or would it?

A furtive shudder of apprehension went through him. He greatly admired his father, not only for his fame and success but also for his handsomeness. His father was as elusive as a monkey, however, when it came to explaining how Gold Star worked. Nor was he at all keen about his following in his footsteps.

His mother's game was equally baffling. She had a disconcerting way of reminding him that there were other ways of making a living besides business.

Such parental attitudes had driven him to the conclusion that he had to depend on himself to make his way in business. To that end he assiduously went through the magazines on construction, banking and economics that his father sometimes left around the house. He also tried to eavesdrop on conversations conducted in low tones between his father and his closest associates when they came for dinner or for a game of mah jong. His mother, however, always seemed to have the knack for sending him off on untimely missions, to fetch her a handkerchief from the bedroom or to get one of the Filipina maids to replenish the tea.

As Chu Wing-seng trudged through the rough, wooded hillsides near Pokfulam, he recalled some of the recently overheard remarks. They centred on the war in Korea, balancing politics, profits and patriotism, exploiting loopholes in the United Nations embargo, using trans-shipments with ambiguous particulars. He couldn't make head or tail of much of it, though he gained the impression that deception was at the heart of those discussions.

He was not averse to deception himself. The afternoon's escapade was a deception. He loved his mother and did not want to worry her. But it seemed to him that deception was a fact of life.

Actually, he had been in two minds over the present outing. He had a natural fear of snakes. They made his skin crawl. They were associated in his mind with evil and treachery. The story of *Lady White Snake* showed how a snake could change form and seduce a man. His teacher in Bible class talked about of the serpent in the Garden of Eden and his English teacher had explained the meaning of the term "snake in the grass". The only thing he liked about snakes was their meat, made into soups and taken steaming hot with chrysanthemum petals, slivers of lime leaves and dough crispies. His father could be counted on to provide such treats when friends came for mah jong or bridge during winter.

Chu Wing-seng's fear of snakes was part of a wider fear over his own inadequacies. He was undersized for his age and that bred physical timidity and aversion to pain. Twice in the course of primary school he had been hit by a bigger boy and twice he had slunk away, even though he had right on his side. He had represented his retreats as turning the other cheek, practising the Christian behaviour recommended by his teachers. But in his heart he knew his retreats had been caused by terror and he suspected his classmates and fellow Scouts knew it. He soon gained the reputation of being a brainy little sissy. His mother didn't help by being overly protective when she turned up for Parents' Day.

It was to slough off such general perceptions that he had manoeuvred Little Ho into teaching him to catch snakes. His Patrol Leader had once brought a Banded Krait pickled in methylated spirits to a troop gathering. That immediately transformed him from a colourless, accommodating lad into a popular hero. Everybody including the Troop Leader and other Patrol Leaders gathered around with faces radiating admiration. They wanted to hear about the characteristics of the creature and how it had been caught. They wanted to see other specimens and when Little Ho brought in a bright green Bamboo Snake the following week, his reputation was made.

Getting Little Ho, a boy almost four years older than himself, to teach him to catch snakes was not at all difficult. Little Ho believed the best about everybody. He behaved in the exemplary manner expected of Boy Scouts, being always ready to put himself out for others. People with such a nature were rare in Hong Kong, although Little Ho seemed to be genuinely one of them.

As Chu Wing-seng stumbled his way along the hillside, he felt slightly guilty over misleading the older boy. He glanced at the harbour, crawling with motor launches, cargo junks, car ferries and ocean-going ships, and at the tenements of the Central and Western Districts below. The buildings appeared like distempered blocks from some discarded toy set. He wondered how he might one day leave his mark.

"Hey, Little Ho, we've been walking for an hour. How come we haven't found anything yet?" Chu Wing-seng called out.

Little Ho halted and retraced his steps. He had a pleasant, open face and a pair of friendly brown eyes. He was sixteen years old and a head taller than his companion. He too had a haversack on his back and a staff with a fork in his hand.

"You have to be patient. You can't be sure of always finding a snake," Little Ho said, good-naturedly. "You see, during the Japanese occupation, lots of people were starving and many came to these hills to hunt for food, including snakes and lizards. I used to come with my father. A lot of wild life disappeared as a result. It's rare nowadays to come across a civet cat or a barking deer. Snakes are still plentiful, however, so it's just a matter of being patient. If you're tired, we can have a drink of water and rest a while."

The two boys found a shady spot and sat down on some granite rocks. In the midst of that parched landscape, where neither wild flowers bloomed nor birdsong sweetened the air, they took off their haversacks and helped themselves to water and biscuits.

"When you hunt snakes, you must always remember to include a clean, sharp razor blade in your first-aid kit," Little Ho said, between bites on a tea biscuit. "Should you get bitten, don't panic. Cut across the fang marks with the razor blade and squeeze or suck out the blood. But don't suck if you've got a cut or an ulcer in your mouth. Let the blood flow freely and then head for the nearest clinic. Cutting your own flesh may sound

12

gruesome but, if you do it with a quick stroke, it shouldn't be very painful. I've done it. A bit of pain is better than dying."

"I thought you said most snakes in Hong Kong are not poisonous," Chu Wing-seng said.

"That's correct. But unless you know them well enough to know which is which, it's better not to take chances."

"What made you hunt snakes? It's not something very many people do."

"I'm not sure. At the beginning it was probably because I felt sorry for them, with everybody hating them and giving them a bad reputation. I wanted to show people they were not horrid and that many of the myths about them were untrue. They never attack people unless provoked or cornered. They are in fact quite useful in keeping down rodents and pests. Their gall bladders provide a popular tonic, their venom can be used for medicines and their meat makes delicious soup. I thought if I mastered handling them I might one day open a snake soup restaurant and make a good living."

"Not a good idea."

"Why not?"

"People only take snake soup during winter because snake meat warms the blood. No one wants to warm their blood in summer. Besides, winters are quite short in Hong Kong. You'll have no business for most of the year. It's better to open an ordinary restaurant and put snake soup on the menu during winter."

"Gosh, never thought of that. I'll have to think again. No wonder everybody says you're smart, that you're going to end up as successful as your father. You're only one form behind me, aren't you? You must have got double promotions in primary school."

"Yeah. That's kid stuff. Does everybody at school know about my father?"

"Sure. They read newspapers. My father's an admirer."

"Really? How come? Does he do business with my father?"

"No, my father's a locksmith. He runs a small roadside stall in Western, near where we live. A few years ago he read about your father building a mansion up the Peak where the gweilos used to keep out Chinese. He was over the moon. He thought it

13

was time someone showed gweilos that we Chinese couldn't always be kept under their thumb. He went out and put his savings in Gold Star shares, not that he had very much, mind you, or knew much about what Gold Star does. When I told him you were in my patrol, he was very pleased."

"My mother told me we used to live in Western during the war. Strange thing, I can't remember much about that. We might have been neighbours."

"Unlikely. Your family must have lived in one of the rich neighbourhoods. Our whole family lives in one room in a tenement building, right along the tram tracks. The place is so old it doesn't even have a flush toilet. We have to use metal buckets, which are taken away at night by night-soil collectors. The contents get shipped by barge to China to be sold as fertilizer."

Those descriptions nudged some blurred, pre-memory impressions buried deep within Chu Wing-seng. "Really?" he said. "How awful! My father still frequently goes for breakfast in Western, you know, at some place called the Evergreen Tea House. Has your family ever eaten there?"

"The Evergreen is very old. I think it started out as an ordinary local tea house but it has now become too expensive for us."

"It can't be *that* expensive, can it? My father has offered to take me there but I've always thought it was one of those crummy old places he goes to for sentimental reasons."

"It may not exactly be posh but you don't know what you've missed. The food there is supposed to be excellent. Its teas are particularly renowned."

"Well, I don't care much for tea. The next time my father offers, I'll ask if I can invite you along. If your family is so poor, how did you manage to get into our missionary school? Fees are high and there's a long waiting list."

"My mother's a Christian. She went to her pastor for help and he got me a free place. Otherwise I would never be there. Come on, let's see if we can't catch you a snake."

The boys resumed their walk, with fierce sunlight riding high upon their shoulders once again. Black granite rocks erupted through the thin top soil here and there and radiated heat like furnaces. Little Ho, walking in front, systematically turned over rocks and fallen branches.

"Sometimes, when you spot a bit of sloughed-off skin, you can count on a snake being around somewhere," Little Ho explained, as he continued to poke into nooks and crannies. "The outer layer of skin has a pattern but no colour. The pigment cells are in the deeper, living layer of skin. There are no really big snakes here, like the anaconda or the African rock python. Those grow to well over thirty feet. The biggest snakes we have are the hooded Chinese Cobra and the King Cobra, both growing to around fifteen feet. Most snakes can put away large meals and live for a year without eating. Not enough is known about their life-spans, however. Some have lived in captivity for over thirty years."

After a while Little Ho turned over a rock and immediately lifted a hand to deter Chu Wing-seng from approaching. He then took aim with his forked staff and pinned a snake to the ground.

"It's a Krait," Little Ho said. "Quite deadly."

Chu Wing-seng approached and saw a two-foot snake with black and white bands twisting around with its head pinned on the ground.

"Quite young. Not a good specimen," Little Ho said, bending to catch the snake by the base of its head.

The reptile thrashed about in an attempt to free itself. When that failed it wound itself around Little Ho's arm.

The snake's jaws were opening and closing. Chu Wing-seng could see its fangs and white throat. His own throat went dry and he took a step backwards.

"If you grip it as I'm doing, it can't bite you," Little Ho said, seeing his companion step away. "Don't be afraid if it winds itself around your arm. It's not a python or anaconda. It can't hurt you. Do you want to hold it and get a feel of handling a snake? You've got to start some time. If you'll hold it, I'll get a container from my haversack. Or, if you prefer, I'll hold it while you get the container."

Chu Wing-seng's heart thumped wildly as he caught the insinuation in Little Ho's words. He either had to prove his interest in snakes or reveal himself as a coward and a fake. "I'll hold it," he said, after a slight hesitation.

Little Ho unwound the Krait from his arm with his other hand and held out the creature like a sceptre to his companion.

Chu Wing-seng reached out with trepidation. Little Ho told him where and how to hold. After Little Ho was satisfied with the grip, he said: "That's right. You've got it. Are you comfortable enough for me to let go?"

"Yeah."

Little Ho released his hold and immediately the snake began thrashing about.

Chu Wing-seng's heart pounded. The creature's jaws were working menacingly. Its coils felt cold and clammy around his skin and its undulating movements seemed unbearably disgusting. Suddenly, a mixture of fear and guilt took possession. The notion of being bitten and dying an agonizing death frightened him. He remembered his mother's admonition against taking life. What if the snake was really the reincarnation of a person? Killing it might lead to his being condemned to a similar fate. Besides, could the evil in snakes be transmitted through its coils?

That jumble of thoughts caused him to disengage the coils hurriedly with his other hand as Little Ho had done. With a cry he flung the snake away with all his might.

"What's the matter? Have you been bitten?" Little Ho asked, rushing to his side.

Chu Wing-seng recoiled from where he had thrown the snake and held up his hands in disgust. He slowly shook his head. His face had gone white and he was on the verge of tears as he watched the reptile slither away into the undergrowth. He was trembling and sweating as Little Ho examined his hands and arms for a possible bite.

"Never mind. You haven't been bitten. It wasn't much of a specimen anyway," Little Ho said, at the end of his examination. "Let's sit down and have another drink of water. We'll catch a more splendid one next time."

"There won't be a next time, will there?" Chu Wing-seng responded, still breathing heavily and wiping his hands and forearms on the seat of his trousers.

"Why not?"

"Because I've let you down. Everyone will be laughing at

me for being frightened. They will laugh at you too for taking someone like me to hunt snakes."

"How would anyone know whether another person has been frightened, unless that other person chooses to say so? I don't know whether you were frightened. All I know is that you held a living Krait in your hand. It was a highly venomous snake and you decided to free it for some reason. Perhaps to spare a life. Not a single member of the troop or a single student in our school has ever held such a dangerous creature with his bare hands. Apart from us, of course."

Chu Wing-seng looked at the older boy and marvelled at his goodness. Here was a person in possession of damning information about a lapse by another. It bestowed upon him the power to ruin a reputation or to exact a price for silence. Yet he was exploiting neither.

Chu Wing-seng judged his secret safe. But he couldn't figure out whether Little Ho was acting out of genuine friendship or whether he was just too simple-minded for his own good. In either case he owed his companion a debt of gratitude. He was determined that one day, after he had become as rich and powerful as his father, he would repay it.

Letter from the blue

2

It was not the best of times for Chu Tung-po, the Chairman of the Gold Star Industrial and Financial Corporation. China's involvement in the bitter conflict in Korea depressed him and the United Nations embargo on trade that resulted had disrupted business for both himself and his friends. His son, Wing-seng, had apparently been acting up in school. Serenity had asked him to contact the Scout Master to resolve the boy's failure to fulfil certain requirements for proficiency badges. Problems big and small seemed to be piling up. The last thing he needed was to be accused of causing deaths. And yet, there it was in front of him, the accusation in damning black and white.

"You are responsible for the deaths of my parents," the letter read. "You have pushed them into a corner, tormented them with the slow ruin of their lives. You gave them no quarter. Capitulation or death. They have chosen death. I hope you have profited mightily. Some may regard you as a pillar of society, but I know you for what you are — a disgrace, a blood-sucker, a destroyer of innocent lives!"

Chu Tung-po knitted his brows as he read on. He sometimes received missives from cranks but this one seemed to carry the ring of truth. It purported to come from a young man named Yam Tin-chee, though it gave neither the names of his parents nor his own address. It stated that his parents once owned a grocery store, inherited from a previous generation. They sought only a decent living and sufficient income to send him, their only son, to university. They were on their way to achieving their goal when Gold Star came along.

When Gold Star opened a supermarket across the road, the business of his parents suffered. They soon found it impossible to compete. They worked harder, stayed open longer, shaved their margins. But it remained a hopeless struggle. The old folks should have sold out and been done with it. He had urged his father to do so. His father was proud, however. He had spent his life preserving his patrimony and he did not want to be taken for a quitter. He felt an honest man had a right to make an honest living. It shouldn't be taken away for no reason. He would not accept defeat. He mortgaged his premises to the hilt and when that proved insufficient, he started using money set aside for his son's education. He sank deeper and deeper into debt. When the bank foreclosed, his parents swallowed arsenic and died in each other's arms.

Chu smoothed out the pages of the letter on the glass top of his mahogany desk and looked across to the four paintings on the opposite wall. They had been done by a local artist he admired. The painter had used plants to symbolize the seasons, pink plum blossoms to denote spring, orchids to represent summer, then golden chrysanthemums and pliable bamboos.

The paintings, with their insinuations of eternal things, evoked in Chu a peculiar sadness. Seasons came and went but the old dilemmas remained. Deaths were eternal. He thought he had finished with them until his own came along. Now another two to justify. Everything he had done had been with good intentions, to succour those he loved, to improve the temper of the times. He had no need for more wealth. Money was only a means to an end, a counterpoint to the political power held by others. It was to enable his views and those of his close associates, dubbed "the Evergreens" by the popular Press, to be taken into account. Had he not allowed Serenity to give whatever she wished to charities? Had he not himself been unstinting in support of worthy causes?

He had tried to play the game according to the rules. He never set out to harm anyone. Every move he made seemed an abstraction, a figure flashed on a dealing screen, a barely noticeable blip in the hurly-burly of the marketplace. For every winner there had to be a loser. He had taken losses with good grace on many occasions. Why couldn't others do the same? Why should losers take their own lives? That was not playing the game. How could he be blamed? If Serenity knew of the letter, it would distress her enormously.

He ran the fingers of his right hand through his fluent hair. It was a gesture he had first made years before, out of nervousness during his first Press conference as Chairman of Gold Star. One of the women journalists told him afterwards that the gesture gave him an appealingly casual air. That mannerism gradually developed into a habit.

His thoughts turned to a response to the letter and he pressed a button on the underside of his desk.

Mrs. Ada Leung entered, notebook and pencil in hand. She was a middle-aged woman wearing black-rimmed spectacles and a dark, loose-fitting business suit. Her hair was unfashionably permed. She gave the impression that no secret could be extracted from her even under torture.

"Any commitments this morning?" Chu asked.

"No, Sir, not till 12.30, when you are to lunch with Mr. Chambers of the Chartered Bank at the Victoria Cricket Club."

"Good. Get Mr. Wong at Gold Star Insurance on the phone and then run off a copy of this letter for Detective Chan. Stamp it confidential and ask Detective Chan to come and see me after he has digested it."

"Yes, Sir." Mrs. Leung disappeared from the room.

A good, dependable woman, Chu thought. One of the few nowadays who took loyalty and discretion to heart. It was not that he was paying her excessively. It was just part of her character and he wished there were more like her in the company.

A few moments later one of the three telephones on the left side of Chu's desk rang and Mr. Wong was on the line. "Good morning, Mr. Chairman. You wish to speak to me?"

"There's a young man named Yam Tin-chee. His parents died recently. I want him made beneficiary of an endowment policy sufficient to get him through university. Shouldn't be too generous, but not too mean either. Something normal and comfortable. Make it appear his father had taken it out before he died. Not through Gold Star, however. Nothing must appear in our books. Call in a favour from one of your shadier confreres. I'll pick up the tab personally, plus whatever commission is deemed necessary. Payment should not be traceable back to me. Got it?"

"I'll need more details, Sir. What is the father's name and where can the beneficiary be located?" Mr. Wong asked.

"Don't know. Will let you know the moment I do."

"I'll work on it right away, Sir. I understand your requirements."

The moment Chu put down the telephone, there was a knock on the door. Mrs. Leung entered.

"Detective Chan is out of the office, Sir," Mrs. Leung said. "I've left a message for him to come the moment he returns."

Chu nodded and Mrs. Leung retired.

Left to himself, Chu looked with distaste at the pile of documents and files in the in-tray. Payments to approve, cheques to sign, proposals to read, contracts to study, inter-company squabbles to settle. How intolerable it was all becoming. And to add to everything, a libellous letter and more deaths on his conscience.

He pushed back his chair and walked to the window. His suite was on the penthouse floor of the Gold Star Plaza. He stood before the tinted glass with his hands clasped behind his back, taking in the panoramic view of the harbour and the Kowloon peninsula.

Cranes, gantries and pile drivers were everywhere. Putting up more characterless tower blocks, he thought. Cutting corners as well. He shook his head slowly. Some of them belonged to him or at least to Gold Star. Land was scarce, population bloated, demand high and profits good. A steady stream of refugees had been flooding in since the end of the Pacific War. The government chanted the mantra of development, prosperity and progress. Investment bankers, stock brokers and shareholders chanted "More! More! More!" It was so easy to get carried away.

He looked with dismay at the spreading canyons of concrete and steel into which the sun scarcely shone. The devouring of green and open spaces seemed unstoppable, the decimation of old buildings a foregone conclusion. Traffic lights and road signs sprouted where trees had once been and urban muck lay where grass and spring flowers would never grow again. It was a blight, a disfiguration, a corruption, eating into a society where the God of Wealth smiled too readily. What could anyone do? People needed somewhere to live and to earn a living. In some areas of Kowloon the population density was the highest in the world. If he stopped building, someone else would pick up the slack.

Beyond that dispiriting sprawl loomed the eroded hills of the New Territories, marking time, awaiting the pleasure of developers and speculators. And beyond those hills lay his ancestral home and reminders of unspeakable guilt. But goodness was also buried there. Traditions, truths, myths, songs of the soul, links with the past, commitments to the future. That beloved land and the burial plots of his ancestors were now barred to him by cruel politics and outrageous fortune.

He caught a reflection of himself in the tinted glass, sporting his hand-made clothes, seemingly debonair and without a care. Women fawned upon that handsome image. It was a mirage. The only woman he loved was Serenity, wife and keeper of his conscience. He could visualize her face, so heartbreakingly beautiful and serene. Yet looking at it inevitably reminded him of what they had once shared and lost.

Why was it so difficult to be a decent man, to lead an untroubled life? He sought simply to be a good son, a good husband, a good father, a good employer, a worthy custodian of money entrusted by others. Yet accidents and exigencies perpetually conspired against him. An unresisted temptation, a small bending of the truth, some convenient rationalizations here and a few white lies there, and suddenly the whole moral balance was askew. One found oneself pounding ever faster on the treadmill of competitive pressures, simply to avoid tumbling into the abyss. Things done could obviously not be undone. But was there really no way to recapture any of the simple hopes and aspirations of youth?

The letter from Yam posed those conundrums anew. He was the originator of the very concepts that had driven Yam's parents to suicide. The claim of offering wider consumer choice was a sham from the start. Had he not laid down the rules for targeting affluent neighbourhoods with existing traders? Had he not expounded on economies of scale, promotional items, loss leaders, snappy advertising, financial muscle and lower borrowing costs? Even now, was he genuinely trying to make amends or was he merely mounting a salvage operation?

His mother used to take him to a neighbourhood grocery in Canton. The owner knew everybody and would pass the time of day with regular customers, chatting about births and marriages, ailments and misfortunes.

He remembered the owner particularly, a jolly old man who always asked him about his studies. If he could recite a new poem the owner would reward him with a piece of candy or a liquorice plum.

Why had he eliminated that human element from his supermarkets? Prices and quantities were fixed. Goods standardized and pre-packaged. Transactions quick and anonymous. A few punches on a keyboard were all that was required. Efficiency and profitability were the watchwords. No staff would ever ask a child about his studies, let alone reward him for progress. If anyone paid attention to children at all, it would be to try to catch them pilfering.

What a cold and bloodless world he had helped to create! How could that represent prosperity and progress? He feared Wing-seng was already being lured by the riches and glamour of modernity, like a fish being lured by a brightly coloured fly. That was why he had tried to distance himself from his son's upbringing, hoping that his wife would be able to teach him Buddhist virtues and help him understand the duality of things, the negative and the positive, the soft and the hard, the deeds hidden in shadows and those in the light. But the auguries were not good.

A telephone rang and the Chairman returned to his desk.

"Detective Chan is here, Sir," Mrs. Leung said.

"Show him in."

The door opened and Detective Chan offered his greetings. He was of medium height and solidly built, with a head of short, iron-grey hair. His face was lined and his features rough and peasant-like. He had retired from the Police as a Detective Sergeant after thirty-five years of service and had been engaged by Gold Star a couple of years back as Deputy Head of Security.

Chu was glad he had engaged the man. He had turned out to be another loyal and trustworthy employee. At the time, people in the Personnel Department had expressed reservations about the man's suitability. They claimed he was old, an ex-copper who had spent his life on the streets, and was unlikely to know anything about installing infra-red security devices, positioning surveillance cameras or debugging rooms. What they had overlooked was that Detective Chan was street-wise and had contacts in useful places. He had lived up to those expectations.

"Please take a seat. What do you make of the letter?"

"Doesn't seem to be an attempt at extortion, Sir. More like a desire to let off steam, as I see it. Can't recall having read about a double suicide or any inquest into such. Could have passed unnoticed, as routine. The boy's been stewing on this for a while, I reckon. Can't judge whether he'll do anything else though, like writing to the Press."

"I agree. Have to end it before it goes any further, regardless of whether he has a legitimate gripe or not. Run this through your connections and see where it leads. Is the inquest over or is it pending? Find the names of the parents, where the boy is staying and as many other details as possible. But don't make contact. Whatever you find out, pass it to me or Mrs. Leung and not to anybody else. I need to have your assessment before determining whether to get lawyers and others in the company involved."

"Understood, Mr. Chairman. I'll get on to it right away."

Father to a village

3

Some eight hundred miles north of Hong Kong, in the Anhui village of Thirsty Hills, Cheng Yin hobbled on his crutches towards the shed housing the sow and its litter. Where his left leg ought to have been there was only a stump, ending above the knee. He had lost the leg during the assault on Luting Bridge during the course of the Long March. As he was about to lift the wire loop securing the wooden gate to the farrowing quarters, he heard the voice of his wife.

"Let me do that," Ah Dun called, from outside the pen where the barrows and gilts were cooling in the mud.

Cheng Yin rested one hand on the gatepost and watched his wife waddling towards him in her cheap black rubber boots. She was, like him, dressed in a patched, short-sleeved, blue cotton shirt. The only difference was that she wore long trousers with the legs tucked inside her boots. She placed her hand on top of his, rubbed it affectionately, and said: "Why don't you attend to things nobody can help you with?"

Cheng Yin saw the obvious tenderness in his wife's eyes and her hand, strong and callused, felt reassuring upon his. Her plain, weather-beaten face pleased him more than ever. He could not help wondering, however, whether he had been right to take her away from the secure routine of the Soo mansion for the vagaries of a pig farm. She might no longer be a bondsmaid but there remained servitude just the same. The shifting political orthodoxies of the day could be more oppressive. Thoughts and feelings he wanted to share with her had to remain unexpressed. Even in the privacy of their own bed, some things had to be left unsaid.

"There'll be time enough for other things," Cheng Yin said, forcing a smile. The summer day had been brutally hot, without even the whisper of a breeze. He recognized the smell of Ah Dun's sweat. It mingled with the odours of the farm, the parched air of the village and those of his own body. He felt a comforting sense of familiarity.

"You're a hopeless liar," Ah Dun laughed, as she entered the farrowing quarter, shutting the gate after her. "Don't forget you're father to a village of sixty-one households, totalling three hundred and twelve mouths. You'll never have enough time to attend to all their needs."

A father to sixty-one households, Cheng Yin reflected. What a struggle it had been! The very name of the place was uninviting. Thirsty Hills. Located in the uplands of Anhui, it was connected to the nearest town by seven miles of dirt track. It had been a triumph of endurance merely to survive. He first came across it when he accompanied his father and the bodyguards to collect rent for a landlord.

The village had no school, clinic, electricity, running water, irrigation or community organisation. Two communal wells served the handful of families subsisting there. Trees in the neighbourhood had been progressively sacrificed for fuel, so that it was a trial to make anything grow in the eroded, sun-baked earth. The will of landlords and rent collectors was law.

Because of what he had seen, he had run away at the age of sixteen to join the Red Army to create a better China. In the course of the Long March he had fought innumerable skirmishes and killed more enemies than he could remember. He had been one of the twenty-two members of the Second Company of the Fourth Shock Regiment selected to capture Luting Bridge. The assault had succeeded, though it claimed the lives of four of his comrades. And he lost a leg in the process. Each survivor was given a fountain pen, a notebook and some eating utensils as a reward.

He also received ten silver dollars as severance pay after losing his leg. Later he received another ten dollars as dowry for Ah Dun from her master, Herbalist Soo, the kindly man who tended his wound. Marriage led quickly to a son, whom they named Cheng Ching or Cheng the Righteous.

By the time he got back to Anhui with his family, however, his father had died. He and Ah Dun decided to rent a plot at Thirsty Hills to start a pig farm. Since he could no longer fight for the ideals he believed in, he thought sharing the hardships of the peasants would demonstrate his commitment to his fellow men.

"Only a litter of ten this time," Cheng Yin said, as he watched his wife nudging the piglets into the farrowing stalls. "We have to be careful the sow doesn't crush another young one. We've enough trouble maintaining meat rations as it is."

"I'm sure you'll think of something," Ah Dun said. "You always do. This lot should be right by the Lunar New Year."

Cheng Yin felt a weariness he could not express. He knew the problems he faced as Party Secretary. He was responsible for finding solutions. He would gladly pass the job to someone else, except there was no one else.

Two years before, after thirteen years of struggles and failures, he had finally managed to produce enough pork to provide each family with six ounces of meat per week. The villagers had been so pleased they marked that milestone with a celebration. He had not been able to improve on that ration since.

To increase production he needed feed in the form of corn, barley, oats and sorghum. But where was he to find them for pigs when even people went without? Animals needed antibiotics too, and there had been none for sick villagers. Pigs needed better accommodation than that of his family, richer pastures to graze for snails, earthworms and insect larvae, and a dozen other requirements. Without them how could sows produce three litters a year as they did in America, with offspring growing to over a thousand pounds in weight?

How could he explain why America produced bigger and better pigs with that terrible war in Korea? Everything American had to be demonised and denounced. As Party Secretary, it was his job to fire up villagers against American imperialism, to get them to volunteer for war in the frozen wastes of a foreign land. He knew he had not done as well as he should and the greatest reminder of his deficiencies was his own son.

"Is Ah Ching still not back?" Ah Dun asked, as they moved towards their mean brick home. Blackie, their dog, was asleep on the doorstep.

"Don't fret. He's a responsible lad," Cheng Yin said. "He'll be back in time to collect the swill. Don't forget he has a seven-mile ride from town, even if his bike doesn't suffer another puncture on that miserable road."

"Sixteen's an unpredictable age," Ah Dun said. "All very

well for him to attend secondary school in town and join the Communist Youth League. The more he learns the more he will grow restless with village life."

"He's an intelligent boy," Cheng Yin said, as he watched Ah Dun exchanging her boots for a pair of rubber sandals before entering the house. "Can't expect him to collect swill and help in the fields for the rest of his life. Everyone must discover for himself what he wants to do with his life."

Cheng Yin sat down on a bench outside their home, parked his crutches against the wall and ruffled the dog's neck. Blackie was growing as old as himself, he thought. He was only thirty-six by the calendar but his hair had turned prematurely grey. So too had his wife's. The untidy stubble around his mouth, once so resolute, added to the impression of weariness. He felt dried up and used up, like some beast of burden required to do too much for too long.

For fifteen years he had struggled to improve things in that desolate village. He had studied tomes on herbal medicine given by Herbalist Soo, in order to provide rudimentary health care. He had dug more wells and tried to pass on knowledge about irrigation and water hygiene. He had started a primary school to prevent the next generation from growing up as ignorant as their parents.

When Liberation came, he thought the threshold to a better life had been reached. True, land was soon confiscated from absentee landlords and given to the peasants. The bullying rent collectors and rapacious moneylenders disappeared. But a quota on production still had to be given to the state and those who fell behind accumulated debts just the same. As Party Secretary, he was the representative of the authorities, the enforcer of official demands.

Perhaps it was in the nature of the world to change slowly. Only his blind conceit caused him to think differently. Improvements in drainage and irrigation took time but could be nullified overnight by a rock slide. Trees took ages to grow and frost or drought could undo months of painstaking work. He felt tired. Fifteen years of unremitting toil had all but snuffed out the fire of commitment. The light had gone out in his eyes. Each generation had to cope with its own vanquished dreams.

Others had done better. Old Yeh, his former company commander and leader in the assault on Luting Bridge, was now a Major General in the People's Liberation Army. They had kept in touch. But at the moment he did not envy his command in that impossible war. Old Yeh was in Mukden, on the staff of General Peng Teh-hwa, the Commander-in-Chief of all Chinese forces in Korea. He could sense a secret pain behind words in his former comrade's letters when he talked of the courage of men prevailing over technology and machines. They had both been left with only grand words.

He had no ambition left. He recognized his own failure. To look after the sixty-one families, to join them in their dumb, obstinate struggle for existence in their godforsaken wilderness, was all he could do. Both he and Ah Dun sought consolation in their son. Perhaps a better world might be possible for him.

Korea now threatened like an approaching storm. It threatened to suck their son and other young men in the village away, perhaps to die unnoticed and alone on some alien plot. A creeping, unarticulated terror possessed him. He sensed the same terror possessing his wife, as she turned restlessly in bed. Neither could give voice to their common distress, however, because in the world they inhabited, every word or deed could be weighed by others in political terms. Fears for the safety of a son implied doubts over the leadership of the Communist Party and the inevitability of victory in Korea.

Blackie stood up suddenly and wagged his tail. He wheezed out a couple of senile barks and Cheng Yin knew his son had returned. He looked towards the path leading down into the village and saw Cheng Ching coasting home on his bicycle. His heart skipped a beat, for the lateness of the return filled him with a premonition of disaster.

Cheng Ching greeted him cheerfully. Constant exposure to the sun had given him a healthy tan. Tiny pearls of perspiration glistened on his youthful brow. He parked his antiquated bicycle against the wall of their house and bent down to pet Blackie. "Sorry I'm late," he said. "Haven't forgotten about the swill."

Ah Dun came to the door at the sound of her son's voice. "Look at you!" she remonstrated. "You're soaked in sweat! Come in and have some tea."

Cheng Ching followed his mother in and re-emerged some time later dressed in a worn blue shirt, a pair of green drill shorts and rope-soled sandals. He was a lean and healthy lad, with the well-defined muscles and grace of movement of an acrobat. He appeared quite mature for his age, however, in spite of bright, innocent eyes. He went to the rear of the dwelling to fetch a bamboo carrying pole and two wooden swill buckets before beginning his journey through the village. He strode in a jaunty fashion, with the pole balanced on his right shoulder and a bucket dangling from each end.

Cheng Yin watched his son go with a sinking heart. He had noted the raptness in the lad's face. There was also a certain spring in his gait, suggesting possession of a satisfying secret. He imagined that he, too, must have betrayed similar signs on the eve of running away twenty odd years ago. That reflection strengthened his apprehension.

Dinner passed uneventfully. His son's bright eyes appeared more subdued. After the evening meal it was customary for Cheng Yin to share the sole rickety, work-scarred table in the home with his son, he to do the paperwork befalling a Party Secretary, such as keeping records of ration coupons for oil, sugar, cloth and other necessities, while his son completed school assignments. That routine had enabled him to keep an eye on the extra-curricular readings he had imposed on his son. From time to time father and son would interrupt each other to discuss some point of fact or principle or to mull a question.

Cheng Yin had no wish to follow that routine this particular evening. Instead, he left the table to his son and settled himself on the bench outside, to gaze reflectively into the gathering gloom.

After homework, his son came out and asked: "Father, would you care to stroll a while?"

Cheng Yin rose and gathered up his parked crutches. They made off in the direction of the fields, away from the frail, flickering oil lamps of the village. Blackie followed at their heels. The intense heat of the day had cooled and there was even the hint of a breeze. The arid fields were like a darkening immensity, harsh, unamenable, eternally mocking. A faint orange smudge on the horizon was all that remained of the dying day. Neither moon nor stars were to be seen. Silence buzzed all around, punctuated by the occasional chirping of cicadas.

Father and son stopped on a slight rise close to a crude wooden shack erected to serve as a primary school. Blackie whimpered and settled at their feet. During their walk dusk had thickened surreptitiously, turning them from visible forms into felt presences.

"Father, I have something important to tell you," Cheng Ching began abruptly. "If I have caused disappointment, please forgive me. I need your help to explain to Mother."

"What have you done?" Cheng Yin replied, keeping his voice as bland as possible.

"I've volunteered for Korea. I report in four weeks."

"How is that possible? You're not of age." Cheng Yin fought desperately to maintain a casual, dismissive tone.

"I told them I was seventeen and a half."

"You told an untruth to Party officials?"

"I didn't mean to. It just came out. Two members of the Youth League decided to volunteer. We all went to support them. In the excitement I said I wanted to volunteer too. The others cheered me on. Since the other volunteers said they were seventeen and a half, I said the same."

"Didn't the officials question you?"

"No, not when I told them you were the Party Secretary in our village and a veteran of the Long March. They were more than eager to sign me up."

A silence descended between them. Cheng Yin saw at once the impossibility of remedying the position. To raise the issue of his son being underaged would reflect upon both his son's integrity and his own lack of enthusiasm for the war.

He could, at a pinch, try to prevail upon Old Yeh to assign Ah Ching to duties out of harm's way. But that would be a shameful and undignified request. They would think less of each other for it. He saw no alternative to letting his son go.

"You have volunteered to serve your country. Why should you need forgiveness?" Cheng Yin said finally, choosing his words carefully. Even in the dead of night, away from the huts of the village, there was still a chance of being overheard.

"It occurred to me while I was collecting swill that I would be leaving you and Mother in an impossible position. You can't collect swill or distribute pig manure with a missing leg and Mother already has too much to do. I didn't think when I volunteered. It was selfish of me."

Cheng Yin reached out and placed a hand firmly on his son's shoulder. The shoulder muscles felt taut beneath his touch. "It's all right, Son," he said. "When I ran off to join the Red Army, I didn't even pause to say farewell to my father. I was afraid he would stop me. I've regretted that ever since because your grandfather died before I got home. At least we will manage a proper leave-taking. Don't worry about the swill. We'll get along somehow. It only needs a small re-allocation of duties among two or three villagers. Why are you so anxious to volunteer?"

It was now Cheng Ching's turn to be silent. "Father, I was ashamed of the record of our village," he replied eventually, swallowing hard. "Newspapers and radio broadcasts tell us each day the Americans are committing rape and murder, bombing civilians and killing innocent children. How can any decent human being stand by while such atrocities continue? At the Youth League we are required to report on the number of anti-American rallies held in our respective townships or villages and the number who have volunteered. No one has volunteered from our village and our rallies have been few and far between. I felt I had to make a gesture.

"Father, we are taught to regard the men and women in the 6,000-mile Long March as national heroes, fighting and dying for what they believed in. Whenever we discuss the assault on Luting Bridge in our political studies, my heart swells with pride because you were part of that. I want to be like you, Father, to fight for things I believe in. That's why I want to go to Korea."

Cheng Yin tightened his grip on his son's shoulder as he tried to choose the right words. He felt his heart was about to break.

"The Party is in command of the nation and we must respect the line set by the Party," he said. "But the Party also recognizes that special circumstances can prevail to prevent the application of a general policy. That is the case here. It has been hard keeping this village going. It is poor, with an ageing population. If its small number of able-bodied men go off to fight, who will do the sowing and planting and reaping? The village will die. I cannot allow that. Too many people have invested their lives here. They have endured winters as sharp as razors, summer air too hot to breathe, droughts tasting of dust, hunger, diseases, decades of sapping toil. They deserve a victory against Nature, their ancient enemy."

"Oh, Father, please forgive me!" Cheng Ching cried. "I never thought I was needed so much in the village. I only thought of winning glory and returning a hero like you. When I come back, I will devote my life to the village, as you have done."

"Wars seldom make heroes. Heroes are created afterwards, to lure future generations into risking their lives for some catchy slogan or a piece of coloured ribbon. I was never a hero. I simply obeyed orders. Who would have ever heard of the assault on Luting Bridge if we had failed? It would have disappeared into the mists of history as a foolhardy attempt by a group of stupid outlaws to capture a bridge. Don't try to be a hero in Korea. It is a dirty war, with no winners. Discount the talk about pushing imperialists into the sea. Each man must discover for himself the actualities of his world, the terms of his existence and the price that has to be paid. It is like eating and sleeping. No one else can do it for you.

"You have volunteered. The only thing your mother and I can do is to help you prepare. Just do your duty as you see fit and don't take unnecessary chances. Come back safely to us. The best thing that can happen would be for the ceasefire talks at Panmunjom to bear fruit before you reach the front. We had better head home now, before your mother starts worrying."

With those words, father and son, followed by Blackie, retraced their steps. As they walked, Cheng Yin realized that his missing leg was merely the first link in the long chain of destiny that fettered him to the village and from which there could be no escape. He hoped his son's destiny would be kinder.

News of the boy's imminent departure for Korea spread throughout the village. Neighbours came in twos and threes to congratulate Cheng Yin and Ah Dun for raising so patriotic and public-spirited a son. They showed up with their simple, honest, rough-hewn faces, shuffling their feet at the door or taking a tentative seat on the edge of the bench outside. They expressed their approval through awkward exclamations and deep-throated grunts, pulling meditatively upon cigarettes during pauses. Those well-meaning sentiments were the hardest for Cheng Yin to bear.

*   *   *

Two weeks later, after the evening meal, Cheng Yin brought out a pile of small packages and placed them on the battered family table. Each was wrapped in rice paper and labelled.

"These are herbal pills and powders," Cheng Yin said. "I'm sure the government has everything needed in spite of the United Nations embargo. But some medicines may not be readily available at the front. There are bound to be cases of dysentery, fever, pulled muscles, skin rashes and, unhappily, bullet wounds. Each package is marked, to identify what it is suitable for and the right dosage. The ones wrapped in red contain a powder to staunch bleeding. Always carry one. In case a comrade is wounded, you can use it to help him before the medics arrive. If the wound is not big, spread the powder directly on it. It will check the bleeding."

Then it was Ah Dun's turn. She handed her son a canvas belt with many small compartments. "I've made this for you," she said. "It'll make it easier for you to carry medicines."

Cheng Ching hugged his mother and tears welled up in his eyes.

On a clear, sunny morning, Cheng Yin and Ah Dun put on clean clothes and patriotic faces to send their son off. A gaggle of villagers joined in and one of the village youths, a particular friend of Cheng Ching's, offered him a pillion ride into town on a bicycle.

Except for a bagful of herbal medicines, Cheng Ching's personal possessions were meagre. The lad kept his final farewell for Blackie.

War of the hills

4

Cheng Ching got his first taste of the front on a dreary day in April. Winter snows had given way to spring rains and the blood-soaked mud of the previous season had reverted to primordial ooze. That slippery mess splattered shoes, clung to clothing and caked weapons. Life in the deep bunkers and trenches was dominated by it.

Death seemed a perpetual presence around the pock-marked hills, amidst the litter of rusting barbed wire, cartridge casings, dented helmets, camouflage webbings, remnants of ripped clothing and abandoned human parts. Blasted stumps of spruce and pine stretched their mangled fingers towards the sky, signalling the threat of booby traps, trip wires and mines.

Yet, after a few days of sunshine, nature reasserted itself. The ooze dried and timid sprouts of grass and tentative buds started colouring that martyred terrain again. Larks, thrashers and the odd butterfly returned. But none of them were signs of hope, as Cheng Ching had learned. Rather, they represented fresh dangers. Anyone trampling on new growth left tell-tale trails to bunkers and gun emplacements. The enemy was observant. More circuitous routes when discharging duties and greater care with camouflage became essential.

Cheng Ching was assigned to a salient that had already changed hands five times during the year. Fierce fighting in late March left almost half the company killed or wounded. Among the replacements were two other volunteers, Lee and Lai, who had trained with Cheng Ching just south of the Yalu throughout the bitter winter.

Lee was a touchy, muscular giant with a bull neck and a swagger to match. Lai was a swarthy, foul-mouthed smart aleck who smoked at every opportunity. Like the majority of volunteers, they were peasant lads who had signed up on a whim, a dare, or an irresistible impulse to discover what lay beyond their villages. Neither possessed much political consciousness and had not even been selected for the Communist Youth League.

Cheng Ching remembered how frequently they had complained during training, particularly about the back-breaking work of digging and filling sandbags for defensive positions.

"Fuck!" Lai had exploded. "I volunteered to fight Americans, to defend socialism, not to dig fucking tunnels and trenches! Our fucking instructor's never satisfied. He keeps blasting our work with his artillery and telling us it's no fucking good. What the fuck does he expect?"

"Yeah," Lee responded, cracking his knuckles. "I came to fight too. At this rate we'll never see action. The truce talks have been going on for eighteen months. If war ended tomorrow, what would we have to show for it? We'd go home without a single trophy, without a single tale of beating the imperialists to hell. Everybody would laugh at us for freezing our balls off digging holes in the frozen earth!"

Cheng Ching did not share their lust for danger. He had learned from his father what to expect and had secretly hoped the war would indeed end before he got there. But that hope had been vain.

All along the front, the opposing forces confronted one another, seldom more than a mile apart. But at his particular salient, identified only by a number or a set of co-ordinates on operational maps, the enemy was barely two hundred yards away. They were looking down each other's throats. It was a war for snipers.

Because Cheng Ching was one of the very few in the company who could read and write, the commander, Old Tung, took him under his wing. Old Tung was a regular army man, aged about forty, who had originally been in the 135th Regiment of the elite 15th Army. Before that he had done a spell as a merchant seaman on a British freighter.

He had been assigned to the command two years earlier, after his predecessor had been killed in action. He had a squarish face and a personality like a warm stove in winter. The loss of every man weighed with him. For that reason he never allowed men to take unnecessary risks. And they loved him in return. But Chinese commanders below battalion level had little room for initiative. Old Tung could only carry out his assignments, with the Political Commissar looking over his shoulder.

Two or three others in the company had been at the front longer than Old Tung. There was no fixed tour for either regulars or volunteers. No pay, either, for volunteers. Home leave was virtually unknown. Everyone fought till he was wounded or killed, or till the war was over. Living conditions in the subterranean caves and bunkers were appalling. But morale remained high because Old Tung managed to convince the men they were fighting for a just and noble cause.

The soldier with the longest service was Mad Fan. He relished fighting. He volunteered for every dangerous mission and somehow always managed to return with no more than a few scratches. His obsession was rifling the pockets of the enemy dead, not so much for valuables, but for photographs of their families. Like most of the others, he had no pictures of his own, cameras being virtually unknown in his village. When Mad Fan brought back new photographs, they all crowded around to look and to offer comments.

Mad Fan never tired of staring at his captured photographs. He studied them for hours on end, pretending the images in them represented members of his own family. Once he broke down and confessed he could no longer visualize the faces of his children. Sometimes, looking at the pictures, he would suddenly wail: "Your Papa's never coming back. Your Papa's coming back no more."

No one could figure out whether he was crying because he genuinely felt the pain suffered by those in the photographs or whether he simply wanted to give vent to his own loneliness. Old Tung warned replacements to stay away from Mad Fan.

The first thing Cheng Ching noticed about the bunkers and tunnels was the stench of human odours and stale cigarettes. Bunkers could be massive affairs, sometimes big enough to house a company or even a battalion. The four at his salient were more modest. They were on the reverse slopes, connected to both the fighting trenches zig-zagging ahead for over a hundred yards and to the maze of tunnels and communication trenches reaching back for miles to successive defensive positions. That enabled troops under pressure to fall back to pre-prepared positions. On the forward side, tunnels and trenches led downhill to outposts and look-outs designed to alert the main garrison of any attack.

Ventilation in the bunkers was poor. Sunlight seldom penetrated. The sweat-soaked uniforms stank and provided an ideal breeding ground for lice. Most men smoked because cigarettes were the only luxury, being issued free. For a non-smoker like Cheng Ching, the tobacco fumes were a trial. During the rainy season, stagnant water and mud added to the stench.

Another horror for Cheng Ching was the blaring of foreign words from loudspeakers located somewhere out in no-man's-land. They called out intermittently and incomprehensibly, throughout the day and night. At first he thought they were simply a form of harassment. What was the point, he wondered, of broadcasting words practically no one understood? What messages were they trying to convey?

Later, out of curiosity, he asked Old Tung. His company commander responded with a throaty laugh. "You'll have to get used to that jabbering," he said. "After a while it becomes background noise. It beats the whine of approaching shells. You want to know their purpose? Well, what did Kung Ming advise back at the time of the Three Kingdoms? Did he not say that when attacking an enemy, one must first attack his heart? That's the reason for the broadcasts. They're attacking the enemy's will to fight."

"You mean those broadcasts are made by us and not the enemy? What do they say?" Cheng Ching asked, amazed.

Old Tung cocked his ear and listened for a while. The voice in English came through loud and clear. "American soldiers, greetings!" it began. "You're fighting on the wrong side. Come over and join us. Don't be misled by wicked war-mongers and greedy Wall Street capitalists. Don't let them turn you into cannon fodder. Think about why you're here. Are you volunteers or have you been drafted to fight? And what are you fighting for?

"The Korean people want self-determination. They want to rule themselves and to live in peace and freedom. They have not attacked Americans in Kansas or Alabama. They have not travelled across the oceans to harm your families and loved ones. So why have you come here to kill them?

"We are Chinese volunteers. We have come to help our Korean brothers defend their homeland and their families. Don't be tricked by the lies of militarists and war profiteers. We are peace lovers. Today is Saturday. Think of what your wives or girl friends might be doing tonight. Don't throw your lives away. Throw down your weapons and go home to them. We are not your enemies. Your enemies are in Washington."

As Old Tung conveyed the gist of the words, Cheng Ching felt as if the reasons for his involvement in the war had suddenly been articulated. The broadcast seemed to explain why he had volunteered.

"Can you teach me those foreign words?" he asked at once. "They reflect my sentiments. If I come face to face with an American I want to explain my point of view. That might spare us killing each other."

"You think you can talk to the enemy? You'll get a bullet before you can open your mouth," Old Tung said, curtly. "Leave peace-making to the generals in fancy uniforms. You can learn all the foreign words you like when the war's over. For now, just keep your eyes peeled and your head down."

When the front was quiet, as it was during April and much of May, the fear of annihilation receded and an intense boredom settled upon the men. For relief some tuned in to Radio Peking. The more sober-minded played Chinese chess or took the opportunity to learn to read and write. Those who could sleep did so. Others gambled.

Mad Fan and the volunteer Lai were fond of gambling. One day, Mad Fan played poker with Lai and four others and totally cleaned them out. His haul included a Parker fountain pen, a pair of sunglasses belonging to Lai, a penknife, a mouth organ and a gold wedding band.

"See, I'm in luck," Mad Fan crowed. "I'm always in luck. That's why in spite of all my years at the front I've never been on the receiving end of a bomb or a shell or a bullet."

"Everyone has a quota of good luck and a quota of bad luck," Lai retorted. "I've deliberately used up my ill luck by losing at poker! It seems others want to lose theirs outside."

The others, cheered by Lai's remarks, chimed in along similar lines. Mad Fan glared at them malevolently as he gathered up his winnings.

Since most of the company were illiterate, Cheng Ching

assisted them to write letters home. But what words could he use to comfort their families? The truth was disheartening. It would in any case never get past the censors or the local cadres in charge of reading out letters from the front. In his own case his father could read between the lines. If he wrote: "The powders you gave were much appreciated by my comrades," his father could gauge their situation. But what prospect was there of peasant families finding out what was actually going on?

Old Tung and the Political Commissar did their best to take the men's minds off the poor food, perpetual damp, chronic trench foot, recurring fevers and constant danger. It was a daunting task. Slogans about defeating imperialism and establishing world peace were too abstract to deflect men from their miseries.

They dreaded night duties most. Mines, booby traps and trip flares, destroyed or damaged through shelling, had to be restored. Bushes used for camouflage needed to be replaced when they withered. Then there were the patrols to set up ambushes, to destroy enemy outposts and to gather intelligence. The risk of stumbling on some rotting body part was always there.

Prior to Cheng Ching's first night patrol, Old Tung had gathered the new replacements for a pep talk. "Night patrols are not picnics," he warned. "Remember what you have been taught during training. Man is naturally fearful of the dark, but darkness is the friend of those facing a stronger or better equipped enemy. Make darkness your element. Learn to move in it as silently as fish in water. By doing a few simple things well in total darkness you can cancel out most of the enemy's advantages.

"Be light of foot when the enemy is the opposite. Train your ears to distinguish between the rustle of leaves and the rustle of clothing. Learn to draw the right conclusions from the sounds of shifting gravel and snapping twigs. Use retreats and ambushes as well as advances to gain your objectives. Master those skills and you will be able to destroy the enemy before he realizes you are there."

During his first patrol on a moonless night, Cheng Ching's heart thumped as he moved towards what lurked menacingly ahead. The highland winds seemed to carry the moans of the wounded and dying. To avoid being separated, men moved with one hand either on the shoulder of the soldier in front or by holding a part of his tunic. Once that tenuous contact was lost, men seemed to melt into the shadows or disappear like objects in a conjuror's hand. Whenever the enemy fired a magnesium flare or scanned no-man's-land with their searchlights, everyone had to fall instantly to the ground, to avoid being exposed or temporarily blinded.

During a subsequent patrol, Cheng Ching had thrown himself down in such haste that he did not realize till afterwards he had pressed his face against a putrefying body. That was preferable to stepping on a mine or a booby trap, a likelihood that increased as a patrol got closer to an enemy position. That turned out to be the fate of volunteer Lee. He became the first fatality in the company after six weeks. Although he was not particularly popular, his death cast a pall over the men.

"Lee had small ear-lobes. Fortune-tellers regard that as a sign of a short life," a soldier named Koo remarked.

Cheng Ching had frequently played chess with Koo and the observation caused him to reflect upon the size of his own ears. They were well-shaped, with long, fleshy lobes like those commonly depicted in images of Bodhisattvas. But that did little to remove the dread of venturing out at night.

Old Tung seemed satisfied with his progress, however. "You're doing all right for someone barely out of his nappies," the company commander said. "You know how to be afraid, not like Mad Fan. Stay cautious and you might just live to tell your grandchildren about this war."

Then the heavy artillery barrages began.

"Sounds like we're going to have a bit of fun, probably a ground attack," Mad Fan observed, matter-of-factly.

There was nothing anyone could do except to huddle in the tunnels and bunkers, clenching teeth and pressing lips. The bunker supports groaned under the falling shells and loose earth cascaded down on the men, making them curse and bellow like animals in terror. Some fouled their trousers.

"There goes our returning fire," Mad Fan announced. He sounded like a radio commentator reporting on a sporting event.

The next day the Americans sent in bombers, but the salient only suffered one direct hit on a forward observation post, killing three. Veterans knew, however, that in spite of the shells and the bombs, their real ordeal was yet to come.

Old Tung saw to it that every member of the company was briefed on what to expect. The People's Liberation Army was extremely democratic in that respect. High Command believed that men would be more committed if they knew their roles in an overall plan. So every foot soldier was briefed in detail. For that reason Americans invariably tried to capture Chinese prisoners while Chinese soldiers often preferred death to capture.

The attack came just before midnight, after more than forty-eight hours of shelling. The lightly manned outposts, radiating from the main fighting trench like points of a star, were the first to engage. Reinforcements were despatched as necessary along the communication trenches.

Cheng Ching watched the unfolding drama from a slit hole prepared for snipers. It was his first taste of fighting on such a scale. He saw the formidable blackness of night being punctured by the tracery of flying bullets, the explosions of phosphorus grenades and the brightness of magnesium flares drifting down on parachutes. The rattle of gunfire erupting from every outpost suggested a large-scale attack.

When trip flares and booby traps close to the fighting trench were triggered, Cheng Ching knew the forward positions had been overwhelmed. The company's heavy machine guns opened up and he himself sent burst after burst into the darkness, without knowing precisely where the enemy was.

The confused battle raged for three hours before the first enemy gained the fighting trench. Old Tung gave the signal to retreat. The men melted away into the darkness.

The enemy was given time to occupy the fighting trench, where explosives had been buried to detonate upon a counter-attack. When it came, bugles sounded and whistles blew. What was left of the company, reinforced by fresh troops, let out blood-curdling yells and swarmed back to the fighting trench. Those with good pitching arms took the lead, lobbing grenade after grenade as they went. The main body reached the fighting trench in the morning light. A brief period of hand-to-hand combat ensued. The enemy had been badly maimed and it took less than thirty minutes to put them to flight.

The fighting trench was littered with the fallen from both sides, their smashed bodies frozen in the undignified postures of death. Among them was the body of Lai. So many young lives obliterated, before adulthood could begin, thought Cheng Ching with a numbing sadness.

He wondered about his own part in the carnage. He had fired his burp gun into the blackness, in a fury of rage and fear. At one stage, he really felt murder in his heart. He was filled with hatred for those who had turned him into a wild beast. The sensation frightened him. How many dead had he been responsible for? Perhaps it was better he did not know. He saw how right his father had been. How could there be victors in such a mad conflict?

He was assigned by Old Tung to search for survivors and to disarm possible booby traps. He did the work slowly and methodically. It was common to find booby traps under corpses. After twenty minutes he had found no booby trap, but he did discover one member of his own company alive, with three bullet wounds in his body and legs. He did not know the man's name but he had him moved to the field hospital. The enemy wounded looked beyond help. The explosives and grenades had done their job well.

As Cheng Ching rounded a bend in the fighting trench, he saw a young American soldier lying flat on his back, whimpering, his eyes wide with fear and pain. A grenade had wounded him in either the stomach or the pelvis, for the lower part of his uniform was stained with blood. He seemed half-paralysed, though he still clasped an M-1 rifle to his chest, with a finger on the trigger.

Cheng Ching judged he had the advantage, for the wounded man's gun barrel was pointed towards the ground whereas his burp gun was aimed directly at the man's head. At last he was face to face with the enemy.

But the wounded man did not look like an enemy. His helmet had fallen off, to reveal short golden hair. His features were unclear because his face had been smeared with camouflage paint. But his eyes were blue. They did not seem like the eyes of a murderer or a rapist or a ruthless aggressor. He appeared only a frightened boy, hardly older than himself.

What was he here for, Cheng Ching wondered. Why was he

risking his life so pointlessly? What principle or point of honour was he trying to establish? He wanted to find out and to explain his own position. But, before he could do that, he had to save the man.

"Don't be afraid," Cheng Ching said slowly, in Chinese, cursing himself for having no command of English. "I want to help you. I have medicine to stop your bleeding."

The wounded soldier showed no spark of understanding. He made a frightened, garbled sound, with fear intensifying in his eyes. In desperation, Cheng Ching removed his left hand from his burp gun and opened his palm. He wanted to indicate that he meant no harm, that he sought only to remove the M-1 rifle so that his father's blood-clotting powder could be used pending the arrival of the medics.

As Cheng Ching reached down for the rifle the wounded man swung it up with what was left of his strength and fired.

Cheng Ching felt a searing sensation on his cheek and his right eye was immediately blinded by blood. He fired instinctively in return. He clasped a hand to his wound as he stumbled against the wall of the trench, breathing hard. With his good eye he saw the wounded man's head had been smashed open by the burst from his burp gun. Blood, brains and spinal fluids were bubbling out of the American's shattered skull.

The sight caused Cheng Ching to vomit.

Aftermath of peace

5

"The war's over. We should be going home soon," Ying said. She was bright-eyed, clear-skinned and a picture of pride and high purpose, the kind of socialist beauty often used to decorate billboards to extol proletarian virtues.

"Will it ever be over for us? Inside our heads, I mean. Can we really bury our dead?" Cheng Ching replied.

"At least you've got through in one piece, as you had promised. Your whole life is ahead of you, to do with as you will." Ying's voice was warm and sisterly. She was twenty-three and had been among the first contingent of Chinese nurses to volunteer for service in Korea.

"Too many didn't made it." Cheng Ching's voice sounded bitter. He had been involved in fighting for less than three months but during that period he had seen far too many deaths. Some of them had been caused by his own hand and each one left a shadow upon his soul. The memories of fallen comrades also haunted him. Old Tung, Mad Fan, Lee, Lai, Koo, the men he had written letters for were all gone. Others had been left maimed or captured. So many sacrificed in such an incomprehensible conflict.

"They didn't have to die," he added, after a long silence, still tormented by his memories. "Why order attacks so late in July, when the ceasefire had been all but signed? What was the point of capturing another two or three desolate hills nobody's even heard of? The whispers in the bunkers are that twenty-five thousand were killed during those final assaults, with possibly twice that number wounded or captured. Don't know if that's true. Why so many lives thrown away? What did their deaths achieve?"

"A ceasefire on our terms, according to my Political Commissar," Ying whispered, placing a cautioning hand on Cheng Ching's arm. Her bright eyes misted over. "You shouldn't talk so openly. Others may hear you. Do you think I feel nothing? We've got to put everything behind us."

Volunteer fighters and nurses had been brought together for an outing to Sepo to boost morale. It hadn't worked. Both groups were self-conscious and hesitant about mixing, except for a few who already knew one another, like Cheng Ching and Ying. The rest kept to themselves.

It wasn't much of an outing, Cheng Ching thought, and Sepo wasn't much of a town. But he was glad that Ying was strolling by his side and drawing envious glances. She was from Soochow, that ancient city of hump-backed bridges and picturesque canals not excessively far from his village in Anhui. He wished they had met during a time of peace and hope. Then he would not have made such a fool of himself by crying. The ancients held that a man should be able to shed blood without shedding tears. He had failed to live up to that ideal.

The memory of his unmanliness made him flush. It had happened in May, during his second day at the field hospital, in a ward filled with the wounded from the engagements of two nights earlier. He had recognized two or three belonging to his company, but most had been from other units further along the front. There had been so many severed limbs, torn bodies, punctured chests, moans, gurgles, imprecations and whimpered pleas to absent mothers. And all the while a confused traffic of orderlies, nurses, doctors, stretcher-bearers and supervisors in the field hospital.

In the middle of all that he had been shocked to see on the bed next to his a member of his company — Koo. The sober intelligence that used to shine from the man's brown eyes when they played chess together seemed to have deserted him. Now they stared blankly out of an ashen face, like two dull, bone buttons. His chest was heavily bandaged and he seemed lifeless, except for a faint, laboured wheeze coming from his throat and a trickle of pink froth dribbling from a corner of his mouth.

The sight of a human being in such a state, let alone a comrade, pained him. He went over to Koo to attempt to ease whatever torment the man might be suffering. He knelt down beside him and whispered his name.

"Brother Koo, Brother Koo, I'm Cheng Ching. How are you?" he asked. "What happened in the fighting? Is there anything I can do for you? You're in good hands. Don't worry about anything. Just rest quietly. You'll get better soon. Doctors here are good. When you are better we can play chess again."

He failed to elicit the slightest response. When he touched Koo's hand it felt cold as ice. Then he noticed a tear forming in a corner of Koo's eye. The tear fattened and rolled down the face. Otherwise, the injured man still did not react. He knew then that Koo was beyond help. At the same time he noticed that Koo's ears too were small, like those of the volunteer Lee. In less than three hours Koo was gone and his bed taken by someone else.

While Cheng Ching lay dazed by the loss of Koo, by the realization of how easily life could be snatched away, Ying came to change his dressing. He had noted her beauty the previous day, while she stitched his wound with her face close to his. To judge by the filthy state of her hospital gown, she must have had an appalling twenty-four hours.

"We've found no evidence of concussion," Ying said cheerfully, as she removed the bandage from his cheek. "It looks like you've escaped with only a flesh wound and a slight fracture of the maxilla bone. There's not much anyone can do about that. It will heal itself. So will the wound, if you keep it clean and don't get it infected. You'll be right as rain in a few days. I'll get you some antibiotics. Come back next week to have the stitches removed. You can to go back to your unit today."

"I don't want to go back. I never want to go back," he said, very quietly, and suddenly tears rolled down his cheeks.

Ying, mistaking his remarks and his tears as a sign of fear, placed a hand firmly around his shoulder and whispered: "It's natural to be afraid, but it's your duty to go back. Look around you. You're luckier than most. You'll feel better once you're back with your unit."

"I'm not afraid," he said, flushing. "I just don't want to kill any more or to watch other people being killed. Yesterday I looked into the eyes of a stranger and blew his brains out. I watched them spill onto the ground. It was revolting. Today I knelt beside a man whom I had played chess with and watched his life ebb away. It was every bit as bad. Such things are too hard for me. I can't stand them any more. I would rather die."

"You were just doing your duty, resisting aggression,

defending the freedom of the Korean people. The man you killed yesterday was an enemy, a heartless killer."

"No, he was just a young man like me. He had blue eyes and golden hair. I've never seen someone like him before. He was badly wounded and terribly frightened. I wanted to help him but I couldn't make myself understood. Then he panicked and I panicked and I killed him."

"It wasn't your fault. Such things happen in war. He was up to no good. He came to kill. He got what he deserved."

"He did not look like a bad man, not someone out to murder or rape. He was just a teenager doing his duty, like me."

"Well, looks can deceive. He came with a gun and a blackened face, didn't he? Only evil men out to do shameful deeds need hide their faces. All aggressors are murderers by definition. I've attended many women and children injured in American air raids. If dropping bombs on the innocent isn't murder, then what is?"

"The man wasn't dropping bombs. Killing someone face to face isn't like dropping bombs. You can see right into a man's soul. Something speaks to you, touches you, when you snuff out a life like that. It was horrible. This is supposed to be a hero's war, to end with a great victory and a hero's home-coming. Killing a wounded man didn't make me feel like a hero. I felt like a murderer, a barbarian."

"All right, all right," Ying said, gently. "It must have been a terrible shock. I'll give you something to calm you down and keep you under observation for another night. You should feel a lot better tomorrow. I'll come back to see you then."

When Cheng Ching returned to the front the following day, a great fuss was made of him by Old Tung, Mad Fan and the others for having acquitted himself so well in his first battle. Old Tung seemed particularly pleased and excused him from night patrols till his stitches had been removed. His own joy over seeing old comrades again, however, was dampened by too many missing faces. He could not bear to count the number of new men or to ask after absent friends.

In the meantime, Mad Fan appeared to have acquired many new photographs. But he had become much more solitary and secretive in studying them. The day after Cheng Ching rejoined the company, he handed Cheng Ching a photograph of a golden-haired man with an arm around a smiling girl in a printed calico dress. Their faces seemed to radiate hope, affection and happiness.

Cheng Ching recognized the man as the one whose brains he had blown apart. The memory sickened him again.

In the nights that followed, he could not sleep. He kept visualizing the face of the young man and speculating over the anguish the girl must be going through. What cruel destiny had brought them face to face, on a desolate hill far from their homes on that cool May morning? He had been fated to be there because his nation had urged him to resist aggression and repel imperialism. He had also wanted to honour his father. But what of the man with the golden hair? Had he gone there to enslave others, to commit murder and rape, as the Party newspapers said?

He remembered his father telling him that Dr. Sun Yat-san had launched his revolution against the Manchu dynasty on the basis of his Three Principles of the People. Those principles had been based on the ideals of Abraham Lincoln, an American President who had opposed slavery. His father had also told him the American constitution was very idealistic, holding liberty and freedom of the individual in high regard. How could it make sense for Americans to come to Korea to enslave others?

He might have gained a better understanding if the Americans had made broadcasts from no-man's-land explaining themselves, as his own side had done. Or if he had been able to talk to the man he had killed or to other Americans. How could there be understanding without talk and how could there be talk without a common language? He suddenly felt as if he had stumbled upon a truth. Different peoples, with their differing values and cultures, had to be able to communicate. Otherwise they would remain forever trapped in the dead end of their own prejudices and beliefs. He began badgering Old Tung to teach him English, convinced that sooner or later he would have to master that language.

The following week, he returned to the field hospital to have his stitches removed. He still felt depressed, both over the blue-eyed American and the dead in his company.

"Your wound has healed well," Ying said, noting his mood.

"It will leave a scar, though not a very big one. I've been told that Prussian officers used to consider a scar on the cheek a badge of honour."

"My scar can only be a reminder of my disgrace."

"What has been done is done," Ying said. "It's no good brooding."

Cheng Ching took out from his pocket the photograph of the dead American Mad Fan had given him. "This is the man I killed," he said. "How can I ever forget?"

Ying refused to look at the photograph. "Why do you have to feel sorry for dead foreigners?" she flared. "Why don't you go through the wards and look at what the Americans have done to your countrymen? Do you feel sorry for them? I used to have an older brother. He was killed last year. Did anyone feel sorry for him?"

Cheng Ching was taken aback by the vehemence of Ying's reaction and the revelation about her brother. The reddening of Ying's eyes flustered him. "I'm sorry, Elder Sister," he stammered. "I didn't mean to upset you. I didn't know about your brother. It's wrong of me to saddle you with my problems."

Ying shook her head and fought back her tears. After a while, she said: "No, it was wrong of me to shout at you. My brother and I were very close. He was also a volunteer. After he was killed I used to look at his photograph and cry. I thought I'd got over it. Your trying to show me that picture did something to me."

"I'm sorry, Elder Sister. I really am sorry."

"I'm all right now. You keep addressing me as 'Elder Sister'. Are you suggesting we should adopt each other? I don't have a brother any more. Do you have a sister?"

"No, I'm an only child. It would be an honour to become your adopted brother."

"You must first promise me you're going to live through this war. I couldn't stand losing another brother. Also promise to come and see me when you're sent to the rear for delousing or for a rest."

"I promise," Cheng Ching said.

It had not been difficult to keep his promises during the month of June and the first part of July. The front was quiet and the routine of the trenches had resumed its tedious pattern, with only occasional sniping and minor clashes. He drifted, like Mad Fan, into a more solitary existence and shied away from new friendships.

There were persistent rumours of a ceasefire about to be signed and everyone hoped that it would come into effect without more fighting. That proved a vain hope, for the artillery opened up again in mid-July. This time it was Chinese guns firing the first salvoes, to presage an offensive.

After the heavy guns had pounded one another for two days, Old Tung informed them of a general attack along the entire front. The specific task for the company was to capture an enemy strongpoint a mile away. The attack would begin at midnight the following night.

At the appointed hour the men slipped out of their trenches. Another company took over their vacated positions, ready to move out when the time came.

It was Cheng Ching's first offensive action and he went into the night wondering if he would ever see tomorrow. Old Tung ordered him to stick close to him so that he might learn some of the craft and cunning employed in battle.

The company moved stealthily across no-man's-land until they were close to the enemy outposts. Then Old Tung sent out small teams to eliminate the outposts. The ploy was successful. The signal for attack was given, and they threw themselves into the assault, oblivious of barbed-wire, buried mines and machine-gun fire.

They fought throughout the night. The following morning rain reduced visibility to a matter of yards. Still they fought on, clinging tenaciously to every inch of captured terrain. By the end of that wet and miserable day the strongpoint was captured. But the price was high. Old Tung, Mad Fan and sixty per cent of the company had perished.

As Ying and Cheng Ching turned into another of the unremarkable streets of Sepo, Ying said: "I hope they send us on an outing to Pyongyang. That's usually a sign they're about to send us home."

"Do you think we will ever get home? According to my Political Commissar, the British imperialists are now organizing provocations near the Hong Kong border. They're in league with the Americans and the Kuomintang in Taiwan. They'll never leave us in peace. If we do get home, what do you intend to do?"

"Try and get into medical college and become a doctor. What about you?"

"I'll study English, in honour of Old Tung, and eventually try to gain admission into the Party."

"You should have no trouble with your family background and your war service. We might visit each other during holidays since we'll be in adjoining provinces."

"Wonderful!"

Cheng Ching was not yet seventeen but he could sense that another power as mighty as the Party's was laying claim to him. He had learnt in the Communist Youth League that socialist love had to be pure, selfless and noble. He could go along with that. What baffled him was whether that held true if the object of his love happened to be his adopted sister.

Between two worlds

6

What was he doing here? How could he endure such soul-destroying duties? Lieutenant Sebastian Baxingdale of the First Battalion Light Infantry asked himself, as he trained his field glasses on the border. He was in charge of one of the four border posts manned by the British Army, the rest being the responsibility of the local police. The land border meandered for some twelve miles between Sha Tau Kok and Man Kam To and his job was to detain illegal immigrants crossing it and hand them back to the Chinese authorities on the other side.

The people being rounded up, including women and children, were officially classified as economic migrants, but he knew in his heart that they were simply desperate folk fleeing poverty, hunger, disease or persecution. They chanced their lives by either floating across the Sham Chun River with inflated tyre tubes or traversing the treacherous terrain of the border zones in the dead of night. And to what purpose? What awaited the successful was usually a precarious existence without piped water, electricity or sanitation and constantly preyed upon by fires, typhoons, landslides and diseases. For most, the only succour available was from hard-pressed charities.

What had happened to human compassion, Baxingdale wondered, when people seeking so little had to be turned back to uncertain fates? The whole exercise grated upon his British instincts. Local rules seemed idiotic as well. If a refugee managed to evade border patrols and reach the urban area, then he or she would be allowed to stay. It seemed an arrangement designed for corruption and rackets. The best estimates suggested a quarter of a million had slipped through since the establishment of the Communist regime in 1949.

Guarding the border in battle fatigues struck him as a charade, a farce. His men joked that Chairman Mao could take Hong Kong without a single soldier. All that was needed was a telephone call. The withdrawal of the People's Liberation Army from the border would send tens of thousands of refugees swarming over.

Three divisions couldn't stop them, let alone the handful of men under his command. In any case, what British officer in the middle of the twentieth century would order his soldiers to fire on a bunch of unarmed and half-naked peasants? Those days were happily long past.

Earlier that day, among the dozen illegal immigrants caught by his patrol was a young woman. What made her different was the look of utter desperation in her eyes. She was bleeding from cuts sustained while climbing through barbed-wire barriers and perilous terrain. She had every appearance of a trapped animal at the end of its tether.

"This one looks all in, Sir," Corporal Fuller had said, leading her past him. "Got a couple of bad cuts too."

With the aid of an interpreter from the Dictrict Office, Baxingdale discovered she was trying to reach a brother in Hong Kong to tell him their father was dying in China and had asked to see him. He felt sorry for her. But it was not his job to pronounce on the veracity or urgency of her story.

"I'm sorry," he said, as kindly as he could. "Can't let you through. You've got to apply through proper channels and get exit papers. There's a quota. You'll have to follow the rules."

Even as he got the interpreter to convey that message, he knew his words were an evasion, a betrayal of his own instincts. It would take years for an application to wind its way through the bureaucratic maze and by then the woman's father would be long dead.

The woman had appealed to him with her tearful eyes and her pitiful face. Those features seemed to say: "You have it within your power to show a speck of human kindness. Let me reach the urban area. Others have done it with bribes but I have no money. Please, for mercy's sake, look the other way."

But he did not. Instead he said: "Get her cuts attended to and put her with the rest."

As Corporal Fuller led her away, tears streamed down her face and she screamed in Chinese.

Baxingdale felt diminished. Even without a translation he divined what the screaming was about. He had not joined the army for such heartless work and he hated having to smother his humanity because of fatuous rules.

His father, the Reverend Alistair Baxingdale, never did that. His father, a self-effacing man with socialist and anti-imperialist inclinations, was vicar of a parish in the East End of London. When Baxingdale was quite young, he remembered a parishioner seeking his father's help to clear the name of a son shot for cowardice during the First World War. His father had responded with gusto. So had his mother, shouldering the paperwork. But their efforts got nowhere, and that failure caused them to vent their dismay over the bone-headedness of officialdom at the family dinner-table.

Had his father sired a moral coward? Other memories came, in the form of his parents' opposition to the appeasement of the Nazis and their treatment of the Jews. In later years they marched with Bertrand Russell, Canon Collins and others in support of nuclear disarmament, the end of apartheid in South Africa, the abolition of the death penalty and a miscellany of other causes.

His parents had lived out their principles. He had yet to take a stand over his. He felt ashamed. The case of the boy shot for cowardice had left him with a secret fear of being branded a coward himself. A clear nexus developed in his mind between being decent and being brave. To live his principles, as his parents had done, might invite derision and ridicule. One had to be brave enough to bear that. To do the decent thing also meant a willingness to sacrifice oneself for some some larger purpose, like Leonidas at Thermopylae or Regulus before the Carthaginians.

He was conscious of his own bookish habits and refined manners. To compensate, he had taken up boxing and rugby. He had a modest talent for both, but had lacked the killer instinct to be outstanding at either.

Dogged participation resulted in three fractured ribs and a broken nose. He did not regret the latter, however, because it added a more pugnacious cast to a face otherwise too dreamy and handsome. He had always thought the sandy hair, the pale grey eyes and the soft, mobile mouth inherited from his mother lacked heroism.

A vague notion that he might prove his courage by seeking a career in the army grew on him. When the Second World War erupted, he was only nine years old. He was nevertheless determined to display his lack of fear. Much to the consternation of his parents, he refused to be evacuated from London along with other children. Even the prospect of going off to faraway Australia or Canada did not interest him. The war filled him with an excitement bordering on happiness, as he lived through the Blitz and the doodlebugs. He absorbed Churchill's exhortations to fight for freedom like verbal iron for the soul. It mattered little that the exhortations were exaggerated. Peace came as a complete anticlimax.

He continued with boxing and rugby at Oxford, but he was never good enough at either to become a blue. He had just finished a degree in modern history at Christ Church as the Korean War broke. When the United Nations decided to resist the invasion of South Korea, he immediately volunteered for National Service. He never saw action, however. By the time he had finished training, the confrontation in Korea had bogged down into a war of attrition and his battalion was posted to Hong Kong instead.

Baxingdale scanned the horizon again with his field glasses. Nothing much was moving on the other side. Everything seemed peaceful. He saw the yellow poincianas, flames of the forest and sweet gum trees sprouting here and there. The paddy fields appeared normal, tended by only a few farmers and the odd water buffalo. There was no obvious sign of impending intrusion. Just below his outpost, the familiar barbed-wire fence, accompanied by a patrol path, snaked along the boundary for as far as the eye could see.

A small unit of the People's Liberation Army sauntered unexpectedly into his line of vision. They were apparently on patrol, dressed in their shapeless green uniforms and crumpled green caps. How ill-trained and unkempt they appeared! Yet it would be a mistake to underrate them. They were, after all, the victors in a civil war that had raged for a quarter of a century. In a sense that conflict was still in progress, for the vanquished had withdrawn to Taiwan to mull over the possibility of a counter-attack under the protective shield of the United States' Seventh Fleet.

Units just as motley had also fought the combined might of the United States, Britain and fourteen other nations to a standstill in Korea. Their steadfastness under fire and their human-wave tactics had left Western allies gasping. It was reputed that, before truce talks began at Kaesong in 1951, they had lost half a million men. It was a horrendous price to pay for pushing back Western forces from the Yalu. One had to regard with awe men capable of such sacrifices.

What was it, he wondered, that made them so capable of absorbing punishment, so scornful of death? What were they laying down their lives for? Perhaps for an illusion similar to his own. Would they, too, end up one day discovering that their country had played them false? He had signed up in support of a saner world order, not to guard a piece of stolen territory. None of it squared with his democratic instincts or his sense of decency and fair play.

Baxingdale put down his field glasses and lit a cigarette. He felt hot and uncomfortable and he longed for a cold beer. On a nearby flagpole the Union Jack over the command post hung as limp as a damp dish-rag.

There was so much about Hong Kong that confounded him. Its merits were obvious, as were its defects. It wasn't a single society but a myriad of societies, each distinct and separate, all rubbing against one another like beans in a sack, co-existing without merging or integrating. They might have produced friction had it not been for the ready lubricant of money. As an officer of the garrison, he did not really belong in any of those societies, Chinese or European.

The expatriate top brass seemed to live in splendid isolation, oblivious of the fact that ninety-eight per cent of the population was Chinese. He, however, felt troubled by that isolation. He wished he knew Chinese, so that he could discover what made them tick and how they thought British rule impacted upon their lives.

During days freed from duty, he took to wandering through the old Chinese quarters. Each excursion was an education. The streets seemed alive with energy and exotic sounds, smells and colours. The garish hieroglyphics of shop signs teased him with their incomprehensibility, with each establishment offering its own weird and wonderful fare. There were dried sea-cucumbers, gingko nuts, back scratchers, ear cleaners, wooden clogs, herbal ingredients, coffins from Lanchow and live snakes kept for their gall bladders. Bargaining housewives, importuning hawkers, chanting coolies, playful children, hooting traffic and yelping dogs all created a maelstrom, jostling, colliding, laughing, arguing.

He remembered in particular an excursion to the old Western District on Hong Kong Island. It was an area where few Westerners or gweilos ventured immediately after the war. In one of its narrow streets he had come across a traditional Chinese tea house. Its name appeared in five characters over the entrance, though he could not read them. The place looked quite pleasant and inviting. As it was by then well after midday, he thought of sampling its fare. But when he made to enter, a waiter smilingly and courteously barred his way and indicated he should go elsewhere.

He could not understand why his patronage should be turned down. He saw, on closer examination, that the tea house was in fact half-empty. Was his money not good enough or was it a kind of reverse prejudice? Or perhaps a form of resistance to the foreign rule that he had been taken to represent? Was a demand for an end to colonialism also taking shape in Hong Kong as well?

He and the waiter eyed each other for a moment in mutual incomprehensibility. Then he walked away, smiling in return.

He raised the subject subsequently with his old Oxford friend, Christopher Knight, when they met for drinks at the Victoria Cricket Club.

"The chap probably ca-ca-can't cope with foreigners. The lo-lo-locals know what's good for them. They may have their resentments, but we have rights un-un-under international treaties," Chistopher Knight replied.

Knight was a heavy, ungainly and tow-headed lawyer. He came from a family of undertakers. Self-consciousness about his roots probably accounted for the slight impediment in his speech. He had built a reputation as a wag when he was studying law at Oxford. He joined the Public Prosecutions Section of the Hong Kong Legal Department after his articles and had since begun to assume a more sober air.

"Yes, but the Chinese regard their treaties with us as unequal, just scraps of paper extracted under duress. If people resent our presence, what's the point of staying? It is not as if they needed us. They can probably run the place themselves better than we can."

"The Ya-Ya-Yanks won't let us leave. They need us to halt the spread of Communism, wha-wha-what with Korea on their minds and the Taiwan Straits ho-ho-hotting up."

"That's just the point. We've seen what the Chinese are capable of in Korea. If they turned nasty, we wouldn't stand a chance. We have no idea what the locals really think of us. Would they turn on us? Would they want to pay us back for the century of humiliations and defeats they've endured and the snobberies they're still enduring?"

An attentive waiter, noting that their beer tankards were empty, asked if they wanted another round. They did.

"It'll ne-ne-never come to that, old boy. The Ya-Ya-Yanks would face down the Chinese soon enough. Good old Sen-Sen-Senator McCarthy'll see to that."

"What? That maniac! He'd have us fighting World War III if he had his way! I don't think America is crazy enough for a land war in China. It held back from doing so for Chiang Kai-shek. That's why McCarthy has been ranting about subversives in the American government who — in his terminology — lost China.

"Do you realize that every nation that tried to swallow a part of China got Sino-ized for its trouble? The Eastern Huns, the Hsiungnus, the Khitans, the Manchus, the whole lot. The only ones to escape were the Mongols and that was because they had the good sense to withdraw in the nick of time. I'll need a lot of convincing that the Americans will step in to save our bacon, special relationships and McCarthy's ravings notwithstanding."

Baxingdale was by then in full flow and Knight made no attempt to interrupt him.

"And it's not only races that get absorbed and transformed in China," Baxingdale continued. "Also ideas. Just look at what happened to Nestorian Christianity and Buddhism. Communism is bound to go the same way. There's something both admirable and frightening about the Chinese. The world is littered with the rubble of fallen civilizations. Where is the Babylon that once astounded Herodotus? Look at the decline and fall of mighty

Rome. By contrast, Chinese civilization simply marches on and on, adapting and re-shaping itself around a central core of values and beliefs. It's amazing."

"I see you're back on your old ho-ho-hobby horse — the decline of the West and the rise of the yer-yer-yellow races," Christopher Knight said. "Spengler's quite out of fa-fa-fashion, you know. I don't see much to support his theory. In any case, the Chinks'll never get anywhere till they stop their disgusting ha-ha-habit of spitting all over the place."

"Well, most races have a few bad habits. But look at how energetic they are, the way they're transforming Hong Kong. We're largely irrelevant."

"Like it or not, Britain getting out of Hong Kong wo-wo-won't happen till long after my retirement and that's th-th-thirty years away."

"How can you count on that sort of time horizon? The People's Liberation Army could barge in here tomorrow. What would you say to them then?"

"I'll tell th-th-them this club is for mem-mem-members only and ask them to leave!"

Dinner with father

HONG KONG
APRIL 1954

7

Except for Sundays, when his father invited friends around for bridge or mah jong, and with their wives joining for dinner, Chu Wing-seng seldom ate at the great, round rosewood table. Its fine grain and rich colour, fretted with intricate carvings and protected by glass, threw back the light of the enormous crystal chandelier hanging over it. A dozen upholstered chairs with similar carvings circled the table. But by some miracle, his father was dining at home without company on a weekend and he had to make the most of his opportunity.

Chu Wing-seng occupied a seat between his parents, as if he were some kind of link between them. His mother was dressed in a white linen suit. His father was in shirtsleeves. It occurred to him suddenly that the last time the three of them dined together his mother had also been dressed in white. Why? White was the colour of purity or of mourning. Was a message being conveyed? About what? There was always something strange between his parents, as if a mysterious undercurrent flowed constantly between them. He never managed to figure out whether that was caused by love or by a certain discomfort with each other's company.

As he waited patiently for the food to be served, his mind went over the questions about financial and business matters he wanted to put to his father. It would be a pleasant change from the boring topics woven around his studies, his scouting, his next set of examinations and his larger ambitions that formed the staple of conversations with his mother. There would also be respite from those worn-out tales about the Lord Buddha's enlightenment under the Bodhi tree, about a Chinese monk's journey to India to acquire holy scriptures, or about Zen masters using impossible parables to defeat the mind. He would have to avoid posing direct questions about making money to his father, however, because he knew his mother's temperament and did not want to upset her.

In front of him, the table was laid out with all the formal

accessories. Personalized ivory chopsticks with names engraved in red. Polished silver chopstick rests. Little square dishes of sauces and condiments. Embroidered linen napkins, immaculately starched and ironed. A centrepiece filled with fresh pink flowers whose name he did not know. It was a far cry from the simple dinners eaten with his mother in the small alcove in her private quarters.

His mother's vegetarian dishes of tofu, mushrooms, beansprouts and stir-fried pak choi were the first to arrive. Then came the dishes meant for himself and his father — pork cooked with dried mustard greens, eggs scrambled with shrimps and Chinese broccoli fried with beef seasoned with oyster sauce. It occurred to Chu Wing-seng suddenly how ridiculous it was to have two Filipino maids serving three people seated at a table meant for twelve!

The meal proceeded in relative silence, except for Chu Wing-seng's occasional protest when his mother placed a helping of her vegetarian fare into his bowl. After a while, the questioning began.

What were the most important requirements for a stock-exchange listing? Why had the Hong Kong and Shanghai Banking Corporation restricted ownership of its shares to a maximum of one per cent per investor? When would the next Gold Star luxury housing project be completed?

Chu Wing-seng ate steadily as he listened to his father's unhurried replies. When he was into his second bowl of rice, he felt more venturesome. "There was a leader in yesterday's newspaper arguing that insider trading ought to be made a crime," he said. "What's insider trading?"

"The use of confidential or privileged information by people to trade shares to their own advantage," his father replied.

"An example, please."

"Suppose Gold Star is in discussion to take over Company X. If the public knew, the price of shares in Company X would soar. If I had bought Company X shares for my personal account before making a public announcement, that would be insider trading."

"What if Mother knew about the talks and bought Company X shares?"

"That would be insider trading too. An executive must keep price-sensitive information to himself. Can't share it, even with his wife."

Chu Wing-seng's eyes shone bright with interest. This was the kind of exchange he had longed for, exchanges that opened the door to business practices. "An executive can't always keep things secret, can he?" he asked. "What if the takeover created so much stress you can't sleep? You might go to Dr. Chow for sleeping pills or tranquillizers. Dr. Chow would want to know why you've been stressed. Discovering the cause, he might decide to buy Company X shares. Would that be insider trading?"

"Dr. Chow wouldn't do such a thing. That would be unprofessional. If a doctor did it in those circumstances, it would be insider trading."

"What if the doctor's nurse saw the medical records and told her husband and the husband went out and bought Company X shares. Would that be insider trading?"

"That's more debatable. That gets into difficult areas of guilty knowledge, intent and proof — the very reasons why insider trading has not yet been made a crime in Hong Kong. We live cheek by jowl. Gossip and rumours fly around all day. Hard to pin down who told what to whom and when. Even harder to prove. If the stock exchange thinks someone has been naughty, it gives him a public ticking off. A blot on his reputation. People criticize that arrangement as too cozy for those in the know. But there's no point having a law that can't be effectively enforced."

"Do the Evergreens ever engage in insider trading?"

"What do you mean? What are you driving at?"

"There was an article a while back hinting that you and Uncle Yue belonged to a group of entrepreneurs known as the Evergreens. The group was supposed to have made fortunes immediately after the war, through shrewd dealings in stocks and shares and in contraband goods. Did the Evergreens use insider information to score?"

"You should eat some more greens," his mother intervened, spooning a helping of fried pak choi into his bowl.

"I don't want more greens, Mother. I've had plenty of broccoli already."

"Pak choi is good for you."

Chu Wing-seng felt irritated. Both he and his father knew it was his mother's way of indicating they were approaching inappropriate territory.

The rest of the meal continued in silence. However, after the dishes had been cleared and tea had been served, his father returned to the topic of his own volition.

"Shouldn't believe everything you read in newspapers, my boy. The war left many people in ruins. A few friends and I were trying to pick ourselves up again. We met for breakfast at a tea house known as the Evergreen. I've told you about it before. It was a wonderful middle-class place located near the boundary of the Central and Western Districts. It served delicious food and over forty varieties of famous Chinese teas. I would gladly take you there, if you can overcome your preference for flashy French food.

"Anyway, to continue. We went to the tea house to exchange gossip and to play the market. Got lucky. Just a bunch of hungry young men, not a secret society. We kept our ears to the ground, sniffing out opportunities. Couldn't rely on insider information because we had no access to important people. One or two of the group might have done some smuggling on the side. Shortages and corruption were rampant in those days. Still a lot of corruption around. Everybody was on the make, including government officials charged with preventing smuggling. Most of us did well after a while, in stockbroking, money-lending, construction, shipping and trading. Still meet regularly at the Evergreen, for old times' sake."

When his father paused, his mother stood up and excused herself. She had barely touched the tea.

After she had disappeared, his father said: "You'll be going to university in a couple of years. I've left your upbringing to your mother, I fear. It's time we talked a bit. Let's do it in the study."

His father flung an arm around his shoulders as they walked. Chu Wing-sen had sometimes been uncertain about his father's love because his father was seldom around and had seemed such a remote figure. Now, as they headed towards the study, he felt his right to participate in worldly affairs was finally being acknowledged.

His father unlocked the door. He always kept it locked when he was not around, on the grounds he didn't want servants banging into his antiques. The only other key to the room was kept by his mother, who opened it once a week for servants to clean it under supervision.

As his father switched on the light, Chu Wing-seng saw that the desk was cluttered with numerous documents and that boxes and crates were all over the floor. Some were still sealed and others had necks of vases and other ornaments sticking out of them. Otherwise, the room was not untidy.

His father took a chair on the other side of the desk. A minature pine, gnarled and partly hollow, stood on a stand next to the desk. The plant, in a buff-coloured clay pot, was set among tiny rocks in mossy soil to resemble a mountainside scene. His father had once tried to explain the intricacies of creating miniature landscapes, or what the Japanese called bonsai, and how a lifespan of fifty or sixty years was not uncommon for such plants. But he had no interest. Tending a dwarf plant seemed a waste of precious time.

Chu Wing-seng saw his father gazing fondly at the twisted pine, more fondly perhaps than he ever remembered his father gazing upon him. The shrunken plant was a grown-up's toy, an irrelevance, he thought, as he watched his father fish a cigar out of a silver cigar-box.

His father's attention seemed to drift towards two scrolls of calligraphy on the wall, as he lit his cigar and blew a cloud of smoke into the air. The scrolls had been executed by one of his father's former tutors, Teacher Tam. The text was by an anonymous Tang poet. It read:

"The bright moon shining overhead,
The stream beneath the breeze's touch,
Are pure and perfect joys indeed —
But few are they who think them such."

Chu Wing-seng followed his father's gaze. Silly poem, he thought. No dynamism, meant for doddering old men on their last legs. His mother had often praised the brush strokes of Teacher Tam and held them up as a skill he should emulate. Who had time to practise with the brush these days?

A restlessness stole upon Chu Wing-seng as the silence

lengthened. He cleared his throat to attract the attention of his father.

"Ah!" his father said, with a start. He ran a hand through his hair. "Your mother has asked me to talk to you about your education. Seems you're inclined towards studying business administration. No need to make that kind of a decision now. You still have two years to go. Something else might strike your fancy."

"Nothing else will. I've made up my mind," Chu Wing-seng replied, blinking behind his spectacles. The tone his father was adopting was not quite what he had expected. It was more father-to-son than man-to-man. He at once felt less at ease. He wished he were older, more of a match for his father.

"You sure you want to go into business?"

"Certainly. I thought you understood that. Wasn't that why you left those economics and business journals around the house? To encourage and stimulate me?"

His father laughed. "I brought them back to have them thrown away, without letting people in the office know. Just forgot to tell the maids. Never did more than skim them. Can't waste time on stuff like that."

"To throw away? I don't understand! Why buy them for your staff and put yourself on the circulation list if you don't intend to read them?"

"To give staff the impression I'm reading the same fancy rubbish they are, so they don't start palming off borrowed ideas as their own. Business is mainly about commonsense and understanding human nature, knowing who is blowing smoke and who can be relied upon. I despair when so-called management gurus pretend it's a science.

"Have you noticed anything about the circulation lists? Doesn't my name always appear last? Everyone on a list has to sign off, together with a date, before passing the magazine on to the next person. That obviously records how long a person has kept it. Passing it along too quickly suggests it hasn't been read. Retaining it too long creates an impression of lack of diligence. Keeps everyone on their toes."

"I see! That's brilliant! Splendid tactics!"

"Business isn't about smart tactics. It's more about not doing things one might regret afterwards. The ancients used to look down upon those engaged in commerce and barred them from ancestral temples. They had good reason. It's not easy for decent men to live in the real world. That's why your mother and I prefer you not to go into business. I've made sufficient provisions for you both. Making more money when you already have enough is pointless."

"It's not about money, Father. It's about achievement and proving your own worth. I've read your magazines. They talk about taking on all comers, becoming dominant, like De Beers in diamonds, Rockefeller in oil, J. P. Morgan in steel. I want to shake the world that way. I want you to be proud of me."

"Your mother and I are already proud of you. We love you. You're highly intelligent and can do whatever you set your mind to. No need to shake the world on our account. We would rather you study a subject that contributes to the betterment of the self and of society as a whole."

"Not you too, Father! Mother always presses me to become some sort of do-gooder, a social worker, a teacher or a seeker after metaphysical truths. To her, anything's better than business. But how can someone like you think that way? You don't expect me to spend my life auditing boring accounts or probing rotting molars, do you?"

His father blew more smoke into the air, watching it curl towards the ceiling before being snatched into the louvres of the central ventilation system.

"Life is ridiculous," he said, with a sigh. His voice had lost some of its crispness. His face became more serious. It was no longer that of a self-confident tycoon but that of a worried father, not knowing how to handle his son.

"Your mother has from the very beginning been worried about your being sucked into Gold Star. I tried to nudge you in another direction. Wanted to send you to boarding school in Britain two years ago. Brits in Britain are quite different from the ones here. They're much more like us, placing the family at the centre of things, respecting scholarship, tolerating the views of others and displaying a strong sense of fair play. Like ourselves, they follow maxims such as 'My word is my bond' and 'Death before dishonour'.

"But your mother wouldn't hear of it. She wanted you by her side. Understandable, I suppose. To allay her anxieties, I left your upbringing to her. Now that your ambitions have hardened in spite of her best efforts, she wants me to dissuade you from business. Not sure I know how. Have you read Mencius? Do they teach him at school?"

"No."

His father got up from his black leather chair and stepped over to a bookcase. He extracted a well-thumbed volume and placed it in front of his son. "Here's Mencius," he said. "You can borrow it."

Chu Wing-seng picked up the book, printed on yellowing rice paper and bound together by white threads. He turned a few pages. "It's in classical Chinese," he said. "I'll have difficulty with that."

"Yes, that's true. You'll need a tutor to take you through it. Pity I haven't an English translation. When I was a boy, I had tutors for both English and Chinese. The Chinese tutor concentrated on classics like Mencius and got me reciting them by rote. Made no sense at first, just parroting sounds. After I learnt the characters, however, meanings began to emerge. I can still recite all of Mencius, just like devout Moslems can the Koran.

"This is what happens in the First Book of Mencius. The sage calls on King Wei of Liang and the king immediately asks for advice on ways to profit his kingdom. Mencius chastises the king for dwelling on profits rather than on righteousness and benevolence. He points to the dangers of emphasizing profits because people obsessed with gain must ultimately plot usurpation. The throne, after all, represents the greatest source of profit in any kingdom."

His father paused, as if he were trying to recall his childhood lessons, and Chu Wing-seng did not know whether he should say anything. His father was beginning to sound like his mother and he wanted him to stop, to revert to the kind of topic raised at dinner.

At last his father spoke again. "Not easy to heed Mencius when both government and society extol enterprise, self-interest, profits and prosperity. Creating wealth is unquestionably good.

But it can easily degenerate into greed. My own actions have sometimes caused distress to others, to people who had done me no harm. By the time I realized it, it was often too late. Too late for regrets."

"What have you got to regret, Father? You've created an empire. You've demonstrated that not only gweilos can create great hongs in Hong Kong. You've given them more than a run for their money. Perhaps one day you and the Evergreens can oust them altogether. This is our territory. Gold Star and the Chu name are already household words. What's there to regret?"

"Deception of the self and of others," his father said, shaking his head and sighing. "Employing sophistry to justify dubious actions. Ignoring the well-being of others in the scramble for profits. Deceiving with inflated claims. The list is long. Not long ago a young man blamed me for the deaths of his parents."

"Who was he?"

"His name doesn't matter. He was a young man who cared."

"Must be a crank. You're not in the business of killing anyone."

"Not as simple as that, I'm afraid. I'm culpable to a degree. The young man's parents owned a neighbourhood grocery store. Gold Star came along with a supermarket. Drove their business into the ground. The old couple lost everything and committed suicide."

"Father, how can you be held responsible if people kill themselves? Just sore losers. In an open economy people have to take their chances. Survival of the fittest. The inefficient must perish, so that society can progress. That's the law of the marketplace, of economics."

"Is it? Is there no room for compassion, for kindness, for consideration of others? Are there no moral imperatives left? What of the Golden Mean? Are the teachings of Confucius and Mencius to be forgotten like last year's pop songs? They spoke of sharing, of displacing selfishness and materialism, of devotion to duty, of an end to intrigue and conniving for gain. Forget all that and we begin to turn nasty and brutish."

"Father, you're a businessman, not a dreamer or a priest. Business is about making money. Has anybody ever seen a commercial contract pledging high moral or ethical standards?"

"More's the pity. But it's not too late for you. Go study a rewarding subject. There're plenty of careers outside Gold Star."

"This is cruel, Father! To tell me like this that you don't want me in Gold Star!"

Frustrated, angry, Chu Wing-seng tore off his spectacles and wiped his eyes with his hand. In his crushing disappointment it came to him that his father had judged him and found him wanting! His father had identified his weaknesses, seen through his deceptions and noted his failures of courage. He re-lived in a flash the fear experienced when tossing away the black and white snake on the Pokfulam hillside.

"You don't think I'm good enough. That's it, isn't it?" he cried. "All my life, I have wanted to follow in your footsteps, to become part of what you've created. You've never nurtured me like that stupid potted pine! You never gave me a chance. Now you want me out! I'll prove to you how good I am! I'll make it on my own! I won't be put off what I've set my heart on!"

"Ah Seng! Please! You've misunderstood. I *know* you're good enough! I *know* you can run Gold Star better than I can. You're very single-minded. That's why I'm afraid. That's why your mother's afraid."

Chu Wing-seng had read somewhere that attack was the best form of defence. His father had regrets, his parents had secrets, perhaps as guilty as the one he shared with Little Ho. He was not going to give up his ambition without a fight. So he attacked instinctively, with the first thing that came to mind.

"Father, if you and Mother don't want me in Gold Star, that's all right. But don't employ trickery against me, your own son. You and Mother are both the same, full of little secrets and deceptions. You don't even love each other. You're just putting on a show."

The Chairman of Gold Star sat up with a start. His cigar had gone out but he made no attempt to relight it.

"What in heaven's name gave you such a notion? I love your mother above all else. We may have our differences, but no two persons in the world can care more for each other."

"I'm not a fool, Father. If this is going to be an evening for truth then let me speak it first. I've got eyes. You two are too considerate, too polite. You never argue or row like other parents.

You don't stay together in a room for more than a few minutes. You sleep in different quarters. Sometimes you don't come home. What kind of marriage is that?

"If Mother's so opposed to my going into business, why has she tolerated your activities? You told me yourself you've caused deaths. Why expect me to accommodate her wishes when you have not? What are the two of you hiding from me?"

"We are hiding nothing. We may not tell you everything, but that is not hiding. That's privacy."

Chu Wing-seng stared boldly at his father. "That's not true. I can sense it. Mother never mentions her parents. Neither do you mention yours, except that they died in Canton during one of the rectification campaigns. You can go into endless detail about using fermented rapeseed husks for your stunted tree, adding charcoal to strengthen trunk and roots. But you never teach me masterstrokes in business or talk about how you and Mother met or what you did before the war.

"Now let me tell you a secret I've been puzzling over. When I was nine, I caught Mother crying in her room and cradling an old Chinese mandolin. I tried to comfort her but she wouldn't tell me what the matter was. She just hugged me and in the end I cried too.

"The memory of that day has troubled me ever since. Why was she crying and holding an old pei-pa? Where did the instrument come from? I had never seen it before. She must have hidden it in one of the cupboards. Why hide it? What is its significance? Why have I never heard her play? She never explained anything."

Chu Tung-po shook his head and sighed again. "Your mother used to play the pei-pa and I used to love listening to her," he said. A remoteness came into his eyes. "She could pluck the most heart-breaking melodies from those strings. That was a long time ago, before you were born. The pei-pa you saw was possibly the same one she used to play."

"Why did she stop playing?"

"I'm not sure. That is something for your mother to tell you, if she wants to. The only thing I can say is that what human beings strive for and what they achieve are two quite different things. If you insist on a business career, I won't stand in your way. It will be a huge disappointment to your mother and me. I ask only that you mull it over. I hope that you will not regret your life twenty or thirty years from now, as I sometimes do mine."

Days in May 8

"This is Tienanmen, the Gate of Heavenly Peace," the tour guide explained through a megaphone, as Cheng Ching and his group of volunteers stared in rapt attention. A short distance away, other guides shepherding other groups bellowed similarly into their megaphones, creating an echoing din.

"This gate used to be the entrance to the imperial complex lying to the north, previously known as the Forbidden City. The Forbidden City was built during the Ming Dynasty and was used by a number of Ming and Ching emperors. The former royal gardens of Chung Nan Hai inside is where the nation's top leaders now reside. We will be visiting public parts of the Forbidden City presently.

"To the south you can see construction in progress. The government is building the largest square in the world in Peking, as a showplace of the new China. A magnificent memorial to martyrs of the Revolution will stand at the centre. Foundations have already been laid. A Great Hall of the People, where legislators will meet, is to be erected on one side of the square and museums displaying the heritage and achievements of the nation on the other.

"The Gate of Heavenly Peace itself, as you can see, is a red brick structure with a roof in imperial yellow. There are five openings. Above the central opening, a portrait of our beloved leader, Chairman Mao, is permanently on display."

Cheng Ching gazed up at the portrait. Chairman Mao seemed to beam benignly upon him. Cheng Ching wanted the tour to end, so that he could find Ying and exchange experiences with her. But the guide droned on.

* * *

Cheng Ching had arrived in Peking a week earlier, having been plucked unexpectedly from his unit in Korea to participate in the celebrations and parades normally scheduled for May. Then he would be discharged, to return home after almost twenty months in Korea.

Except for a few from his own company, the others accorded similar treatment were strangers. Their haunted looks suggested they belonged to outfits that had suffered high casualties. He himself had spent a gruelling winter manning the ceasefire line. The freezing cold and the boredom of inactivity had been nearly as unendurable as the fighting.

His orders to move out had come so suddenly that he had no time to inform Ying. To his utter amazement, however, he discovered during the journey to Peking that Ying and some other nurses were on the same train.

"Elder sister!" he almost screamed, when he spotted her while he walked through the carriages.

"Little Ching!" Ying responded, in that cheery Chinese form of address adopted towards juniors. She rushed to hug him. "What are you doing on this train?" She looked as radiant as ever.

"I tried to reach you. I've been selected to take part in the May Day parade. And the May the Fourth commemorations afterwards. Then I'm going home! My stint is over!"

"Me too!" Ying trilled. "I wrote to you. But I don't suppose you got my letter. We must explore Peking together. I'm so excited. I've never been there. Have you?"

"No, never. They must give us some free time before we go home. I'm only worried it won't be enough. There's so much to take in here, unlike poor Sepo."

Their fortuitous encounter confirmed his belief that their fates were intertwined.

But their quarters turned out to be located in different parts of the city and rehearsals for the ceremonies prevented any meeting. They could not even spot each other's units among the innumerable groups and contingents. The May Day parade itself was a heady affair. The procession snaked for miles and took hours to pass the review podium where Chairman Mao and other leaders took the salute. The cheers of the crowds and the music from numerous bands were deafening.

Cheng Ching had anticipated he would be free after the May Day parade. But he was wrong. Organized visits to the Great

Wall and the Ming tombs had been arranged for the following day and rehearsals for the May the Fourth commemorations the day after that. It appeared that the only free time was a half-day of unescorted sightseeing on the day before dispersal.

After the May Day parade, he returned weary and downcast to his quarters. He resented being kept from Ying. The moment he reached his quarters, however, his group leader handed him a new blue cotton Mao suit and told him to get cleaned up for a function. Knowing that cloth was rationed and that a new suit was a windfall, he realized something momentous must be in the wind. It turned out that he was one of a small number selected to represent his group at a reception hosted by national leaders.

After a hurried meal he was loaded with the others onto a bus, which picked up further contingents along the way. He neither knew where he was heading nor what to expect. He was eventually deposited outside a large building of venerable design and led into a sumptuous reception hall, with lacquered latticed panels, high gilded ceilings and tall curtained windows.

A band, dressed in white uniforms covered in braid, occupied a small dais at one end of the vast chamber. Except for an area of polished parquet in front of the dais, the floor was covered with a thick-piled Tientsin carpet of an intricate design. Tables piled with food and drink stood at strategic locations around the room.

The young men and women stood expectantly in small groups. Most had volunteered for Korea as engineers, mechanics, doctors, nurses, anti-aircraft gunners, infantrymen, cooks or stretcher-bearers. The men were dressed mainly in blue Mao suits. The small number in uniform represented units of the People's Liberation Army that had volunteered en masse. The women were in white blouses and navy-blue skirts.

Cheng Ching noted also a good sprinkling of Communist Party cadres. There was a quality about them that reminded him of his father. They bore the stamp of strongly held ideals. They were dressed like him in blue Mao suits, though theirs were more worn than his own but of a better cut. Another distinguishing feature was the fountain pens clipped to their breast pockets.

He remembered that his father had been awarded a fountain pen after storming Luting Bridge. His father had passed the pen to him when he entered secondary school, but he had considered it too precious to bring to Korea. He wished he had it with him now, so that he might clip it onto his own breast pocket.

He surveyed the room in search of Ying but could not find her. The possibility that she might not have been chosen as a representative for her group suddenly occurred to him and his heart sank.

Clapping broke out suddenly from the other end of the room and he saw Chairman Mao and other leaders entering, followed by a large entourage. He recognized Liu Shao-chi and Chou En-lai. The clapping swelled into a wild current of enthusiasm that was picked up by those standing around him. The leaders responded by clapping in return.

Cheng Ching watched them moving off in different directions to mingle with guests. Their bodyguards and aides followed. As the Chairman moved steadily in his direction, Cheng Ching's heart began pounding furiously. His throat felt as if it had turned to sandpaper.

Before he knew it, the Chairman was in front of him, glowing like the sun at dawn. His face was smooth and ageless and he radiated charisma. He was dressed in a grey suit of the style he had made fashionable. But there was no fountain pen clipped to his breast pocket.

"How are you?" the Chairman asked. "Did you get that scar in Korea?"

"Yes, Chairman Mao. A mere trifle," Cheng Ching replied, unable to recognize his own voice.

"A wound received in battle is no trifle. It should be worn with honour. What is your name and where do you come from?"

"My humble surname is Cheng and my given name is Ching. I'm from a village in Anhui." As he uttered the words it seemed everything he had done in Korea had served some higher purpose. He had been a mere instrument, a foot soldier, in some masterly plan devised by the man standing in front of him. He felt all eyes on him. He was no longer a nobody, a collector of swill and pig manure. He had played a part in the destiny of his nation!

"Your parents are farmers?"

"My father was in the Red Army, till he lost a leg. My mother was a former bondsmaid. They now rear pigs."

"Splendid! Two generations of veterans! How did your father lose his leg?"

"During the Long March, on the assault at Luting Bridge."

"Ah! Luting Bridge! A hero of the Revolution! What is your father's name?"

"Cheng Yin."

The Chairman beamed but showed no sign of recognizing the name. "Capturing Luting Bridge was a critical event," he said, with a sudden seriousness. "If it had not been taken, the whole course of the Revolution would have altered. You have done well to follow in the footsteps of your father. You are also a hero. I believe your period of service is about to end. What do you intend to do?"

Cheng Ching was momentarily lost for an answer. He had promised his father he would devote his life to the village at Thirsty Hills. But it seemed ridiculous to say that to the Chairman. He felt light-headed for an instant.

"Study hard, join the Communist Party and serve the nation," he replied, falling back on the answer drilled into him at the Communist Youth League.

"Good! That's what I like to hear!" the Chairman exclaimed. Mao turned to one of his aides and said: "Make sure to send a message to the Anhui authorities. Tell them a young man by the name of Cheng Ching is about to apply to join the Party. When his application comes in, I want them to know it has my personal endorsement."

"Thank you, Chairman Mao," Cheng Ching said, hardly believing his good fortune. At that moment he would have done anything for the Chairman, even returning to the mud and snow, to kill again and perhaps to be killed. The Chairman had once asserted that deaths weighed differently in different circumstances and that death for a just cause was as light as feather.

The Chairman extended his hand and Cheng Ching clasped it firmly.

"You come from good revolutionary stock," the Chairman said. "You have the makings of someone from whom great things can be expected. Good luck in your endeavours. Our country has need of men like you."

The Chairman moved on.

Cheng Ching remained rooted to the spot, almost fainting. Those around him congratulated him on finding favour with the Chairman. When a waiter passed with a tray of drinks, Cheng Ching grabbed one and gulped it down, indifferent to whether it was fiery mao tai or aerated water. It turned out to be beer.

It took minutes for him to calm down. Everything and everybody in the room seemed to have dissolved into a blur. Slowly, questions crept into his mind. Why had the Chairman favoured him? Was it mere chance he stopped where he did? The Chairman's skill at winning hearts was legendary. Was it all show or was he genuinely extending recognition to a loyal follower?

The sound of strange music floated towards him. It seemed to come from far away. "Ah, the band's playing a medley of foxtrots and waltzes," someone remarked. "They're the Chairman's favourites."

Being a village lad, Cheng Ching had never heard Western music and had no idea what foxtrots and waltzes were. He listened to the tempo and after a while saw to his utter amazement the Chairman dancing with Ying.

"Hey! Look! That's my elder sister dancing with the Chairman!" he cried excitedly.

"She's a beauty," his companion said, admiringly. "Your family must be blessed."

Soon other couples joined the dancing and his view of the the Chairman and Ying became obscured. He had never seen Western dancing before. It seemed to be a form of rotating hugging set to music. If he had not witnessed the Chairman and Ying indulging he would have considered it decadent. Now he thought only of how pleasurable it would be to whirl with Ying in his arms.

* * *

"The tour of the Forbidden City is concluded." The guide's announcement jolted Cheng Ching out of his reverie. "You are now free to continue sight-seeing on your own. The coaches to take you back to your barracks or hostels will be parked in that car park over there. They will leave at precisely six o'clock. Please remember the number of your coach. If you miss the departure time and cannot find your own way back, report to the nearest Public Security Bureau for assistance. I wish you all pleasant journeys to your homes tomorrow."

Released from the tour, Cheng Ching rushed back to the Gate of Heavenly Peace where he found Ying already waiting next to the middle entrance, below the portrait of Chairman Mao.

"Elder Sister!" he shouted, running forward. "At last we are together. Where would you like to go? What should we see first?"

"Let us walk a while and talk," Ying said.

"All right. It was marvellous watching you dance with the Chairman and the other leaders the other night. Democracy must be working in our country. I never imagined we could get so close to our leaders and engage them in conversation. None of them put on airs. They behaved just like ordinary people. You must tell me everything. I've got exciting news. I've been saving it for today. Can you believe it, Chairman Mao has given me his personal support to join the Communist Party!"

"Fantastic! Congratulations!"

Cheng Ching began recounting in detail his encounter with the Chairman. He was so caught up with his own narrative that he did not notice a growing pensiveness in Ying. When he had finished, he said: "How about that? Isn't that like a dream come true? Now you must tell me your story. How did it feel dancing with the Chairman?"

"He was a very smooth dancer and a charming talker. It was certainly an experience I shall never forget."

"What did he say to you?"

"I can't go into that," Ying said, with downcast eyes. "I've been warned by security people that whatever the Chairman says is a state secret, not to be repeated to anyone else. I will not be going home tomorrow."

"Oh? You mean you're staying a few days longer? That would be nice. I'd like to stay too, except that I don't have enough money. I had thought of escorting you to Soochow before I head for Anhui."

"It's not a matter of staying for a few more days. I may have to stay for a very long time."

"What? Why?"

"Chairman Mao has asked me to become one of his personal nurses. The Central Bureau of Guards is conducting security checks on me. If I pass, if no black mark can be found in my family background, I will be moving behind the vermilion walls of the Chung Nan Hai compound."

"To serve the Chairman is a great honour. But what about your medical studies?"

Ying shrugged. "Everyone has to make sacrifices. Chairman Mao has taught us that self-denial is a political virtue. He sacrificed eight members of his family for the sake of the Revolution. How can I think of myself when I am required to serve him?"

Her voice sounded oddly flat, as if she were engaging in a debate with herself. "He is a very important person, the personification of our nation," she continued. "His health is of the utmost importance. His wisdom is needed to guide us through the next stage of China's development. How can I put my personal wishes ahead of the needs of the nation? Haven't you and others shed blood for the nation? Should I do less? If I pass the security checks it will be my duty to join his nursing team."

All Cheng Ching's hopes for a relationship with Ying seemed to shake and crumble like buildings in an earthquake. "We can at least stay in touch, write to each other," he said in desperation.

Ying shook her head. "That will not be possible. Inside Chung Nan Hai, everything is a state secret. It will be dangerous to communicate with anyone outside. Innocent remarks may be misunderstood. I'm sorry to be cut off from another brother. This time, I'm to blame."

The bright Peking sunshine seemed to sear Cheng Ching. He felt as if he were being roasted in an inferno.

They were passing a photographer's shop. "Let's have our photograph taken together," Ying said. "Then we'll have something to remember each other by."

Cheng Ching acquiesced without enthusiasm. The proprietor promised to have the prints ready by the following morning. Ying paid for the pictures and they left the shop.

Seeing that Cheng Ching was still downcast, Ying slipped her arm through his. "You told me Chairman Mao had spoken of you as a man from whom great things might be expected. I expect that too. The Chairman has given you a head start in the Party. Make the most of it. Once in a while spare a thought for your Elder Sister, for she will be thinking of you often. Now I must run. I have to present myself at the Central Bureau of Guards for questioning."

Ying dashed away and Cheng Ching watched her receding figure disappear among the crowds. Slowly he retraced his steps to the Gate of Heavenly Peace. The portrait of Chairman Mao looked down. In spite of being his benefactor, Mao's face now appeared smug and self-satisfied and less benign than before.

The Chairman had a million nurses to choose from, Cheng Ching thought. Why did he have to choose Ying? Why did he have to snuff out his hope of finding happiness?

Sugared liquids

JUNE 1955

9

"Why are you wasting your Saturdays here?" Chu Wing-seng asked Little Ho, as the troop started to disperse. "I have to keep up with this nonsense, but you've already graduated."

Little Ho, whose khaki uniform and beret displayed the insignia of Troop Leader, did not reply. After they were out of earshot, however, he said in a low, chiding voice: "You shouldn't say things like that in front of others. That's the reason the Scout Master has never allowed you to rise above the rank of Patrol Second."

"Don't give a toss! What I want to know is why you're still in this stupid farce."

"There wasn't anyone to take over as Troop Leader, if you must know. The Scout Master asked me to continue. What's wrong with that? A couple of the boys, like you, got interested in snakes. I couldn't abandon them."

The mention of snakes discomfited Chu Wing-seng, reminding him of his failure of nerve. Although Little Ho did help him to catch three snakes eventually, he never attained much standing or respect.

He left his catches with Little Ho for fear of upsetting his mother if he took them home.

"Why not tell the kids the truth? The Brits want us nice and well-behaved, with every bit of rebellion scrubbed out of us. That's the whole idea behind scouting, isn't it?"

Chu Wing-seng deliberately sought to provoke, because he wanted to pierce Little Ho's carapace of good nature.

"That's not fair," Little Ho answered, in a tone of sweet reasonableness. "Scouting's supposed to help people develop character. I see nothing wrong with promoting truthfulness, honesty and consideration for others."

"Let's not argue. Let's go for snacks."

Taking snacks after assembly was a custom initiated by Little Ho. It had been an adventure for Chu Wing-seng at first, wandering through the old Western District filled with the noise

82

of clattering trams and the pungencies of the dried seafood and poultry markets.

The shop at Centre Street Little Ho had introduced him to delighted him with its mouth-watering fare, some of which he had never tasted before. Its concoctions, commonly called "sugared liquids", included snow fungus stewed with papaya, black sesame gruel, lotus seeds cooked with lily pods, tofu jelly with syrup, red beans seasoned with dried tangerine peel and gingko nuts prepared with barley. Each preparation was credited by tradition with a beneficial effect on a particular part of the body. A walnut gruel, for example, was supposed to be a tonic for the brain, while a preparation made with dark-green lentil seeds reputedly produced a cooling effect on the blood.

The shop was close to where Little Ho lived. The route they took was by way of a network of narrow cobblestoned streets lined with stores and workshops offering a staggering array of goods and services. Wooden tubs, scrubbing boards and clogs; paper lanterns, red plaques and banners with propitious sayings; palm-leaf fans, chicken-feather dusters and coir-fibre brooms; writing brushes, seal stones and seal ink-pads impregnated with crushed cinnabar and oil; buttons, needles and spools of coloured thread. There were bakeries, noodle shops and small eateries, as well as the odd letter-writer, cobbler, barber, herbalist and seller of tropical fish.

Chu Wing-seng eyed the cluttered premises with contempt. They reeked of obsolescence and unfulfilled lives. The shopkeepers sat indolent, smoking, gossiping, playing cards, listening to the radio, indifferent to promoting sales. It seemed absurd that such establishments could survive.

Chu Wing-seng was irritated by their proprietors' inability to foresee their doom. Who would want scrubbing-boards or wooden clogs a few years hence? How many would require writing brushes in another ten years? Schools were already turning to ballpoints. Stone seals! How antiquated! They were for old women and illiterates. If the articles in the magazines brought home by his father were anything to go by, market forces would soon see off such deadbeat stores.

He hated the backwardness they represented. It seemed to reflect the unprogressiveness of his race and its resistance to change. Yet their stubborn survival seemed to mock his modernizing instincts.

"They're all heading for extinction," Chu Wing-seng cried, in sudden frustration.

"What? You mean the scouts?" Little Ho was taken aback.

"No, I mean these stupid shops. They'll all die out."

"They've been here for generations. My father and I often patronize them. They're nice and friendly. Why should they die out?"

"Don't be romantic. How can you believe that crap about the unchanging East in tourism brochures? Just look at these places! They're dusty and cluttered. The war has blown our world apart and it can't be put back. We had better realize that and start doing things the American way. That's the wave of the future. That's where the big bucks are."

"Is that what your father has taught you?"

"No!" Chu Wing-seng replied vehemently. "He wants me to stay away from business. But I'm going to prove I can make more money than he can."

"Life isn't just about money."

"You sound like my parents. I may not be in university but I know that money is the ultimate power."

"Not everybody looks at life in terms of money."

"Don't they? Let me tell you about one of our Filipina maids. She's a university graduate, a qualified teacher. She would rather work for us as a maid than as a teacher in the Philippines. Why? Because she earns four times more than as a teacher back home."

"Perhaps she needs the money to support her family."

"It doesn't matter whether she needs the money or not. The point is that it's available and she wants it. Wanting to have more is a basic human instinct. That's why everybody wants to be rich, because they can then buy whatever they want, whoever they want. How can the poor compete? We want one more maid and forty Filipino kids are deprived of a teacher. That's how the world operates. You've got to make as much as you can so that you can call the shots."

"Ah Seng, you're much smarter than I. But you make the future sound so depressing. Shouldn't people simply make an honest living and be content with what they get?"

"Didn't they tell you in Bible class that to those who have more will be given? That means we should grab what we can. Biology taught us that only the fittest will survive. Didn't you learn that?"

Little Ho flushed. "Survival of the fittest is intended for jungles, not civilized societies. In civilized societies people have to help one another. T. P. Choy is a great believer in that."

"Who the devil's T. P. Choy?"

"He's President of our Student Union. He's been trying to start a discussion group on social questions, since political topics are out of bounds under the law. Unfortunately, not many have taken him up. Most are too busy studying or dating."

Chu Wing-seng shook his head. "A discussion group on social questions! A fat lot of good in a colony. Another dreamer! You two must be real Boy Scouts!"

"I see nothing wrong in that. Scouts are supposed to be helpful to others. Choy's ideas are quite stimulating. They make me think. At the last meeting we discussed the resettlement of the fifty or sixty thousand victims of the 1953 squatter fire at Shek Kip Mei. We tried to work out why it had to take such a horrendous fire for the government to start a rehousing programme. The appalling conditions in squatter areas have been known for years. The government must have anticipated the need for better housing. It had the money. Why didn't it act before? Was it... ?"

Chu Wing-seng cut Little Ho short. "Pragmatism. Decent conditions'll attract more refugees. We're a small place. We can't accommodate everybody from China. Misery's a useful deterrent."

"Choy says that sort of argument may sometimes be used by our foreign rulers, but not by us. The refugees are our brothers, people of our own blood. Many have relatives here. Choy says relying on misery as a deterrent betrays a meanness of heart. A person facing starvation, torture or even death would still flee, even if the alternative is far from good. Civilized societies should do what they can for the less fortunate. I agree with Choy. I've given up the idea of opening a restaurant. I'm going to devote my life to helping people."

It was now Chu Wing-seng's turn to flush. The words

wounded him, as if this unknown person named Choy had attacked him and the ideas he believed in. But then, he was used to being misunderstood. "Don't be sentimental!" he declared. "You'll end up a loser. We're not here to solve the problems of the world. Life's a fight for survival and it's every man for himself. If you don't go after what you want, you'll get trampled underfoot."

"Lots of people are already being trampled underfoot. That's why I want to help them, to repay some of the good fortune I've enjoyed."

"You're joking! What good fortune have you ever had, for heaven's sake?" Chu Wing-seng's voice rose in disbelief. "You live in some grubby sub-divided tenement, sharing a kitchen and a latrine with no flush with umpteen other people. You haven't a decent suit to put on your back and you live surrounded by muck and noise."

Little Ho showed no sign of being upset. "Quite a lot, actually," he said calmly. "My free place at school gave me the chance of making friends with you and Gold Star is putting me through university. Otherwise I might have followed my father to spend my life fiddling with locks. With a good education I can one day do something better for myself and for others. Isn't that a lot to be thankful for?"

"You got a free place because your mother's pastor wanted to convert you to Christianity, can't you see?" Chu Wing-seng declared in exasperation. "He had an ulterior motive. Gold Star has nothing to do with your being at university. Your father made an investment and it worked out. That's capitalism, pure and simple."

"Can't be that simple. Fate must have come into it. My father would not have bought Gold Star shares if it had not been for your father standing up to the Brits. One way or another, he thinks we owe somebody a debt of gratitude."

"Tell your father he doesn't owe anybody anything. His investment paid off. That's all."

"Investments need money. What about people with none?"

"They'll have to remain wage slaves."

"That's not very fair."

"Life's never fair. You're tall and I'm short. You've got good eyesight and I haven't. What's fair about that?" Chu Wing-seng's voice rose again with irritation. "I don't like to see people live in poverty any more than you do. But that's the way the world is. The poor can only get out of poverty if they sincerely want to be rich. Stirring things up like this fellow Choy doesn't help. You may not believe me now, my friend, but in time you'll see that I'm right. If you continue to think the way you do, I guess I'll have to keep an eye out for you."

Little Ho looked bemused. "You mean you're not going to let me be ground into the dust by the laws of natural selection?"

"You're different. You're my friend."

They reached Centre Street. There were two shops selling "sugared liquids" and they headed for the one whose offerings they liked better. The entrance was flanked by a glass display case on one side and a black painted counter on the other. The glass case exhibited a wide variety of non-liquid snacks, including red-bean rolls, almond biscuits, walnut cookies, coconut tarts and sesame cakes. Behind the counter sat a shrewd-looking old woman with a gold tooth. She was loud in her welcome. There were two servers inside the shop, a middle-aged man and a teenage girl. All three appeared to belong in the same family. As customers finished, the servers would cry out the sums due and the old woman collected them.

The shop was well-patronized. Three ceiling fans provided a modest breeze. The sweet concoctions attracted flies and two strips of brown fly-paper dangling from the ceiling displayed many captives.

Chu Wing-seng and Little Ho had arrived just in time to commandeer a booth being vacated at the rear. They sat down and took off their khaki berets. The offerings of the shop and their respective prices were set out on coloured paper pasted on the walls.

Chu Wing-seng ordered a red-bean gruel while Little Ho went for a bowl of lotus seeds prepared with dried lily pods.

Halfway through their treats, Little Ho asked in a low, worried voice: "Judging from your earlier remarks, I suppose this place is in danger of going too?"

"Certainly."

"I can't see why. Business is good. People are keen on

sugared liquids. I love the stuff. You and I come regularly. Why should it go out of business?"

"Just look around you. This place probably hasn't changed in fifty years. The people in charge are too dumb to realize they're cheating themselves. These premises have probably been bought by an ancestor and nothing much has changed since. Because they pay no rent, they haven't factored that into their prices. Nor notional wages. They don't advertise or do promotions. No idea of creative accounting. They just chug along, expecting the business to carry on forever."

"But the place is crowded most of the time. What's the point of advertising for more customers when there's no room for them?"

"It's not good enough to rely on steady customers. Tastes change. Western confections are becoming popular. Soon this place'll be competing with chocolate bars, milk shakes and multi-flavoured ice creams. A business has to keep winning new customers."

"Well, I still prefer the desserts here. There are some I haven't even tried."

"That's precisely the trouble. There's too much choice. That leads to inefficiencies. Soon the younger workers will get sick of learning the skills needed to prepare so many different types of specialities. They'll resent the long hours and the meagre returns. Places like this deserve to go under."

"You're always so hard on people."

"I'm not hard on anybody," Chu Wing-seng said. "I just want people to see their situations realistically. The aim of an enterprise society is to change the instinct for keeping up with the Joneses into a passion for overtaking the Joneses. Muddling along means no growth, no prosperity. Capitalism demands that everybody should want more. It's like riding a bicycle. You have to keep pedalling or else you fall off. Only with everybody going hard at it can market forces be kept efficient."

Little Ho shook his head and stopped eating. "People talk a lot about efficiency and market forces these days," he said. "I wish I could get all the arguments straight in my head. I sometimes wonder what's so good about being efficient in luring people into becoming smokers or alcoholics. Or being efficient in cutting down forests, killing wild life and manufacturing weapons of war. It just seems we're increasingly moving away from what our forebears have taught us for thousands of years."

"The world is changing. It's now all about market forces, guided by the invisible hand of self-interest."

"But what about other forces? T. P. Choy says human dignity, social cohesion and cultural identity must be taken into account. We must care for people too weak to look after themselves. We have to create a fairer society."

Chu Wing-seng sighed. "The Communists tried to do that across the border and look at the result. Would you rather have what we've got here or what the rest of China has?"

"I get so confused," Little Ho said, meekly. "When I listen to you, much of what you say makes sense. But when I talk to Choy, I find myself agreeing with him too. I ought to get you two together. I can't hold a candle to either of you."

"By all means."

Chu Wing-seng felt elated at the prospect of a challenge. Although his opponent was a university student he was confident he could hold his own. He had had discussions with the Filipina maid and though she was also a university graduate she did not know half as much as he did.

"I don't know whether I can arrange it, though," Little Ho said. "Choy's graduating and I might not see him again. I'll let you know. We might get him to meet us here after assembly next Saturday and enjoy some sugared liquids as well."

"Fine."

The two friends made their separate ways home after the snacks, Little Ho on foot and Chu Wing-seng by taxi.

Conversations

10

The sky was thick with the promise of rain as the 4,000-ton freighter, recently re-named the *Rising Star*, steamed at twelve knots towards Taiwan. It was flying Liberian colours. Apart from its cargo-carrying capacity, it featured four passenger cabins, two of which were occupied.

Chu Wing-seng, who occupied one of the cabins, climbed the metal rungs leading to a small sun-deck. He was glad he was not seasick. It was his first sea voyage. In fact, it was his first journey out of Hong Kong. He had been pacing the main deck for an hour to take his mind off the gentle rolling of the ship.

On the sun-deck, Chu Tung-po, the other passenger, was standing by the starboard railing, gazing out to sea. A breeze teased a few strands of his hair.

"Love the sea," the elder Chu said. "Gives a man room to think. That's why I enjoy taking the pleasure boat out at night. You should try it." His voice was wistful.

To Chu Wing-seng his father looked like a matinee idol in a white open-necked shirt, checked Bermudas and blue canvas deck shoes. An ultra-thin Piaget gold watch with a black face added a touch of class. Everything seemed to come so easily to his father. He drew admiration simply by standing there. He didn't have to wear absurd horn-rimmed glasses.

Chu Wing-seng resented his own appearance. His clothes, though identical to his father's, did not produce the same effect. His shorts reached below his knees like a clown's. He was five inches shorter than his father and, at seventeen, he might never grow any more. Was he destined to be stunted, like that miniature pine in his father's study?

"You said we had things to discuss," Chu Wing-seng said abruptly, joining his father at the railing. "Why have you asked me on this trip?"

Two white-breasted sea gulls circled above them, scavenging for food, and Chu Wing-seng felt as if he, too, were scavenging for his father's approval.

His father turned and gave him a faint smile. "For a chance to talk before you leave home," he said, running a hand through his hair. "Your mother's worried you might not cope in America."

The mention of his mother made Chu Wing-seng wince. He loved her. Yet she always found ways to embarrass him. Whereas other mothers came to Parents' Day in nylon stockings and high-heeled shoes, his mother would appear in plain, sombre cotton clothes, looking like a servant in spite of her beautiful face. She wore neither rouge nor jewellery. She would also try to hold his hand. It made him look a sissy. Even now, when he was about to enter university, she still fussed over him and watched his every move.

"To Mother I'm always a little boy," Chu Wing-seng said, grudgingly. "What about you? Do you think I can't cope?"

"Well, the Confucians used to hold that a person embarking upon learning had to be thirty before he could stand firm and sixty before his ears became obedient to truths. It would not be until seventy that he could follow his heart's desires without transgressing what was right. You have barely begun. Society is made up of all kinds of people, some more essential than others. We can always do with more doctors and teachers. On the other hand, we would probably be better off with fewer lawyers and currency speculators. You have many options. Why decide so prematurely on business administration?"

"Because I want to be like you, though you discourage me at every turn. So I might as well learn about business at university."

"There are few things about business that can be taught in a classroom. Circumstances often dictate what a man has to do. Many of the things I did, I did for you and your mother."

Chu Wing-seng detected a note of either unhappiness or regret in his father's voice. "What are you talking about, Father?"

A Filipino steward appeared with two glasses of chilled lemonade.

"I didn't order any," Chu Wing-seng said.

"I did," Chu Tung-po said. "Thought you might get thirsty pacing the deck."

Chu Wing-seng accepted the glass gracelessly. Dusk was creeping in. The smell of rain suffused the air.

"Have you ever imagined what starvation might be like? Your

stomach twists itself into knots, you know," Chu Tung-po said.

"I've heard about famines. But Hong Kong's passed that stage, surely?"

"You can never be sure, if war comes again."

"You think war will flare again?"

"No, but it does no harm to be on the alert. A stable situation can deteriorate quickly, like during the last war."

"Tell me about the last war."

"When the Japs bombed Pearl Harbor and captured Hong Kong in 1941 no one had any inkling what was in store. You were just a baby then. The occupation was really bad. The Japs rewarded collaborators with food but kept supplies at subsistence level for the rest. Trade in foodstuffs was disrupted and prices soared.

"The Japs also closed banks and froze accounts. Many businesses had to shut. People were left with only what they had in their pockets. Most didn't have a bean to fall back on. The Japs also required all public transactions to be conducted in their new occupation currency. Violation meant execution. The exchange rate was set at four Hong Kong dollars to one of theirs. Purchasing power fell. Food supplies stopped coming from China because no one wanted Japanese occupation currency. You sure you want to hear about those miserable times?"

"Why not? I lived through them. Might as well know what really happened then."

Chu Wing-seng was not particularly interested in the Japanese occupation. But he thought if he kept his father talking about the occupation his father would be prevented from going on about his choice of studies at Princeton.

"The Japs intended life to be hard," his father said, reflectively. "They had a war to fight and didn't want to feed civilians. They imposed rationing of rice, oil and sugar and limited the maximum amount of each item anyone could purchase at any one time to three or four days' supply. Prices were also set at many multiples of the pre-war ones. Worse than that, each ration had to be purchased from a different depot, so you had to keep going from one depot to another.

"Queueing became a daily chore. Your poor mother! She got the worst of it. We had to queue separately to make the best of things, but your mother refused to be separated from you. She carried you, day after day, in her arms or strapped to her back. I'll never know how she endured all those interminable hours of waiting her turn, sometimes standing overnight. She refused to allow me carry you when I queued."

"I never knew it was as bad as that!" Chu Wing-seng exclaimed. "Why haven't either of you mentioned this before?"

"Your mother doesn't like to be reminded of those times. So we never mention them."

"Mother's not here now. Tell me more." Chu Wing-seng's interest was now engaged. "How did you and Mother survive?"

"Sheer luck and the help of friends," Chu Tung-po replied. "If you really want to know the details, let's begin with the food depots. Their operating hours were erratic. So were supplies. Stocks often ran out before everybody could be served. Depots opened or closed according to whim. The choice then was either to remain in the queue overnight or to lose your place. Scuffles and arguments were common. The Japs met disturbances with rifle butts.

"Each adult was only allotted six taels or about eight ounces of rice per day! Babies like you weren't even counted. The quality was abysmal, full of husks and sand. Unrationed food was simply too expensive for ordinary people.

"People soon got the message and fled. By the beginning of 1944 three quarters of the population had vanished. As the tide of war turned, the Japs became even more indifferent to the plight of civilians. They scrapped rations altogether and left people to fend for themselves. Those unable to flee were really up against it. The rich slaughtered their pets to stave off starvation. The poor hunted rodents and reptiles. Those who couldn't hunt were reduced to eating roots and leaves. Malnutrition, tuberculosis and beri-beri became endemic. Corpses appeared in the streets with pieces of flesh missing, particularly buttocks. Cannibalism was whispered about."

Chu Wing-seng shook his head in disbelief. "How appalling! One of my friends told me he had hunted reptiles with his father. I didn't realize things got that bad. I didn't eat any human flesh, did I?"

"No." Chu Tung-po smiled reassuringly. "No human flesh

for any of us. You'll have to thank an uncle by the surname of Fung for that. You'll meet him when we get to Taiwan. His nickname's Buck-toothed Fung and he's quite a character. His looks would frighten the living daylights out of most people. He invited me to join a group of companions— one of whom was Uncle Yue — to sail to Chinese-controlled territory where food was cheap and plentiful.

"I told him I had no money, even if cheap food was available. He laughed. He said the middle class was hopeless. In good times it wasted money on Swiss watches, German cameras, French perfumes, silver cigarette-cases, malt whiskey, heaven knows what. We all had a few such items at home. Selling them would produce the money needed to buy food, he said. The middle class in Free China was the same. People there were prepared to pay handsomely for baubles that enhanced their status. The dangerous part was making the trip there and back.

"I was desperate because I couldn't bear to see you and your mother wasting away. I gathered up the few items I had and joined the group. We made our runs after dark, through a gauntlet of Japanese patrols, pirates, bandits, treacherous seas and Allied air raids. Getting caught was something none of us wanted to think about. The initial run was a great success. Came back with rice, beans, Yunnan ham, dried shrimps, wind-dried ducks, sausages and other goodies. Each of us had enough to feed our families for weeks."

Chu Tung-po paused and took a drink of lemonade.

"I immediately began thinking ahead," he continued. "The food could not last long. No one knew how long the war might drag on. Having sold most of my disposable items, what had I left to trade with the next time? I had to find new things. So I experimented. I took some food and went around offering it in exchange for suitable objects.

"I was amazed by what was pressed upon me. People begged me to go into their homes to select whatever I wanted in return for a few miserable sausages or a couple of catties of rice. I was offered jewellery and heirlooms, exquisite embroideries and antique vases, jades and stamp collections.

"My former English tutor, Teacher Tam, whom you'll also meet in Taiwan, had taught me a few things about antiques. I knew some of the items were far too rare to be bartered away at provincial marketplaces. They needed to be kept for better times, to realize their true value. Hunger and suffering were immediate, however. People were living skeletons, surrounded by precious paintings and artefacts that could not dull their hunger. Some signed away whole buildings for a couple of sacks of rice."

Chu Tung-po paused again, as if troubled by his recollections. He then continued with a sigh.

"I wanted to help them. But I also saw the opportunity to become rich, so that neither you nor your mother would ever be in want again. I was learning about supply and demand and risk/reward ratios in the raw. I pointed out the opportunities to other members of the group and we decided to make our fortunes by continuing our runs.

"Your mother was unhappy, however. She was all for relieving hunger, but did not think we should go after profit. She did not appreciate that other people were not like her. They would not risk their lives without the prospect of big rewards.

"We traded some food and gathered a fresh supply of items for our second run, everything from Movado watches and ebony cigarette-holders to Church's shoes and fine British suits. But we hit trouble. Pirates tried to board us one night. We resisted. Uncle Fung fought like ten men. I knocked some into the sea. One or two pirates might have been killed in the fighting. Eventually we chased them off."

"You mean you all turned killers?"

"No! We only defended ourselves. Except for Uncle Fung, I don't think any of us killed anybody."

"You said you knocked pirates into the sea. You must have injured them."

"Yes, I suppose. It was self-defence. A number of us got hurt too."

"Did you continue with the expeditions after that?"

"Of course. Continued till the end of the war and for a while afterwards also. Profits were too good. No one wanted to stop."

"Did you have to fight off more pirates?" The almost childish eagerness in Chu Wing-seng's voice elicited a smile from his father.

"We were lucky. Had only one other run-in with pirates plus

one attack by robbers. Both at night. Successfully fought them off, though one of our companions lost his life. The gods must have been with us. We missed the Japanese patrols.

"It's one of life's little ironies. Just when we were getting enough to eat, your mother turned vegetarian. She gave away part of the food to help neighbours. I traded surplus food for land and buildings. I was convinced that Hong Kong would boom once the war was over. I was right. So you see, being successful comes mainly from luck and opportunity. It has very little to do with mission statements or synergy or the rest of that business-school rigmarole."

"But you were still motivated by profit and you had to work out whether the rewards were worth the risks."

"I suppose so."

"And you all ended up rich?"

"Well, those who stuck together and followed my advice did. But not Uncle Fung."

"Why not?"

"He took a different view. He wanted to live for the day. He feared he might not survive the next fight. Squandered his money on women and gambling. Also left Hong Kong too soon. When the Communist armies swept across the Yangtze, he thought they would over-run Hong Kong. Didn't fancy his chances with his Kuomintang connections. So he headed for Taiwan. Great pity. Could have become rich. That's why I'm inclined to be generous when he does a job for me or touches me for a loan. But I never expect any loan to be repaid. He's not very good with money."

"He's a welsher then?"

"Well, I wouldn't put it that way." Chu Tung-po paused, emptied his glass of lemonade and gazed into the sea. "I suppose he has human failings, like the rest of us. You can make up your own mind when you meet him."

"So the Evergreens did get their start from smuggling, as the newspapers have been saying."

"Since time immemorial, when a territory is under enemy occupation, circumventing enemy restrictions has been considered an honourable activity. It would be as true to say we got our start by famine relief. But I suppose describing it as smuggling sells more newspapers."

"And this boat? Have you bought it for more patriotic business?"

Chu Tung-po laughed. "No, nothing like that. It's just handy to have a couple of vessels at your disposal. One never knows when they might come in useful. Airports can be closed easily during an emergency, but the sea is always wide open."

* * *

The next evening, the *Rising Star* docked at Kaohsiung. Buck-toothed Fung was waiting with a chauffeur-driven black Merccdes and three uniformed army officers.

"Elder Brother Fung!" Chu Tung-po cried and embraced his old friend.

Chu Wing-seng was surprised by the warmth his father displayed towards a known killer. He certainly did not look like his father's other friends. Though no taller than his father, he was thickset and barrel-chested. He moved with the lumbering gait of a gorilla and probably had the strength of one as well. His face was misshapen and lopsided. The right half was squashed, leaving one narrow, cunning eye glaring an inch or more out of alignment. His ill-fitting Western suit seemed a throwback to the bootlegging thugs of the Roaring Twenties in America.

Yet, for all his ugliness and bulk, Uncle Fung appeared to Chu Wing-seng to be more comical than menacing. Four buck-teeth protruded over the man's lower lip like some ridiculous miniature snow-plough. They fixed his crooked face with a simpleton's grimace. His hair was close-cropped. Its greyness argued for a degree of respect.

"So this is Little Seng!" Buck-toothed Fung boomed, clapping a heavy paw on Chu Wing-seng's shoulder and regarding him with his unbalanced eyes. "He seems not to have grown very much since I bounced him on my knees. Ha! Ha! Looks a brainy type though, with spectacles and all. Must take after his father."

Chu Wing-seng thought the patronizing tone an unwarranted liberty.

His father whispered something to his ugly friend and then

handed him some documents. Uncle Fung in turn passed them to the army officers who then boarded the *Rising Star*. The new arrivals were whisked away by Uncle Fung in the Mercedes with a minimum of formalities.

"What was that about?" Chu Wing-seng asked in the car.

"Uncle Fung wanted a favour for some friends," Chu Tung-po replied.

"You want me to explain the ways of the world?" Fung asked, teasingly.

"Oh, no, Uncle Fung. That's not my concern. Just curiosity."

"Yeah, imagine you've got plenty to be curious about at your age!" Fung laughed and slapped Chu Wing-seng on the thigh. "You stick with your Uncle Fung and he'll show you some of the deepest mysteries of life."

After they had checked into a hotel, Uncle Fung took them out to a superb dinner, during which the two older men steadily drank a pale green wine from Chekiang Province. The wine, made with fermented sorghum, glutinous rice and herbs, was potent. Chu Wing-seng confined himself to soft drinks. After dinner, he was surprised to see the two men engaging in a boisterous Chinese drinking game. He had never associated his father with that type of blue-collar rowdiness. Nor had he imagined him to be so good at it, defeating Uncle Fung three bouts out of four.

The game was a simple one, rhythmic and fast-moving. The players faced each other, with a clenched fist and a glass of wine. Upon a signal, each chanted a series of numbers ranging from zero to ten. With every chant each extended a varying number of fingers. If a contestant shouted a number matching the sum of the fingers extended by both, his opponent had to empty his glass.

Buck-toothed Fung turned ruddy-faced to Chu Wing-seng after his defeats. "Do you play this game, my lad?"

"Of course," Chu Wing-seng lied with bravado. Having watched his father he thought he could manage. He didn't want to lose face by backing away from an ugly brute.

"All right then. Let's see if you're cut from the same cloth. No fizzy drinks in this. A man's drink," Fung said, planting a glass of the greenish wine before him.

Chu Wing-seng's throat felt dry as he settled down to the

match. He lost the first bout in record time and the fiery wine seared his gullet as it went down. His head began to swim. He expected his father to come to the rescue, but he didn't.

He had no choice but to redeem himself through another bout. He saw Uncle Fung re-filling his glass and heard him say: "You need more nimble fingers, my lad, a woman's touch to loosen them up."

The second bout went no better than the first. After the second penalty, the world spun and his head began pounding like a drum in a dragon-boat race. He only had the vaguest recollection of his father carrying him to bed.

The next day they drove to Tainan and visited a range of temples — Confucian, Buddhist, Taoist, ancestral and a number of hybrids. Chu Wing-seng's head throbbed with increasing agony.

The day ended with dinner and a further session of the fingers-guessing game. But this time Uncle Fung invited two young women to join them. The women were high-spirited and good at the game, but each nevertheless was defeated by Chu Tung-po.

Then one of them challenged Chu Wing-seng. He felt trapped.

"Come on, my lad," Fung egged him on. "Even if you lose, you win. These ladies can take care of you in ways you can't imagine." He laughed uproariously.

Chu Wing-seng took up the challenge and to his surprise he won the first bout as well as the second. Just as he was beginning to enjoy the game, he lost the next bout and the one after that. Again his father had to put him to bed.

The third day in Taiwan began much as the second for Chu Wing-seng, with an excruciating hangover. When he met his father for breakfast, he was filled with dread over another evening of alcoholic punishment. He said gloomily: "How much longer do we have to run around with Uncle Fung? I don't think my head and liver can survive another evening."

"Sorry you got thrown in at the deep end," Chu Tung-po replied. "One has to learn when to pick up a challenge and when to let it pass. We'll be driving up to Taipei today. Over the last two evenings, proprieties have been observed, hospitality exchanged. Once in Taipei, we'll be on our own, with time to do whatever you wish. I still have to have some minor discussions with Uncle Fung, but there'll be no need for you to see him again, unless you particularly wish to."

"Thank heaven for that!" Chu Wing-seng said. "Can't understand why you want to keep up with a brute like that. He's not at all your type."

"My type? Businessmen have to deal with all types, not just those with bespoke suits and clean fingernails."

"I see!" Chu Wing-seng opened his eyes wide and smiled across the table at his father. "You're teaching me something at last! If a man wants to get to the top, he must have villains like Uncle Fung to do the dirty work! Right?"

Awakening

11

It hit Chu Wing-seng suddenly, while travelling in the hotel limousine with his father to call on Teacher Tam. The traffic was moving on the wrong side of the road! How strange he had not noticed earlier! His hangovers must be to blame. From that moment, other differences between Hong Kong and Taipei manifested themselves. Streets signs appeared only in Chinese, in white characters on green backgrounds, instead of bilingually, in black on white. Names resonated with Eastern evocations. The Road of Philanthropy. The Road of Benevolence. By contrast, streets back home glorified departed imperialists — Connaught, Wyndham, Pottinger and Wellington.

Flags fluttering over buildings and monuments were red, with a blue upper-left quadrant setting off a white sun. There was not a Union Jack in sight. Gone were red pillar-boxes and cricket pitches. Money no longer carried the head of a foreign woman with an ungainly crown. No doubt Christmas and Easter meant nothing except for their commercial aspects and English was no longer the common language.

He realized with increasing alarm that he was in another part of China, possibly under false pretences. He had come on a permit issued for "returning overseas Chinese". But neither his nationality nor his instincts conformed. He was a British subject, a citizen of a fracturing empire, drilled into different habits and patterns of thought. He even thought in English rather than Chinese! Was that another bit of Pavlovian conditioning? When did it begin? Had he already turned into a yellow-faced European?

He heard the voice of his father cutting into his reflections. "It might be an idea to tell you something about Teacher Tam before we arrive. He was from Kwangtung originally, now relocated here. He's a great collector of antiques, which he intends to bequeath to a reunited China. But that day seems decades away. He lives in a villa with his wife, spinster sister, four sons, their wives and — at the last count — ten grandchildren. One or two grandchildren are around your age. The sons followed different disciplines but have all ended up as teachers. Father and sons call themselves 'the five voices in the wilderness'.

"Teacher Tam belongs to a family of officials. Got a viceroy and two provincial governors in the family tree. Studied for the imperial examinations like his forebears, but also immersed himself in English. By the time he was ready, the examinations had been discontinued. When the empire itself disappeared, he became a teacher. My father — who was well acquainted with his father — persuaded him to teach me English. I was eight. He was thirty-three. He taught me for ten years."

"Ten years? That's hell of a long time to be studying English!"

"Wasn't just English. He taught me many other things. Made me soak up history, literature and philosophy. Like Socrates, he stressed that the unexamined life was not worth living. Left me hankering after a scholar's life instead of selling crockery."

"Why didn't you do that? You could have become a teacher."

"Family obligations. English was needed for the export trade. Letters of credit, bills of lading and all that stuff. My father sent me to Hong Kong in 1936 to open a branch. Teacher Tam left Canton shortly before then."

Father and son continued in desultory conversation during the rest of the journey, about the former family business and how Taiwan fell into foreign hands, first Dutch and later, Japanese.

They arrived eventually at the entrance of a villa in a tranquil valley. "You can see that in keeping with Chinese tradition the villa is located to the west of the plot, with the garden and its pond at the centre," Chu Tung-po pointed out.

Wing-seng noted that verdant hills formed a backdrop. Oaks, cypresses, bamboos and cherry trees were in abundance. A lotus pond stood in the garden, like a mirror reflecting the peacefulness of the surroundings. Traces of valley mist and sounds of tumbling water enhanced the setting.

"Present these to Teacher Tam," Chu Tung-po said, as he handed his son a bag containing two bottles of Armagnac brought over from Hong Kong. He then ordered the driver of the limousine to wait.

An aged gate-keeper bowed greetings. "The Master is expecting the honoured guests," he said, as he led them through a forecourt into a reception hall, formally laid out with traditional blackwood furniture. It was dominated by a portrait of a bearded man in the official robes of a provincial mandarin. Wing-seng presumed it to be a picture of the father of the host.

Teacher Tam appeared almost immediately. He was of medium build and completely bald. He wore a wispy, white goatee. Otherwise he might have passed for someone younger. He greeted the visitors warmly while a servant served tea.

"For a teacher to be visited by a student of eminence is an honour indeed," Teacher Tam said, with a loud chuckle, as he accepted the gift from Wing-seng. "For him to bring along a son is a double honour. For a humble teacher's partiality to Armagnac to be remembered as well is honour beyond expression."

"A student's indebtedness to his teacher can never be repaid," Chu Tung-po replied, continuing in that vein of ritual banter favoured by Chinese scholars.

"It is I who must beg forgiveness for my many deficiencies. Your commercial successes resound throughout the Four Seas. A worthy teacher would have rendered his students incapable of becoming tycoons."

"Teacher Tam has delivered me from an even worse fate. For that I shall be eternally indebted. It is the bent of my character that has been deficient. Like Confucius, Teacher Tam has urged me to find pleasure in water and virtue in hills. But I failed to heed such wisdom and allowed myself to be caught up in the trammels of worldly things. I must seek the forgiveness of my teacher."

"Each man has a choice. Each must be drawn by his heart's desires. Eternal truths are always there to be grasped."

"Easier said than done. A couple of wrong moves and one soon finds oneself trapped by obligations towards others. One is sometimes tempted to throw it all up, but conscience makes cowards of us all."

"I see you have not forgotten your Shakespeare. To be affected by conscience is to be a step closer to wisdom. Too bad all my sons are at work. They relish discussions of this type," Teacher Tam said. Then, turning to Wing-seng, he added: "And you, young sir, are no doubt weary of old men's chatter. I'm afraid my grandchilden are at school. You're stuck with us, I fear. I can deliver you to the women of the house, if you so prefer. There are enough of them around."

"Oh, no, Sir. I'm honoured by the opportunity to learn from Teacher Tam," Wing-seng replied. But in truth he thought the exchanges stilted and pointless. "My Mother has often told me to emulate your masterly calligraphy. My Father has spoken of your renown as a collector of antiques. Might I be favoured with a sight of your treasures?"

"Ah, it is indubitably true that a tiger never sires a cur! It is rare these days for the young to be interested in calligraphy and antiques. I hope the bits and pieces I have managed to salvage do not disappoint. Please excuse me while I turn off the alarm."

Teacher Tam disappeared from the room for a moment before returning. Then he led his guests into a small courtyard through a set of latticed side-doors. Matching doors stood across the courtyard. Between them lay a small rockery against a connecting wall.

The remaining side of the courtyard took the form of a six-foot wall with an opening shaped like a cherry blossom. Above that opening, four moulded characters proclaimed: "The Fragrance of Antiquity Lingers Forever."

"Walls and doors," Teacher Tam remarked, as he led his guests towards the second set of latticed doors. His black cloth shoes made no sound. "Foreigners mistakenly think they're for privacy and separation of spaces rather than for generating depth and mystery."

He nodded towards the cherry-blossom opening and said to Wing-seng: "Gardens are beyond. You are no doubt aware that in archaic script the characters for 'garden' and 'circle' and 'universe' are all interchangeable. Isn't that worth pondering, young sir? Have we lost something by being too precise and clever?"

"That's a thought, Sir," Wing-seng said, politely, though he knew nothing of archaic characters nor what his host was driving at. The gush of words sounded like babbling pedantry.

Wing-seng followed Teacher Tam and his father into the study. He had never seen a traditional Chinese study before. It was bright and spacious. A large redwood writing desk took pride of place and upon it rested the usual paraphernalia for writing — an ink slab, a thick stub of ink, a sheaf of brushes in a blue-and-white porcelain container, a matching brush rest and a flower-shaped rinsing dish in a pale green crackled glaze. There was not a fountain pen or ballpoint in sight. It was like stepping back in time.

Books in both English and Chinese were everywhere, on the desk, in bookcases, on shelves, on chairs. They jostled for space with vases, candy dishes and ashtrays on side tables. Some were opened while others had pieces of paper sticking out as markers. Two scrolls of calligraphy hung from one wall. The characters were too cursive and impressionistic to decipher. A large blue porcelain bowl, entwined outside by a four-clawed dragon in relief, stood on a low stand beneath the calligraphy. It held a collection of rolled-up scrolls. A black-lacquered folding screen, decorated with golden chrysanthemums, stood at one end of the room.

Teacher Tam folded back the screen to reveal a steel-plated door. "A requirement of the insurance company," he said, apologetically, inserting a key into the lock. "Sometimes I wonder why I bother. What good is money if a masterpiece is destroyed? Insurers are Philistines. They fear children breaking things. Art should be freely accessible. My grandchildren have to see my collection under strict supervision."

Behind the steel-plated door was a large room with barred and shuttered windows. Air-conditioning gave off a steady hum. There were a number of illuminated display cases filled with porcelain plates, dishes and stemcups, bronze incense-burners and ceremonial wine vessels, lacquer vases and covered boxes, ivory seals and ornaments, jade teapots and wine pitchers. Between the display cases hung a number of landscape paintings.

"There are a few items from the Imperial Collection over here," Teacher Tam said, leading the way. "That," he added, indicating an elaborately decorated red lacquer vase, "carries an inscription by the Emperor Chien Lung. That is supposed to enhance its rarity and value. Quite frankly, Chien Lung did not always have the best of taste. The workmanship of the vase is in fact third rate. But for those not knowing any better, the praise of an emperor obviously counts for more than the opinion of a lowly bookworm."

"Product endorsement," Wing-seng observed, "like a Wimbledon champion singing the praises of a brand of tennis racquet."

"Ah, so that is what they call it nowadays," Teacher Tam said, nodding.

Wing-seng wandered slowly around the room. Some of the objects were beautiful enough, though he couldn't see why celadon bowls and dishes should be worth so much. He figured many could be mass-produced for a song and few would notice the difference. What was the point of keeping a dish worth tens of thousands under lock and key when a million reproductions could be sold for ninety-nine cents each? They would probably sell even faster if images of Mickey Mouse or Popeye the Sailor were added.

He stopped in front of a landscape painting extensively covered with red imprints of seals. There were in excess of twenty. He had never seen so many on a painting before. He was trying to divine the reason when Teacher Tam came and addressed him.

"I should be interested in your opinion on the Southern School."

"Southern School? I fear I know nothing about it, Sir. I was just surprised by the large number of seals on this painting," he replied.

"This is by a Ming master and the seals are those of successive owners. At the top, one of the previous owners had added a poem of comment. That is the seal of the painter and that of his studio. That one belonged to a minor poet, a friend of the painter's and the original recipient of the painting. Now, that is the seal of a former Secretary to the Board of Rites. That is my great-grandfather's seal, that my grandfather's and that my father's. It is fascinating to try to trace previous owners through seals. It is like unravelling a puzzle."

"Which is your seal, Teacher Tam?"

Teacher Tam laughed and stroked his goatee. "I'm too ashamed to place mine among such illustrious company. I haven't even identified all the previous owners yet."

"Teacher Tam spoke just now of the Southern School. What exactly is it? What does it represent?"

"It is a style of landscape painting reputedly started by Wang Wei in the eighth century. You mean your father has not yet acquainted you with the rudiments of painting? More than twenty years ago I presented him with a primer by Wang Kai known as *The Painting Manual Of The Mustard Seed Garden*. Has he not shown it to you?"

Chu Tung-po, who had caught Teacher Tam's comment, quickly intervened. "My fault, Teacher Tam," he said. "I have allowed myself to become preoccupied with other things."

"Other things? What is more important than the upbringing of children?" Teacher Tam replied, severely. "To bring children into the world is to assume a responsibility for their development. That cannot be delayed or set aside for what you call 'other things'."

"I've been negligent. I have Wang Kai's primer still and I shall see to it that my son becomes acquainted with it."

In order to spare his father further embarrassment, Wing-seng spoke out. "Father did speak on occasion about knowledge of painting being important in the make-up of a cultivated man. But, frankly, people lead such busy lives nowadays that there is little time for scholarly pursuits. There does not seem to be much variety in Chinese landscapes in any case. They all appear much the same. Trees, mountains, rivers, mists and so on, with people appearing as afterthoughts. Why can't Chinese artists be more innovative, do something different?"

"They *are* innovative and different," Teacher Tam said, "though originality is often not uppermost in their minds. On the face of it, they may appear much the same. But would a truth not remain a truth for all eternity? An artist, glimpsing a truth in nature, would naturally try to capture it. Successive generations of Chinese painters have followed that tradition of getting as close to nature as possible. Hsieh Ho, the fifth-century painter, spoke of capturing the chi or life-spirit in paintings. Tung Yuan, the Sung artist, had sought to distil what he called 'the very truths of Heaven' in mountains, trees, rocks and streams.

"Artists in other cultures may have different aims. You do not see severed heads or scenes of rape and pillage in our paintings. Those misfortunes are considered too ephemeral to be worthy of attention. The aim is to find a path to Nature and its mysteries, to lead mankind away from materialism and conflicts.

"One of the Six Principles of painting codified by Hsieh Ho is to copy and perpetuate the old masters. The assumption is that old masters have caught something of the deepest truths in nature. Therefore painters often state quite plainly that their works have been executed after the style of so-and-so. That might account for the impression of sameness you mentioned."

"I see," Wing-seng said. But he did not see. Teacher Tam's gushing exposition struck him as pedantry and humbug. It was like the Buddhist obscurities peddled by his mother. He lived in a commercial and scientific age. Knowledge had to serve some utilitarian purposes and not be accumulated for antiquarian amusement. He could not understand why his father should waste his time calling on such an old codger.

After the visitors had finished viewing the antiques, the older men spent a further period reminiscing over tea. It bored Wing-seng.

The visitors eventually took their leave and as the limousine carried them back to the hotel, Wing-seng said: "What a to-do Teacher Tam makes of paintings. Are you going to make me study that manual?"

"Not if you don't want to," Chu Tung-po replied.

"That stuff is a waste of time. I couldn't read the characters in the scrolls in the study. Too flowery, not like the scrolls in your study."

"Ah, my son, you are missing so much! There are many types of calligraphy. Some are not meant to be read but *felt. Absorbed.* It's art, it's rhythm, it's movement. It isn't copybook writing. In calligraphy, you ignore the meaning of characters and concentrate on the vitality of brush strokes. Great calligraphers, like painters, try to lead viewers to the essence of nature, which is movement."

After having endured Teacher Tam's expositions, Wing-seng was in no mood to hear another spiel on calligraphy. He deflected his father by closing his eyes and pretending to doze.

It had been an altogether unsatisfactory day, Wing-seng thought. The sense of alienation experienced during the drive through Taipei had been exacerbated by Teacher Tam's long-winded erudition. What had any of that ancient babbling got to do with him? Mere curiosities. He was a British subject, armed with a British passport, about to embark for a new life in America. The imprisoned antiques did not represent his heritage any more than the Magna Carta or a haul of Roman coins. They elicited neither reverence nor emotional satisfaction.

He realized suddenly the enormous debt of gratitude he owed to his colonial education. It had stuffed him with useless information about distant European squabbles, about Drake and the Spanish armada, Wellington and Napoleon, Wolfe and Montcalm. It was all utterly forgettable. During that dreary process his expatriate teachers had expunged every attachment to race, nation and culture. In teaching him about self-interest and the survival of the fittest, they had set him free, free from the ethical considerations weighing upon his father, the religious imperatives shackling his mother, the cangues of tradition restraining Teacher Tam. He could shake off all that rubbish like raindrops from an oilskin cloak. What was freedom, after all, but the shedding of inhibitions and restraints? And, until a man was free, how could he know what he might be capable of?

The British had also given him a language that was more creative and ambiguous than Chinese, one he could slip in and out of and exploit its peculiarities. He saw himself as the prototype of modern man — savvy, quick-witted, amoral, contemptuous of the past and focused on the future.

Certainly, even if the heavens fell, he would see that neither his mother nor himself would ever have to queue for a few taels of worm-infested rice. He would owe allegiance to nothing but money and serve no master except himself. He would be like the *Rising Star*, flying any flag that suited his convenience. If international capitalism was to become the new imperialism, he intended to be among its leaders. In a month he would be off to America. There he would begin his preparation for the conquest of the world!

* * *

Two days later, Wing-seng was awakened at dawn by a knocking on the door. He opened it to find his father standing there, fully clothed. "What's the matter?"

"Have to fly to Japan."

"Want me to go with you?"

"No, you can't. You haven't a visa. Can't wait for you to get one. Shouldn't be away more than four days. I've spoken to Uncle Fung and... "

"You're not going to leave me with Uncle Fung!"

"Relax. You don't have to spend time with him. He's got a distant relative in Taipei, job-hunting. About your age. You'll have some company to see what we had planned, Fa Lien, Sun Moon Lake and so on. Hotels all paid for."

Chu Tung-po took out a wad of banknotes and handed it to his son. "This should be more than enough for fun and incidentals," he said. "If you need more, ask Uncle Fung. I'll settle with him later. If I'm held up, I'll get word to you from Japan. You must then make your way on schedule to Kaohsiung and take the *Rising Star* back to Hong Kong. Understood? Now go back to bed."

Wing-seng nodded and watched resentfully as his father disappeared down the hotel corridor.

Fei-Fei

12

It was two o'clock in the morning and Fei-Fei was wide awake, staring distractedly at the oddly shaped shadows on the ceiling. For the past two hours, after Young Master Chu had fallen asleep, she had been re-living the events of the previous six days.

The words of warning uttered by Mama Mui kept echoing inside her head. "Love's not for the likes of you. Sweet talk by men can only lead to heartaches. I know. I've lost my head once. Just treat your customers as shadows cast across your life, shadows without names or faces, each no different from the next. The best hope is for a rich merchant or a powerful official to take to you. Then you may enjoy a period of ease as a concubine or mistress, until he tires of you. When that happens you'll become like me, drinking too much, smoking too much, trying to teach other unfortunates their trade."

The trouble was that Young Master Chu was not a shadow. He had a name and attractive features. During the past six days she had grown accustomed to his round, smiling face, to his voice that seemed at once shy and coaxing. Now lost to sleep he looked as innocent as the brothers she had helped to raise in their village near Su-Ao. At daybreak, however, he would be heading for Kaohsiung to take the ship back to Hong Kong.

"Come with me," Young Master Chu had urged. "The ship belongs to my father. I can sneak you on board. We can get married and travel the world."

"How can I leave?" she had replied, laughing at such fantasies. "I have no papers, no passport, no exit permit. I'm sure to be arrested and punished."

"Don't worry. My father's a magician with money. You've heard the old saw that with enough money even the devil can be made to do one's bidding? Well, my father has lots and lots of money and he has a way of making impossible things possible."

"Will the Hong Kong authorities allow me to stay?"

"Certainly. Once we're married that will make you — in the official jargon — a Hong Kong belonger."

"Please don't joke. Marriage is a serious matter."

"Who's joking?"

"You're teasing me. We're too young to get married. We're only seventeen."

"If we're old enough to do the things we've been doing, we're old enough to get married!"

"You're wicked!" She blushed and thumped him on the chest, as she remembered the pleasures his lips and tongue had given. "I hate you!"

"But I love you."

"Stop it! Stop it! We're not suited. You're from a wealthy family; I'm a fisherman's daughter. I can't even read or write properly. Your family will never permit it."

"You may be surprised. My parents can be quite broad-minded. I can get you all the education you need. Education is a commodity, to be acquired like any other. You buy it with money. Just say you'll marry me and everything'll come out right."

"What about my mother and my brothers and sisters? I just can't up and leave. They are expecting Uncle Fung to get me a job so that I can support them."

"What kind of a job can Uncle Fung get you? The pay wouldn't be enough for you to live in Taipei, let alone support your family. Don't be taken in. My father can take care of your family."

He made everything sound so easy. In the still of the night, however, not only Mama Mui's words but also Uncle Fung's instructions troubled her.

"I want you on something important," Uncle Fung had said. "Play your cards right and you'll hook a big fish. I've a rich friend, suddenly called away on business. He wants his sonny looked after for a few days. Right up your alley. The boy's the same age as you. A 'green-headed lad' for sure, so you'll have to play the bashful virgin. You know what to do. Say you're a distant relative of mine, looking for a job in Taipei. There'll be money in it, to be sure."

It was supposed to be a business transaction, like all the others. How was she to know that Young Master Chu would be so attentive, so gentle, so loving? How was she to know she would fall in love so fast?

She recalled strolling with Young Master Chu through the centre of Taipei when they happened upon a shop specializing in jade ornaments. They had stopped to glance at its window display and were about to move on when the elderly owner came out.

"Do come in," he invited, with a broad, welcoming smile. "A plentiful selection inside. Take your time. You are not obliged to buy. Come in to have a cup of tea on this hot summer's day. If the young lady finds an item to strike her fancy, well, then that must be fate."

She had been reluctant to enter, for she had neither the means nor the intention of buying anything. She also did not want to give the impression of angling for a gift. But Young Master Chu had responded to the invitation and had pulled her in.

Once inside, an assistant served tea and the owner showed tray after tray of jade ornaments. There was a bewildering array of bracelets, rings, earrings, necklaces and pendants. They came in many colours, ranging through white, grey, yellow, brown and mauve to various shades of green. There were also pieces with marvellous combinations of colours, like abstract pictures etched in stone.

"See anything you like?" Young Master Chu asked, in his quaint, Cantonese-accented Mandarin.

"They all look nice, but I don't know anything about jade," Fei-Fei replied.

"Please permit me to advise," the owner intervened. "I have a special place in my heart for young people in love. Oh, yes, I can tell you're in love! I was young once. First love, it's wonderful! It is good to have a memento to mark such glorious days. They come but once. How about this?"

He dangled before them a circular jade pendant in lustrous emerald green. He then placed it in her hand.

"Feel its quality, its warmth, its magic," he said. "A superb piece of the finest Burmese jade. Not Taiwanese nephrite, you know. See the brilliance of the green, the blended striations in white."

"You sure this is Burmese?" Young Master Chu asked. "I've been warned of fakes."

"The reputation of my shop is my guarantee. Jade evokes all

the qualities revered by Chinese people. How can a dealer in jade act against what that stone represents? Jade is smooth and glossy like benevolence, compact and strong like intelligence, full of radiance like good faith. It's like courage, for it cannot be bent, only broken. It's esteemed by all, like the paths to truth and duty. When worn as a necklace or a pendant, it falls naturally towards the ground like humility. One can easily feel those qualities in a piece of jade. No stone colours the imagination as much. Would a humble man who deals in it violate everything is stands for?"

"We do not mean to doubt your word. It is just that we know little about jade. We do not even know why pendants are shaped the way they are."

"This humble person would be happy to explain whatever the gentleman wishes to know about jade," the owner said. "Pendants shaped like a peach denotes longevity, that of a bat represents wealth. This particular pendant is in the form of a circle. Circles have no beginning and no end. They are like the unendingness sought in love.

"This pendant is fashioned after the bi, the symbol of heaven, a symbol familiar since the Shang Kingdom of 3,500 years ago. Note the hole in the centre. It represents the opening through which the soul can ascend into heaven. What more fitting token can be offered to a loved one?"

As he spoke, it seemed to her that the pendant in her hand actually took on the attributes described. She quickly put it down on the counter, afraid she might become attached.

Young Master Chu asked the price and the shop owner quoted a figure that seemed astronomical.

"If the young lady is pleased with it, I can offer a discount of ten per cent, as a token of my good wishes," the owner added.

As Young Master Chu reached for his wallet, she became flustered. She did not know what to say. She was not sure that so expensive a pendant was actually meant for her. It was only when he hung it around her neck that she understood.

"It's a perfect adornment for a charming young lady," the shop owner beamed.

"No, I can't accept so valuable a gift," Fei-Fei protested, fearful about how Uncle Fung and Mama Mui might react.

"Hush," Young Master Chu said, and led her from the shop, to the bows of the owner and his assistants.

Now Fei-Fei looked over to the man sleeping next to her and fingered the emerald-green pendant lying between her naked breasts. It was the most beautiful thing she had even possessed. She would have to hide it, lest Uncle Fung or Mama Mui took it from her. But, if she hid it, would it turn into an everlasting reminder of her deceptions and lies? She silently cursed the unfairness of life.

Her childhood had been one of poverty, helping her mother with household chores and her father with mending fishing nets. When she was fifteen, her father was lost at sea during a typhoon and the family sank progressively into debt.

Then the village money-lender brought Uncle Fung into her life. She heard this stranger with buck teeth and uneven eyes telling her mother: "I can get your daughter a job as a waitress in a Taipei hotel. The pay should support your family and help pay off debts. But I'm not going to train her only to have her skipping off after a few months. I'm only prepared to do it if you and your daughter sign an agreement to work for five years."

Her mother broke down in tears. "That's a very long time. What about two years?"

"Take it or leave it," Uncle Fung said. "I have to invest a lot to make her presentable. She's pretty enough and lively enough, but she can't show up for work in a classy hotel like that. Just look at her skin, dry as old leather. Her hands are full of calluses and her feet are as big as sampans. She doesn't even walk properly, stomping around like a manual worker."

"It's all right, Mother," Fei-Fei said. "Don't cry. Five years will pass quickly. The younger ones will be ready for work then. I don't mind."

Uncle Fung did not get her a job in a hotel, however. Instead he took her into a frightening labyrinth of alleys and warrens hidden behind the modern thoroughfares of Taipei, and passed her over to a woman he addressed as Mama Mui. She was in her late forties and was pleasantly plump and jolly.

The woman clucked her tongue. "She'll need a lot of work."

The next three months with Mama Mui seemed, in retrospect, like living in the lap of luxury. She shared quarters with two other village girls. Food was plentiful. Tasty meat and fowl she used to enjoy at her village only during Lunar New Year were available almost daily. The rest of the time was spent in what she regarded as pure fun. She and the other girls doubled up with hysteria each time they tried walking on high heels. They also giggled helplessly when misapplying rouge or mascara and slapping gooey creams and lotions on their faces and bodies. A regime of exercises soon re-shaped their waists and firmed their breasts.

Mama Mui took a special interest in her, showing her how to walk with a slightly indolent swing to her hips. Her hair was trimmed and permed and gowns of silk and brocade were made to measure for her. Looking into the mirror she was amazed by her own transformation. She never dreamt she could become such a beauty.

When Mama Mui began teaching her to dance to Western music she expressed surprise. "Why must a waitress learn to dance?" she asked.

"Do you think we've spent all that time and money to have you wait at table?" Mama Mui replied. "You won't earn enough to live. We all have to make the most of what we've been given. For the moment, you've got youth and beauty. You'll be a hit as a dance hostess. I'm the manageress of a dozen girls like you at the Starlight Rendezvous. That's a classy nightclub, with a rich clientele. You'll enjoy working there."

"But I don't want to work in a nightclub. My mother only agreed to my working as a waitress."

"Don't be a silly goose. Why struggle against fate? I would hate to see anything unpleasant happen to you. If you don't work in a nightclub, you'll have to pay back the money given to your mother and what we've spent on you. Can you do that? Be sensible. Being a dancing girl is much better than mending fishing nets under a boiling sun."

When she still resisted the idea of becoming a dancing girl, Uncle Fung reappeared. "It's wiser to do as you're told," he said, glaring at her. "You're in territory controlled by the Green Bamboo Triad. You can't run away. If you try, their boys will catch you and slash your face. Or pour sulphuric acid over you. For the sake of your family, behave! Start earning your keep."

She began learning dance steps.

When she finally made her debut, she found the Starlight Rendezvous both exciting and frightening. It was a vast, dimly lit hall more luxurious than any place she had previously seen. The air was machine-cooled and pinpoints of light in a dark, domed ceiling twinkled like stars. The darkness was filled with a steady stream of soft, sentimental music from a band. On a small dance floor, hostesses sheathed in Chinese dresses with side slits moved indistinctly with their customers, like shadows locked in languid, amorous embraces. Clustered around the dance floor were a succession of high-backed sofas, set at discreet angles and separated from one another by lattice screens and broad-leaved plants.

What held her back, however, were the crude gropings and importunings Mama Mui had warned her to expect. Back in her village, she would simply clout or kick boys who tried to be fresh and she knew the village elders would always be on her side. At the Starlight Rendezvous, she had been briefed that customers were always right.

"Men do not pay good money to cuddle a block of wood or to gaze into a sour face," Mama Mui had said. "They can get that at home for free. They pay to feel good about themselves, to imagine they could impress girls half their age and escape with them to paradise. They want to forget their professional and family responsibilities, the state of the war, the conscription of their sons. Your job is to help them forget. If anyone propositions you, send him to me. Don't negotiate yourself. I can get you better deals."

The trouble was that she never sent anyone to Mama Mui. Instead, customers descended upon the manager, complaining about the lack of success with their overtures.

"What's the matter with you?" Mama Mui asked one day, taking her aside. "Don't you want to make money?"

"I don't want to do what they ask," she replied. "I feel dirty, being pawed and fondled every night."

"Ah, I see! You've never gone beyond fondling before! You're protecting your precious pearl! That's a good selling point. A premium is in order."

Uncle Fung appeared in her room again shortly afterwards.

"Mama Mui tells me you have hesitations," he said, darkly. "We can't allow anything to stand in the way of business. Are you going to stop this nonsense or do you want me to deal with you?"

"There's nothing in my mother's agreement about sleeping with strangers."

"Well, I'm no stranger. Strip!"

When she refused Uncle Fung slapped her across the face and tore off her dress. She fought furiously but Uncle was too big and strong.

After he had finished, Uncle Fung said, not unkindly: "You may hate me now, but one day you'll thank me. If the Green Bamboo Triad had done the honours, you would have had four or five thugs here and you wouldn't be able to walk for a week afterwards."

She felt numb, too hurt for tears. In the subsequent days she seemed to acquire a look of infinite sorrow, as if something irretrievable had been lost. Paradoxically, the customers found that quality charming. She quickly became the most sought-after hostess at the Starlight Rendezvous and queues formed to hire her for those brief, regulated minutes of simulated romance.

It was during this period of semi-torpor that Young Master Chu was pressed upon her. The young man's initial shyness suggested he might indeed be the "green-headed lad" Uncle Fung had supposed. She suffered his clumsy initiatives, as if he were courting the girl next door. But when he spoke about his ambitions he seemed a young man in a hurry, confident of what he could achieve.

His talk was grand. She thought at first it might be adolescent bravado. But there was a consistent refrain to it, about reshaping the world and one day laying it at her feet. It was refreshing to listen to his earnest talk about his ambitions instead of the puppy prattle of other customers.

When he presented her with the jade pendant she realized that in his quaint, boyish way he was trying to make a commitment to her. It came as a surprise that his love-making came with a passion she could not resist. He had unlocked some secret part of her, liberating her, enabling her to give of herself. She could no longer engage him in the soul-dead fashion she had adopted with other men, with simulated grunts and groans.

With him, making love was akin to physical annihilation or the agony of creation.

She had a big black mole on her left buttock which she had always been a little self-conscious about. Her sisters and some customers teased her about it. But Young Master Chu appeared to love it. "That's my star of destiny," he had said, stroking it and kissing it. "It's going to link us together forever, in life and in death."

The realization that she meant something special to him, coming as it did in the Sixth Moon of the lunar year, caused her to muse again about life. That month contained the anniversary of the lotus. Back home, villagers took the lotus to represent redemption. They marked its anniversary with prayers and offerings. Though grown in filth, the lotus was capable of rising pure and clean above the foulest mud. Could she not do likewise with this strange boy-man? Could she not leave behind all the past deceits and corruptions and become worthy of his love? Or was she already beyond redemption?

The dreadful uncertainty of her fate, the tenuous clinging to hope when there was no hope, caused tears to flow at last. Sorrow, sorrow. Was there to be no end? What crimes had she committed in a previous existence to warrant her present suffering? Was redemption available only in story books? The more desperately she sought answers, the faster her tears flowed.

Her sobbing woke Chu Wing-seng. "My love, why are you crying?" he asked, embracing her. "Is it because I am leaving today? There's no need for tears. I'm not disappearing for good. I'll get my father to arrange travel documents and send for you. He can get you a visa for America. You can go with me to Princeton and learn English. We can study together. We can settle in America."

Fei-Fei shook her head, sobbing more convulsively than ever. After another bout of love-making they fell asleep.

At daybreak, Fei-Fei awoke to the lingering spoor of love on the bed. Young Master Chu was still asleep. She was clear-headed now. To attempt to cling to the happiness of the past few days was self-delusion. She had been blessed with a gift of love she had never expected. Now was the time for courage and sacrifice. Her life was a ruin. Nothing could alter that. If sorrow had to come, let it fall upon her for being party to the plot of Uncle Fung and Mama Mui. She would come clean. That was better than a lifetime of longing and pain. She might then disappear from his memory like an insignificant misadventure.

She got quietly out of bed and went into the bathroom. She dressed carefully, steeling herself for her ordeal. She re-entered the bedroom to find Young Master Chu already awake.

"Good morning," Chu Wing-seng said, sleepily. "You're dressed early. Are you thinking of going down for breakfast?"

"No, I'm going back to Taipei," Fei-Fei replied. "You have been good to me. I ought to tell you before I leave I'm not related to Uncle Fung."

"Good, Uncle Fung has never been one of my favourite characters. Now I don't have to treat him with the consideration due a relative when we marry."

"You don't understand. We're not getting married."

"Why not? Because you're from a poor family and haven't much education? What does that matter so long as we love each other? When you get to America you'll find that nobody cares about your origins so long as you have money. And I do promise you we are going to have lots of money."

"I'm not who you think I am. I've been hired by Uncle Fung to keep you company for a few days, that's all."

"That's the smartest thing he's ever done. We fell in love during your employment. What's so strange about that? We're going to be together forever."

"You're not listening to what I'm saying. I will bring sorrow to you and your family. Uncle Fung means to extort money from your father."

"Fiddlesticks! My father's got the measure of Uncle Fung. Come over and kiss me."

Fei-Fei did not move. She had to be more brutal, to inflict a sharper and more vicious hurt. Her heart ached at the prospect and she prayed for the strength to bring it off.

"Why do 'green-headed lads' always think they're in love with the first woman they bed?" she said, with an air of cynicism. "Why get all hot and emotional over a simple business deal? If you like what I do, come back and see me the next time you're in Taipei. You can find me at the Starlight Rendezvous."

Chu Wing-seng looked half-stunned. It was as if he had just been told he would be shot at dawn. He groped for his spectacles on the bedside table and looked at Fei-Fei in disbelief. "Are you telling me the last six days meant nothing to you? That everything has been an act?"

Fei-Fei saw the pain in his eyes and knew she would have to live with that vision for the rest of her days. She forced herself to smile.

"I'm sorry," Fei-Fei said. "You're a sweet boy. I never meant to hurt you. And thanks for the jade pendant. You've got to learn to be less generous with dancing girls, no matter how much money you may eventually make." She then headed for the door.

Chu Wing-seng hesitated for a moment before scrambling naked out of the bed. He cast aside the tangle of bedsheets and blanket and yelled: "Wait! Fei-Fei!"

But the door slammed before he could reach it.

When old friends meet

13

Sebastian Baxingdale came out of Knightsbridge underground Station and ran straight into the heavy tourist traffic swirling around Harrods. The press of people reminded him of Hong Kong, though the pewter skies promised yet another drizzly English March day. He was wearing a much abused mackintosh, with a button missing and a torn pocket. Underneath he had on a heavily stained Shetland sweater and a pair of tattered jeans. His hair had grown to shoulder length. A beard, crying out to be trimmed, hid much of the gentleness around his mouth and extinguished all remnants of his military past. His eyes were bloodshot.

Across the road, outside the side entrance to Harrods, he spotted Christopher Knight waiting. A prematurely receding hairline had eaten into his friend's unruly mop during the last few years, but his chin now conveyed a more confident cast. He had put on weight. A developing paunch, snugly encased in the waistcoat of a three-piece suit of charcoal grey, bestowed gravitas. The only element missing from that picture of settled prosperity was a gold watch-chain.

Baxingdale stood studying his friend for a moment, assessing whether his altered appearance was due to marriage to Phoebe Sweetman. The wedding had taken place four years earlier, in a village church in Dorset. He had been best man. He might have been the one walking down the aisle with Phoebe instead of Christopher, if she hadn't realized in time that a clergyman's son had little to offer in terms of material needs and social aspirations.

He crossed the road and extended a hand to his friend. "Hallo, Chris. Where's Phoebe?"

"Jesus Christ, Seb! What's happened to you? I hardly recognize you with all that hair!"

"My Bohemian phase. Where's Phoebe?"

"Back in Hong Kong. I'm here on a quick business trip. Leaving the day after tomorrow."

Baxingdale nodded.

"What's going on, Seb? You look awful! You're my best friend. You don't answer my letters. You don't respond to our Christmas cards. I had to contact your father to locate you."

Baxingdale was surprised his friend had lost his stutter. Marriage must agree with him. "I just dropped out for a bit, that's all. I'll fill you in later."

Christopher Knight shifted his weight uncertainly from one foot to the other. "I've booked at Marco's, just round the corner in Brompton Road. Hope that's all right."

"Sure, if the headwaiter doesn't kick up a fuss. If he does, you can say you're entertaining the greatest Austrian poet of the twentieth century."

"Why Austrian?"

"Because the blighter might actually know the leading French or British ones."

"Are you really writing poetry?"

"Not exactly."

"Are you still teaching then?

"No."

"Well, what *are* you doing?"

"Contemplating my navel."

Christopher Knight shook his head in exasperation as they reached Marco's. The headwaiter took custody of Baxingdale's mackintosh with a distinct lack of enthusiasm.

Baxingdale ordered a beer while Knight opted for a dry sherry.

"Is Phoebe well? Have you got children?"

"Phoebe's fine, throwing herself into the Hong Kong social whirl. No children yet, but in the planning stage."

"Glad to hear that. Still in the Public Prosecutor's Department?"

"Seb, I wrote to you three years ago telling you I would be leaving for private practice."

"Did you? Guess it never registered. So now it's game warden turned poacher, is it? When you were swotting up Roman Law you said you intended to devote your life to fighting injustices. What's happened to that?"

"When one's a child one speaks of childish things." Knight

shrugged to indicate a disinclination to pursue the topic. After a pause, he added: "You know what Phoebe's like. She's got grand ideas and none of them fits in with a civil-service salary. Besides, someone made me an offer I couldn't refuse."

"Oh?"

"There's an old codger named Harry Rand who's worked up a nice practice in conveyancing, company law and wills and probates. Not the thing to set the world on fire, but good bread-and-butter stuff. He's got a passion for Chinese snuff bottles. Since he's made money, he wants to devote more time to his passion rather than his practice. He has three quite good Chinese solicitors in the firm. But he's a bit conservative. Can't quite reconcile himself to a Chinese partner just yet. So he offered me a partnership."

"You mean the chap's a racist."

"Well, I wouldn't put it like that. He's not a bad sort. Just a bit odd. Now you're looking at a partner in the flourishing firm of Rand and Knight, making more money than I've ever dreamt possible. What about you? What have you been up to? When I got married you were teaching at some ghastly secondary modern in inner London."

"Hackney. Ended two years ago. Couldn't have stood it a moment longer. The head was a twit. One of those avant-garde types who believed in allowing children to develop at their own pace. Giving rein to their creativity, as he put it. The result was chaos. Lessons became geared to the pace of the least gifted. I had my hands full dodging ink pellets and coping with rowdiness and vandalism."

Christopher Knight chuckled. "I can imagine you looking very unflappable amidst that chaos," he said.

"Something happened that wasn't funny at all. I reported one of the most obstreperous lads, a fourteen-year-old. The father was a bricklayer. The father stomped into the classroom one day, clouted the lad in front of the whole class and dragged him out by the ear. 'I said school's a bloody wasta time,' he shouted. 'You stick with yer trade, lad.' That was the last I saw of the boy. I had unwittingly ruined his life. I had not accounted for his low self-esteem and had completely misunderstood his behaviour. I couldn't continue after that."

"You can't blame yourself."

"But I do. Has it ever crossed your mind, Chris, that some people are just not meant to do good? They only make things worse. Perhaps I'm one of them. Perhaps I'm meant only to be an onlooker, to watch with folded arms as the world rushes towards the Apocalypse, to bear witness to greed, drug addiction, perversions, sexual promiscuity and war without being able to act."

"Tell me quick, where's the sexual promiscuity? My neighbourhood's dull as dishwater, hoity-toity all round," Knight said with a laugh. After a slight pause he added: "Come on, Seb, you can't be so pessimistic. The fact you went into teaching implies a degree of faith in the future."

"Awfully easy to misread motives. Haven't you noticed there's no queue forming to hire someone with a degree in modern history and a few years of military service? I needed a job, that's why I went into teaching. I knew I couldn't do anything about the world going to pot."

The chicken masala they had both ordered arrived, together with a bottle of Chianti.

"So what have you been doing since?" Knight asked, between mouthfuls.

"Philandering with tobacco, exercising my spleen through my typewriter."

"You mean you've become a writer?"

Baxingdale allowed himself a hollow laugh. "Collecting rejection slips doth not a writer make."

"Gosh, Seb, I didn't realize things had been so bad. Macmillan says people've never had it so good. Things have been booming nicely in Hong Kong, so we thought it must be the same over here. Why don't you go back East?"

"I've thought about it, except I don't have the language."

"Don't talk nonsense. English is the official language. I do quite well with only a few phrases of Chinese. You shouldn't have difficulty getting by."

"That's the trouble. I don't want to just get by. The population is overwhelmingly Chinese. Yet we make them deal with us on our terms, under our rules. Not knowing their language conveniently absolves us from finding out what they're actually thinking and what their real aspirations might be, though we're supposed to be running the place in trust, on their behalf."

"They're being well governed. Needn't lose sleep over that."

"Are they? Isn't the government making such a virtue of laissez-faire because it doesn't know what to do? In any case, what can I do back in Hong Kong? Guard the borders again against 'economic migrants'? Join one of the princely *hongs* of reformed dope dealers? Or become a police inspector to put the squeeze on hawkers and street walkers?"

"Don't underestimate yourself. There are plenty of jobs you can do."

"No, if I ever go back I'd want to have a good command of the language. I'd want to get into the soul of the city, to connect with its people. There's something unique there. It's full of enigmas, contradictions and strange beliefs. It's alive with notions that steal into one's psyche — auspicious or inauspicious days and numbers, geomancy, hexagonal mirrors hanging outside buildings, acupuncture, herbal cures, praying to ancestors, the notion of being rewarded or punished in the next life, all that and more.

"When Buddhists talk about 'the wisdom of the other shore', I know there's something there I can't quite grasp. It's infuriating. I never managed to get beneath the surface the last time. I was cut off because I couldn't speak or read the language and being in the army didn't help. In the end I never managed to decide whether I loved the place, hated it or feared it."

"Don't romanticize. Hong Kong's just a mongrel city, a new Babylon, more freebooting by the day. It's entirely market driven. The realization of everything that Adam Smith wrote about, except the emphasis on education. Between now and 1997 there're fortunes to be made for those with enough gumption to find their own niches."

"For any dog willing to eat dog."

"Do you remember a chap named Chu Tung-po? He was already making quite a splash when you were there."

"Yes, vaguely. Wasn't he the one who built a magnificent home on the Peak and put a lot of expat noses out of joint?"

"That's him! There are plenty of others like him now, all coming up fast. They want membership to our clubs and before you know it they'll be stewards in the Jockey Club. A frightening thought! It just demonstrates what money can do. We may not abide their outlandish ways — slurping their soup and talking too loudly. But they're on everybody's invitation list now.

"Yet behind our backs they call us gweilos or foreign barbarians and gab about their ancient traditions. Perhaps old Spengler did stumble onto a thing or two about the yellow races. Just look at the way the Japanese have picked themselves up from atomic devastation! If we don't want to be elbowed out, we need to counteract the Eastern races in some way. Or at least make what we can while the going's good."

Baxingdale took out a packet of cigarettes. "I'm not sure I'm cut out for money-grubbing," he said.

"Sooner or later you've got to start earning a living. You can't continue forever writing stuff nobody wants to publish."

The remark cut Baxingdale to the quick. His money was indeed running out and he couldn't contemplate falling back on his parents. He did not have the courage to breathe to anyone that he had been cleaning windows for the last six months to make ends meet. If more gainful employment did not turn up, he would soon not have the wherewithal to pay his rent, let alone enjoy the kind of meal he had just finished. But the wine was beginning to make him carefree. "Something'll turn up," he said.

"What if something doesn't? What then?"

"Kill myself, I suppose."

"Come on, Seb! I mean, seriously."

"I *am* serious. Don't worry, Chris, it isn't so easy to kill oneself. Since you're paying for lunch, the least I can do is to earn my meal with an amusing story. You know, I've got a gas cooker in my bed-sitter. My landlord has hooked it up with one of those wretched coin meters that swallows shillings like a whale. You have to keep feeding it. I've discovered that the maximum number of shillings that can be put into that infernal machine remains grossly insufficient for a lethal dose! The moral of that story is that one should attempt suicide only in a more respectable class of digs. Otherwise it's a waste of money."

"Don't tell me you've tried!" Christopher Knight exclaimed. "Look, Seb, I've got an idea. You're a smart chap. Why don't you muck into law for a couple of years and join me in Hong

Kong? The name Rand, Knight and Baxingdale has rather a nice ring to it."

"Thanks. I've read enough Dickens to be put off."

"No, Seb, be serious about my suggestion. It would be marvellous seeing you back in Hong Kong."

Baxingdale stubbed out his cigarette, lit another and sighed. "My father wants me to spread the gospel to dark corners of the world. My mother wants me to take up the pen like Zola. You want me to practise law. Well, you know, D. H. Lawrence once said something about our getting rid of our sicknesses through books. That's what I'm trying to do. I rather enjoy pouring venom out of my typewriter."

Baxingdale picked up his wine glass absent-mindedly and discovered that it had already been drained. He eyed the empty glass with disappointment.

Christopher Knight reached for the Chianti bottle, only to discover that it too was empty. "Care for more wine?"

"No, just fiddling. I've had enough."

"Look, Seb, I'm not sure I know how to say this. But what's the point of bashing away at your typewriter if no one gets to read what you've written? If you have a yen for writing, why not try journalism? I would hate to see you… "

"Turn into a bum?" Baxingdale interrupted.

"No, I was going to say 'wasting your talents'. Look, my mother has a distant cousin who's married to one of the senior editors at the *Daily Globe*. My mother could set up an interview. Maybe there's an opening."

"The *Globe* might not contain the abominations of the gutter press, but it's still a pretty low-brow sort of rag, isn't it?"

"It's got two million readers and that's not to be sneezed at. I don't suppose you can count on anything very grand to begin with. Probably chasing ambulances, hanging around magistrates' courts, covering coming-out parties and that sort of stuff. I'm going to try and set something up."

"Thanks, but I don't think so, Chris. Finding gainful employment is my problem, not yours."

"Seb, I'm not going to argue with you. I'm going to put my mother on to you and you can argue with her. And that's final."

Lucille

14

"Golly, getta load of this," Lucille Mong said, as she peered at the label next to the Chinese painting. "It says this is a copy of a famous painting by the Sung artist Li Lung-mien, entitled *Gathering Of Scholars At Western Garden*. Why is the Metropolitan Museum of Art hanging a *copy* of a painting? We've just seen Botticelli's *Last Communion Of St. Jerome*. They wouldn't dream of displaying a copy of that, would they? So why should they do it with a Chinese painting?"

"It's different with Chinese paintings," Xavier Chu replied, as if the point was obvious. "A fundamental principle of Chinese painting is to copy old masters. Therefore many copies of famous paintings are around, some done by painters quite famous in their own right. Originality's not the deciding factor. When copiers become masters themselves, their copies acquire artistic standing as well."

"No kidding! Learn something new every day."

When they came to two scrolls of Chinese calligraphy, Lucille Mong asked: "What do those characters say? Wish I could read them."

"You're not supposed to read them," Xavier said. "Calligraphies are not meant to be read. Characters as such should be ignored. Calligraphers often choose famous poems or passages from the classics for their work. They expect people to concentrate on the rhythm and vitality of the brush strokes and consider how they come together to form — not just characters, but larger abstractions, with their own contours, contrast, balance and rhythm. Rhythm is most important, for it represents movement and movement is an essential element in nature."

"Gee, I've never approached calligraphies that way. They just shame me because I can't read them."

Lucille wished she had met Xavier earlier. He was good at illuminating Chinese obscurities. Her parents ran a small fruit store in San Francisco's Chinatown, squeezed between a shop dealing in Chinese sausages and preserved ducks and an unpretentious noodle restaurant. It was situated in one of the less salubrious streets running off Grant Avenue. Her elder brother also worked along the same street, as a waiter in another restaurant. She had long sought to break free from that confinement. Helping her parents move crates of fruit had already roughened her hands and the prospect of being trapped in the family store during the best years of her youth was disheartening. It was not simply a case of getting off the bottom rung of the social ladder, but also of coming to terms with her own identity as an American-Chinese.

At first she thought herself special. It seemed an advantage to have a choice of being American or Chinese, as the fancy struck her. From the age of ten, however, she began puzzling over what she actually was and to which of those two cultures she actually belonged. If to both, then how could their contradictions be resolved?

At school she pledged allegiance to the American flag each morning, just like other American children. She spoke the same language as her classmates, wore the same brand of clothing, played the same games and nursed the same fantasies and ambitions.

But at home, her parents spoke the Toi Shan dialect and drummed into her she was not a "foreign devil" but a Chinese. Paradoxically, her parents never allowed her to join the Saturday Chinese classes run by one of the clansmen's associations. They said she was needed at the store. They also intimated that some of the teachers were too progressive and were pursuing doubtful activities. She had no idea what they meant.

Gradually she concluded that being Chinese meant being obedient, studying hard, not going out at night and not fooling around with white boys. Later, when she started menstruating, two additional requirements were added. The first was to guard her virginity until marriage because no respectable Chinese family would allow a son to marry a girl who had lost it. The second was to accept whichever husband her parents might choose. The choice appeared restricted to the sons of Chinese families owning restaurants, souvenir shops, jewellery stores or financial institutions in Chinatown.

Her parents, though formally American citizens and

ostensibly members of the Democratic Party, were proud of their Chineseness. They still regarded China as their real home, in spite of the fact they had little time for its Communist rulers. They drank tea incessantly, joined clansmen's associations, observed Chinese festivals and jabbered away in the Toi Shan dialect with other inhabitants of Chinatown.

But their habits perplexed her. They could not explain clearly, for example, why some of their neighbours preferred green tea and others red, or what their differences were. They seemed to observe Chinese festivals only for the sake of form. When pressed to explain why moon cakes had to be eaten during the Mid-Autumn Festival or the origins of the Chung Yeung Festival, they hummed and hawed. They did not know half the things Xavier knew. She concluded that being Chinese meant essentially spending the rest of her life in the ghetto of Chinatown, acting out some Oriental stereotype for tourists.

As she grew into adolescence, her confusion increased. When her breasts began to develop, her mother made her bind them every night before bed, declaring it indecent for Chinese girls to have large breasts, let alone to take pride in them. This, her mother claimed, was standard practice among girls in respectable society. She had observed them while working as a servant for a rich family in Canton.

Later, her parents were aghast when she secured, at the age of fifteen, a place among the cheerleaders in high school. They could not abide her publicly displaying her shapely legs in an abbreviated skirt. It took many arguments to convince them that being selected was considered an honour by American girls. Her parents' reservations made little sense in the age of sweater girls and Jane Russell. It did not take her very long, prancing around waving pom-poms at football and basketball games, to discover with a devastating certainty that her legs and breasts were centres of attraction and objects of desire.

Lucille and Xavier came out of the museum into brilliant sunshine. People were sitting on the steps in scattered clusters, reading, chatting or soaking up the sun.

"How about a walk in Central Park?" Lucille asked. "I want to see all of New York before heading home."

"Fine with me," Xavier said.

They made their way into the park. She noted again with a slight disappointment that Xavier was quite short. Hardly more than her own five-foot-three. In high heels, she would embarrass him. She was glad she had on flats.

Nevertheless she felt comfortable with him. He did not appear the type she had to fight off in the back seat of a car. Indeed, she would probably never get into that situation with him. He was too reserved. He didn't talk much, though once he had thawed he could be a knowledgeable guide, opening doors to a world previously never quite intelligible to her.

When they examined the round, discoloured jade discs in the museum, he explained the symbolism Chinese associated with jade. The discs themselves represented the ancient Chinese symbol for heaven. The holes at the centre were meant for souls to pass through. She felt that she, too, had at last found a hole through which she could reach her own identity and culture.

At the same time, however, she puzzled over the hesitancy and correctness in his behaviour. It was as if his mind was occupied with something else. He had never once attempted to make a pass during the parties and nightclubbing of the previous week. Even when they danced, he kept a distance. It bruised her pride to think he did not find her attractive. She usually had to fight off American boys, even on first dates. Could Xavier be sexually otherwise inclined?

"Tell me, how did you get to be such buddies with Bob Winchell?" Lucille asked.

"We were at Princeton together," Xavier replied. "We were the best economics students in our class. We both wanted to prove who was better. Couldn't settle it, however. We both got straight A's, made the Dean's List, got elected to Phi Beta Kappa and all the rest of that stuff. Gradually we got to respect each other and became friends.

"When it turned out we were both heading for Harvard, we decided we wouldn't go head to head any more. It was simpler just to divide the world between us. After graduation, Bob suggested a couple of weeks of high living before getting down to work. I agreed, on condition he fixed me up with a date because I didn't know any girls in New York. And here we are. What about you and Helen Winchell? How did you two get so close?

You're from San Francisco, aren't you, and she's from New York?"

"You might say we're both refugees from our parents."

"Oh?"

"Helen went to study at Berkeley to get as far away from home as possible. You see, she's Jewish and her parents are very conservative. They won't allow her to date anybody except Jewish boys. She didn't like that and opted for the greater freedom of California. My story's roughly the same. My parents considered it normal for them to pick a guy for me to marry. Not my idea of romance, not that I'm aiming to marry a non-Chinese. When the chance came to study at Berkeley, I took it. Actually I was aiming for Stanford, but couldn't make the grades.

"At Berkeley, one of the first things I did was to sign up to study Chinese. I wanted to get into Chinese culture, but it ended in tears. They taught Mandarin at Berkeley but I spoke Toi Shan. It was bad enough trying to remember the characters, let alone two different pronunciations. I was never a very good student. After one term I gave up. I did a couple of courses in Far Eastern history and comparative religion, though."

Lucille was afraid she might be boring Xavier, but he appeared attentive. So she continued.

"After a while I thought it easier just to settle for being American, particularly that bit about the pursuit of happiness. That meant forgetting a lot of stuff my parents drummed into me, like not dating American boys and all that. That didn't work either. Whatever I may try to be, I didn't *look* American. The point was driven home the hard way. When I upset a guy who got fresh, he hit me and called me racist names. I realized then that I was neither fish nor fowl.

"At that low point I met Helen Winchell. We were both sophomores. We bumped into each other browsing in one of the bookshops along Telegraph Avenue. Talk about coincidence! Both of us ended up buying Simone de Beauvoir's *The Second Sex*! We got talking. After reading de Beauvoir we started thinking of ourselves as women first, rather than as Chinese or Jews or Americans. Began discussing Women's Lib and became a little more radical as a result.

"Gosh! I'm sorry! Am I boring you? I don't know why I'm

dumping my life's history on you! I've never talked like this to a man before."

"Hey! Go on! Don't stop! It's interesting," Xavier said, touching her encouragingly on the elbow. "I had a similar problem with parents. They fed me a lot of notions about being Chinese. But it just wasn't my scene. I'll tell you about it after you've finished your story."

"Okay. Well, I started rooming with Helen in our junior year. Just before summer break Bob asked Helen to bring home a girlfriend as a blind date for a Chinese buddy from Hong Kong. Bob only knew Jewish girls and didn't think that would work. I'd never been to the Big Apple and it sounded like fun. As they say, the rest is history. I hope you haven't been disappointed."

"Of course not! You've been the most wonderful blind date a man could have hoped for."

Lucille did a mock curtsey. "Flattery will get you everywhere," she said, and they both laughed. They were nearing the pond for sailing model boats and they paused to watch children at play.

"Now tell me your story. Helen said your father's some kind of Hong Kong Rockefeller. Is that right?"

"Well, my father's quite rich, but I won't be relying on his dough once I start work. He's got this thing about being Chinese and has a lot of moral hang-ups about the way business is done. I don't buy that. Business is business. Nothing else comes into it. It's like running the fastest mile or climbing Everest. You've got to aim to be the best. I want to become the richest man in the world. I've given myself twenty-five years to achieve it. That's why I've been studying like mad. Haven't found time for girls. Now that I've signed up with Morgansteen, Dillon and Preston, perhaps I can take things easier."

"Bob's going to work for Merrill Lynch, isn't he? You said you two had divided up the world. Which is your half?"

"I'm after both halves! Only I haven't told Bob yet."

They both laughed again.

"You're fantastic," Lucille said, slipping an arm through Xavier's. "You're so full of confidence. I guess that comes from having everything: rich family, MBA from Harvard, swell job on Wall Street, a wealth of knowledge about Chinese things and a future without limit. I'd give an arm and a leg just to have a quarter of your understanding of Chinese culture."

"You won't look half as beautiful without an arm and a leg!" Lucille laughed again, partly to hide her blushes.

"What are you going to do after graduation?" Xavier asked. "Are you going for a Master's or a job?"

"Don't know. Haven't thought that far ahead."

"When you do get around to deciding, please consider the East Coast. Closer to Wall Street, you know. It's been real fun the past week. I've almost forgotten what it's like to enjoy myself. It would be nice meeting you again."

"It has been great fun for me too," Lucille said. "I'll certainly bear that in mind."

She felt a shiver of delight. Xavier was inching out of his shell. The relationship had possibilities. He was Chinese and rich. Her parents should be impressed and couldn't possibly object on either score. A Harvard degree and a job on Wall Street. What more could any girl want? If things worked out, Hong Kong and Taiwan were prospects on the horizon. She could explore her roots to her heart's content. She had to be either Chinese or American, not some undefined half-breed belonging nowhere.

The only snag was she was no longer a virgin. She had lost it half-unwillingly to a quarterback on the previous year's football team. A few unmemorable men followed. None provided that earth-moving experience she had expected. She wished she had kept it now. She did not know whether Xavier or his family understood women's need for sexual freedom. If they didn't, should she attempt to thrash out the issue before getting more deeply involved? Or simply disguise her loss of virginity and hope for the best?

"Could I write to you at Berkeley? Sort of keep in touch?"

"Sure, I'll give you my address before I leave," Lucille said. "But I've got a confession to make. My real name isn't Lucille Mong."

"Good grief! You're not telling me Bob has played a trick, that you're not his sister's room-mate after all? Who are you then? An actress hired to keep me entertained?"

Lucille recoiled from the outburst. The sudden coldness in

Xavier's voice took her by surprise. "Oh, no! Nothing like that!" she reassured him quickly. "Helen's my room-mate all right. Let me explain. There's no trick of any kind. You've gotta believe that. I've never told anyone before, not even Helen. My real surname is Lee, not Mong. I wouldn't have told you either except that I want very much for us to become friends. I figured that with your knowing all sorts of Chinese stuff, you'd sooner or later start questioning what a queer surname Mong was. I didn't want to have to explain then, so I thought I might as well be straight with you from the start.

"You see, my father's name is Lee Mong. When he came to this country, he didn't know English and the guys at immigration didn't realize that Chinese always put their surnames first. So 'Lee' got registered as his given name and 'Mong' as his surname. When my brother was born, my father got scared of raising the issue. He didn't know how to explain why he had used a false surname for so long. He thought he might get into trouble. My mother's entry into this country wasn't on the up and up either. My father thought it best to accept 'Mong' as a surname to avoid trouble."

"A common enough mistake among overseas Chinese," Xavier said, reassuringly. "I thought I had fallen for one of Bob's pranks! Why not come back to the hotel for a drink? Then we could plan a few more fun things for the remaining week."

"Why not?" Lucille answered, brightly. "I would love to compare the dim sum in Mott Street with those in San Francisco."

They strolled arm in arm out of the park towards Xavier's five-star hotel on Madison Avenue. As they walked, sexual chemistry began to take over. If she could manoeuvre Xavier into inviting her for drinks in his room, the problem about her virginity might get resolved.

Picking up the pieces

15

It was a Sunday afternoon. The French windows offered a vista of sunlit lawns and blossoming flowerbeds, but Xavier Chu Wing-seng was oblivious to them. He was hunched over his father's desk, furiously taking notes from balance sheets spread before him. Stacked around was a mountain of files and financial documents.

Only twenty-five, he thought, and in charge of a conglomerate comprising seventy-nine companies. His father had never had such an opportunity at that age. Mastering so many inter-company relationships was infinitely better than merchant banking at Morgansteen, Dillon and Preston. Digging through Gold Star's corporate maze was like playing simultaneous games of three-dimensional chess. He felt exhilarated as he absorbed the intricacies of his inheritance.

His father was a genius, obscuring the financial strength of Gold Star from prying eyes through inner reserves, cross-holdings and inter-company loans. He noted with surprise that the once highly profitable supermarket chain had been sold and was no longer part of the group. Then he remembered what his father had told him about being accused of causing the deaths of an old couple.

Among the documents he found a bill for meals taken at the Evergreen Tea House during the previous three months. It had been sent over from the office together with other personal papers by Mrs. Leung, his father's secretary. She could throw no light on it, however, except to say that such bills had previously been settled personally by his father. But how could that latest bill be possible? According to the dates, it was for meals consumed months after his father had died. And the amount demanded seemed grossly excessive.

He recalled his father offering more than once to take him to the tea house, to sample its selection of famous teas, but he had never taken him up on it. Unlike his father, he never developed a taste for tea and hence never found the need to delve into the

Cha Ching or *Book Of Tea* written thirteen hundred years ago. To him, tea was just a beverage made with dried leaves. He couldn't understand why his people made such a fuss over it or spent so much time investigating its taste, aroma and supposedly health-giving properties. He had got used to coffee and Coca-Cola in America. It seemed he would have to visit the tea house after all, to discover if someone was trying to pull a fast one. In any event, the bill might reveal something of his father's hidden life.

Poor Mother. She had spent her life sloughing off worldly attachments. He wondered how she really felt about his father's death. On the surface she appeared unperturbed. Her only outward signs were some loss of weight and a slight greying of her hair. But she must have loved him in her own way.

What an ordeal for a woman who rarely left the home to cope with. The death had caused a scurrilous Press to write articles full of insinuations and libels. Some actually went so far as to allege relationships between his father and various women, hinting at lovers' quarrels, a suicide pact and even murder.

Those allegations had offended him. Though his mother had dismissed them with indifference, they had left him with a lingering doubt. He was in the dark concerning much of his father's life. The connections with rascals such as Buck-toothed Fung and with scholars such as Teacher Tam demonstrated what a complicated man his father was. In death he remained a conundrum. What secrets had he taken to the grave? The bill from the tea house could be the beginning of a trail of discovery.

The coroner's findings left further mysteries. He needed explanations, but where could they to be found? His mother was tighter than a clam.

He glanced idly around the room, wondering if he had overlooked clues. Nothing seemed fundamentally changed from eleven years ago, when that traumatic after-dinner discussion with his father took place. The only thing missing was the miniature potted pine. His mother had commandeered it for her own quarters.

Otherwise, everything was much the same. Half-opened and unopened boxes were still stacked everywhere. Teacher Tam's scrolls of calligraphy hung as before. The words of the Tang poem sounded more silly than ever. Who had time for bright moons and gentle breezes? He had enough trouble getting through his father's business papers.

Across from the scrolls, the glass-fronted bookcases stood against the wall on the opposite side of the room. He got up to examine their contents. They were not showy and leather-bound like those in the library. Both the English and Chinese volumes were well-thumbed. They lacked order in respect of subject and language, however: Homer, Socrates, Milton, Marx, Adam Smith, Bernard Shaw and Bertrand Russell. Spengler's *The Decline Of The West* and Gibbon's *Decline And Fall Of The Roman Empire* stood like pillars in some temple of knowledge.

The Chinese works included the Books of Mencius, the analects of Confucius, the writings of several Taoist sages, collections of Tang and Sung poems and a number of volumes on Buddhism. *The Painting Manual Of The Mustard Seed Garden* was there, as was an ancient encyclopaedia entitled *A Discussion Of The Essential Criteria Of Antiquities*.

He remembered his father showing him *The Painting Manual* after their return from Taiwan, but he quickly became bored with it. As his eyes moved from one Chinese title to another, he discovered that he had barely heard of most of them, let alone read them. He searched for books on macro and micro economics, on management and corporate case studies, over which he had pored at Princeton and at Harvard. He found none.

What struck him also was that nothing in the room celebrated his father's life as a tycoon. No Rotary Club plaque, no Chamber of Commerce trophy, no photograph taken with the high and mighty. It was as if that part of him never existed. The study exuded an air entirely alien to business and high finance.

He was distracted by a timid knocking upon the door.

"I'm not disturbing you, am I?" Serenity asked, in her gentle, musical voice. Her smile radiated affection and kindness. Her hair was done in a chignon and she was dressed in a loose Chinese suit of rough mourning grey. She had a string of prayer beads in one hand and something he could not make out in the other.

"Not at all," Xavier replied, turning to remove a pile of documents from a chair to make a seat for his mother.

"What a mess this is! All those crates and boxes! Your father never found time to deal with them. You sure you have enough room? You can use the library until some of the things are removed."

"It's all right, Mother. I've enough room." He was pleased to see that his mother's face still had that old beatific look of a person in a state of grace.

"I'm sorry I had to call you back," Serenity said. She glanced around the room and let out a sigh.

"It's all right, Mother. No big deal," Xavier said, as he resumed his seat. "Merchant banking's a dreary business anyway."

"In ancient times Confucians held that a filial son had to retreat from the world upon the passing of a parent, to leave his hair uncombed and his beard unshaved. On the other hand Buddhists believe the physical self is but a shell, a carcass, to house the spirit as it journeys from one existence to the next. To slough off a temporary casing is of little significance. Both points of view seem to make sense. I suppose I'm more Buddhist than Confucian."

"I'm glad."

"I've brought you your father's watch." Serenity opened her hand to reveal the thin gold watch with the black face. "I'm sure your father would like you to have it."

"It's a lovely watch, full of class. I've long admired it." Xavier took it and turned it over in his hands. "Yes, I'll certainly wear it with pride."

"I wouldn't have sent for you if I could have coped. I hope you understand. Many of your father's papers are in English. I couldn't make anything of them. I trust I haven't done anything wrong. I wouldn't want anyone in Gold Star to lose his job because of me."

"You did fine, Mother. Father was a genius. He left everything ticking over like clockwork. Built up massive cash reserves. Gold Star's solid as a rock."

"That's a relief. We must decide what to do soon. It has grown too big. I don't want you working day and night like your father."

"We don't have to deal with that now. You must have been run ragged the last few weeks. Let things settle down first."

Xavier looked into his mother's gentle eyes. He felt sorry for her life, wasted on useless religion. At the same time he suspected her inclinations might work against his grand designs. Donating her stake in Gold Star to charity would probably be uppermost in her mind. That would be disastrous. He needed her holdings to maintain control. He would have to secure his succession first and bide his time. Whether her affection for him was sufficient to bend her to his wishes remained uncertain.

"I hope you've not been hurt by the rubbish in the papers," Serenity said, misreading her son's silence. "Your father was a good man. A great tree often draws the whirlwind. Don't take idle gossip to heart."

"Oh, no, I was thinking of something else," Xavier said. "I'm still trying to fit all the bits of the jigsaw into place. Our family has never been very good at telling things to one another, has it?"

"What do you want to know, Ah Seng?"

"Did you accept the coroner's findings? They don't make sense to me. Good heavens! I've seen Father drink! A few pegs of whisky to him would be like raindrops on a desert. How could he fall into the sea and drown?"

"Yes, your father certainly could hold his drink. But what could anyone do? The coroner concluded it was an accident."

"The facts just don't add up, Mother. Father would at least have cried out if he were in difficulties. The crew didn't hear a thing. There was no sign of a struggle. There has to be something more."

"I've told the coroner all I know. Your father decided on an evening at sea after dinner. Nothing unusual in that. He never came back. They found him drowned the next morning. The coroner's verdict might not explain everything, but what else can we do?"

Xavier's eyes narrowed. "Why should Father be in bathing trunks?" he asked. "When the boatswain took me to the spot where they anchored, he said Father told him and the other crew member to go to sleep. Father said they wouldn't be returning to town till dawn. He left Father happily drinking and taking the breeze, fully clothed. Father's not the sort of man to go swimming alone at night, in the middle of nowhere. The coroner seemed to have ignored that and seized upon the fact that Father's clothes and personal belongings were in the cabin. I've had that ex-detective in Gold Star's security department — what's his name? Chan, isn't it? — sifting through the evidence again, but he couldn't come up with anything either. That fellow's getting too old for his job. I ought to get rid of him."

"Your father always allowed long-serving staff to leave of their own volition, unless a person has been seriously dishonest. If you want to let him go, at least give him a pension."

"Pension? Nobody at Gold Star gets a pension. They're all on month-to-month terms, including myself, for that matter."

"That may be the case, but your father always saw to it that long-serving staff could enjoy a contented old age. Detective Chan has given your father good service. He deserves some sort of reward. If Gold Star cannot provide it, please arrange a pension to be paid by me."

"All right, Mother, though I'm not sure he deserves one. He failed to come up with a single logical explanation to the questions I had about Father's accident."

"One cannot always find explanations. Some things cannot be explained."

"I doubt if that's true. I hate loose ends. You didn't notice anything bothering Father before the accident, did you?"

Serenity gave a laugh: "The only thing he fretted about was your adopting a foreign name. He went on about it for weeks."

"I know. He telephoned me. I tried to explain that 'Wing-seng' didn't carry the right ring. The guys at Princeton and Harvard kept asking me what it meant. I felt stupid telling them it means 'Forever Successful'. Everybody is supposed to be successful in America. Xavier, on the other hand, makes a neater statement. It gives the impression that your money is safe with a person so named. A banker needs a reassuring name rather than one that trips over the tongue. Father didn't accept that. I've never heard him so upset."

"I should think so! When we chose your name, we intended you to be forever successful as a decent and upright human being, not as an accumulator of wealth."

"You never told me that. I just wanted to follow in Father's footsteps, to make Gold Star a name to be reckoned with. He almost ordered me to stick with my Chinese name. Sent me a jade seal."

"He showed me. A really exquisite piece of Burmese jade. I loved the lion carved on top as the grip. He went to a lot of trouble to find it and engaged a master carver in Taiwan to do the engraving. He had it done in ancient script to remind you of the best of Chinese traditions when you use it. Have you been using it?"

"Mother, a person can't use a thing like that on Wall Street. It's messy. You need a vermilion ink pad to begin with and it's also too big to lug around. People'll think I'm cranky."

"Why be put off by what others think? Seals have been in use in China for thousands of years. Vermilion is the colour of life, of eternity. If foreigners do not know our ways you should explain things to them, not shy away from following tradition."

"Mother, Americans don't accept an imprint from a seal as a binding signature on a contract."

"That's strange. I remember your father telling me during the early days of Gold Star that he had to get corporate seals made for it and for its sister companies."

"Corporate seals are of a different order. In any case, I've given my seal to Lucille as a keepsake."

"Your father would be heartbroken if he knew. You might use it now that you're back here. Lots of people still use seals instead of signatures. An imprint with well-formed characters can make a very impressive statement."

In order to turn the conversation away from the subject, Xavier said: "I ought to call on Uncle Yue and some of Father's other associates. I'll need all the support I can get until I'm firmly in the saddle. Do you think Uncle Yue would put in a good word for me with the rest of the Evergreens?"

"Why are you so interested in the Evergreens?"

"Why shouldn't I be? A number of them have business connections with Gold Star. We ship garments to America on Uncle Yue's vessels, we are partners in construction projects with another uncle, we buy machinery from a third. It seems logical to preserve such relationships. Did Father eat frequently at the Evergreen Tea House?"

"He used to breakfast there three or four times a week.

Sometimes lunch as well. I would rather you distance yourself from those people. They were good friends of your father's but they belong to the past. They've made too much money too quickly. There's gossip about them, manipulating land prices and things like that."

"Nothing wrong with being quick-witted or stealing a march on others."

"That depends on how it's done. We are rich enough. You don't have to make more. I'd rather you spend more time with your family. When is Lucille bringing my grandson home? I'm longing to see both of them."

The switch in topic came as both a relief and an annoyance to Xavier. It seemed his mother had an instinct for touching on matters embarrassing to him.

"I'm sorry we didn't bring Ah Yuen for the funeral," he said. "He had been ill on and off since birth. We didn't think the long flight and the noise and wailing at a Chinese funeral would do him any good. We left him in San Francisco with Lucille's parents. Lucille'll bring him as soon as she's negotiated a release on the lease of our New York apartment."

"Good. Dr. Chow will look after him once he's here. Doctors don't come any better than Dr. Chow. Should I start looking for a nanny for Ah Yuen as well?"

"Thank you, Mother. I'm sure Lucille will appreciate that."

"You sure Lucille will be comfortable here?"

"Certainly. Why not? This is one of the best houses in Hong Kong, far better than anything she's been used to."

Serenity hesitated for a moment. "I didn't mean physical comfort," she said. "Lucille's American, but I sense she's not very comfortable with our ways, living with a mother-in-law. She asked a great many things about our customs, particularly about mourning rites, after the funeral. She seemed anxious not to put a foot wrong."

"I presume you told her the minimum necessary for the sake of form, Mother. That should be good enough. She's born and bred American. Let's keep her that way. Don't confuse her with mushy Chinese customs and ideas."

"I don't mean to interfere, Ah Seng, but you must help her adjust. She doesn't know any characters and does not even speak

Cantonese. She has only a smattering of Toi Shan village dialect. People may make fun of her."

"Mother, please let her be," Xavier pleaded.

If his mother got Lucille started, Xavier thought, there was no telling where it would end. With his father gone he did not want to be reminded any more of his own lack of interest in Chinese ways. He was a modern man, used to the get-up-and-go of Americans. If his mother started giving pointers to Lucille on what was or was not in the best Chinese tradition, domestic life would become more complicated. He needed the time and freedom to pursue his own ambitions, not to have both eaten up by a wife badgering him about Chinese obscurities.

"Please don't complicate Lucille's life," he continued. "She already has a hang-up about her heritage. She can speak English. The Filipino maids understand English. That should be enough. It took me years to get rid of the rubbish they taught me at school. Just look at the stuff around this room. Mouldy old books and antiquated knick-knacks. Americans have things better organized. They're not weighed down by their past. If Father had freed himself from all this stuff, he might have made more of his life."

"Made more of his life?"

"Yes. He might have become richer and more famous."

Serenity rose from her chair, shaking her head. "I'm going to the Meditation Room. Has it ever occurred to you that your father might have seen through the illusions in life, except that for him it was too late to turn back? He had accumulated too many obligations, done too many things he could not undo. For you, it's not too late. Please reflect upon what I've said. Perhaps I should have left you in New York and tried to handle Gold Star in some other way."

Xavier watched his mother head for the Meditation Room across the hall. He felt sorry for upsetting her. He was only trying to be honest and not mealy-mouthed. He could imagine her kneeling before the great bronze Buddha in the Meditation Room, with her head bent to the ground, praying for the salvation of her unrepentant son.

He leaned back and recalled his father's mesmeric voice recounting the conversation between Mencius and King Hui of

Liang. Why were people so fond of telling others how to lead their lives? First his father, now his mother. He did not have the heart to tell his mother it was his father's opposition to his adopting "Xavier" as a name that had driven him into a spur-of-the-moment marriage. He had wanted to be modern, to assert his right to do whatever he wished.

In doing so, he had not been entirely fair to Lucille. She had asked for it, however, flaunting her physical attractions and allowing herself to be seduced in his hotel room in New York. His father's criticisms had come when he was in the middle of a bout of loneliness. To shake it off he had invited Lucille to join him for a weekend in Las Vegas. Once there, Lucille's charms again got the better of him after a few drinks.

To compound that mistake, he had sired a sickly son. Lucille had spoken of having many children. That had not been in his calculations, at least not till his career had settled. No sooner was his son born than his father died. Was that an omen? If so, of what? Of ill-luck to come or of an accelerated opportunity to rise in the world? Only time would tell.

Meanwhile, he had to get to the bottom of the bill from the Evergreen Tea House. His mother had spoken of manipulation of land prices by the Evergreens. It would be worth getting the inside dope on that. He would give Uncle Yue a call.

The Evergreen Tea House

16

"How are you, Uncle Yue? Good of you to invite me for lunch."
Xavier Chu bowed as he spoke and felt slightly absurd. Nine
years in America had stripped him of that Eastern habit and
reverting to it seemed an imposition.

"Ah Seng!" Mr. Yue cried happily, half-rising and gesturing
with one of his large hands for Xavier to take a seat. He was
dressed in a traditional Chinese suit of grey cotton. "A pleasure
to see you again, under happier circumstances. A meal's the least
I can offer the son of a dear friend."

Xavier took a seat on the bench opposite his host and gazed
once more into a face he used to see regularly at his father's
mah jong games. With its thinning hair, bushy eyebrows and
broad, flat nose, it struck Xavier as too unrefined for someone
owning the largest shipping fleet in Asia and countless other
businesses.

The Evergreen Tea House, too, seemed like a throwback to a
former age. It was set in a row of two-storied tenements, each
with its own outdated charm. The marble cloud-patterned table
top, set in a blackwood frame, had long gone out of fashion.
Four identical booths, separated by high latticed wooden panels,
flanked both sides of the room. The space between was occupied
by three round tables, each with six matching stools. A large
brass spittoon stood next to each booth. Lazy ceiling fans made
a pretence at ventilation.

"I'm drinking Dragon's Well. Does that suit? If not, you can
order something else. There are dozens to choose from,
fermented, semi-fermented and unfermented, the very best of
each kind."

"I'm not much into teas. A Coke would be fine."

Mr. Yue laughed. His laughter was good-natured, as he bared
large discoloured teeth. "Have you not been here before?"

"No. Father did offer to bring me but I never found time
before leaving for America."

"Didn't your father tell you anything about this place?'

"Nothing beyond his meeting you and other uncles here."

"Ah Seng, you're in for an experience! I'll have to explain things, then. See that old man sitting over there behind the counter? He's Proprietor Ng, the owner. What do you see on the wall above him?"

Xavier turned his attention to a large black frame hanging on the wall behind the counter. It contained a passage in Chinese ascribed to an eighth-century scholar, asserting that tea could temper the spirit, harmonize the mind, arouse thought, refresh the body and clear the faculties.

"Impressive claims," Xavier allowed.

"Now look at what's in front of the counter."

There was a stand with three layers jutting out like steps. Each layer was lined with large, wide-necked glass jars with metal lids holding different types of tea. Cloud Mist. Pearl Tea. Kee Mun. Luk On. Kar Sow. Gee Sheng. They went on and on and Xavier, in spite of his years of university education, could make no sense of those strange and unfamiliar names. "I guess they don't serve Coke," he said, wryly.

Mr. Yue laughed again. "Try some of my Dragon's Well," he said, pouring a steaming cup. "It's one of the best Chinese green teas, full of cooling and refreshing properties. Strictly speaking, to be at its best, it should be brewed with water from a certain spring in Hangchow, but that's being pedantic. How come you never developed a taste for tea? How could you have missed so much, Ah Seng? There are teas to aid digestion, to relieve stomach aches, to cure colds, to stimulate circulation of the blood. All the best ones are here. All fine pluckings, done before the Ching Ming Festival. Do you know the differences between the types of pluckings and when they take place?"

Xavier shook his head and blinked. He took a sip from his cup to hide his annoyance. He hated to have to admit ignorance. The astringent liquid seared his tongue.

"In fine pluckings only the bud and the top two leaves are harvested. In medium and coarse pluckings leaves are taken from further down. Leaves are at their most tender before Ching Ming. For green teas, they have to be cleaned and steamed immediately to prevent fermentation. Then rolled and dried several times till they're tightly curled. The Japanese like to spread jasmine over the tea for fragrance. Some connoisseurs like to season leaves inside lotus blossoms. I suppose not having a taste for tea is better than drinking it like foreigners, with milk and sugar or lemon. What abominations!"

A waiter in a white jacket buttoned up to the neck and a pair of black trousers, came up to the booth. "Is Mr. Yue ready to be served?" he asked.

Mr. Yue nodded and the waiter shouted something unintelligible in a high-pitched voice towards the rear of the room. From somewhere an echo of the order came back.

It dawned on Xavier the room they were in was not enclosed, as he had originally supposed, but connected to the kitchen. It was then that he caught a slight whiff of food being prepared. Closer observation revealed that the wall behind the counter was an illusion. There were in fact two other parallel walls, each about six feet wide, set behind the first. They created the impression of a complete barrier, but left an opening for waiters to fetch food from the kitchen.

"You might think me mean inviting you to lunch in a tea house," Mr. Yue said. "But this place is special. It serves the usual dim sum, but for special customers it lays on the best and freshest foods from the markets each day. It means pot luck, of course. We'll just have to enjoy our tea and wait to see what we get."

Xavier pretended to sip his tea as he studied the novelty of the premises. On the wall of each booth was an underglazed enamel painting set in an intricately latticed redwood frame. They were pictures of individuals in ancient garb, enjoying tea in gardens or parlours. The picture in his booth showed a man and a woman holding tea cups.

"Do you know the people in the picture?" Mr. Yue asked.

"Haven't the foggiest."

"The man was Tsai Shiang, a famous Sung Dynasty calligrapher, and the woman a state courtesan named Chou Shao. They were both great connoisseurs of tea. Chou Shao was very knowledgeable and often bested Tsai Shiang with her knowledge of teas and tea drinking. Ah! Those were the days! Courtesans were beautiful and well schooled. They could play musical instruments and match couplets with the best poets. They served the needs of the intellect and the soul as well as those of the body. Where can such treasures be found today? It's now all topless bars and Suzie Wongs. You know, Chou Shao was eventually released from her duties by a high official and she became a nun."

"Paintings like that must be worth a pretty penny these days," Xavier observed.

"I suppose so. But only to collectors. They used to be plentiful but have gone out of fashion. Nobody paints or makes them any more. I image our Marxist-Leninist comrades have already banned them as decadent art. They lose meaning in any case when people don't know what they're about."

Xavier noted that all three round tables were apparently being shared and occupied in relays. As soon as some customers left they were replaced by others from a queue outside. The room resounded regularly with the cries of waiters placing orders and echoes of acknowledgement. When not serving food, the waiters did the rounds with large brass kettles of boiling water for replenishing teapots.

Xavier noticed, however, that all the booths, except for the one he was in, were empty. "They're not making the most efficient use of the booths," he observed.

"The booths are occupied," Mr. Yue said.

"You mean they're reserved?"

"No, they're occupied. See that second booth on the other side? That's occupied by your father."

"My father! But... "

At that moment a waiter arrived with a steamed red snapper and dishes containing stewed king eel and Chinese broccoli fried with slices of beef.

"Ah, stewed king eel! An unexpected treat! Let's eat."

"Uncle Yue, you said my father occupied that booth. I... "

"Yes, Ah Seng. Don't be like an American, always in a hurry. You telephoned me about a bill from this tea house. I will explain later. First, let us enjoy this splendid meal."

Xavier ate in silence, his head in a spin. The food was the kind he normally fancied, but somehow it seemed tasteless. He had spent the best part of an hour listening to inconsequentialities about tea and tea drinkers. If it had been about shipping he might have at least picked up a useful tip or two. He was anxious to get down to brass tacks. But Uncle Yue seemed determined to take his own sweet time. Was he toying with him? Was he trying to size him up as a business partner, now that he was head of Gold Star?

After the meal, a waiter cleared away the dishes and brought a new pot of Dragon's Well. He tipped the dregs in the cups into the spittoon next to the booth and poured fresh cups. Meanwhile, a steady turnover continued at the round tables, but the seven booths remained empty.

Mr. Yue sipped his tea with relish for a while. Then, suddenly, more than a dozen people from the queue outside were ushered in. They made for the empty booths.

Mr. Yue looked at his watch. "Two o'clock," he said. "I guess none of the regulars is coming. That's exceptional. Normally at least two or three of us are here. Those lucky fellows will get their treats. Now we can go upstairs and I'll answer your questions."

Xavier followed Uncle Yue out of the booth and headed towards the wizened old man at the counter. Uncle Yue effected introductions and the two exchanged bows.

"My humble establishment is honoured by your presence," Proprietor Ng said. The rich baritone voice coming out of the proprietor's frail frame took Xavier by surprise. "My deepest condolences over the passing of your father," Proprietor Ng continued. "He was an exceptional man to whom my family and I are much indebted. I'll have tea sent upstairs."

It was only when Xavier turned from the counter that he discovered a flight of stairs behind the booths. He followed Uncle Yue up to a floor considerably larger than the one they had left.

The space was divided by a partially drawn red velvet curtain. A similar curtain had already been drawn over the windows at the far side of the front section.

The only light came from a table lamp on a corner stand. A powerful air-conditioning unit beneath the windows fed in a steady stream of cool air.

The section contained half a dozen sofas of the type used in first-class aircraft cabins, arranged in a semi-circle, with teapoys and brass spittoons next to each. An armchair held a stack of neatly folded blankets. The arrangements reminded Xavier of a luxurious private cinema.

In the rear section there was a round table similar in design to the ones downstairs, except it was capable of accommodating at least ten persons. Matching chairs stood around it.

Mr. Yue led Xavier into the front portion and invited him to take one of the sofas. He took another next to him. A waiter arrived with a pot of tea. He poured two cups before retiring, drawing the second set of velvet curtains.

"No doubt you're bursting with questions," Mr. Yue said, teasingly. "You might be wondering why your father, myself, Uncle Kan and the others, all very wealthy men, should wish to continue patronizing a place like this. Fond memories, Ah Seng, and gratitude for the good fortune we have enjoyed since gathering here. Wise men do not forsake such places. First, some history.

"Before the war, I wasn't a shipping tycoon. I was just a fisherman with a boat. Uncle Kan, who was a plumber then, and I used to live in this neighbourhood. We came 'to drink early tea'. This place was a favourite haunt of bird-fanciers. They brought their birds along in handcrafted cages. Canaries, skylarks, mynahs. We enjoyed the birdsongs with our tea. It was like a morning tonic. We were fond of the teas and the dim sum here, too.

"When the Japs came everybody landed in the shit. I got together with a few friends to find a way of keeping our families alive. One was a nightwatchman with connections in the underworld, a brute of a man, full of courage and game for anything. He was known to us as Buck-toothed Fung."

"I know Uncle Fung," Xavier interjected. "My father introduced us in Taiwan."

"Good, then I can skip some details. Uncle Fung introduced us to your father. He said your father was well-educated and full of ideas. He was certainly right. We took my boat and brought in food from China, right under the noses of the Japs. A dangerous enterprise but exceptionally rewarding. Not everybody survived. Nine of us did and, because of the foresight of your father, each of us found ourselves at the end of the war with a comfortable nest egg in buildings, land and valuables.

"See this ring?" Mr. Yue lifted his left hand to display on one of its thick fingers a stunning oval of green and translucent jade set into a gold ring. "I got it in exchange for just a scoop of soya beans. It has brought me luck ever since."

Mr. Yue's eyes took on a misty and reminiscing look as he recounted the origins and growing influence of his band of friends known popularly as the Evergreens.

It appeared that he and Uncle Kan had invited the others to the tea house for early tea after the war. Soon it became a regular thing. The floor where they used to meet was in public use then, dominated by bird-fanciers. The tea house opened, then as now, at 5.30 am and the friends gathered at around six.

Their exploits during the occupation had turned them into brothers, with few secrets among them. A nod of the head was all that was needed for business to be transacted. No hassle with lawyers or pieces of paper. They all had dreams. Some wanted to start factories, others to found utilities or to engage in commerce. They wanted to become both respectable and rich, though none had enough liquidity to start what each wanted.

They knew little about bank financing and mortgages then. The obvious way to raise cash was to sell assets. Uncle Fung was all for selling everything and getting out with the money. He had Kuomintang connections and was afraid of the Communists.

Chu Tung-po, on the other hand, wanted them to hang on to what they had and to wait. He said the civil war was likely to continue for a good many years because the Americans were supporting the Kuomintang. Whoever won would be left too weak and with too many internal problems to take on the Brits, at least for a good while. He said land and property prices were bound to rise once former residents started returning to Hong Kong, not to mention the rich from China escaping the civil war. Most thought his arguments made sense. Only Uncle Fung disagreed. He sold out and headed for Taiwan.

Uncle Yue paused and Xavier noted that the older man had a real knack for story-telling. His tale was providing increasing insight into how his father's mind worked.

After a moment Uncle Yue continued. He recounted how a suggestion was made that, while waiting for land prices to rise, the group might continue with smuggling in supplies to meet market demands. Uncle Yue still had his boat and there was always money to be made with a daring crew. Capitalism and free enterprise were all the rage. However, most of the group no longer wanted to run risks, even though the dangers were in fact much less than during the Japanese occupation. Only two wanted to chance their arm. Uncle Yue and one other. They made money hand over fist and were able to advance money to the others to get them started.

Chu Tung-po turned out to be right about land prices. Within a year the million people flooding into the colony sent prices soaring. But still Chu didn't want anyone to sell. He said conditions were not ripe. Many sites had been acquired for a song. Or for a few bags of beans or rice, to be more precise. Most were war damaged. Many had been taken over by squatters or were being used as rubbish dumps. Clearing them prior to sale would cost money. Chu told everyone to sit tight. He got each to form a company to hold their properties.

At last, when Chu judged the time right, the group selected one of its member to test the water. Before beginning, the group determined a minimum acceptable price. When the lot came up at public auction, the other seven bid up the price. That created a perception of high demand and nudged prices up. That, in turn, boosted the value of their holdings. Any excess arrived at over the minimum price agreed was shared out equally among all.

Each had to bid correctly, so as not to push the price beyond what outsiders might be willing to pay. Getting it wrong meant one of the group being stuck with the winning bid. In those circumstances the seller would privately refund the buyer the difference between the sale price and the minimum agreed price. The whole thing worked beautifully. It might be said that the group was responsible for starting Hong Kong's first post-war property boom.

Mr. Yue paused again to enjoy his tea.

"Sounds like my father masterminded a bidding ring! Was that legal at the time?"

"Don't rightly know. If you looked closely, everything in this town could be illegal, including this tea house."

"This tea house?"

"Yes, it hasn't got a separate fire exit, as required by law, but that doesn't prevent it from providing a service people want. It just means working out an accommodation with those enforcing the law. It was no different then. We were looking after our own self-interest. We didn't ask too many questions. We found the liquidity we needed to specialize and branch out. Construction, financing, trading, insurance, warehousing, stockbrokering. I concentrated on shipping, Uncle Kan on property development, and so on. Your father wanted to test himself against everything. He had genius but also seemed wrapped up with deeper, more non-business considerations none of us fully understood."

Genius and non-business considerations. That sounded like his father all right, Xavier thought.

"We continued to meet here for early tea," Mr. Yue continued, after a few sips of Dragon's Well. "As we prospered, we began attracting attention and envy. Financial journalists, stockbrokers, commodity traders and gossip columnists discovered our meeting place and descended upon it. They eavesdropped on our conversations. No doubt they paid some of the waiters to pass on anything they picked up. We couldn't risk our discussions being overheard. Yet we didn't want to abandon the Evergreen. We struck a deal with Proprietor Ng. We wanted him to reserve the upper floor exclusively for our use during early tea. In return we paid him one and a half times what he normally earned from using it for the morning trade. The arrangement didn't please the snoopers. Nor the bird-fanciers who got restricted to the lower floor. But it cemented our relations with Proprietor Ng.

"That relationship deepened two or three years later, by accident you might say. Uncle Kan and I often lunched here, with friends and family members. The place was conveniently close to both our offices. On a number of occasions, however, we turned up to find the place full. That annoyed us. We thought it reasonable that Proprietor Ng should reserve a booth or two for regulars.

"We raised the subject at early tea. Most thought it a good idea, except your father. He said that in business one must ensure that all parties made a profit. Otherwise relationships would turn sour. Although we were regular customers, it would be wrong to place Proprietor Ng at a disadvantage. It was inevitable, your father said, that we would lose the Evergreen quite soon. Tea houses were disappearing as buildings got knocked down for redevelopment. No new tea house was likely to be established because it was patently more profitable to sell other things than to run a tea house. The question was whether we could be reconciled to the loss.

"None of us could be. The Evergreen was like a second home to us. We had made our fortunes here and our luck might change if the tea house disappeared. Your father laughed at our agitation. Some of us were angry he was treating the matter so lightly.

"After we had calmed down, he chastised us, demanding to know what we had done to preserve what we claimed to value. Had we explained the benefits of tea to our children, encouraged them to drink it, schooled them in the subtleties of the 'after-taste', or had we merely stocked our refrigerators with fizzy drinks for them to help themselves? New beverages were being advertised massively, but none had been tested on human beings over centuries like tea. Some might actually be harmful to health. Instead of promoting tea drinking we were turning ourselves into accomplices in the brainwashing of our children. None of us should be against change, he said, but change did not necessarily mean progress. We had to help our children make informed choices and not to allow them to follow fads."

Xavier picked up his cup of tea and made a pretence at drinking it. The words sounded like a rebuke delivered by his father from the grave. It made him self-conscious of his ignorance about tea and tea-drinking.

"Your father left us feeling more than sheepish," Mr. Yue went on. "Then someone suggested buying the land on which the Evergreen stood, to allow it to continue. Your father shook his head. He said buying the premises, far from preserving the tea house, would only hasten its demise. It would make it easier for Proprietor Ng to retire. If he did that, we would be left with a tea house that none of us knew how to run.

"Incentives for Proprietor Ng to continue were needed, your father said. The first step would be to acquire the land on either side of the Evergreen. Once that had been secured, we could put it to Proprietor Ng that circumstances had turned him into our partner. Sooner or later we would redevelop the adjacent sites and we would then need his property because it straddled ours. When that time came he could name his own price. In the meantime, he could watch his asset appreciate steadily with Hong Kong's building boom. He and his family would do well to continue with the tea house because no one, apart from ourselves, would want a site incapable of redevelopment by itself."

"Did everyone agree with the plan?"

"Ah Seng, when your father comes forward with a proposal, it is usually so sound that none of us would disagree. In this instance, your father was also emphatic that we shouldn't be seen as predators or bullies, but to present Proprietor Ng with an obviously good deal. To that end we guaranteed Proprietor Ng's profits by each of us taking up permanently a booth on the ground floor for lunch. It did not matter whether we actually came for meals. We would each simply pay Proprietor Ng for four meals every day, since each booth accommodated four. He could bill us quarterly or half-yearly. That would work out at only a few thousand dollars per month. Since every one of us was already a millionaire many times over, that was neither here nor there."

"And that accounts for the bill landing in my father's office long after he had passed away!" Xavier said.

"Correct. Your father had insisted on two further rules. First, meals might or might not be eaten. But, if eaten, they must be in the company of the payer. In other words, wives, children or friends could not turn up by themselves to demand meals charged to us. That would confuse both Proprietor Ng and the waiters. Second, if any of us did not turn up by two o'clock, then the meals paid for could be offered to the public at a discount, with the proceeds split equally between Proprietor Ng and his staff. That kept the staff happy and accounted for the daily queues outside. That also accounted for your father's booth being left empty till two o'clock."

"That explains the queue and the rush at two o'clock!"

"Precisely. The bill also covers one other item that crept in some years later. As we grew older, someone suggested it would be wonderful to have a place to nap for half an hour after lunch, before returning to our offices. Since we already had an arrangement over closing the upper floor during early tea, it seemed logical to extend it to lunch as well. That's why there are sofas here instead of tables and chairs. The bills cover all three arrangements. Your father's passing has affected us so much that we didn't rearrange anything. We miss him terribly and that's not just out of sheer sentimentality. Nothing seems the same without him."

"Thank you, Uncle Yue. I'm sure my mother appreciates your sentiments. May I thank, through you, all the other uncles for being so considerate and helpful at the funeral. I don't want to sound presumptuous, but would you and the other uncles object to my taking over my father's place? I want to learn from all of you, though I have only met some for the first time during the funeral."

"You've hardly touched your tea, Ah Seng," Mr. Yue said.

"I'm not thirsty."

Mr. Yue drank from his cup, emptied the dregs into the spittoon and poured a fresh cup. He remained silent for a while. Then he said: "It's premature to speak of taking your father's place. You're still in mourning. Your father's passing has reminded us of our own mortality. It would be unseemly to raise the subject at this stage. Your presence among us would also raise larger issues. We all have sons. None of us has brought them into our circle. It's obvious that the younger generation must take over one day. But most of us find it difficult to speak as freely if youngsters are among us. We've been through so much together that we can communicate without words. It won't be the same with our sons present."

"I understand. I'm sorry I raised the matter."

"Ah Seng, leave this with me for the time being. We can talk about it again. Give me a chance to sound out one or two of the others. Meanwhile, I suggest you pay your father's bill. I don't think anyone can object to your lunching here. You might ask Proprietor Ng if you could take over your father's arrangement for a booth at lunch. Future bills can then be made out in your name. That doesn't mean you can join us for early tea or afternoon naps, mind you. But it'll give you exposure before the other uncles, allowing them to get to know you a little better. It might even convert you into a tea drinker!"

"Thank you, Uncle Yue. I'll do as you've suggested. Do you mind if I ask your opinion about something else?"

"No, unless it's going to land me in a libel suit!"

"Do you think my father's death was accidental?"

Mr. Yue paused for a long moment. "Deaths are never accidental," he replied. "They are fated. We all have our appointed hour. For some people, death can be a release, eagerly awaited. For others, a mere passage into another existence. For a very few, death produces consequences. Some lives can only be fulfilled through death. Your father's might be one of those. But this is not the time to go into such abstruse matters. We must leave. The tea house closes at 3.30. Proprietor Ng and his staff have already worked for ten hours. It won't do to detain them further."

Pipe dreams

SAIGON
APRIL 1966

17

The noise and confusion of afternoon traffic enveloped Sebastian Baxingdale as the trishaw took him from the Chinese opium den in Cholon to Rue Catinat. The pleasurable after-effects of four pipes lingered still. The thring-thring of bicycle and trishaw bells sounded like the tintinnabulation of Eastern music. The rocking movement of the vehicle lulled him. Vietnamese women floated by like beckoning sirens in white, flowing dresses.

He closed his eyes and dreamt of the lotus-bulb protuberance of the long-stemmed pipe, the sizzling of opium paste over a bright lamp and the soothing pungency of the drug as he sucked it in.

After what seemed a dreamy eternity, a rough Vietnamese voice interrupted his reverie. He opened his eyes to find the sweaty face of the trishaw pedaller turned towards him, asking where he wanted to be set down. The face was gaunt, impassive, nut brown.

Baxingdale smiled sheepishly and noticed for the first time the grotesque varicose veins worming up the pedaller's exposed calves. He picked up the copy of *Iron In The Soul* from the seat next to him and paid more generously than he needed. He felt guilty about using another human being as a beast of burden. Perhaps that was what this whole senseless war boiled down to, a struggle by people like the pedaller to live with less misery and more dignity.

Rue Catinat was a handsome, tree-lined thoroughfare with many bars, cafés, restaurants and nightclubs. It would not be out of place on the Left Bank in Paris, except that it lacked the literary ghosts and the intellectual ferment of the Sixth Arrondissement. Instead it was pervaded by the same get-rich-quick atmosphere he had encountered in Hong Kong. Only there seemed even greater urgency, as if each transaction had to be completed before the next grenade or bicycle bomb nullified it.

It was remarkable how quickly people adjusted to the possibility of death. It seemed as if some stabilizing instinct lulled them into thinking it could only happen to others. He strolled a little along the boulevard and felt the sense of lightness and well-being induced by opium seeping slowly out of him. He selected a quiet café and ordered coffee to cope with returning sobriety.

The rush hour had started and, sitting on the pavement in one of the café's rattan chairs, he watched the gathering flow of motor vehicles, bicycles and pedestrians. In another couple of hours, Rue Catinat would blossom with whores, pimps, pickpockets, beggars, money changers and drug pushers, drawn by the irresistible smell of Yankee dollars.

The more popular restaurants and nightclubs had metal grilles fitted over their windows to prevent grenades landing among customers. Such premises, after all, were the regular meeting places for influential politicians and diplomats and for foreign correspondents sniffing for gossip. And drifting among the regulars, like Homer's ghosts, would be the lost souls from Kansas or Montana, fresh-faced young men sent to fight for a cause they could not comprehend and who, if they survived, would return home scarred in body or soul or both.

He himself had turned increasingly to opium to dull his disgust at so much bloodletting. As correspondent for the *Daily Globe* he was supposed to report the truth. But everybody, from his Press-baron boss to the two million readers of the newspaper, expected truths to be simple, palatable and digestible. But truths in Indochina were both complex and unpalatable. It was an Oriental Balkans. Every truth was cocooned in deceit, illusions and wishful thinking.

Journalistic work would be simple if one stuck to superficialities and military handouts. America assisting freedom-loving peoples to beat back the tide of Communism. Sorties flown, bombs dropped, enemies bodies counted dead or wounded. But that would be far from the total picture. The most powerful country on earth had manufactured an incident in the Gulf of Tonkin in order to participate in a many-sided conflict in an impoverished Asian land. Little did Pentagon planners realize they had stepped into a quagmire.

They had ignored the centuries of rivalries and hatreds, of racial and religious antagonisms. Their roots stretched back to the ancient kingdoms of Annam and Tonkin, to the Khmer empire, to French colonial legacies, to contests between Buddhists and Catholics, to nationalist aspirations and minority races, to the wealth of the few and the enslavement of the many, to outlandish sects like the Hoa-Hao and the Caodists, to bishoprics with private armies, to criminal syndicates and primitive hill tribes preyed upon by all. Those tangled roots bound everyone in a benighted land.

When he stumbled into journalism, he did not realize what he was letting himself in for. His mother had spoken blithely of his becoming a new Zola, to shed light on the injustices of the world. What endearing naivety! More than eighteen months in Vietnam had convinced him of his utter impotence. No matter how pregnant his words, how graphic his descriptions, they became grotesque and unwelcomed when served up in print at the breakfast tables of middle England.

He had written about corruption in high places, misuse of American aid, student leaders spirited away by the secret police, self-immolations by Buddhist monks and nuns, and the oppressions by a Catholic puppet regime. He had detailed the deadly effects of the defoliant Agent Orange and terrorist bombs slaughtering off-duty Americans in bars and nightclubs. He had shed helpless tears watching children ignited by napalm rained upon their villages. The smell of burning human flesh was such that he could no longer bear the thought of eating roasted meat again.

His justification for his grisly occupation was that his words might make a difference, might one day cause people to protest against the recurring barbarities in the world. But they only earned him a reputation as a trouble-maker, undermining the efforts of a just war. American and South Vietnamese authorities angled for his replacement. He was more than willing to go. But the *Daily Globe* couldn't find a substitute and he was left for a further period recounting the death rattles in a war that everyone was doomed to lose.

What had enabled the Vietcong — and the people who had supported them — to endure so much? They had taken everything that modern military technology could inflict and yet had stayed defiant. Were they merely fatalistic or had they been born with higher thresholds for pain? Japan had risen from the ashes. So had South Korea. No doubt, given peace, the Vietnamese would too. The rest of the world ought to take note of these yellow races. It was not for nothing that Spengler had warned of their rise.

Baxingdale reached into one of the pockets of his tan safari suit for a packet of cigarettes. As he blew a cloud of smoke, he wondered how much longer he could bear the carnage and butchery. Why had he been condemned to this? He had joined the *Globe* just to make a living. He had not signed up to spend the rest of his days as a professional onlooker, chronicling the inanities and madnesses of the human race. If that was his inevitable fate, he would rather die.

The notion of death gradually took hold of him and grew increasingly attractive as he smoked. He was, after all, a white man, a foreign devil, as the natives would say. He was sitting on an exposed pavement in one of the most deadly cities in the world. He could easily be taken for an American, a legitimate target of opportunity for any Vietcong patriot. A well-aimed grenade or a bicycle bomb would do the trick. It would be over in a flash.

The only snag, he supposed, would be the indignity of being scooped over his own death. That would be rich! Getting killed was an occupational hazard. Perhaps he ought to file the circumstances of his demise in advance. Doing his own obituary could be fun. It wouldn't take long. Dead journalists never rated more than a couple of paragraphs at the bottom of a page.

"Correspondent Killed By Terror Bomb". No sooner had he thought of the headline, he rejected it. Opium must have addled his brains. No headline writer worth his salt would use a word like "correspondent". It was too long and clumsy. He was bound to go for something snappier. Also a verb with more immediacy. He began playing mentally with different combinations and eventually settled for "Bike Bomb Kills Newsman".

It occurred to him that being blown apart might not necessarily result in death. If the Buddhists were correct, there was no such thing as death. One merely transmigrated from one existence to another. Any existence was bound to be better than the one he was stuck with.

On that note he ordered another cup of coffee and opened Sartre's novel. The words somehow failed to register. He lit another cigarette and as he did so he sensed someone passing in front of him.

"Hello, Joe," a female voice said.

He looked up and saw a Vietnamese girl in a sleeveless red dress with a hemline ending six inches above her knees. She was young and svelte. A small white handbag dangled from a long strap on her left shoulder. Her right hand rested akimbo on a jutting hip. She was pretty enough, in a forward sort of way, and he could see at once that both her beauty and her youth had been overused.

"Hello," he replied. "The name's Sebastian, not Joe."

"Ah, Sebastien! Nice name. You not American, no? I'm so sorry. Your name is name of saint, no? They killed him with arrows. I remember that, see? I learned at convent. My name's Françoise." Her English cooed with pleasing French intonations.

"Well, Françoise, I'm afraid the convent taught you wrong. Saint Sebastian didn't die from arrows. He survived those. He was actually clubbed to death later."

The girl gave a shrug of the shoulders, obviously put off by his pedantic response. She recovered her importuning form quickly, however, and gave a knowing laugh. "You like a good time, Sebastien?" she asked. "I can give you *very* good time."

"I'm already having a good time, Françoise. I'm enjoying a fine cup of coffee and I'm reading a good book."

"I can show you better time. I have special talent," she said, smiling and shifting her weight from one foot to the other. She thrust her pelvis at him.

Baxingdale regarded her brown, slender legs and the proffered pelvis. Why not? he thought. Anything to hold back the awfulness of the conflict. Sex was as good an escape as opium.

He was about to say something when he caught the flash out of the corner of his eye. A fraction of a second later he heard the explosion and felt something hitting him with great force. He toppled over backwards on the rattan chair, striking the back of his head against the pavement.

He remained dazed for a few moments. Then sounds came

back as through a filter. Muffled screams, shouts and the sound of whistles. He became conscious of a weight pressing upon him. There was also an annoyance of hair in his face. Then he saw the red dress and realized it was Françoise. Her limbs were straddling him awkwardly, as if in an unnatural posture of copulation.

"Françoise, Françoise! Are you all right?" he whispered urgently into the mess of hair next to his face.

There was no response. He tried to lift her but could not find the strength. When his hands came away he saw they were covered with blood.

"Oh, no!" he cried, not certain whose blood it was. He felt no pain and that alarmed him even more. Was it the blood of Françoise on his hands or his own? Was his wish for death about to be granted? What about Françoise? He tried to lift her again but failed again. He took hold of Françoise's head to turn the face towards himself. A pair of lifeless eyes stared back at him. "Someone please help me!" he called with all his might. "A woman's been badly hurt."

Eventually the young Vietnamese waiter and some other people came and lifted Françoise off him. She had a piece of shrapnel sticking out of her back.

"Fini," the waiter said, phlegmatically.

Some people helped him up and sat him down on another rattan chair. His safari jacket was covered with blood. An ambulance arrived and a medic examined him and pronounced him unhurt, save for a few scratches on his legs and the bump on his head. A Vietnamese customer sitting at another table had suffered a serious arm injury. Except for the Vietnamese and Françoise, nobody else had been badly injured.

He asked for another cup of coffee and a cigarette, which the waiter readily supplied.

Police and the security men were fussing around the twisted mess of bicycles at the stand in front of the café, watched over by a knot of onlookers. When satisfied that no other device had been planted, a security official came over to take Baxingdale's particulars and his account of events.

"The girl was your companion?" the security official asked, after Baxingdale had told him what happened.

"No, never saw her before."

"Then why were you talking to her when the bomb went off?"

"She was asking the way to a convent. I couldn't help her."

The security official nodded. "You're a very lucky man, Monsieur," he said, closing his notebook and re-joining his colleagues.

In the meantime the medics had led the injured man to an ambulance and Françoise's body had been bundled away.

The waiter was busy straightening the tables and chairs toppled by the blast and picking up the shards of broken coffee cups and saucers. Next to where Baxingdale had sat, a copy of *Iron In The Soul* was resting on the ground in a small pool of blood. The waiter picked up the book between thumb and forefinger. A few drops of blood dripped from it. He looked at Baxingdale questioningly. Baxingdale shook his head and the waiter consigned it to the rubbish bin brought along for the clean-up.

Baxingdale felt wrapped in numbness. The bomb had been meant for him. He must have been mistaken for an American. If he had not engaged Françoise for a few minutes in pointless banter, if he had either dismissed her or gone off with her more quickly, she might still be alive. Her death was his responsibility. He was on the scene. He was an eye-witness. Yet it was a tragedy he could not write about. What wholesome British family would be interested in a foreign whore dying half a world away while propositioning a john?

He finished the coffee. When he felt sufficiently composed he stood up and hailed a taxi. His safari jacket was covered with blood. He told himself he ought to head home to change.

Once inside the taxi, however, he asked to be driven to Cholon.

The battle of the loudspeakers

HONG KONG

JULY 1967

18

Cymbals clashed, drums rumbled and the falsetto laments of a
Cantonese aria reverberated outside the office of Derek Soames
at Beaconsfield House. Ordinarily, such an irritating invasion
of his peace and quiet would cause the Senior Press Officer of
the Hong Kong Government Information Service to decamp
immediately for a drink at one of the shrinking number of places
where his credit remained unquestioned. Contrary to expectation,
however, he seemed uncharacteristically unbothered. Indeed, he
appeared to be positively revelling in those ear-splitting sounds.

They were, after all, his idea. He had masterminded the
current battle of the loudspeakers. The deafening decibels
underscored a deadly contest with the Chinese Communists,
holed up across the road in the Bank of China Building. The
expressions registered on the faces of passers-by suggested they
were enjoying the silliness and, in the sober Communist view of
things, to be regarded as silly was tantamount to having lost.

Derek Soames allowed his florid features to break into a self-
satisfied smile. Opera was an acquired taste, particularly
Cantonese opera, he reflected, as he rose from his desk. He
waddled across the room to a steel filing cabinet, waving his
arms as he went, in parody of those performers with grotesquely
painted faces. From the bowels of a filing cabinet he extracted a
clear plastic bottle printed with the popular Gold Star brand of
mineral water. He took a hefty swig and smiled again as he closed
his sly, intelligent eyes. He would have preferred gin, but its
aroma was too revealing in the office. Vodka had to do.

Soames, at forty-one, was already rapidly going to seed. His
bulbous nose, his flabby, insolent mouth and his retracted chin
inspired little confidence in superiors or associates. That
accounted for the briefness of his previous careers in advertising
and with a British tabloid. But he had luck, and through some
kindly twist of fate he had been offered a job in Hong Kong as
Senior Press Officer. It came just in the nick of time, for creditors
and landlords in the slums of Liverpool, where he had digs, were

167

already closing in like quicksand. The pay was nothing to shout about but the hours were mercifully short and the standard of work undemanding even for someone of his slackness.

His relocation suited his two main indulgences. Alcohol was his lifeblood and its cheapness in Hong Kong a godsend. Added to that was the plentiful supply of clean-smelling Oriental women. There was something about them that excited both his libido and his imagination. Their smooth magnolia skins and their sweet Eastern scents stirred him. Their voices tinkled soft and musical, whether in excitement or rebuke. It seemed he had escaped not only from his unsympathetic creditors but also from the shaved legs and sweaty pungencies of Merseyside women. Yes, gin and womanly tonics were all he desired.

His notion of heaven was a place filled with petite Oriental maidens, plying both. He could almost hear, in those recurring moments of reverie, their delightful, child-like propositions.

"Dellick, dalling, you gimme sixty dollahs faw all night, okay?" they would wheedle at the bars he frequented. He never managed to find strength to say anything other than "okay", even though each affirmation increased the precariousness of his finances.

He could have winged things on the never-never, got by somehow cadging from colleagues. But those damned Communists had upset everything with their Great Proletarian Cultural Revolution. What had hitherto been an amusing game of wit and luck and soft living had turned into something resembling hard work. He loathed hard work, almost as much as the deprivation of his nocturnal routine of drink and women.

It had all started unremarkably enough. A tedious labour dispute in a major shipping company in March had culminated in a victory of sorts for a Communist union. Then, a couple of months later, a rash of co-ordinated disputes erupted, involving a textile factory, a cement factory, four taxi companies and a manufacturer of artificial flowers.

When pickets illegally prevented the management of the artificial-flower company from removing goods from the premises, police intervened and twenty-one of the pickets, including its leader, were arrested.

A collection of Communist unions demanded the immediate

release of the pickets and government compensation. When the demands were rejected, rioting broke out in Kowloon. It lasted three days. The Chinese Ministry of Foreign Affairs entered the fray, protesting against British brutality and alleging that two hundred compatriots had been killed during the disturbances.

At that point only one person had been killed — and probably by rioters rather than the police. But chanting students soon marched into the centre of town waving little red books containing the thoughts of Chairman Mao. Demonstrations also flared up in front of Government House. Powerful loudspeakers were installed at the Bank of China and at other Communist-controlled buildings. They began broadcasting seditious propaganda and incitements to violence. Intermittent riots erupted, forcing the authorities to impose curfews.

On June 3 the *People's Daily* in Peking called on Hong Kong people "to organize a courageous struggle against the British and to be ready to respond to the call of the Motherland for smashing the reactionary rule of the British". The call was reproduced in local left-wing newspapers. That led to mob assaults on the police. On June 24 a general strike was declared and on the same day a mob of two hundred attacked a police post in the border village of Sha Tau Kok. The post was attacked again on July 8, this time with machine guns, and five policemen were killed. Eleven more were wounded.

The local moneybags had long sent their families to boltholes in North America and Australia and their liquid assets to numbered accounts in Switzerland. Now, even ordinary citizens formed lengthening queues for visas at foreign consulates. British officials began thinking the last jewel in the crown of empire was about to be snatched away. Discreet telephone calls to airline offices were made. Plans to bring children out for summer holidays were cancelled. Family heirlooms were quickly packed and shipped away.

But Derek Soames remained unfazed. It was not that he was made of sterner stuff. It was just that the unintelligible racket emanating from the Bank of China Building opposite had rendered him incapable of thought. It also drove him with increasing frequency to the mineral-water bottles in his filing cabinet. To add to his confusion, journalistic idiots in London,

Washington and other capitals, utterly ignorant of time zones, kept ringing up at all hours to demand backgrounders and sitreps.

An excess of alcohol and a deficiency of sleep soon combined to shroud everything in a not unpleasant haze. It was in that merry condition that Soames attended a staff meeting called by the Director of Information Services. Neither the Director's nervousness nor his desperate tones registered with Soames.

With a comforting sense of detachment he heard the Director articulate, seemingly from a vast distance, the sombre assessments of the great and the mighty. The Director revealed that umpteen meetings had taken place at the highest levels and everyone had had his say. The Attorney General held that broadcasts from the Bank of China Building constituted a criminal offence, a public nuisance at best and sedition at worst. They had to be stopped if the law was not to be brought into disrepute. The Director of the Special Branch warned, however, that arms had been stockpiled in the vaults of the Bank of China. Any attempt to interfere with the broadcasts or to confiscate the loudspeakers was likely to be resisted and might lead to a bloodbath.

The Commissioner of Police opined that his men, while remaining ready to serve the Crown, would probably baulk at storming a fortified building owned by the Chinese state. A number of them had already been killed and attacks by mobs were becoming more frequent. The Political Adviser pointed out that forceable entry into a Chinese state institution would bring diplomatic repercussions. The Defence Secretary said shooting could bring the intervention of the People's Liberation Army. The limited British forces would be quite incapable of offering meaningful resistance. The Economic Secretary said stock and property prices were plummeting and the exchange rate for the Hong Kong dollar was coming under intense pressure. The Commissioner for Banking reported massive outflows of hot money. The Director of Commerce and Industry said business confidence would crumble completely unless law and order were quickly restored.

It seemed, according to the Director of Information Services, that the only action so far agreed was the issuing of a summons for causing a public nuisance. Everybody thought moderation a virtue. But beyond that there were divisions. How was the summons to be served, on whom and by whom? London was no help. It raised questions about the effect on British exports to China, the security of British investments there and the safety of British nationals. While London was being consulted, the Director said, it would be as well to marshal ideas on how best to serve a summons should one be ultimately issued.

"Forget the summons. Just give them a bit of their own medicine," Derek Soames said, languidly and unsteadily.

"What do you mean, Soames?" the Director asked, frowning.

"That racket across the road is driving me round the bend. Why not pay them back in their own coin? Rig up a few loudspeakers and blast them with *Rule Britannia*. It probably won't be legal, but what the hell! See how they like that!"

"Wait a minute! That's not a bad idea," an Assistant Director interjected. "Fighting fire with subterfuge! *Rule Britannia* might be too provocative, but what about Cantonese opera? That's noisy enough to drown anything. Most locals know and like the stuff. Just think, operatic arias against the mouthings of Mao! Should be no contest!"

"Brilliant!" the Director said. "I'll float that at the Chief Secretary's Committee."

Thus it came about that the battle of the loudspeakers was launched.

Soames took another swig from his mineral-water bottle and a germ of resentment grew in him. No one had given him so much as a verbal pat on the back for his brainwave. Probably his name never even rated a mention in the Chief Secretary's Committee. That was about par for the course with those old farts. Stealing the ideas of others without so much as a by your leave.

His resentment grew by quantum leaps as he visualized them with their la-di-da Oxbridge accents, their old-boy networks and their secret masonic understandings. He hated the way they dropped crumbs of information to demonstrate their access to top-secret papers. They turned their noses up at him at the Victoria Cricket Club as if he suffered from some unsociable disease. There was no need for that. He was only trying to make a living, just like them. He might have faults but at least he never tried to pretend he was something he was not. Well, he'd got their measure, seeing them flustered and indecisive over a small local difficulty. They were nothing more than fifth-rate brains masquerading as third-rate mandarins!

He had helped in their scams for years, putting out all that guff about how well they were running the world's most successful economy, bringing stability and the rule of law. Well, where were their stability and rule of law now? They couldn't run a wimpy stand, let alone an economy like Hong Kong's. It was the hard work and enterprise of the locals that had brought the place its success. Those old frauds merely stole the credit.

Soames pulled generously on the mineral-water container and as he did so his resentments, real and imaginary, sharpened and multiplied. They had always done him down, never appreciated his talents. They had given him the most obnoxious assignments and passed him over for promotion. They blamed him whenever their pathetic speeches failed to make the newspapers. And all the while they pretended they were little tin gods bestowing good governance upon a heathen population.

Until the recent troubles, where in the world had there been a place requiring less governing than Hong Kong? Virtually all the essentials of modern living were in private hands. That was the real secret of Hong Kong's success. Electricity, gas, telephone, telegraph and television were all run by private companies. So were buses, trams, ferries, cable cars, dockyards, wharfs and civil aviation. Three commercial banks issued local bank notes. Defence was provided by Britain, for an annual fee, though the efficacy of that defence was highly questionable. There were no elections to speak of, no labour exchanges, no unemployment benefits, no old-age pensions, no social security. Even in a vital area of economic and political development such as education, the government operated little more than five per cent of the schools.

Basically, government was in the hands of amateurs with little clue about how things ought to be run. They had a streak of shrewdness, to be sure. They realized that by sloughing off responsibilities to others, to business enterprises, voluntary organisations or private individuals, they could not be blamed should things go wrong. Malfeasance might be a crime, but nonfeasance was difficult to call to account. They hit upon fancy terms to justify avoidance of responsibility. Laissez-faire. Free enterprise. Positive non-intervention. What a laugh! They effected surprise and buried their envy when private individuals got on with supplying services and made fortunes at it.

They contented themselves with cutting ribbons, officiating at charity balls and mouthing platitudes. In time, as they watched boom after boom enveloping the colony, they actually began thinking it was their genius, their masterly inaction, that had brought prosperity to millions. They rewarded themselves with perks and lived on the Peak, attended by official servants and uniformed chauffeurs. They waited with bated breath for the gongs and knighthoods they regarded as their due.

In reality, they had only the vaguest notion of how things worked. They remained blissfully ignorant of the rampant insider-trading at the stock exchanges, the knavery among land developers and contractors, the gold smuggled from Macau inside the disembowelled bodies of babies, the bribes paid to the "no money, no water" fire service, the protection fees extracted from streetside hawkers and prostitutes, the syndicated corruption within the Police, the "snake heads" who brought in illegal immigrants by the boatload.

How complacent they were! How out of touch! Derek Soames felt a perverse desire to see the boot up their backsides, even if it had to be a Communist boot.

He took another drink and cursed himself for playing their game, doing their dirty work. How often had he refrained from exposing their frauds! How often had he trotted out dreary statistics about GDP growth, full employment, increases in exports, budget surpluses, hefty reserves and foreign investments to save their bacon! How off-handedly had he covered up the current parlous situation by posing a rhetorical question: "Would anyone be so stupid as to kill a goose that lays golden eggs?"

Even in his state of semi-inebriation he realized the question assumed that rational human beings rather than demented ideologues were calling the tune over Hong Kong. A risky assumption at the best of times and the present was decidedly not the best of times. And then there was a quirkiness in Orientals that had to be taken into account. In spite of an increasingly materialistic world, there were still many who placed face, pride, honour and other intangibles above money.

Well, the game had a long way to play yet. Pity he couldn't count on too many of his own countrymen to play it with him. The allies he needed were some of the brighter local civil servants, like T. P. Choy, who had been done down like himself by the eunuchs at the top. People like Choy would understand the real situation and would appreciate that so long as ordinary citizens did not lose their nerve, Communist bullyings and Whitehall ineptitudes could be surmounted. Hong Kong was supposed to be an anachronism, a colony without a magna carta or a bill of rights. It had been deprived of elected representation. Yet the common sense and pragmatism of its people managed to turn it into one of the truly free and thriving places in the world.

They deserved better than to be left to the tender mercies of bullies and incompetents. The eyes of the world were on Hong Kong and he wondered if he might, for once, spill the beans and expose the bureaucratic fault-lines to the journalists now flooding in like competing undertakers.

He had been assigned to pick up yet another journalist that evening. This one, by the name of Sebastian Baxingdale, he had heard of before, as the Far Eastern correspondent of the *Daily Globe*. He was coming direct from Saigon, where for the last three years he had been getting up the nose of the Pentagon with his weekly "Letter From Vietnam". He had also won Press awards for his coverage of the conflict. Well, it was about time somebody got up the noses of those in the ivory towers of Hong Kong and London. Baxingdale might be just the man. He had previously served with the garrison in Hong Kong. They couldn't pull the wool over his eyes so easily!

Soames emptied the contents of the mineral-water bottle and discovered to his dismay that all the bottles were empty. He gathered them into a carrier bag and headed out of his office, leaving Beaconsfield House by the back exit. That led into Battery Path, whereas the front entrance was directly opposite the Bank of China.

It was best for a gweilo carrying a load of empty bottles to avoid chanting Communist sympathisers, he thought. Otherwise the encounter might turn out a shade too Noel Cowardish.

Bombs and banquets

19

The atmosphere was surreal, Sebastian Baxingdale thought, as he waited in the lobby of the Victoria Cricket Club for Derek Soames. Out on the streets, bombs were going off, people were being maimed and policemen were under attack. Communist newspapers were screaming for armed insurrection. An assassination list of people deemed either too pro-British or too anti-Chinese had been published. The first victims had been a radio commentator and his cousin. In Peking, the Reuters correspondent had been placed under house arrest since July and an officially inspired mob had sacked the old British Embassy building.

Yet, so far as the Victoria Cricket Club was concerned, those events might have taken place on another galaxy in another age. The quiet, dated charm of its lobby was reminiscent of clubs along St. James's. Columns of dubious architectural lineage and acres of red velvet curtains exuded an air of solidity and uninterrupted tradition. Although the Club had long since been fitted with air-conditioning, wooden-bladed ceiling fans still churned overhead to retain the illusion of an earlier era.

A mahogany newspaper rack, standing as stolidly as a Grenadier, paraded copies of British newspapers such as *The Daily Telegraph* and *The Times*, though the *Daily Globe* was not among them. Included on the rack were copies of the two local English dailies, the *South China Morning Post* and the *Hong Kong Standard*. A long oak table displayed two neat, fan-shaped arrangements of magazines, including the *Tatler*, *Country Life*, *The Economist, The Spectator* and a variety of regional publications.

A steady expatriate traffic passed on its way to one of its several dining rooms and bars. Some men were in dinner jackets and their ladies wore dresses clearly traceable to Knightsbridge or New Bond Street.

Two Chinese waiters in starched white jackets and white gloves stood attentively by. Every sparkle of the crystal chandeliers, every swish of taffeta, suggested affluence and social order.

Baxingdale settled himself in one of the Queen Anne chairs in the lobby. He felt desperately weary. Was there to be no respite, he wondered. He had just endured three years of the Apocalypse in Vietnam. Now he had been selected for an even more bloodcurdling assignment, to recount the horrors of a quarter of the world's population gone berserk. Because Britain was in such bad odour with Peking, however, visas were unavailable for correspondents of British newspapers. That meant being spared, for the moment at least, the blood and gore of the Great Proletarian Cultural Revolution. But the sideshow in Hong Kong was sufficiently unpleasant.

He asked a passing waiter for a dry sherry. While he waited, he speculated on why Derek Soames had invited him to the club. He had developed a certain fondness for that frequently inebriated mouthpiece of government. There was a gentle chemistry between them, as if each recognized in the other a fellow outsider, compelled to live a life not of his own choosing.

Unlike less forthright publicists, Soames did not lie about unpalatable facts. He simply neglected to mention them, though he always came clean when the chips were down. For that reason, Baxingdale considered Soames a source worthy of cultivation.

Baxingdale's thoughts were interrupted by a woman's voice crying: "Seb, darling, fancy seeing you here!"

He found Phoebe Knight bearing down on him. She had grown plumper in the intervening years but was still attractive in pink. Christopher Knight was in tow. Phoebe quickly proffered hand, cheek and décolletage.

Baxingdale took the hand, kissed the powdered cheek and kept his eyes clear of the décolletage. There were memories buried there he had no wish to revive. "You look very well, Phoebe," he said. "Motherhood must agree with you."

"Liar! I know where the extra inches are. Chris told me you had arrived. I wish you had come before all this awfulness."

"I only get sent to places where awful things are happening, I'm afraid. Is there some gala going on? Everyone seems dressed to kill. I can hardly believe there's a crisis."

"Stiff upper and all that. People are popping by for a drink before *Tosca* at the City Hall. Behaving normally, Chris calls it. I'd rather take the children home till this blows over. But can't even do that. Been roped into government service."

"What? A British Mata Hari? Has it come to that?"

"Stop being wicked, Seb. It seems the Minister of State at the Colonial Office is coming to show the flag. He's a friend of Daddy's and the government thought I might help organize a banquet for him. Oh, dear! Have I said something I shouldn't? The trip is supposed to be hush-hush for the moment."

"You certainly have, my dear," Christopher Knight interjected. "But so long as the Minister displays a flag that isn't white we should be all right." Then, turning to his old college friend, he asked: "What are you doing here? At this club, I mean."

"Waiting for Derek Soames."

"That old soak!"

"He's my minder."

"Come and have a quick drink with us. We have to rush or we'll miss the curtain."

"Thanks, I'll pass. I'd best wait for Soames."

"All right. I'll be in touch."

"Darling, you must come to dinner and meet the children," Phoebe Knight said, proffering cheek and décolletage yet again, before heading for the bar with her husband.

As Baxingdale watched his friends leave, he wondered whether it was British phlegm or sheer lack of imagination that ruled the behaviour of expatriates. He had already finished his sherry when Soames arrived.

"Sorry, old chap," Soames cried, rushing up with an extended hand. He looked tired and uncharacteristically tense, his nose a shade redder than usual. "Got frightfully held up. More bombs, I fear. Fortunately, no one hurt. Let's get lubricated. First things first."

The two men made their way to the Members' Bar. It was almost empty now that the opera crowd had dispersed. They took a corner booth. The walls were cluttered with images of long-departed cricketers frozen in postures of bowling or batting. There were photographs of former Interport teams from treaty ports up and down the China coast. The most striking ones were sepia coloured, taken more than half a century ago, of hirsute players and hatted ladies sipping tea in different pavilions.

"What'll you have?" Soames asked, signalling for a waiter. Baxingdale ordered another sherry, Soames a gin and tonic.

"You've lived here before, haven't you?"

"Yes. In the army. A long time ago."

"Then I don't have to tell you what a screwed-up place this is. Screwed-up mainly by us, mind you."

"Can't be more screwed-up than Vietnam. How's London reading the situation?"

Soames made a face.

"Hear they're sending out a minister."

"Where did you get that?"

"A little bird."

"Shit! This place leaks like a sieve! Nothing's firm yet. Just in the preparatory stage. Depends on how things develop. Appreciate your keeping that under your hat for the time being."

Baxingdale nodded. "Look, I know you're supposed to accentuate the positive but you don't have to soft-soap me. What I want is the genuine low-down, of how things stand. What has the Special Branch got to say about the current chaos? Who is in control on the other side? Or is anyone in control at all?"

"I'm not senior enough to have access to SB assessments, not that they're much good in the best of times. My guess is that a power struggle's still going on, among the central authorities, the provincial overlords and the local cadres here. The boys at the centre probably wants to keep a lid on but can't count on being obeyed by local hotheads. Things a bit iffy, I reckon."

"I'm supposed to be in China. Waiting for a Chinese visa. But if things are going to hot up here, I might as well hang around for a while."

"You'll have to hang around, I fear. They won't give you a visa while Sino-British relations are in their current state. Even if they did, they'd restrict your movements so you wouldn't see a thing. I wouldn't be saying this to anybody else, but my advice is for you set up shop here. You may get a better idea of what's happening in China here than over there."

"How can that be, unless you rely on speculation and the usual rumour mill? Most of the killings and chaos are across the border."

Soames took a drink and eyed Baxingdale for a moment, as if weighing him up. "Refugees," he said.

"How can I possibly reach them? They're rounded up near the border and shipped back before anyone can say 'Boo!' I've been on those sort of details in the army."

"Things have moved on since then. There's a secret Anglo-American intelligence operation going on, right inside the Immigration Department. Each refugee is being quizzed exhaustively, on where he comes from, what has happened in his town or village, the numbers killed or injured, what he has seen on the way and so on. When you put thousands upon thousands of those eyewitness accounts together, you begin to get a pretty good idea what's going on in China. Now, I have no access to those reports. But if you'll do something for me, I just might be able to put you in touch with someone who has."

Baxingdale saw at once that Soames was a smarter operator than others had given him credit for and that he was pursuing his own agenda. "What do you want me to do?"

"The international media haven't been particularly helpful in our present difficulties," Soames said. "They're after headlines and have blown things out of proportion. The injuries and deaths here have actually been fewer than the number on any given day caused by drunken driving in London or street crime in New York. But their alarmist articles are shaking confidence. I'm sure you can see that. I've come across some of your pieces on Vietnam. They were good, fair and constructive. What I would like you to do is something similar for Hong Kong. I don't think our masters in Whitehall know what they're doing and I think the people here deserve better."

"I like the people here too. If Whitehall is leading them up a gum tree, I'll be glad to say so."

"Fair enough. Those Whitehall weasels haven't a clue. They're despatching diplomatic notes like farts. Their usual rubbish, filled with ifs and buts and blame-shifting clauses. If they knew their onions the embassy in Peking wouldn't be up in smoke. They reckon they can read the Chinese like an open book, except the book they're using has been devoured long ago by the flames of revolution!

"Whitehall's ambivalence is giving vested interests here cold feet, particularly foreign ones. One major American bank has panicked and pulled out. A couple of the British hongs followed. Then the hot-money boys and some local bigwigs started screaming for exchange controls. Unless stopped, that rot will spread. Fortunately, our Financial Secretary is standing firm. And with some success."

Soames stopped talking when a waiter brought the drinks. "Cheers," he said, gulping down half his gin and tonic and immediately ordering another. He smiled broadly. "Don't often get to drink at government expense."

"Saw a lot of black ties and evening gowns earlier. Does that signal steadying confidence?"

Soames laughed. "That lot's probably too far gone to be scared. They're shining examples of those who have learnt nothing and forgotten nothing. Probably expecting a replay of the Boxer Rebellion, with John Wayne riding in at the head of an international force.

"We're never going to get out of the hole we're in until we marshall the locals. The population, by and large, don't like the chaos, neither here nor across the border. There's no question they prefer us to the Communists at this point in time, if only because our intrusions into their lives are as nothing compared with the other side. Yet they're reluctant to support us openly because they don't trust us. We've dumped them in it too many times before. They also see that we don't trust them. They're not blind. They know we suspect them as potential enemies.

"Look at the schoolchildren demonstrating against us. You may say they've been misled or brainwashed by radical teachers. But what about their parents? No father would expose a child to tear gas and baton charges unless he harbours some genuine resentment against us. But we're not getting the message."

"What do you think the administration must do?"

"To begin with, give some real power to the more senior local officers. Make it obvious they can really speak for the administration. They can reach the local population in ways that we can't. See our waiter and his chums behind the bar? You think they'll ever talk heart-to-heart with a gweilo? Yet they've got their ears much closer to the ground than some of our so-called China experts. Most important of all, the administration has to convince locals that it intends to end racism and discriminatory practices."

"It's all down to making local officers feel they have a stake in what's going on, isn't it?"

Soames nodded and waved to the waiter for another round.

"What about the solid citizens? Will they be prepared to stand up and be counted too?"

"It's a question of finding someone to take the lead without appearing a British stooge. The bosses in my department are averse to risks. They operate at the mental level of traffic lights. They feel more comfortable with stooges, so they can't get the message across. We need somebody independent, like you, to shake some sense into them, to interview a few community leaders willing to speak out in favour of public order and an end to violence. Would you?"

"Have you people in mind?"

"There's a young Turk by the name of Xavier Chu. Do you know him?"

"No, but I've heard of him. Isn't he the son of that tycoon who built that lovely mansion up the Peak after the war?"

"That's him. He came back from New York a couple of years ago, after his father died in a boating accident. Took over Gold Star, the family firm, and made quite a splash. Got many admirers. He's got balls. When some of the foreign firms started pulling out, he jumped in and bought them cheap. He's got to be either one hell of a gambler or he's got foresight. I'm not saying you have to like him. But if you could get him to go public on why he thinks this place still has a future, that would be a tremendous boost for confidence. He might well be the evolving face of Chinese capitalism."

"Isn't he a bit young?"

"Yes, but he's got a good track record and good pedigree. His father had a reputation for being anti-British. It was before my time, but he apparently slammed us for taking on people who had collaborated with the Japs as our advisors. That's why my bosses shy away from the son. The father turned Gold Star from nothing into one of the most popular names. The son picked up where the father left off. The younger Chu, however, sprouts that type of business-school claptrap that flies over the heads of oldies like me. In a sense that's a plus because Americans are partial to that stuff and the United States *is* our biggest market."

"What else makes him worth interviewing? There must be dozens of successful business-school types around."

Soames ordered another round although Baxingdale had not yet touched his last glass. "This one's dangerous. He might turn around and bite you. He's got the balls to play both ends against the middle. I haven't figured out what his deeper game might be. But he's at least putting in money here when others are pulling out.

"Let me tell you a couple of stories. When Xavier Chu got back from the States, one of the first things he wanted was to join this club. So far as anyone could tell, the bugger hasn't even a nodding acquaintance with cricket. There's a crusty old sod on the Membership Committee, a solicitor by the name of Harry Rand, who doesn't fancy wogs at all. He blackballed Chu. Not once but twice. Our boy somehow found out. Instead of kicking up a fuss, he simply got hold of Rand's partner and offered the firm a retainer for a number of his companies. The partner, a chap named Christopher Knight, accepted and — surprise! surprise! — the next time Xavier's name popped up, no blackball."

"I know Christopher Knight. Just bumped into him and his wife here. I was at Oxford with him."

"Small world. No doubt you can get the gory details from the horse's mouth."

Though Soames's known capacity for alcohol was impressive, he nevertheless surprised Baxingdale by ordering a round of brandies.

"Mixing your drinks?"

"You must try this and tell me what you think before my second story."

When the brandies arrived, Soames downed his in one go while Baxingdale sipped his.

"Well, how do you like it?"

"Good cognac, smooth on the throat, enjoyable."

"Does it put lead in your pencil?"

Baxingdale laughed. "No, don't think so. What has that to do with the second story?"

Soames stared reflectively at the bottom of his empty glass. He ordered another and perked up. "Everything!" he said, smiling. "It goes like this. Years ago, the elder Chu secured the sole agency for Connoisseur cognac. The brand sold steadily for years, but nothing spectacular. After Xavier took over, sales shot up. He ran an ad featuring a local film star with many known concubines and a reputation for womanising. The ad showed that actor clutching a beautiful model with one hand and a glass of Connoisseur cognac in the other. The text had the actor saying that Connoisseur gave him zest for life. The message was unmistakable, brilliant. It got the job done. Nobody could accuse anybody of false advertising or making misleading claims.

"At the same time, hostesses in the red-light districts began spreading stories about men showing increased sexual prowess after a few snorts of Connoisseur. No prize for guessing who put them up to it.

"Hong Kong now has the highest per capita consumption of cognac in the world. Throughout Southeast Asia, wherever there are concentrations of Chinese, consumption has shot up. Of course they often mix it with such unspeakable stuff as Coca-Cola and Seven-Up! But just imagine the possibilities when China opens up. If I were you, I'd invest in cognac without delay. The whole thing has been such a howling success that the Frogs are thinking of awarding Chu the Legion of Honour for services to French exports!"

"What a story! I suppose that's marginally better than peddling carbolic smoke balls!" Baxingdale laughed. "If he's considered a top entrepreneur, how does one distinguish between that and a spiv?"

"By using your imagination. That's why Xavier Chu's a dangerous customer. He's not afraid of skating on thin ice if there's money in it."

"Well, he might be worth immortalizing in the *Globe*. I'll have to get him to say something like: 'The troubles will blow over. Let the faint hearts run. I'm buying them up. The good times are bound to roll again.' Has he the balls to say that?"

"If you can convince him that the Brits won't forget a good deed done in a time of need. He's a young man in a hurry. If he thought the Brits might give him some sort of official appointment in return, he would go for it. Something like being made a Justice of the Peace, for example. There's something else he's got balls for."

"What?"

"His wife, Lucille. She's got half the men in this town panting after her. She's from San Francisco, American-born Chinese. Amazingly easy on the eye, particularly when she appears in a low-cut ball gown. Some wag once said hers was the bosom that launched a thousand wet dreams! I'm afraid that has stuck. Chu's got to have something to be able to keep such a woman under control. You may get to meet her as a bonus."

"On that note, I had better go home and dream about it."

"Come on, the night's still young. I'm still thirsty. I can show you interesting places that have popped up since your last stay. There's a bar in Wanchai I guarantee is right up your street. Szeto's Bar. Intellectual types gather there for good conversation and cheap drinks. It has turned into a watering hole for academic and artistic types, political activists and some senior local civil servants. You'll get a completely different slant on our colonial administration from them."

"Sounds interesting. I'll take you up on that when I'm better settled."

"Hey, don't put off till tomorrow what you can do today. If you're more into flesh and blood, I can fix that too. There are fascinating worlds out there, some the average white man hasn't even dreamt about."

"I know. Dangerous too. But tonight's not the night for adventure. I have a piece to write."

Soames shrugged and asked for the bill. After he had signed it, the two men left the Members' Bar, making their way back to the lobby down photograph-adorned corridors.

At the club entrance, Baxingdale said: "Thanks for the drinks and the background briefing. I'll follow things up. Be sure not to step on a bomb, wherever you're heading."

"Don't worry," Soames replied. "Don't you know an angel protects those who've tippled a wee dram too much?"

Baxingdale watched Soames enter a taxi before he began his short walk home. An anomalous man in an anomalous town, he thought. Perhaps he himself was one too.

Debits and credits

20

Baxingdale leaned back against the chair and stretched himself. He had been practising Chinese characters with a brush for an hour. The orthodox way of holding the instrument, not yet entirely familiar to him, had tired his wrist and cramped his hand. He set down the brush and wiggled his fingers. The bold, black pictographs on the rice paper gave him a sense of accomplishment. Each character, though less than perfectly formed, still appeared respectable and pleasing to the eye. They struck him as more attractive than the emaciated script of the Latin alphabet!

When he first expressed an interest in learning Chinese and mastering the brush, his tutor, Madam Shek, had reacted with surprise. "A traditionalist, are you?" she had cried with delight. "An unusual aspiration for a Westerner, especially when our own schools are abandoning the brush for the ballpoint. Acquiring even a passable competence requires hard work and much practice. You sure you're prepared for that?"

"Yes," he had replied, unhesitatingly.

"Good. You have a choice of approaches. You can either begin as Chinese children have done for centuries with the *Three Character Classic*, or follow a system popular among foreigners, based on learning a thousand basic characters."

"The former, please."

Madam Shek then explained briefly the practical philosophy embodied in the *Three Character Classic*, governing learning, filial piety and human relationships. At the first lesson she taught the basic strokes in forming characters, the appropriate way of holding the brush, how to tease on the right amount of ink and how to steady the wrist while writing.

Baxingdale discovered that the classic, written in the thirteenth century, had been in universal use until modern schooling edged it out of dominance. Its name was derived from the way its text was presented, in phrases of three characters making up 356 alternately rhyming lines. It began with a brave and optimistic assertion: "The nature of Man at birth is good." It then went on to stress the importance of education in developing that innate nature in children.

The ideas expounded were not dissimilar to those held by his parents, Baxingdale reflected. Studying hard, bringing honour to ancestors, behaving decently towards neighbours, acting with fairness towards all. His parents had taught by example, supporting pacifism, opposing imperialism and pursuing ideals that often ran counter to the temper of the times. "A man must not just mouth his beliefs but live them," his father had emphasized.

The recollection brought a smile to his face. Bless his parents. The trouble was that each time he tried to follow their teachings he had ended in a mess. He had joined the army at the start of the Korean War to defend freedom against tyranny. Instead, he found himself at the borders of Hong Kong driving back refugees. His teaching efforts at Hackney also went disastrously wrong, probably doing more harm than good.

Writing fiction ended no differently. His scribblings found no acceptance among publishers. It took him a while to realize he had not lived enough. The characters he created had been too deficient in human failings. They hardly ever got skewered by mismatched or unrequited love! His portrayals of love had come across as dreamy abstractions, half created and half plagiarized. His brief and unsatisfactory affair with Phoebe Sweetman was all the experience he had to go by. No one had previously excited him like Lucille Chu. It was only after meeting her that he understood how love could turn the world upside down, that man without woman was incomplete. The Taoist imperative of keeping the Yin and the Yang in balance then began to seep into his consciousness.

Thoughts of Lucille stirred the sediments of loneliness and despair within him and gave him a thirst. He stood up, rotated his head to loosen the neck muscles and strolled over to the refrigerator for a bottle of the local San Miguel beer. He uncapped it and took a swallow. The coldness rushing down his gullet struck him like an internal douche.

Lucille continued to invade his thoughts as he drank. In spite of the advance billing by Derek Soames, he had not been prepared for her devastating beauty. He now relived the moment of their meeting. Dark, phoenix eyes, smooth magnolia skin, succulent lips. The lips, in particular, seemed designed for whispered endearments and immaculate kisses. He had betrayed himself hopelessly upon being introduced, by retaining her hand longer than was appropriate. Her unabashed voluptuousness and her open American manners, so different from the usual shyness and hesitancy in Chinese women, left him unhinged.

No woman had a right to look so damnably desirable, he reflected. A line from Marlowe struggled for recollection. What was it? Something about whoever loved who did not do so at first sight?

When he discovered that she was also taking Chinese lessons from Madam Shek, he wondered whether their meeting had been fated. She had to be in search of something. What? Knowledge, roots, identity, purpose? What better relationship than one between two misfits, unsure of what they wanted out of life?

His instinct had been to give chase, to surrender to that wondrous tingling in his soul. The fact she was married to a powerful man merely added the spice of risk.

But at the same moment he also saw himself as he was, a foreigner, a gweilo, a common object of disdain among the Chinese. Even allowing for Lucille Chu's American egalitarianism, he had no money or illustrious connections to fall back on. He was just a paid voyeur of human tragedies, a hired chronicler of the poverty and enslavements blighting the world. What kind of a future was that to offer any woman?

Yet another line from Marlowe occurred to him and he wanted to cry: "Sweet Lucille, make me immortal with a kiss!" But how absurd to fantasize about a woman in his situation. He ought to stop behaving like an infatuated schoolboy! It was an impossible love. She had come too late into his life and he was too old for self-delusions.

Baxingdale returned to his desk with the beer, sat down and heaved a sigh. He gazed down upon his exercise sheets. He had been fiddling with Chinese calligraphy because he couldn't concentrate on his work. The deadline for his next "Letter From Hong Kong" was only a day away. The prospect of getting down to it depressed him further. He reluctantly stacked away the exercise papers and brought out his Remington portable. What should he write? Another account of the mayhem and bloodletting in the Great Proletarian Cultural Revolution?

He was thoroughly sick of the subject. In a way he was glad diplomatic wranglings over a visa had kept him out of China. The British Embassy building had been sacked and the Reuters correspondent was still under house arrest. If he were there he would no doubt suffer an equally unpleasant fate.

Yet he could not escape knowledge of what was going on. Soames had put him in contact with an operative in the secret Anglo-American intelligence unit in the Immigration Department. He had seen some of the debriefing transcripts of refugees and illegal immigrants. They recorded in soul-blanching detail the disasters occurring in towns and villages across the southern provinces.

He had had his bellyfull of death and suffering in Vietnam. The rattle of gunfire, the cries of the injured, the smell of burning flesh, death agonies in their various shapes and forms. They were all too familiar. So was his nausea of helplessness and disgust. No doubt the gathering protests in Britain and elsewhere against the war in Vietnam must reflect a more universal disgust. Yet the carnage went on. Now China had opened up its entire country to killings and excesses. It was the middle of the twentieth century yet barbarities remained medieval. Was the world going mad? Or was the real nature of Man basically far from good?

Suddenly, the cry of an itinerant hawker penetrated the room, interrupting his introspections. He had heard such cries before, each one touting a distinctive trade. He could normally identify them, but the cry sounded novel this evening. It had the quality of a lament. The sound drew him out onto the narrow wrought-iron balcony of his second-floor flat and all at once the hubbub of his neighbourhood swelled around him, like part carnival and part hymn.

His flat was located along one of the meaner approaches to Victoria Peak. It was wedged in a steep, cobbled street linking Caine Road and Hollywood Road, a stone's throw from the heart of the business and financial district. The *Globe*'s housing allowance was sufficient for accommodation in a more fashionable area. But he wanted to be connected to ordinary people, to the un-Westernised and less well-off, to those whose Chineseness had not yet been eclipsed by the ravages of colonialism.

The bubbling vitality of the neighbourhood washed over him. He closed his eyes and allowed the familiar medley of sounds to overwhelm him. The clip-clop of wooden clogs, the whirr of a sewing machine next door, the garrulous voice of Mrs. Ngan gossiping on the telephone, the shuffling of mah jong tiles, snatches of music, laughter and high-pitched altercations, water gargling down drainpipes, the rumble of vehicles along the intersecting roads. On some evenings, the notes of a flute would float at the far edge of hearing. But not tonight.

Smells, too, wafted around him. Hints of camphor from across the street, where wooden chests with stone inlays were being fashioned. The sour odours of hemmed-in humanity; whiffs of sandalwood incense from ancestral altars or from the Man Mo Temple a short distance away; the fragrances of stir-fried cooking from adjacent kitchens; and the more powerful pungencies of fermented tofu and salted fish from food stalls farther along the street.

He opened his eyes and was greeted by the familiar sight of housewives hanging out washing between garish shop-signs. On the pavements were scatterings of old women and children assembling plastic flowers. Labourers chatted under street lamps or idled outside shop fronts. A few were munching snacks. Stalls, consisting of little more than shallow shelves nailed to a wall, were still trading in cigarettes and magazines, toilet paper and stationery. The area was too far down the economic scale to sprout the kind of neon signs disfiguring the centre of the city or to invite an invasion by international franchisers of junk food.

There was something enduringly Chinese all around him, in spite of more than a century of colonial rule and the pressures of the gathering Cultural Revolution. He knew that many were making sacrifices to send aid to relatives caught up in the homeland chaos. Their bland faces and their practised civilities hid so much, both of their strengths and their weaknesses. He had been living among them for nine months, yet he was far from understanding them. A curious chiaroscuro seemed to obscure them. He had no real idea what they thought of him, a gweilo, camped in their midst. Did they regard him as part of the imperialist order or had they tolerated him as an eccentric touched by too much sun? It was hard to say.

But one thing was certain. Behind their inscrutability, they were a remarkable race. Perhaps that came from what the German philosopher, Johann Herder, had called Volkgeist, the ability of a race to follow its own historical rhythm and maintain its own psychological characteristics. The writer of the *Three Character Classic* had observed that some men left their sons chests filled with gold, but he wanted to leave children only one book. It was possible that the contents of that one book had been part of that nation's strengths.

The Chinese capacity for patience and endurance was amazing. Had that quality enabled their civilization to survive for thousands of years while others crumbled into dust? Upheavals associated with dynastic cycles had been regular features in their history. Yet they seemed to take them in their stride, surviving rectification campaigns, communes and official attacks on Confucian ideas. Seen in that light, the Cultural Revolution might just be one more misfortune to overcome.

But what of the humiliations inflicted by foreigners? Would the Chinese, as a nation, ever forget? The grievances were many. Gunboat diplomacy, annexations of land, extraterritorial rights, the torching of the Summer Palace, the looting of national treasures and the massacres of students and demonstrators in their concessions and colonies. If there was no forgiveness, were they patiently waiting for an opportune moment to settle scores? The riots of the previous year might indicate the shape of things to come.

He could sense resentments at many levels, particularly against Britain, among the local intellectuals Derek Soames had introduced him to at Szeto's Bar. References to British rule were seldom unlaced by contempt.

He recalled a beer-drinking session the previous week. As the only Englishman present, he bore the brunt of many awkward questions. Why should Britain strip Hong Kong British subjects of the right of abode in Britain under the 1962 Commonwealth Immigration Act? Was that not an act of blatant racism aimed at non-white races? Why should Britain preach free trade in one breath and impose import restrictions on Hong Kong textiles the next? Why should the Hong Kong public be denied the air services of foreign airlines simply to protect the profitability of the state-owned BOAC? And how did legislation requiring local public transport companies to buy British Leyland buses square with free-market principles?

The subject that generated most resentment was the huge losses suffered by the colony due to the recent devaluation of sterling. Hong Kong had built up substantial reserves over the years, but London required them to be held in sterling. As a consequence, the colony became the second largest holder of sterling in the world.

It had been apparent for some time, however, that economic bunglings and social disharmonies in Britain would sooner or later force a devaluation. Hong Kong naturally wanted to protect itself by diversifying its holdings. But Whitehall denied permission. When the inevitable came, Hong Kong lost a quarter of its reserves or approximately £79,000,000. That sum could have been better used building schools, hospitals, public housing and other amenities. London took no responsibility and refused to consider compensation.

Such behaviour had been less than defensible, the crowd at Szeto's Bar declared. The duty of care owed by a metropolitan power towards a dependent territory had been breached. He could offer no excuse. He could only respond by saying: "Why haven't you chaps done something about that, instead of crying in your beer?"

The answer came from a senior civil servant by the name of T. P. Choy. "The consensus is that it's best not to rock the boat. Venting our spleen at gatherings like this is one thing but, ultimately, it's better the devil you know than the one you don't."

"Don't quite follow. Your complaints seem legitimate enough. Why not demand redress? Some of you are working for the government, for heaven's sake! Can't you push through change?"

"Some of us do work for the administration, my dear fellow, but we don't make the decisions. The important ones are taken in London. Political poker involves high stakes. Likely gains are not proportionate to possible losses. At the moment, all geopolitical factors favour London. The community here has nothing to gain through protesting, but a great deal to lose."

"Chinese pragmatism," an assistant professor of history named Mun commented.

"You mean cynicism, don't you?"

"We all know Peking wants Hong Kong to remain more or less as it is," Mun responded. "So does Britain and the majority of the local population. Peking needs Hong Kong to gain access to hard currencies and technologies, to gather intelligence and to keep a window on the world. We need Britain for a quiet life. Agitations against the British are likely to lead to instability. No one wants that."

"Everybody knows Britain is milking us," Choy added. "The Chinese are accustomed to paying protection money to triads and gangsters. But they had expected better from the Brits. If Britain wants to squeeze the colony, that's all right. Just don't be so damn hypocritical about it. Our sharper operators would then feel less qualm about making it back speculating against sterling, circumventing British trade rules or simply by being fiercer barracudas when they come up against Brits in the free-enterprise sea they all feed in."

"If what you say is true, then it's going to be quite a job drawing up the credits and debits on over a hundred years of British rule."

Mun gave a merry laugh and intervened again. "Why such unseemly haste in that respect, my dear chap? History isn't journalism. It need not be written fresh upon events. Indeed, it's better without the immediacy of passion and personal involvement. Objectivity tends to increase over time. Political accountings are therefore best left to future generations."

Baxingdale recalled those discussions as he gazed upon the lively street scene below. Successive British governments had refused to countenance giving Hong Kong people a voice. Even socialist ones had retained atavistic attitudes towards democratic accountability and racial distinctions. Centuries earlier, taxation without representation had sparked revolution in the American colonies. The trouble was that London was currently too preoccupied with strikes and the unravelling of the social order at home to consider its trusteeship responsibilities.

Such failure seemed short-sighted. His parents had believed that honesty and fair dealing were absolutes. Even if local people did not kick up a fuss for their own reasons, someone should raise the matter before the British electorate. His country's record of empire had not been one deserving of much glory. But some reputation could be salvaged by relinquishing its last significant colony with a semblance of dignity and honour. The people of Hong Kong deserved it and his instincts as a patriot demanded it. It seemed a modest enough ambition to remind Westminster and Whitehall of their obligations.

With that thought Baxingdale left the balcony and returned to his desk. He inserted a sheet of paper into his typewriter and began drafting his next "Letter From Hong Kong".

The Meditation Room

21

Torrential rain pelted the windows of the Meditation Room like gravel fitfully flung. Xavier Chu came in quietly, closing the door behind him. It was an uncharacteristic entrance for the Chairman of the Gold Star Industrial and Financial Corporation. At annual general meetings and Press conferences his arrivals, if not exactly accompanied by fanfares, carried an aura of self-confidence and panache.

Now he was almost diffident, entering a place intimately associated with his mother and out of his own milieu. It was like stepping into a long, forbidding passage, with promises of revelations if he could get to the end of it. Previously he had ascribed his unease to cautionary tales heard during childhood about good and evil, retribution and redemption. But after three years of having his most cherished plans thwarted by his mother, he no longer knew what to expect.

A giant bronze Buddha, with legs crossed in the lotus position and fingers curled in the posture of meditation, dominated the room. Its face radiated kindness and tranquillity. Its eyes were closed, as if blind to the turmoils of the world. Yet Xavier could not escape the sensation that it was watching him, probing his innermost thoughts.

An altar, covered with an elaborately embroidered cloth, stood before the bronze image with the usual paraphernalia of worship. Two decorated vases filled with pink gladioli flanked a pair of altar lamps. The dim illumination of the lamps was augmented by the flickering flames of two fat red candles. Lazy wisps of incense rose from a bronze burner. The flames and the smoke combined to cast weird shadows upon the tapestries and murals.

This was his mother's world, Xavier thought, as he looked at her small figure kneeling on a prayer mat. He could not tell whether she was meditating or silently reciting sutras. Whichever it was, she was obviously too preoccupied to acknowledge his presence. It made him feel like an intruder. His dark pin-striped

Savile Row suit and smart silk tie seemed to mark him as one who had bartered away his soul for material rewards.

Since the room was devoid of chairs, he lowered himself onto a prayer mat. His clothes had not been designed for such postures. The jacket tightened around his armpits and the trousers cut painfully into his crotch. He shifted position, loosened his tie and took off his jacket, placing it upon an adjacent prayer mat. He then removed his Bally shoes.

He had never had much truck with gods or the supernatural. Money was his religion. He was at his best when plotting take-overs, launching dawn raids or stripping the fat from bloated corporations. He had been sharper than his father. Since returning to Hong Kong, he had saved numerous companies with atrocious balance sheets, undervalued assets or appalling management. He had lived up to the sound of his self-selected name. He had indeed been a saviour, though saving others naturally brought rewards for himself as well.

The Meditation Room was an original feature of the two-storied mansion his father had built three-quarters of the way up Victoria Peak. He had built it with the specific aim of outdoing European residences in opulence and splendour, choosing a design in the shape of a plum blossom first used in China fourteen centuries ago, during the Chou Dynasty. The upper floor was surrounded by a wide balcony. The entrance to the mansion was guarded by doors of studded teak and a massive pair of Chinese stone lions.

Concessions to modernity came in the form of a swimming pool, shaped like an unshelled peanut, a garage large enough for ten cars, two tennis courts and a separate residential block for servants. The mansion was surrounded by gardens and lawns and the entire development was confined within a traditional red brick wall topped with curved green tiles. A team of gatekeepers and watchmen augmented security. The magnificence of the residence quickly turned it into a landmark for the flood of tourists entering the colony, though none could see much beyond the imposing outer wall.

The mansion was a repository for a remarkable collection of antiques and treasures. At every turn something arrested the eye, be it a Tang horse, a Ming vase, a Sung painting or a Chien

Lung cabinet. Grey Italian marble floors, hand-woven carpets and crystal chandeliers set off the exhibits.

Yet the displays somehow seemed to Xavier too faultless, too perfect, like photographs in some interior-decoration magazine. The insinuation of wealth and opulence was marred by a certain want of naturalness or character or taste. That deficiency permeated everything, from the magnificent jade prunus tree and Yuan vases decorating the reception hall to the thick leather-bound volumes standing dustless and unread in the library.

The treasures had not always been so displayed. His father had been the only true art lover in the family. But he died before he had time to enjoy his acquisitions, many of which he left unappraised and uninsured in packing cases in his study. The present arrangements represented a triumph of expensive pedantry over trusting ignorance. He might be no connoisseur but it had to be a mistake to let silver-tongued interior decorators and art experts loose on Lucille.

Only the Meditation Room escaped intrusion. His mother had closed it to outsiders. The bronze Buddha was itself a work of considerable vintage and value. It had stood for centuries in a wat in Thailand before disappearing about a hundred years previously. When it re-surfaced after the war, it was quickly snapped up by his father as a gift to his mother. It now endowed the Meditation Room with an atmosphere of simplicity and piety.

Xavier occasionally exploited the room for his own purposes, much to the annoyance of his mother. Unlike his father, he was fond of entertaining business associates at home. Lucille was a superb hostess. After meals, he would put on an air of sham reluctance and allow guests a peek into the Meditation Room. He would then recount how he meditated there before making important decisions, garnishing his stories with humbug about Eastern ethics and Buddhist obscurities purloined from his mother. He was convinced that such fanciful stories would add colour to his personality when *Forbes* or *Newsweek* got around to writing him up as a titan of Asian business.

Presently, his mother turned towards him. "So you've returned at last, Ah Seng, late as usual," she said, in her musical voice. "You didn't get wet, did you, with that storm óutside? I thought you were coming home for dinner. Have you forgotten? Have you eaten?"

Xavier moved to a prayer mat next to his mother's. "Yes, Mother, I've eaten. Sorry about dinner. I got held up. Besides, you know I'm not fond of vegetarian food."

"Lucille and Ah Yuen are not vegetarians. When you are expected home, the cook makes a point of preparing non-vegetarian dishes for the three of you," his mother said, tartly.

The imputation of filial deficiency in his mother's voice caused him to look into her smooth, saintly face. It radiated so much goodness that he expected her to wag a finger at him, notwithstanding his international reputation as a commercial and financial wizard. It was true he still appeared amazingly boyish at twenty-eight, causing some associates to joke about him being another Dorian Gray.

"Is Ah Yuen asleep?" his mother asked. "He's been having another bout of asthma. Dr. Chow has been and has given him the usual medication."

"I'm not sure. Lucille's with him. I'll look in later."

"Ah Yuen is almost four. Isn't it time you had another child?"

"I thought you wanted to discuss the papers I left for signature, not family planning."

"I see so little of you. You know perfectly well I don't understand English, so why leave a stack of documents in English for me to sign? Is it too much to explain first? I tried to get Lucille to tell me what they were about but she couldn't grasp their purpose either. She said they had to do with the sale of our home and the antiques to a Panama company. Why are we selling? Are you short of money?"

"Of course not, Mother. I'm rolling in it. No one came out better than I did over the last couple of years, in spite of the Star Ferry disturbances, the bank runs, the Cultural Revolution riots and the devaluation of sterling. When old British conglomerates started pulling out, I seized the opportunities they left behind."

"Then why do you want to sell our home?"

"You're not really selling anything. It's just a paper exercise, to save money and taxes. I asked you to sign because I didn't want to bother you with details."

"I don't understand."

"As I've said, you're not selling anything. It's quite simple. It's no use having assets that eat up money for upkeep. Just the insurance on this place and its contents is horrendous, not to mention wages for the cook, the chauffeurs, the gardeners, the Filipino maids, the gatekeepers and the watchmen. Then there are rates, taxes and heaven knows what else. I've worked out a scheme whereby everybody can benefit.

"I've set up a Panama company to which you can notionally sell the house and everything in it. Then, instead of giving me my full salary as chairman and chief executive, Gold Star can cut my pay but provide me with furnished accommodation, complete with servants. We will continue to live here, as at present, except that Gold Star will be paying the Panama company for rental of the house and its upkeep. That means Gold Star also pays for the servants, the rates, the insurance and everything else. You no longer have to pay a cent.

"I, for my part, will save on taxes because of the reduction in my salary. It will be presentationally good, too. Shareholders will see how modestly Gold Star's chief executive is being paid! That will justify stock options. The rent for the house can be easily lost in the accounts under a general item for corporate offices, warehouses and other rentals. Wages for servants can be buried in the corporate payroll. The same goes for insurance and all the other bits and pieces."

Xavier spoke quickly and succinctly, as if he were presenting a proposition to a board of directors. He expected others to defer to him and pass things on the nod. It was an attitude that came naturally to him, given the wonders he had done with Gold Star since assuming control. Every division, from property to trading, from manufacturing to retailing, from financial services to investments, had been profitable. The overseas subsidiaries were also contributing to the bottom line. Those successes caused him to slip into the same curt attitude when dealing with domestic matters. Still, that had not prevented his mother calling him to account. And it had been a cruel form of betrayal for his father to leave her the major shareholding.

"Who owns the Panama company I'm suppose to be selling everything to?" Serenity asked.

"You do, of course."

"Then what difference does it make? Surely if I'm the owner of the Panama company I will have to pay taxes on its income. Is that not more paperwork?"

"No, for two very simple reasons," Xavier replied. He shifted position on the prayer mat. His back was getting stiff from the unfamiliar posture and his legs were developing pins and needles. He massaged the back of his knees and calves as he continued. "First, the beauty of a Panama company is that it can issue bearer shares. In other words, names of shareholders need not appear on share certificates. Whoever holds certificates owns the company. That means one can transfer title at will, to avoid taxes, death duties or whatever.

"Secondly, the Panama company will never make a profit because it has notionally to raise a loan from a company in Anguilla to pay for the property and its contents. It has to repay part of that loan each year, with interest. It also has regular out-goings in wages, insurance, rates, administrative and accounting costs, bad debts and so on. Assets also have to be depreciated."

"I can't follow that. Who owes what debts to whom? We've had this house a long time. Hasn't it been depreciated fully? Or can we keep depreciating it forever? And what about the antiques? How can antiques depreciate over time?"

"Mother, you need not worry your head over such details. That's what lawyers and accountants are for."

"I don't trust lawyers and accountants. What's true or false, right or wrong, can't be altered through a clever arrangement of words. Who is supposed to own the other company, the one in the place I've never heard of?"

"You mean the Anguilla company? Well, that is owned by a company in Montserrat and if you trace that back far enough you will find that it's ultimately owned by me."

"My goodness! Why all these complications? Anyone would think we are trying to hide something. We're not, are we? If not, why go to this trouble to save taxes? We're not poor. We should pay taxes."

"Mother, I assure you what has been worked out is perfectly legal and above board. Everybody with any sense goes in for tax planning nowadays. Everybody seeks out what is in his own self-interest. That's the whole basis of capitalism."

Xavier was growing tetchy with his mother's questions. He had had a hard day. It was not enough that he had started the day with a breakfast meeting and ended it with a business dinner. He had to come home to explain tax avoidance to his mother! He still had to look in on Ah Yuen. And Lucille was unlikely to spare him the wheeze by wheeze account of their son's latest asthma attack. Given half a chance Lucille would also raise the matter of having another child. He longed simply for a nice bath and bed.

Through his weariness he heard his mother say: "What's legal may not necessarily be right. I don't like evading taxes, even if it's legal."

"Not evade, Mother! Avoid. There's a big difference."

"That's just being clever with words. Don't talk like a lawyer. We didn't sent you to America to learn such tricks."

A fierce gust of wind suddenly pelted the windows with rain. After it had subsided, Serenity said: "Ah Seng, I know it must have been hard for you the last few years. After you left for America, your father started cutting back. He didn't explain why. After you took over, you started expanding in all directions. Again, you didn't explain why. Now, out of the blue, you want to sell our home under an arrangement I cannot understand. You're not trying to hide something, are you? Is Gold Star in some kind of trouble?"

"No, Gold Star's fine. It's going from strength to strength. Everything I've done has been in the newspapers. I've nothing to hide. If anyone is hiding anything, it is you."

"Me? What am I hiding?"

"I don't know, Mother. Are there not things you keep from your only son? You and Father are two of a kind. At least Father told me something of his boyhood and what he did during the Japanese occupation. You're a closed book. You're secretive even about that Chinese mandolin you hide in your room. Don't you remember I caught you crying over it once? Father told me that was your secret. You can't blame a son for wanting to know about his mother, can you?"

"I'm sorry," Serenity said. After a pause, she continued: "I learnt the mandolin when I was a girl but gave it up when I got married. That's all. We can talk about musical instruments some other time. For now, I'm uncomfortable over selling the house through a chain of companies. If that is such a wonderful idea, why didn't your father do it?"

Xavier's exasperation intensified. Why couldn't his mother stick to her pieties and leave worldly affairs to him? He had worked like a demon, driven himself to the limit, yet far from appreciating his efforts she was continuing to measure him against his father. Didn't she realize he had already achieved results far beyond those of his father? He had evolved his own vision of the world. It would be a challenge to expound his beliefs before a knowledgeable audience. Before a woman like his mother it would be a waste of time. Yet, if he did not try, she would suspect him of plotting something. If he tried, the apocalyptic nature of his vision would upset her. He resigned himself to making another attempt.

"Mother, I don't know why Father didn't arrange a tax-avoidance scheme," he said, as gently as he could. "I suspect he was too busy. What I'm doing is no more than what any sensible corporate executive would do. Why compare me with Father? We're different breeds. Father was a man from a previous era. He was too sentimental. He never pressed advantages to the limit. I think he foresaw the future shape of the world and had trouble coming to terms with it. Perhaps it was a kindness that he should have died when he did."

Serenity's eyes widened with shock. "How can you say that about your father?" she demanded. "Your father tried to make the best of every situation he found himself in. People admired and respected him because they saw the goodness in him."

"Mother, I'm sorry. I didn't mean to upset you. I didn't mean to be disrespectful towards Father either. I'm just trying to make you understand reality. Power is devolving steadily into the hands of international conglomerates. They're out to corner markets, to create monopolies and cartels. Gold Star has to expand and forge alliances. Otherwise it will be swallowed up. The only hope lies in becoming as powerful as the predators or, indeed, becoming a fiercer predator.

"Modern conglomerates reject religions and ideologies. They do not try to change people or societies. They just want to make money. Eventually they will determine what we eat and wear, what news we hear, what books we read and what entertainment we get. They're already putting governments into their pockets. No single government is strong enough to resist. The run on sterling after the Labour Party victory shows their power. I know, because I punted against sterling on Wall Street. In such a situation one either becomes a decision-maker or a pawn. I don't intend to be a pawn."

"Stop!" Serenity cried. "We've discussed this before. You intend to strengthen Gold Star to exploit the weak? You want to decide whose lives get ruined for profit?"

"Mother, it's inevitable. Someone has to decide and it might as well be me. There's no other choice."

Serenity rose from the prayer mat, slowly shaking her head. "I cannot believe things can come to this. What of piety, duty, compassion and benevolence, of all the virtues taught by our sages and ancestors? We celebrate the birthdays of Buddha and Confucius to remind us of their teachings. I suppose, given half a chance, you would have Gold Star commercialise them like Christmas and Easter. Encourage people to give out promotional begging bowls or bags of fortune cookies! You'd do well to consider their teachings. I'm going to my room."

Xavier Chu rose too, unsteadily. His legs were numb. He stood shoeless and dishevelled, blinking his near-sighted eyes. When he saw his mother's diminutive figure reaching the door, he called out: "What about the transfer papers?"

Serenity turned with only the merest trace of disappointment in her face. "I would like to take my time with that," she replied.

Xavier closed his eyes and remained standing uncertainly in the room. Fresh squalls of rain hammered upon the windows. His conceptions had been far-sighted, he reflected, yet his mother baulked him at every turn.

He looked at his watch, the one with the black face that had once belonged to his father, and noted it was ten minutes to midnight. The end of another day, but the discussion with his mother had left his spirits jangled. Why did he feel so besieged and ill-at-ease when he came home? Was it because of his mother's persistent questions, his wife's hints at more children or his sickly son's demands for attention?

All at once he felt isolated and lonely. No one understood

his needs and no one loved him the way he wanted to be loved. Except Fei-Fei. She at least had giggled with delight when he promised to conquer the world and lay it at her feet. He remembered saying, too, that the mole on her left buttock would be his star of destiny to guide him in his quest. That recollection sent a shiver of desire through him. But she, too, had rejected him in the end and the manner of that rejection had wounded him. Perhaps he should have tried harder, swallowed his pride and begged her to come back to him. But his pride had not allowed him to crawl.

Piety, duty, compassion, benevolence. Those were recurring words of his mother. Of Little Ho too. They were the kind of words that had trapped his father. What was each of them worth? Nothing! They added no extra zero to a bank account. They had lured Little Ho into collecting used clothing for disaster victims and his mother into incoherent mumblings inside the Meditation Room.

He noticed the sightless Buddha looming over the altar. It seemed to be reading his thoughts. He shivered. The incense must be softening his brain, he thought, angry with his own foolishness. He shook his head and stretched his arms. The evening had been a waste. His mother had not fallen in with his proposals. He didn't know why he devoted time on such piddling matters. If his mother didn't want to avoid taxes, let those lousy papers remain unsigned.

He was a free man, owing no loyalty to anyone or any creed. But at times he also felt lonely. Great leaders had spoken of loneliness at the top. If that was to be the price, so be it.

Mortal coils

22

"When can we go to the Evergreen again Mummy?" Ah Yuen asked, as Lucille tucked him into bed. Serenity was engaged in gathering up some Meccano strips and plush toys from the floor. The boy's voice, clear as a bell, reassured the women an asthma attack was not imminent.

"When Daddy finds time, darling," Lucille replied. "Sure you're warm enough? Don't want you catching cold."

"Daddy's always busy. Can't we go by ourselves?"

"No, darling. We must go with Daddy."

"Why? Lots of people go by themselves. Yue kung-kung does and so do some of the other kung-kungs."

"I know, darling. But they still go according to the rules."

"Yue kung-kung said he's going to teach me about teas. He ordered chrysanthemum tea for me. It was really nice. You should've tried some, Mummy."

"Next time."

"If you like chrysanthemum tea, I can make you some at home," Serenity interposed.

"Great."

"What else did you and Yue kung-kung talk about?"

"Yue kung-kung said I reminded him of Grandpa. Some of the other kung-kungs thought so too. I wish I had known Grandpa. Do I remind you of him, Grandma?"

"Yes, my precious," Serenity replied, fingering her string of prayer beads.

"I wish you'd go the Evergreen with us. You'll like it there."

"The Evergreen doesn't serve vegetarian food. Did you offer the kung-kungs appropriate Lunar New Year greetings?"

"Oh, yes! They gave me lai sze. Big ones!"

"Did you thank them properly?"

"Yes, Grandma."

"Good. If you do well in your lessons tomorrow, I'll speak to your father. Maybe he can find time to take you there again."

"Oh, goodie-goodie!" The boy's eyes brightened. "Are both

of you going to stay with me tonight? You haven't done that for a long time."

"Don't get up to your tricks, young man!" Lucille said. "You know the rules. One of us stays on Nanny's night off. Tonight it's me. Grandma's not feeling well."

"Are you going to send for Dr. Chow, Grandma?"

"No, my pet. Dr. Chow has already given me some pills. They make me feel much better."

"Why can't Dr. Chow give me pills to make me feel better?"

"You've a different kind of ailment. Yours is asthma. Mine's angina. That comes with old age. Dr. Chow says you eat too many chocolates. That triggers your attacks."

"But I love chocolates, Grandma."

"Sometimes we have to give up things we love for our own good."

"That's enough talk," Lucille interjected. "Just go to sleep. Your inhaler and your glass of water are on the table. You've nothing to worry about. I'll be here till you're asleep. Now say 'good night' to Grandma."

Serenity bent over the boy and kissed him on both cheeks. Ah Yuen threw his arms around her and returned the kisses.

"Sleep well!" Serenity said, switching off the overhead lights.

In the frail glow of the nightlight on the bedside table, Lucille cuddled her son and whispered endearments, checking once again that he was properly tucked in against the February cold. Then she retreated to an armchair on the other side of the table.

The room was dominated by a large ebony desk, which jarred against the colourful curtains filled with Disney characters. The gleaming desk had once been her father-in-law's. It was too high for Ah Yuen. He needed cushions on the chair and a footstool. But since her mother-in-law was sentimentally attached to it Lucille had left it in situ. It was littered with comics, colouring books, crayons, pencils, copy books, an array of tin soldiers, a black stone ink slab, a stick of ink and a half-constructed aircraft made out of Meccano strips. At one corner a brand new baseball rested in the hollow of a barely used mitt. She had bought both on impulse, before remembering there was no man around to teach her son to pitch or bat.

A large poster of Bruce Lee was taped directly above the

desk. The actor, with his aggressive stance and well-defined muscles, appeared like a ferocious animal defending its territory. The poster disconcerted Lucille. She did not quite approve of her son selecting such a role model at his tender age.

Bruce Lee and the desk gave the room a distinctive Oriental air. Out of sight, in the drawers, were a set of Chinese chess, a string of antique brass cash, a collection of writing brushes and a stack of rice-paper copybooks covered with characters done as homework for Tutor Tsim.

Lucille was slightly envious of her son. He was picking up peasant songs and ditties from his grandmother and making faster progress with written Chinese than she herself. She wanted to immerse herself in her cultural roots, but her twice-weekly lessons with Madam Shek were slow going. Moreover, the more she delved into them the more she became overwhelmed by their complexities and traditions.

It was Serenity rather than her husband she had to rely on to guide her in that bewildering maze. Even obvious things such as dates were a trial. The Chinese dated artefacts and history according to the reigns of emperors. It was difficult enough to get the dynasties right, let alone the reigns of individual emperors. Then, for the dates to make sense, she had to correlate them back to AD or BC.

Even the antiques around the house tested her. She often got mixed up over which porcelain was produced from which imperial kiln and during which period. The outstanding ages for lacquerware and enamel were confusing, as were the different types of chalcedony. Whether a particular piece of carving had been done in boxwood, birch, cedar or aloe wood was too much to keep straight in her head. She felt utterly stupid when quizzed by guests and often had to fall back on mumbled evasions.

Serenity was always patient, guiding her to books that her father-in-law had accumulated and that Serenity had salvaged when Xavier decided to clear them from the study. But those tomes were in classical Chinese and beyond her ability to read. Serenity frequently went through a text with her sentence by sentence. It was excruciating and humiliating, especially when, due to her Toi Shan village dialect, she couldn't get the pronunciation right in Cantonese.

Xavier, on the other hand, turned out to be quite unreliable on Chinese culture. She had been taken in when he talked about paintings and calligraphies at the Metropolitan Museum. When he gave her a jade seal carved with his name, he had detailed the qualities Chinese associated with jade. He had told her of the power of keepers of Royal Seals and said that by entrusting his seal to her he was leaving his fate in her hands.

All that had been a pose. Only his charm and ready smiles enabled him to hold forth before foreigners with a semblance of authority. Before the likes of Uncle Yue, he transformed himself into a Wall Street master of the universe, sounding off about matrixes and synergies, mission statements and leveraged buyouts.

Lucille closed her eyes and listened to the lengthening rhythm of her son's breathing and the familiar sounds associated with deepening sleep.

Whatever made her imagine Xavier capable of leading her back to her Chinese roots? She saw with irony the advantages of being an American now. Nothing of importance had to be accounted for before the Boston Tea Party or the chopping down of that cherry tree. It took little effort to be democratic, sharing the same Main Streets, the same fast foods and the same Sears Roebuck catalogues. Occasionally, however, one had to pay the price of being called "a fucking Commie" or a "dirty Chink whore".

Xavier had turned her into a trophy wife. That was not what she wanted. Beyond material things, her existence was a misery. Living in a magnificent house stuffed with priceless antiques and attended by servants was certainly better than that dingy fruit stall in San Francisco's Chinatown. Fine wines, designer clothes, silk sheets, pleasure boats, exclusive clubs and credit cards with astronomical limits were not to be sneezed at.

But she wanted a big family. In spite of her feminist posture at Berkeley, she secretly yearned for a man who could love, enchant and pamper her. There had been precious little of that with Xavier. Not even sex. The four feet separating her bed from her husband's divided them as effectively as the Rockies. During their early days in Hong Kong, Xavier occasionally climbed into her bed. He had not done so for eight months.

Two weeks ago, when her nipples tingled and her body ached for satisfaction, she had gone over to his bed — only to be met by rebuff.

"Horrible day. I'm exhausted," he had said, before turning his back on her, forcing her to retreat in humiliation.

She felt insulted. She was still young, not yet thirty. Her physical charms and appetites were intact. How could she be no longer desirable? She thought with deepening resentment of the boys who had panted after her at high school and college. Other men still found her attractive. She could detect it in their eyes.

That British journalist, Baxingdale, had displayed interest. She had only met him once before, more than two years back, when he came to the house to interview Xavier and to take photographs. And last week he had been a fellow guest of the Knights at the Red Cross Ball. During the course of the evening he had invited her to dance. He was an excellent dancer and his bigness made her feel safe and protected. She noticed at once his pleasing male smell, not at all like that of callow American youths doused with Old Spice. When the band played one of those Nat King Cole ballads she loved, Baxingdale had said: "That's one of my favourites. They don't seem to write songs like that any more."

"It's one of my favourites too," she had replied. "Could it be that sad songs are out of fashion?"

"I suppose people nowadays prefer dancing to the jingle of money," Baxingdale said and began to hum the tune in a deep baritone.

It appeared, momentarily, that she was being courted and she allowed herself to get carried away. She doubted if Xavier would notice or, indeed, care. As was usual on such occasions, he would be courting popularity by running around selling raffle tickets and practising his community-service routine.

She had closed her eyes and treated herself to the luxuries of dancing and male attention. She had clung to her partner closer than she had meant to and he had responded.

The way they danced did not pass unnoticed by Phoebe Knight. Later, in the powder room, Phoebe had said: "Seb's a darling man. We were at Oxford together, you know. Chris too, of course. Seb's got all kinds of talents. I can vouch for him. He would make a marvellous catch except he's poor as a church mouse. His father is only a vicar, you know."

"Money isn't everything."

"Easy to say when you have it, darling."

Phoebe Knight sucked in her stomach and thrust out her bosom. She obviously harboured residual claims upon Baxingdale's affections. Lucille felt hugely embarrassed that her lapse on the dance floor should have led anyone to suppose she had designs on the journalist.

She had lain awake half that night thinking about it. She longed to be free again, to love again. A divorce was attainable, together with a modest settlement. She had no intention of even denting the Gold Star fortune. But she could not give up Ah Yuen and that was a concession her husband would never allow, unsatisfactory father though he was. Taking Ah Yuen back to America would also hurt Serenity. She couldn't do that after all the kindnesses her mother-in-law had shown.

There were also her own parents to consider. They had a claim on Ah Yuen's company and affections. Soon he would be old enough and, hopefully, well enough for her to take him to visit them on a more regular basis. If she did not, tongues would wag and she would be accused of distancing herself from her family now that she had married into wealth and position. In any case, it would be right to expose Ah Yuen to America, to allow him to discover for himself where he wanted to spend his life.

Serenity had probably detected some of the considerations she was wrestling with and had guessed the cause of her unhappiness. Her mother-in-law had made efforts to draw Xavier and herself closer together. She had taught her to prepare various herbal tonics for Xavier. There was one known as the "Four Gentlemen's Tonic" and another brewed with barrenwort. But her husband seldom returned early enough to take the tonics or would refuse them on the grounds they'd cause him to visit the toilet too frequently during the night.

Serenity also introduced her to Buddhism, telling her that sufferings in life were traceable to human passions and desires. But was it so wrong to desire to be free, to be loved and to give life to lots of children?

How had Serenity coped with her husband and a cold-blooded son like Xavier? Did her daily retreats into the Meditation Room really cultivate the tranquillity she displayed? Or had she merely bottled up her feelings? There was much about her mother-in-law she could not figure out. And yet, when she joined Serenity in the Meditation Room for contemplation or for reciting scriptures, she did feel peace of a sort.

Ah Yuen was asleep. Lucille left the bedroom quietly and made her way down to the Meditation Room. She found Serenity sitting cross-legged on a prayer mat, as if in a trance. She was about to retreat when she heard Serenity say: "Please stay."

"Are you feeling all right, Mother?" Lucille asked. "I didn't mean to disturb you."

"I'm fine," Serenity answered. "Care to read some scripture?"

"Sure, if I'm not being a nuisance."

Serenity smiled and handed her an opened copy of the *Diamond Sutra*. "Let's start with that verse," she said, indicating the place with her finger. "I think you're already familiar with it."

Lucille sat down on a prayer mat next to her mother-in-law and they began to intone in unison:

"This earthly life may be likened to a dream,
It may be likened to a bubble;
It may be likened to the dew and lightning,
For all sentient life must be so regarded."

Rallies and riots

23

It was well past six in the evening but a fierce July sun continued to beat upon several hundred demonstrators gathered at a corner of Victoria Park. They were mostly college students, with a sprinkling of teachers, writers, clerks and factory workers, and they did not seem to mind the humidity. They had gathered for a patriotic purpose, risking comfortable futures in the civil service or glittering jobs in the private sector for what they regarded as a just cause.

Most of them carried small plastic bags containing soft drinks and fruits. Many fluttered palm-leaf fans. The most committed wore white headbands with black characters urging protection of Chinese territorial integrity and the defence to the death of the Diu Yu Toi Islands.

Girls committed to the cause were more restrained. Ruined complexions apparently counted for more than death. Wide-brimmed straw hats and cheap umbrellas, augmented by sunglasses, were much in evidence. The atmosphere, in spite of spasmodic outbreaks of shouted slogans and patriotic songs, was generally festive, like a noisy college outing.

"Protect Diu Yu Toi!"

"Defend the territorial integrity of the Motherland!"

"Resist the revival of Japanese Militarism!"

"Defeat American and Japanese Neo-Imperialism!"

Elsewhere within Victoria Park's forty acres of reclaimed land, the shouting and songs attracted scant attention. High-school students absorbed in football or basketball created a din of their own. The elderly, sitting on benches or strolling by the harbour side of the park, looked upon the demonstrators with mild curiosity. A fair number accepted printed handbills, if only for something to fan themselves with. A collection of local journalists and photographers hovered around the edges jotting notes and snapping pictures.

Sebastian Baxingdale stood about twenty or thirty yards from the growing crowd, under the shade of some scrawny willow and eucalyptus trees. Memories of his own student days came back to him. So many things had seemed possible then. Now there was only cynicism and ennui. He was wondering why he had come when Tony Tao, a member of the Executive Committee of the Hong Kong Federation of Students, rushed up panting, clutching a fistful of handbills.

"Sorry didn't find you earlier, Mr. Baxingdale. Many things to do, you know, besides press relations. English not good but can try to answer questions. Too bad other foreign journalists not at protest."

Tao had a high-pitched Eastern voice and an awkward English accent. He was a thin, unremarkable lad, wearing steel-rimmed spectacles. As he spoke, he continued to dish out handbills to passers-by with a friendly smile.

"Have to be honest with you," Baxingdale said. "I came because I'm a little baffled by the issue. You people have been demonstrating for months, mounting signature campaigns, handing in protest letters. Some of you have been arrested, injured and imprisoned. Still you keep kicking up a fuss over what appears to be a quarrel between the Chinese and the Japanese over a few specks of rock in the middle of the East China Sea. This has little to do with Hong Kong. Can't the matter be settled through diplomatic channels or before an arbitration court? I don't think the British public is much interested in faraway quarrels. The *Daily Globe* certainly does not want to be used by others for grinding political axes."

"Sorry, Mr. Baxingdale. I hope I can explain properly. I'm history student. Diu Yu Toi islands part of China. But because Western oil companies want to drill there, Americans try to hand them to Japan next year, when they return Ryukyu Islands to Japan. Diu Yu Toi not part of the Ryukyus. History, geography, geology link them to China. Every Chinese knows this and is united on this. Many protests in China, Taiwan, United States, Europe.

"I speak for Hong Kong Federation of Students. We are only one of many protest groups. We don't want you to take sides, only to witness British injustice. We are taught British bring rule of law. But we get no justice. We want our feelings known."

"Why do you feel you're not getting justice? There is a

process for applying for public demonstrations but I gather, according to the authorities, your people have not complied with requirements."

"Authorities are tricking us. Public Order Ordinance says police must give permit before meetings in public places. We applied for permit to rally in Victoria Park. Police said park controlled by Urban Council. If Urban Council allows use, police will give permit. But Urban Council ask us to use a football stadium and not disturb other park users. What good is football stadium? Who goes to football stadium except to watch football? Better stay home and shout slogans at walls.

"We want right to express opinions, like Speakers' Corner in Hyde Park. Demonstrate peacefully, like in Britain. Authorities forcing us to break law. They send police to arrest us. We will not resist. We learned about civil disobedience from Gandhi. We want the world to know what's happening here."

Baxingdale listened to the fractured discourse from the young man with growing understanding and sympathy. His natural instincts for justice and fair play were engaged.

"If what you say is true, the administration seems a bit bone-headed," he said. "If it's a matter of colonial injustice, then that is a legitimate concern for the *Globe*. I will look into this more fully. But do you and your friends want to go so far as to risk arrest? You may end up with criminal records, unable to apply for visas to study abroad. Why not fight this through the courts? Seek a judicial review?"

"Takes too long. Whole thing dead before court hearing. Japan gets Diu Yu Toi in one year. Must act now. We know risks, Mr. Baxingdale. We're not heroes or agitators, just people wanting our say."

There was a shout from the crowd. "Old Tao! Where are the staplers? Where did you put them?"

"Sorry. Please excuse a minute," Tao said and raced off towards students erecting a makeshift stand with pieces of plywood and empty fruit cartons. They were trying to fix a piece of cloth with a slogan to the stand.

Tao trotted back to Baxingdale after a short interval. He brushed the back of his hand across his forehead and it came away with perspiration. "Hot," he said, apologetically, before drying his hand on his torn and faded jeans. He seemed anxious to complete what he had started to say.

"During 1967 riots, some called us running dogs of the British because we took no stand, made no gesture. That shamed us. They were partly right. We thought mainly of our careers. The older generations at least opposed the Japanese or took sides in the civil war. But we have been keeping our heads down for quiet life. We wanted to be good boys and enjoy prosperous futures. Now there's a chance to show what we are. We must decide something. Otherwise life is false. I'm sorry, I can't explain well. You understand what I say?"

"Yes, I understand," Baxingdale said. He felt inexpressibly touched.

The number of demonstrators had by now swelled to over a thousand. Riot police had also arrived by the truckload. They were marshalled in front of their vehicles, dressed in khaki, with black riot helmets, rattan riot shields, black wooden truncheons and hob-nailed boots. They were commanded by a tall European Divisional Superintendent who stood conferring with a handful of subordinates. Photographers scurried between the two groups searching for dramatic angles before any melee started.

Baxingdale eyed the display of force apprehensively. He knew that a Hong Kong riot company consisted of a hundred and seventy men. He figured there had to be at least five companies massed. Such a force suggested the authorities were out to teach the demonstrators a lesson. He could feel the tension gathering, like static, ready to be discharged on the slightest contact.

"What are you expecting to happen?"

Tao grinned. "Same crazy game. Police in fix. Can't surround park like other sites. Park too big. Can't disperse us because we're too many. Can't arrest us all. We just sing songs, chant slogans, try to involve public. At seven o'clock, former President of Hong Kong Federation of Students will make address. His name is Yam Tin-chee, now trade union activist. When Yam starts speaking, or maybe before, police will warn us to disperse. But we'll stay. We're committed. Let them beat us again before television cameras. That'll help our cause."

"Tempers are apt to be short in this heat. Things can get out of hand, turn bloody. I've seen it in Vietnam and even in London. You sure there's no other way?"

Tony Tao shrugged his slender shoulders. "Up to police. We want peaceful protest. Many girls here. My girlfriend also. Makes no sense to put her in danger. Her name's Mai. She's in English Lit. That's her over there, in the straw hat and pink pedal-pushers."

Tao pointed to a girl and the girl waved to him.

Tao waved back. Then he pulled a document from his hip pocket and held it out diffidently to Baxingdale. "Mai made translation of history of Diu Yu Toi into English, from our pamphlets."

"Thanks," Baxingdale said. "I'm not up on this dispute, I must confess. The Japanese say the islands have been part of the Ryukyus for a long time. Claimed to have put up a marker there in 1895."

"That's true. But fact is China lost the First Sino-Japanese War in 1895. Had to cede Taiwan and Pescadores to Japan. At end of World War II, Japan agreed to return them to China. No mention of Diu Yu Toi. Chinese assumed position understood. Then, in 1969, America announced intention to return Ryukyus to Japan in 1972, including Diu Yu Toi. New plot became clear. Chinese people protested all over the world. Everything in Mai's translation."

"I'll study the arguments. Thanks."

"Better join others now," Tony Tao said, with a slight bow. "Rally starting soon. Thanks for coming." He trotted back to the main body of students, patting Mai reassuringly on the shoulder as he passed, before taking up a position near the makeshift stand.

At the appointed hour, a tall, lean man with a loud hailer climbed onto the stand. Wrapped around the front was a two-foot wide slogan: "Protect Diu Yu Toi and the territorial integrity of the Motherland."

"Compatriots!" the tall man on the stand called and immediately a roar of approval went up. He punched the air with a clenched fist and shouted: "Defend Diu Yu Toi at all costs!" The call was echoed and met with more roars of approval.

"My name is Yam Tin-chee. I used to be a student like you but I have more recently been a guest in British gaols. It is good to be made a guest of British gaols. I'm told only the best people get that privilege! Many subsequently became presidents and prime ministers!"

Roars of laughter.

"We're here today to protest peacefully — I stress peacefully — against another plot to steal another part of our Motherland," Yam continued. "Though we are not protesting against the British in Hong Kong, their police and lackeys have turned up to silence us. But we will not be silenced, will we?"

The demonstrators responded with a resounding "No!"

"We all know the British for what they are," Yam shouted. "They pervert our educational system. They excise from textbooks the disgraceful facts of history. But no matter. We all know they made us buy opium under the threat of gunboats and under the pretext of free trade. We know they made war again and again against our people and crippled our nation with war indemnities. It was a British commander who ordered the razing of the Summer Palace at the time of the Boxer uprising. It was British police who massacred compatriots in British concessions. Remember the shootings in the Shanghai International Settlement? The killings at Shakee? Have we forgotten the seventy-two martyrs?"

Shouted anti-British slogans greeted Yam's indictment.

"I am not just talking about history," the speaker continued. "I'm also talking about what is happening now. It's the British who talk of democracy, yet denying us a say over our own affairs. It's the British who talk of the rule of law while perverting the law. They make us squander our reserves to bolster their sagging currency. They pass laws to force us to buy their products but restrict our goods in the British market. They are at this very moment trying to use their laws to turn this into an illegal gathering. We must not forget we have a right to be here."

More roars of approval went up.

"It's the British who have occupied our territory and who want us to remain silent while another part of our country is being stolen by their allies. It's time to defend our Motherland, to defend our right to free speech and free association. If blood is shed, then one day blood must be repaid with blood."

The response of the crowd was overwhelming. Baxingdale's

command of Chinese was insufficient to catch everything, but he got the drift. His country did have a great deal to answer for, he reflected, and the prosperity now enjoyed by the colony did not make British actions right.

Then another message boomed out from another loud-hailer. "Attention! Attention! This is the police. This gathering is an illegal assembly under the provisions of the Public Order Ordinance. You are breaking the law. Disperse immediately. If you do not do so within five minutes you will be liable to arrest and imprisonment. Vacate the park at once."

"Stand fast! We will not yield!" Yam cried, and his words were taken up by the entire assembly. A few demonstrators behind the makeshift stand unfurled four cloth banners on poles calling for the defence of the Motherland and Diu Yu Toi and demanding freedom of speech and assembly.

A police detachment immediately rushed towards the stand to arrest Yam and to tear down the banners. Students on the stage tried to protect the banners. Police and students alike got entangled in them. Others attempted to hamper the police, so as to enable their leaders to escape. Officers lashed out with their truncheons. Punches and kicks flew. The demonstrators rushed en masse to the aid of their leaders. The makeshift stand gave way with a loud crack.

Yam was apparently the prime target. A policeman already had his head in an arm lock. Students clambered over the policeman as they tried to free their speaker. Several officers struggled to disentangle themselves from the cloth banners and to confiscate them. Others applied their batons furiously and indiscriminately. The addition of more policemen and demonstrators in the confused struggle reduced the makeshift stand into a dangerous rubble of jagged wood.

Baxingdale watched the riot police crunching towards the main body of demonstrators, ordering them to leave, striking out with boots and batons. Threats, insults, imprecations and pleas filled the air. Girls screamed. The whole vast, heaving mass of humanity altered shape, like some giant amoeba. It began fraying at the edges before splitting off into smaller entities. The new groupings quickly took on lives of their own, charging off in different directions to hurl missiles and abuse at the police.

Those remaining with the main body simply curled up on the ground and covered their heads with their arms to ward off the baton blows.

Tony Tao pushed his way towards Mai. She was sitting on the ground with her arms curled around the straw hat on her head. Four policemen got to her area before Tony and set about dispersing demonstrators with varying degrees of physical encouragement. One grabbed Mai by the shoulder to pull her up. She played possum. In the test of wills that followed, her straw hat fell off and then the blouse she was wearing got either torn or undone. Her white brassiere became exposed. She screamed and tried to cover herself, still refusing to stand up.

At that moment Tony Tao reached her. He tried to loosen the officer's grip on the blouse. A truncheon cracked down on Tao's head and he tumbled on top of Mai. A backhanded blow sent his spectacles flying. Blood was trickling from a wound in his head. Mai gathered him up in her arms and screamed and screamed.

The officer lost interest in Mai. He had a bigger prize — a rioter who had attacked a policeman and obstructed him in the execution of his duty. He jerked Tao away from Mai, threw him on the ground, pressed a knee against the small of his back, and twisted his arms behind to handcuff him. Then he half-dragged his prisoner towards one of the waiting detention vans.

"Please let him go! Please let him go!" Mai cried, stumbling to her feet and retrieving her straw hat to clasp it over her chest. "He's hurt. Please let me take him to a doctor," she pleaded. Tears were streaming down her face.

"You want to be arrested too?" the officer demanded, pointing his truncheon at her.

Mai collapsed on her knees, wailing: "Tony! Tony!"

A rage surged through Baxingdale, the kind he had never managed to summon up in the boxing ring or on the rugby pitch. He rushed towards the officer who was dragging Tony Tao away. He had no idea what he might do once he got there. All he knew was that his instincts had been offended.

He fought his way through the demonstrators in pursuit of the policeman. Before he got near Tao, however, he was barred by two other policemen in riot gear. A red tag on the shoulder strap of one indicated that the wearer understood English.

"Who are you? What you want?" the officer demanded, shield and baton at the ready.

"Journalist," Baxingdale replied, showing his press pass.

"Stay back. This police business."

Baxingdale looked straight into the officer's eyes. He thought he detected a malevolence there, perhaps even a secret hatred, as if the eyes were saying: "You are to blame for this. Because of your kind I'm forced to injure my own countrymen."

Baxingdale's mouth was open and he was breathing hard. He was bigger than either of them. He could bring them both down in a single tackle. But then what? The officers would never leave it at that. Reinforcements would come and far from freeing Tony Tao he would end up joining him in gaol. He was not there to make news, he told himself, only to report it. The messy state of the world wan't his business. His body relaxed and he took a small step backwards, though his heart still pounded furiously.

The officers turned and went back to chasing demonstrators. Many students, joined by local street youths, had already spilled into the shopping streets of Causeway Bay, to vent their anger on rubbish bins, cars and shop windows.

Tony Tao had disappeared into one of the police vans. The crowds began to thin. The injured were helped away by friends.

Baxingdale made for the spot where Tony Tao had been bludgeoned. It looked as if a typhoon had hit. The debris included empty soft-drink containers, broken umbrellas, discarded straw hats, blood-soaked handkerchiefs and torn banners. He spotted among the mess a pair of steel-rimmed spectacles with one lens smashed and an arm twisted out of shape. He picked them up and put them into his shirt pocket. He looked for Mai but she was nowhere to be seen.

He felt drained. He wanted something, anything, to help him forget what he had witnessed. He wished Hong Kong still had opium houses like Cholon. He could do with a pipe or two. Or perhaps, like Derek Soames, he needed different kinds of succour.

Suddenly, he recalled the night he had danced with Lucille Chu at the Red Cross Ball. Her memory intoxicated him still. She would be ideal for soothing his anger and his hurt. He could imagine how healing her embrace could be. But she was somebody else's wife!

Reluctantly he followed the trail of destruction along the crowded streets of Causeway Bay towards Szeto's Bar in Wanchai. If he encountered T. P. Choy and Derek Soames there, he would give them both a piece of his mind.

Law and disorder

24

"Tried reaching you last night. Looked everywhere. At Szeto's too," Sebastian Baxingdale said, plaintively, standing before the desk of the City District Commissioner.

"Sorry. Had to deal with the aftermath," T. P. Choy replied, in a voice full of weariness.

"Christ, T. P.! Why did you let it happen? All those kids hurt, dozens arrested."

"I didn't *let* anything happen. If people participate in illegal assemblies they have to take their chances. The police are there to uphold the law."

"That's bullshit and you know it! The establishment provoked the whole thing. It sent the kids on a bureaucratic merry-go-round, then unleashed the storm troopers!"

Baxingdale leaned over and brought his fist down on the teak desk as he spoke. He was presuming upon his friendship of four years with the Commissioner. The blow, however, produced nothing more than a shudder from an empty out-tray. The desk, like the rest of the furniture in the office, had been made by prison labour and designed for rough usage.

"They were just students, for heaven's sake, not criminals," Baxingdale continued. "They wanted to make a legitimate political point. No call for violence. Don't know how many got hurt but Tony Tao was certainly beaten. Saw it with my own eyes. One moment he was briefing me quietly and the next he was being bludgeoned. He's probably lying in a stifling cell right now, unattended, waiting to be charged!"

The Commissioner allowed his wide, pugnacious mouth to form into a conciliatory smile. "Have a seat, Seb. I know you're upset. But this administration's not as machiavellian as you might suppose."

"I don't want a damn seat."

"The government didn't trick anybody into a demonstration. It just wanted to preserve public order. Local newspapers gave conflicting figures on the injured. For the record, of the twenty-two persons arrested, only four required medical attention. Unfortunately, Tony Tao was one of them. He's not lying unattended in some stifling cell, as you put it, but in a remand hospital. Six stitches on the face and under observation for concussion."

"And he's probably half-blind too!" Baxingdale took the remnants of Tony's spectacles out of his pocket and placed them on the Commissioner's desk.

Both men stared at the mangled remains as if they were a mute reproach against the violence visited upon them.

"I'll get them to his parents," Choy said.

Baxingdale finally sank into a chair. "I want to testify," he said. "Tony's had a raw deal. I'll get him a lawyer. I know a friend who used to work for the Director of Public Prosecutions."

"You mean Christopher Knight? Why such concern over a virtual stranger? Tony merely invited you to a demonstration. What do you know about him?"

"Not much. Struck me as an idealistic young man."

"He was one of the prime movers of the illegal assembly."

"He organized things pretty well then. It had been a totally peaceful gathering till the police tried to break it up. A policeman was trying to drag Tony's girl friend to her feet and in the process just about ripped her blouse off. Tony tried to stop him, as any gentleman would, and was beaten to a pulp right before my eyes. That's not the behaviour of a British administration I'd want to account for."

"You don't have to account for it," Choy said, tartly, his eyes narrowing in his broad, squarish face. "You're a journalist."

"I don't like seeing police brutality or students being treated like criminals. That's not British justice. I'm certainly going to tell my readers what's going on here."

"That's your prerogative."

"Why the hell did you encourage me to attend? The whole atmosphere was almost like a carnival till the police intervened."

"You've forgotten to mention that the gathering was unlawful and that the crowd failed to disperse when ordered to do so. I did encourage you to attend because you told me you wanted to observe how the rule of law operated here. Now you're upset by what you've seen."

"You knew there would be trouble, didn't you?"

"I knew nothing of the sort. I knew a radical trade-union leader by the name of Yam would be addressing the gathering. He's a powerful speaker. Passions are bound to be aroused with him haranguing people on an emotive issue. The police couldn't take chances. They set conditions for a legal demonstration but the organizers failed to comply. Yet they insisted on a demonstration. The police had no choice but to break it up. Regrettably, things got out of hand."

"And kids like Tony paid the price. It's not fair. I want to see justice done."

"Just leave Tony be, Seb. Otherwise you'll ruin him."

"Me? Ruin Tony? That's rich! I'm not the one who's given him concussion or had him locked up."

"Testifying's a bad idea. Are you going to give evidence on behalf of the other twenty-one detainees as well? And what about those who got away?"

"I didn't see what was done by others. I saw people being clubbed and kicked indiscriminately, including girls. Most of them were just sitting on the ground, terrified, like Tony's girl. I don't know who were actually rioting. Fighting was spilling all over the place, in Victoria Park, in Causeway Bay. I had no way of telling who the rioters were."

"Precisely. Over a thousand people disturbing the peace and you concentrated on the behaviour of one boy. How convenient! If I were Tony's companions I'd smell a rat. Why should a gweilo journalist, looking into a sea of yellow faces, focus his attention on a single individual? And come forward afterwards to testify on his behalf no less! Was the gweilo a genuine journalist or a Special Branch operative in disguise? Was Tony an informant passing on intelligence or fingering his associates? It's not difficult to visualize how minds might work."

"I observed Tony because I had been talking to him shortly before trouble started. He handed me an account in English of the history of the dispute."

"That settles it then. He was obviously an informer. Things would only go worse for him if he were defended by an Englishman who also happens to have been an ex-government lawyer."

"I can't believe this! This sounds like something out of Orwell!"

"Just let Tony be, Seb. If he's only charged with illegal assembly he'll probably plead guilty and do his two or three weeks. Let him enjoy his martyrdom. The memory might warm him in his old age. He'll be paying enough for his misguided ideals. Give him that one shining memory to keep, that moment when he spurned the blandishments of the world to do what he thought right."

"How can you, of all people, be so cavalier about a young person being beaten up and tossed into gaol? Chalking up a criminal record to boot. How can you defend the excesses of last night?"

Choy stared into the palm of his left hand, rubbing his thumb slowly against his fingers. "You call them excesses. I don't know that they were. I wasn't there. In any event, I have to defend them. That's my job. I'm part of the colonial establishment, remember? So are the police. That ties us together. Anyway, no one got killed. So far as I can tell, no one except Tony was even seriously injured. By colonial standards that's pretty benign."

Baxingdale shook his head vigorously in disbelief. "You're one of the most senior Chinese officers in this damned administration. Its only legitimacy is derived from a few pieces of paper extracted by force of arms. There's no election or democratic accountability here, even though the people are among the best educated and most intelligent in the world. Except for unique historical and political circumstances they would have been independent long ago. Since they've been denied a voice, they have a right to look to officials like you to look after their interests. It's bad enough you didn't prevent yesterday's disaster. Why play the running dog to defend colonial brutality now?"

"Running dog? You think I'm a running dog after all the time you've known me, after all I've told you about British double-dealings and cock-ups?" The Commissioner's nostrils flared and he waved his arms dismissively at his visitor. "You've no inkling of half the things I'm forced to do. You talked at our gatherings about each individual's duty to become engaged in social issues. What does that mean? Writing an article once in a while for a newspaper on the other side of the world?"

"That's better than nothing!" Baxingdale retorted. "Yes, you gripe over your beer, but where's the action? How convenient to hide behind alibis of not rocking the boat, not upsetting the apple cart and playing up the Communist bogey! Didn't it use to be a Chinese tradition for upright officials to resign or even to commit suicide rather than become accomplices to disgraceful deeds? What has happened to that hallowed tradition?"

As Baxingdale continued his verbal attack he rose from his seat and leaned over the desk again, with eyes blazing. He locked them onto those of the Commissioner.

The Commissioner glared back and barked: "That tradition was meant for another time, for a different society. Officials used to be chosen through imperial examinations for their mastery of our classics. They absorbed their moral content in the process. Resignation or suicide was a gesture, a self-sacrifice to prick the conscience of a harsh ruler. Here the British have introduced the culture of the iron rice-bowl and the obedient servant. No one ever resigns or gets off the gravy train over a principle. For every man of principle in this administration there are a hundred time-servers with none."

At that point the Commissioner's secretary, in a remarkable feat of timing, entered the room with two cups and a pot of the Commissioner's favourite Chinese tea. The two men disengaged their eyes and Baxingdale resumed his seat.

"Would you prefer Lipton's?" the Commissioner asked, with consummate civility, as the secretary set out the cups.

"No, Chinese's fine."

After tea had been poured the Commissioner picked up the damaged spectacles and handed them to the secretary, instructing her to get them to Tony Tao's father.

The men sipped the hot brew and that commonplace act somehow restored their equanimity.

After the secretary had retired, Baxingdale said: "T. P., I'm sorry I shouted at you. I had no right to call you a running dog. I know you're not. That was thoroughly uncalled for. I was just angry with myself for being so useless yesterday. You want to know what happened? For a split second, when I saw the policeman laying into Tony, I almost attacked the police myself. But I hesitated and drew back. Prudence, cowardice or failure of nerve? I don't know. I've been hating myself since. I guess I just needed to vent my frustrations on somebody."

"I'm glad you curbed your impulse. Otherwise I would have had to worry about getting you out of a stifling cell as well! Forget the name-calling. What are friends for if they can't insult each other once in a while? I've said wounding things too. Yesterday was a bad business all round. I was more affected by what happened than I let on. I haven't told anybody before, Seb, but Tony's my own bloody godson."

"What!" Baxingdale was dumbfounded by the disclosure. "Jesus Christ! Why didn't you tell me before? I've been talking way out of turn! I feel like a complete ass. Ought to kick myself. You must be worried sick!"

"Don't feel badly. How were you to know?"

"Can't you at least get him away from the police, pull some strings to get charges dropped?"

The Commissioner shook his head. "That wouldn't be very proper. Justice, even if it's only British justice, must be seen to be done. Got to wait for the medical results first and then find out what he's going to be charged with."

Baxingdale shook his head in despair. "Jesus! What a mess! This might be being wise after the event, but couldn't you have stopped him from going?"

"Could I have stopped the thousand other participants too?"

"Tony's your godson, for heaven's sake. You knew the risks and the attitude of the police."

The Commissioner nodded his head and sighed. "I knew more than I've admitted, my friend. You've hit the nail on the head without realizing it. I *was* partly responsible for what happened last night. I *was* a running dog."

"What the hell are you talking about?"

Baxingdale realized all of a sudden how deeply troubled his friend was. He had lived long enough among Chinese to know about their preoccupation with "face". They always lived a part of their lives in the shadows. Behind their ritualised civility and unfailing good manners, they hid failures and defeats, suppressed vices and abandoned dreams. His friend, on the surface a tough and urbane civil servant, was no different. The man had secrets bottled up inside, though he now appeared exposed and vulnerable. If he were a Catholic, he would probably be heading for the confessional.

"Tell me what you're driving at," Baxingdale said, gently, in the face of his friend's lack of response. He wanted to help him unburden himself.

"My job as City District Commissioner is to smooth out awkward situations," Choy began eventually, in a subdued voice. "I'm supposed to assess grassroots sentiments and come up with solutions. Doesn't mean, however, that my advice is always followed."

All the fire previously smouldering inside the Commissioner seemed to have been brought under control. He continued: "The Diu Yu Toi issue, as you can imagine, raises troubling echoes of events in the previous century. The police have been stirring up additional resentments by breaking up Diu Yu Toi signature campaigns and arresting demonstrators. Though the row is over a pile of rocks in the East China Sea, it nevertheless taps into unhappy Chinese memories. If people got too fired up they might soon direct their anger at the British in Hong Kong as well. The situation therefore had to be defused.

"Knowing Tony's involvement, I asked him to set up a meeting between myself and the other organizers as a step towards finding a solution. I let it be known that the authorities would consider issuing permits for future demonstrations if certain conditions were met. Tony managed to convince his associates that I was serious and a man whose word could be relied upon. The meeting duly took place.

"It became obvious at once that I was not dealing with a bunch of anarchists or rabid radicals. Most were sober, patriotic students, like Tony, who felt — rightly or wrongly — that the big powers were ganging up on China again. The authorities trying to silence them merely reinforced the suspicion that there was indeed an international conspiracy. If being British meant anything, the organizers of the demonstrations asserted, then it should mean the same right to organize peaceful public meetings in the colony as in Britain itself. They pointed to the repeated arrests as evidence of a conspiracy.

"I judged the organizers pragmatic enough not to want to destabilize the colony and, because I was Chinese and spoke their language, I managed to allay some of their fears. I then engaged them in some pretty tough but constructive negotiations. In the end we hammered out a whole range of conditions to be fulfilled before the granting of a permit. They would apply for permission in good time, restrict the demonstration to a designated corner of Victoria Park, limit the duration of the gathering, accept a modest police oversight, cut back on the number of speakers, appoint a sufficient number of stewards for crowd control, disperse peacefully afterwards and so on.

"On my advice, those became the stated requirements of the police. I thought I had the makings of a deal. If those conditions could be fulfilled, much of the heat would go out of the situation. I believed in the peaceful intentions of the organizers and I recommended the granting of a permit under those conditions.

"But the police, after agreeing, had second thoughts. They were afraid of creating a precedent. Because the demonstration was quasi-political in nature, they got scared. They tried to dodge the issue by imposing an additional condition. It was, of course, technically within their right to do so under existing public-order legislation. They told the organizers that since Victoria Park was under the control of the Urban Council, they must first secure permission from the Urban Council. Such a request was also a precedent for the Council. So it dithered. It suggested alternative sites out of the public eye, on the grounds that demonstrating in the park would disrupt the activities of other users of the park. The organizers soon suspected they were being played for fools.

"I was naturally furious. I protested to my superiors and the dispute ended up at Government House. To cut a long story short, that fear of setting a precedent hardened before the Governor. It was decided that the demonstration should be banned and that the police would take all steps necessary to maintain public order and uphold the law. I felt as helpless and outraged after that meeting as you did at the park yesterday."

"Jesus! That's cutting the ground from right under you. That's adding fuel to the fire. How could those clowns be so blind to Chinese realities and sentiments? Didn't your Chinese colleagues support you?"

"What Chinese colleagues? I was the sole Chinese there! We are very few at senior levels. Just window-dressing. Hewers of wood and drawers of water with fancy titles. The debacle last night is certain to be regarded as further justification for keeping us down. After all, arguing for political demonstrations to be allowed and failing to defuse a simple situation must reflect on both the loyalty and the competence of Chinese officers."

"How idiotic, even for blimps! If they value your talents so little, why don't you quit? Leave them to stew in their own juices. There are fortunes to be made in the private sector. Just look at chaps like Xavier Chu."

"That's what I'm terrified of, turning into a man who cares more about his own enrichment than the welfare of his community. He's an Anglo-American product, stuffed with the mouthings of Adam Smith and robber barons. The trouble is that most people in the West have forgotten the educational part of Adam Smith's teaching and concentrated on the self-interest bit. That allows corporate sharks and stupid governments to exploit his ideas. Actions and ideas now have repercussions far beyond narrow national borders. Can't people see where the uncurbed pursuit of self-interest is leading? Can't they see crony capitalism and corruption taking hold, not only in colonies and pseudo-colonies but in the very hearts of the most advanced free-market economies as well?"

Choy paused and picked up his tea cup to drink.

Baxingdale was familiar with the Commissioner's social and economic theories. They'd had many absorbing discussions on the whys and wherefores. But he sensed his friend had not yet finished talking and he did not want to divert him. He therefore remained silent and drank some tea as well.

"I can't quit, Seb," Choy said, finally, still nursing his teacup. "I chose a side a long time ago and, no matter how bad things get, I'm stuck with that. At the time there were qualities I had read in books about the British that I loved — their tolerance and libertarian traditions, their wry humour and sense of fair play, their eccentricities and ability not to take themselves too seriously. I also thought I could do something for my community working within a colonial framework, so I swore an oath of allegiance to the British Crown. An honourable man must be bound by his word, must he not, let alone his oath?

"I didn't realize till later that most of the British qualities I loved never got transplanted here. For some inexplicable reason, your countrymen seem to leave them behind when they come East. Out here they put on the mask of unearned superiority. I also never realized till much later that oaths of allegiance and fealty only worked in one direction so far as ministers of the Crown were concerned. I fear acquiring an empire has not brought out the best in your countrymen."

"You can say that again! Thank God we're in the end game."

"End game or not, they still have the power to be spiteful. That's what I'm afraid of. The police may throw the book at Tony, for the sake of setting an example. Assaulting a police officer, resisting arrest, participating in an illegal assembly, conspiracy to create public disorder, the works."

"If they do, you must let me testify. Ah, I'm beginning to see why you wanted me to attend the demonstration. You were counting on the presence of foreign correspondents to deter the police from being too heavy-handed. And even if things went wrong, you figured there would be independent witnesses. That's right, isn't it?"

Choy smiled.

"You old rascal! No wonder the blimps don't trust you. You keep trying to rescue them from their blockheadedness."

"My manoeuvre didn't prevent Tony getting hurt. If he ends up with permanent damage or if the police throw the book at him, I wouldn't know how to face his parents."

"No point crossing that bridge till you come to it. What about a pre-emptive strike? I could do a human-interest piece about Tony for the *Globe*. Give my eyewitness account of a peaceful demonstration being turned into a riot by unnecessary police brutality. Explain how Chinese around the world perceived the handing over of the Diu Yu Toi islands by the Americans to the Japanese as a fresh encroachment upon China's territory. Finally, a young idealistic lad lying injured, his hopes and dreams in ruins, simply because he was trying to protect his girl friend from police assault. Details of Tony's injuries and criminal charges. That should touch the hearts of a few back home, perhaps spark a question or two in Parliament. The red faces resulting might foil the harsher inclinations of the police."

"Could also provoke them further."

"True. We've got to take that chance." Baxingdale fished for a notebook from his pocket and added: "I'll need details of Tony's family, his school attainments, how you and he are connected and so on."

The Commissioner lowered his head and sighed again. "All right, I guess there's no better alternative. I only hope it works. My wife and I adopted Tony some ten years back. His father and I were good friends at secondary school. We had often talked of entering university together. But Tony's grandfather, who used to own a small factory making canvas shoes, went bankrupt. So university was out for him. He had to get a job and he became a book-keeper in a small trading firm. We kept in touch. The grandfather died a couple of years later. Eventually we both got married. Tony's father married a textile worker and they started producing one child after another. Tony was the first.

"After the first two kids, the wife had to quit work to look after them and the father was forced to moonlight as a cashier in one of those late-closing tourist shops in Tsimshatsui to make ends meet. The father's ambition was to send his children to university, to give them the education he missed. To that end he's been working sixteen hours a day for the last fifteen years. Still does.

"I wanted to make things easier for him, but he was too proud to accept money. Since my wife and I never managed to produce a child, we decided to adopt Tony, according to Chinese custom, as an indirect way of easing the family burden. We paid Tony's fees, bought him books and things like that. Tony has turned out a marvellous boy and a promising student."

"Splendid," Baxingdale said, scribbling furiously in his notebook. "Where do they live?"

"In a multi-storeyed block in a resettlement estate. Eight in a room — grandmother, parents, Tony and four brothers and sisters. You know the standard allocation. Twenty-four square feet per person, including kitchen, 192 square feet in all. You talked about a stifling cell just now. Tony's been in one all his life. Try sleeping eight in a room that size in this heat and you'll get an idea what I mean."

"Great, great! I know that scene. Derek sent me on one of those horrid press tours when I first arrived. Hideous concrete!

Metal gates enclosing each unit. Like penitentiaries with inmates keeping their own keys. Communal bathrooms and latrines. Washing standing up and shitting squatting over trenches. Peeping toms and molesters. Graffiti on walls. Thugs lounging in stairwells. Long corridors like vertical streets, floor upon floor, menaced by shadows after dark. No policeman ever ventured through them, day or night. Not half as easy as bashing students and kicking girls in the park, that's for sure! Yes, Tony rising above that mean environment only to be literally beaten down again."

Baxingdale rattled off his thoughts and jotted them down as if dictating to himself.

"The party line is that those estates are monuments to the administration's public-housing achievements," Choy observed.

Baxingdale snorted. "I've done my research. The fact of the matter is that colonial administrators hadn't a clue what to do with refugees flooding in after the Pacific War. They sent soldiers like myself to the border to round them up and ship them back, to labour camps or worse. Ours was not to reason why. It was the good old Nuremberg defence. We slipped it on as neatly as a glove and came away with clean hands. But not clean consciences, I'm afraid.

"But in spite of everything guards did on both sides of the border, the refugees kept coming. Whitehall began referring to them as economic migrants to justify sending them back. Those who managed to slip through became squatters in hillside shanty towns without any basic amenities. Those settlements multiplied like a rash. It took the Shek Kip Mei fire to force the authorities into some sort of rehousing programme. And those miserable estate blocks were all they could come up with.

"You know something, T. P.? We could have done so much better for these people if only we had had the will or the foresight. We the Brits, I mean."

All of a sudden Baxingdale felt an overwhelming desire to join his friend in purging himself. He wanted to do it not only for the honour of his nation but also for himself, for failing to do nearly enough as a decent human being.

"We Brits had been too full of ourselves," Baxingdale continued. "Too insular and frightened of our own economic decline. So we resorted to every dirty trick to stem it. We didn't fulfil our duty as trustees. We pissed away the reserves of your people to defend sterling, extracted spivvy defence costs from them, restricted imports of their goods and all the rest of it. We didn't even do our duty as decent human beings. You are right about Adam Smith and the perversions of his latter-day disciples. Self-interest has to be curbed, not encouraged, in an inter-dependent world. Otherwise the rich and powerful will grow more so and the impoverished will descend into a new form of slavery.

"You know something else, T. P.? The more I travel around this region, the more I'm convinced that one of these days the yellow races — the Chinese, Japanese, Koreans, Vietnamese — will overtake the West. They had all been bombed out and devastated by years of conflicts. Yet look at them today. They have risen, or are about to rise, like the phoenix.

"They'll soon leave Europe behind because they've got that gritty determination to make something of their lives no matter how bad things get. They've also retained a remarkable faith in learning and are willing to make sacrifices to secure it for their young.

"Tony's father is a case in point. Fifteen years of hard slog without ever wavering. Continuity and the future mattered to people like him. You've got to take your hat off to that. We in the West have lost that kind of faith, that dedication to the future. We've gone soft, living off the intellectual achievement of our forebears and the accumulated fat of empire. All we seek now are material abundance and life served up on a plate."

"Human affairs have ups and downs," Choy interjected. "We've had our dark ages, our dynastic cycles. Great civilizations can sometimes endure by renewing themselves. It all depends on whether they're fortunate enough to come up with the right leaders at the right time."

"I doubt if right leaders will emerge again in my country during my lifetime. I find little to be hopeful about. I look at my father's diminishing congregation and the rising number of school dropouts and despair. The British thirst for learning is fast disappearing. People now just want their places at the trough."

"There has to be hope, Seb. Otherwise we might as well go and slit our own throats."

"Perhaps. At least Tony has given me a chance to redeem myself, to involve myself in a cause that is just. But back to work."

Baxingdale continued to elicit further details about Tony and his family. After a while he shut his notebook. "I've got enough, I think. I imagine it's pointless to ask the police for permission to interview Tony?"

The District Commissioner made a face.

"Pity. I guess you'll have to find out the extent of his injuries and what the police intend to charge him with. Shall we meet at Szeto's for an update? Say, around six? I can then finalize my piece and send it off tonight."

"Certainly. We should both have worked up a mighty thirst by then."

Plotters in Peking

25

Even for a senior Party cadre like Cheng Ching, employed as he was in the most secret of the eight divisions in the General Office of the Chinese Communist Party, being admitted to Chung Nan Hai was still an intimidating affair. The vast complex, formerly part of the royal gardens of the Forbidden City, was reserved exclusively for Party leaders and top officials. It was surrounded by vermilion walls and guarded by more than two thousand elite soldiers of the Central Garrison Corps, known as Unit 8341 in the People's Liberation Army.

Cheng Ching had been invited for dinner there by his adoptive father, General Yeh, who was both the Deputy Chairman of the Military Affairs Commission and the Chief of the General Staff of the People's Liberation Army.

As Cheng Ching presented his identification papers at one of the guard posts, he felt a niggling sense of unease. Ordinarily, his security passes, coupled with an invitation by General Yeh, would have ensured speedy access. But times were distempered. The long-running Cultural Revolution had brought the country to the brink of economic collapse. He had seen the dismal evidence during his journeys to and from his village at Thirsty Hills.

In such circumstances, the hunt for scapegoats and traitors grew more intense by the day. High office offered no protection. General Peng Te-huai, hero of the revolution and General Yeh's former Commander-in-Chief in Korea, was rotting in prison because he had criticized Chairman Mao before the Politburo for using state funds for private pleasures. Liu Shao-chi, the Head of State, argued for General Peng's rehabilitation and got hounded out of office and declared an anti-Party traitor for his principles. His death five years ago had still not been announced, turning him into a non-person.

Cheng Ching waited patiently as the guards examined his documents and the basket of fresh fruit he had brought as a gift. He wondered what the invitation to dinner portended. Had his adoptive father been caught up in some high-level tussle for power?

After the guards had been satisfied, a detail of three escorted him with formal courtesy to the residence of General Yeh.

"Good to see you back," General Yeh exclaimed, extending his right hand.

Cheng Ching took it and proffered the fruits. "A trifle, Erh Fu. My parents send greetings. Thank you for having me to dinner, so soon after my return."

"Why are you standing on ceremony? You're part of the family. Our home is yours," the General said. He was lean and erect, though his closely cropped hair was grey. High cheekbones, hollow cheeks and a pointed chin gave his face a curiously triangular aspect.

"Your parents well?"

"Quite. Thank you."

"Good. Always nice to know that old comrades are well."

Cheng Ching detected a slightly too hearty timbre to the General's voice and his senses triggered an immediate alert.

The sound of conversation brought the General's wife from the kitchen with cups of tea. She was chubby and beaming and was effusive in her welcome.

"Aiyah!" she exclaimed, when the General passed her the fruit. "Why you mess around wasting money?" She smiled broadly and wagged a motherly finger. The Yehs had no children and Cheng Ching was the closest thing they had to a son. After a while, she excused herself. "You two have a nice chat. I'll prepare something special for dinner."

"Don't go to any trouble!" Cheng Ching called.

The mistress of the house dismissed the remark with a wave of her hand as she disappeared back into the kitchen.

"My father asked me to bring a letter of greetings," Cheng Ching reported, presenting the missive with both hands in accordance with etiquette.

"Your father's letters are always pure joy. He can convey things by not mentioning them! The letter will keep." The General pocketed the letter and added: "How's life at Thirsty Hills in general?"

"Improving, I'm glad to say. There was a celebration when I

was there, to coincide with the Spring Festival. Father was very pleased because the villagers finally managed, after ten years, to save enough to acquire a second-hand diesel generator. They now have power to pump water to the terraces and to enjoy an electric light or two in their homes. They feel immensely proud."

Cheng Ching paused and grew pensive. "Nevertheless, I sometimes feel bad when I go home. Seeing Father on crutches reminds me I had promised to return to Thirsty Hills after Korea, to help him and Mother around the village and to train another family dog. My father has aged a lot, but he never says anything about my promise. That makes me feel even more guilty."

"Life often does not offer a man a choice. Your father's a true patriot! Always steadfast. I'm sure he understands that the Party requires your talents. I haven't seen him for close to forty years. Have been meaning to visit, but never found time. Still remember him as he was on the day we stormed Luting Bridge. What a day! Victory or death! We're greybeards now. Perhaps it's better to live on memories, to remember each other as we then were. We probably wouldn't recognize each other should we meet. Come, let's stroll in the garden a while."

The General led the way out, walking stiffly.

The air in the garden was sweet with the smell of damp spring earth. A full moon had risen in the black, cloudless sky. Cheng Ching offered his arm and the General took it. As the pair strolled along the crooked walks, it struck Cheng Ching that the leaves of the pines and cypresses, licked by moonlight, had taken on an unnatural sheen. He had a premonition that something else was about to illuminate itself.

After a dozen yards, General Yeh whispered: "Not safe to talk indoors. Harder for eavesdroppers out here."

"Somebody's been eavesdropping on you!"

"Can't be sure. No harm in being careful. Someone recently tried to bug the private railway carriage of Chairman Mao."

"Really! Who would dare do such a thing?"

"Obviously some group playing for very high stakes. Haven't been able to find out so far. This damnable Cultural Revolution has turned the country upside down. The air is poisonous with intrigues. Everybody's jockeying for power, spying on everybody else. Your father hasn't been troubled by Red Guards, has he?"

"Thirsty Hills's too small and remote for anyone to bother."

"That's a blessing! Your father always had foresight, hiding himself in a place like that, away from all the scheming and back-biting. If we had more cadres like him, this country wouldn't be in the mess it's in. That wife of the Chairman and her coterie are bringing ruin to the country. They must be stopped."

Cheng Ching's heart skipped a beat. People had lost their lives for saying less. His adoptive father had been closely associated with General Peng Te-huai and both his father and himself were closely connected with General Yeh. Chairman Mao did not always distinguish between guilt and innocence when rooting out opponents and conspirators. Cheng Ching suddenly grew fearful for the safety of his parents.

As if reading the younger man's thoughts, General Yeh murmured: "General Peng was the most upright man in the Politburo. You don't know him as I do. He thought only of the good of the country. It had been a real honour to serve under him. How can a man be declared an 'anti-Party' plotter and thrown into prison for speaking the truth? He's sick and they're denying him medicine. That's not right. I can't stand idly by!"

"What are you thinking?" Cheng Ching asked. The hairs on the back of his neck itched with alarm.

General Yeh tightened his grip on Cheng Ching's arm. "Ah Ching, I've put you on the spot. Forgive me. Your father and I have risked our lives many times for the dreams we've believed in. You've risked yours too. If a man can no longer live honourably, then it's time to die honourably. I can't bear to see the progress so many have paid for turn to dust in the clutches of rascals and vultures. Our country is spinning into chaos. We must stop it. Will you join me?"

Cheng Ching shivered involuntarily. It was as if he were back in the frozen trenches of Korea. Whatever he decided, lives would be at stake. Not only the General's and his own, but also those of his parents. There would be bloodbaths and he might have to kill again, in the name of patriotism or duty or Party unity. Had he the stomach for it after so many years of pushing paper in secret offices? He fingered the scar on his right cheek.

"If you're concerned, it's best you denounce me while there's still time," General Yeh continued. "Our families are too closely linked. If you won't join me, you'll have to distance yourself, for the sake of your family."

"Erh Fu, I could never denounce you! You and my father were close comrades in arms. You were one of my commanding officers in Korea and have now adopted me as a son. How can I do anything but side with you, come what may? I haven't been blind during my time in the General Office. I've seen the rot setting in. There was a time, wasn't there, when the revolution really gave the nation hope? We served the common people. We got rid of many of the old evils. Everybody became so honest no one needed to lock their homes at night. All that is now being lost."

The General nodded. His angular features tightened with bitterness. "During the darkest days in our history, under the most despotic emperors, we still had a Censorate to criticise bad policies and give voice to the dissatisfactions of the people. Now we've developed a new class of professional slaves under a feudal-fascist dictatorship, with everyone living in fear."

"That's the Chairman's doing!" Cheng Ching said, vehemently. "I've waited for other leaders to step in after Chairman Liu, but no one did. Chairman Liu's death in disgrace is also our disgrace."

"Too many at the top have kept silent. They trembled as they watched old comrades destroyed. The young, the conscience of our Party and the hope of our country, were executed too. Have you heard of a woman Party member named Chang Chi-hsin, who served in Shenyang in Liaoning Province?"

"Yes, I came across her dossier in the General Office. She was what every upright Communist ought to be. She defended the reputations of General Peng and Chairman Liu on the facts of their cases. But they arrested her. In spite of legal assessors twice finding her without guilt in any crime, she was sentenced to an indefinite term of imprisonment."

"She's been inside since 1970 and repeatedly tortured. Yet she's remained defiant, claiming she was only exercising her right of free speech as a Party member. She argued that if Party members could not speak freely, then who could? There've been a number of public protests in Liaoning in her support, but no one seems to have the courage to set her free. It's a shameful case, a national disgrace! You know who's in charge of Liaoning, don't you?"

"The Chairman's nephew."

"My sources tell me he'll have her executed as a warning to others who defy him."

"That's appalling!"

"I'm afraid so. Unfortunately, I'm helpless to do anything. That is why we must end this chaos as soon as possible."

The two men strolled for a while in silence.

"Erh Fu, I don't think I've ever told you how Chairman Mao came to be my benefactor. By uttering a few words he opened the way for me in the Party. I gained admission to the provincial and national Party colleges and rose in the Party like a meteor, some said. Everybody thought I had been handpicked. Within the General Office I'm still perceived as being unquestioningly loyal to the Chairman. I'm deferred to for that reason. Yet I've spoken with him only once in my life. Isn't that laughable?"

"That's good," the General said. "A Maoist reputation is an asset these days. You'll be more useful for that."

"Actually, I've come to loathe him even as I read his instructions and relay his directives. What have the dead of the Long March died for? Or those who threw their lives away in Korea? What of the millions killed during the rectification campaigns? How many more people must die before our leaders come to their senses? Seeing Nixon in the heart of Peking was an abomination. Seeing him embraced by the Chairman was the last straw. That made a mockery of all our principles."

Cheng Ching's outburst took him back momentarily to the fighting trenches of Korea, to the night patrols with Old Tung, Mad Fan, Koo, Lai and the rest of them. They had laid down their lives. For what? For a vision that the survivors were honour-bound to deliver. Ying, too, had sacrificed herself for that same vision. He had manufactured a pretext to study her Party dossier. She was married now, to some junior cadre in a backwater in Kansu. She has a son and was still working as a nurse. What a waste! His heart ached over what might have been.

He had failed them all, he bitterly rebuked himself. He had settled for being a paper-pusher in the General Office. All at once he wanted to be rid of his guilt, his years of complicity, his cowardly servitude. He looked at the moon. It seemed to shine as brightly as a clear conscience. "I'm with you," he declared.

"Good," General Yeh said. "But don't be too hard on the Chairman. Don't forget, his policies had been endorsed by the Politburo and the Party. Politburo members might occasionally suffer from a loss of nerve, but no one can question the legitimacy of Party decisions. The Chairman has grown old and fallen prey to manipulators. If he had died fifteen years ago, he would have gone down as one of the greatest Chinese leaders. As it is, his reputation and achievements are being tarnished."

"It would have been better if he had died in 1954."

"1954? Why '54?"

"That was the year I met him. I stood before him then, and I was filled with wonder. It was a golden moment. He seemed like a hero, a god, full of charm and kindness. I would have given my life for him if he had asked. Though he extended me a helping hand, he also exploited a girl I loved to satisfy his own lust. When he tired of her, he married her off to some lowly cadre. I did not discover till long after I had joined the General Office what a womaniser the Chairman was. I can never forgive him."

"Set personal feelings aside. There's much to do. I want you to keep your eyes and ears open in the General Office. Identify those who might be sympathetic to our cause. But make no contact. Just let me have the names and I'll arrange the rest. Be careful. I'm not yet sure where the sympathies of your Director lie. Don't forget he used to be the Chairman's bodyguard and is still a big player in the Cultural Revolution. I also want you to study all the files and dossiers on Hong Kong you can lay your hands on. If we are successful, chances are you'll have to go there."

"Hong Kong? What can I do in that den of corruption?"

"Where, except in a den of corruption, can unobtainable things be obtained? The military has been starved of modern weaponry. It has been seriously demoralized by the Lin Piao affair and the arrest of a number of its senior officers. We have to keep the Liberation Army on side. The Chairman's concepts of warfare are outmoded. He hadn't seen at first hand what happened in Korea nor learnt the lessons of our conflict with India. He still thinks wars can be won by raw human courage. That plays into the hands of our enemies."

Cheng Ching nodded in agreement with the General's analysis.

"Since Korea, the West has cut us off from high technology. Even telecommunication products and computers are embargoed, let alone nuclear and space technology. The excuse is that we're harbouring aggressive intentions when it is the Americans and the British who have bases all over the world! We must get better equipment to protect our country. That means buying or stealing whatever we can. Gyroscopes, tracking radar, mainframe computers, guidance systems, production equipment for liquid-fuel missile engines, manuals, maintenance reports, malfunction investigations, everything."

"The Americans'll kick up a fuss once they find out," Cheng Ching said. "They're screaming enough already about infringements of copyright and breaches of intellectual property laws."

"Americans! What gall! When they were establishing their country they were the most unscrupulous stealers of other people's land and ideas. Now they talk of protecting intellectual property. Bah! The fruits of the human intellect should be enjoyed by all. We invented paper, matches, printing, gunpowder, the magnetic compass, the seismograph, the decarburization of cast iron, the making of silk.

"Who has ever paid us a single fen for their use? Even now, others want to learn about herbal medicine and acupuncture from us. We do not charge them. I feel no qualms over taking what we need from the Americans. The trick is not to create waves. Or at least, waves too obviously made by us. It's not for nothing that the Americans keep in Hong Kong their largest consulate in the world."

"Haven't we been getting what we want out of Hong Kong?"

"We have. But not enough. The man there at the moment doesn't carry sufficient clout within the Party. Also he's not smart enough to handle the Americans and his local colleagues. The jockeying for position in Hong Kong is every bit as complex as it is here. You've got the Party's Central-South Regional organisation to contend with. Then there are the ministries for foreign, financial and economic affairs. Add in the Bank of China, various provincial hierarchies and the local Work Committee and the whole thing's a mess. Not sure whom to trust. Security becomes a headache. The putative local head, the Director of the New China News Agency, has mixed loyalties and is beholden to too many people. He's simply past his prime."

"I may not be able to do any better than the person there at the moment. I know nothing about Hong Kong."

"But you're much smarter than he is. Besides, you know the inner workings of the Party and enjoy a much higher standing. You'll be able to cut through the jurisdictional squabbles. I want to deal with somebody I can rely on. Your knowledge of English will also be an advantage. You can deal directly, without an interpreter, eliminating a potential source for leaks. I can place handpicked operatives at your disposal, as many as you want, both in Hong Kong and across the border in Kwangtung. They're highly trained and will execute orders without question.

"But we need to resolve problems here first. Bide our time. When power changes hands, it must be seen as smooth and bloodless. Old Ironsides, Commander of the Southern Military Region, is with us. When it's time for you to head south, I'll fix up the contact. You can go to him if you encounter local difficulties you can't handle."

"I understand," Cheng Ching said. "I'll be ready when you need me."

"Good. Now let's go in and see what's for dinner."

Chance encounter

APRIL 1974

26

Lucille was crossing the lobby of the Siam Inter-Continental when she heard a voice calling her. She turned abruptly, in a semi-pirouette, to find Sebastian Baxingdale approaching with a smile.

"Small world," Baxingdale said, removing a pair of dark glasses. His grey eyes sparkled with pleasure. "You're here with your famous husband no doubt, buying up another chunk of the Thai economy?" In his khaki safari suit he looked like some great white hunter from a bygone era.

"Actually my husband's in Zurich," Lucille replied cheerfully, "buying up a chunk of something else. With the stock market going great guns in Hong Kong I hardly see him."

"Then you must be playing hookey from Madam Shek. That's very naughty!"

"What about you? The pot calling the kettle black!"

"I'm different. I'm on duty."

"Well, I'm off duty. My son's at a Boy Scout camp for a week. So I'm off to Phuket tomorrow, to soak up a bit of sun and solitude."

"Sounds ominous."

"What? The sun, the solitude or the Boy Scout camp?"

Baxingdale chuckled. "Sorry, just being facetious."

"No need to apologise. Why are you here? What kind of story are you working on?"

"Trying to find out what's going on in Cambodia. There are rumours of Khmer Rouge massacres in the civil war. I'm off to Aranyaprathet tomorrow, to try and get in. Legally if possible, via Poipet. Otherwise, through the jungle. I have to finalize travel arrangements and pick up equipment."

"Isn't that rather dangerous, entering a country through the back door? Illegal too, I imagine."

"No alternative, I'm afraid. Got to get at the truth. Verifying misfortunes happens to be how I earn my living."

"Poor man! Do all journalists risk life and limb that way?"

Baxingdale smiled. "I'd like to think at least a few do. Look, what are you doing for dinner tonight? I can expound on professional ethics and sacrifices over a meal."

Lucille hesitated. She had not seen him for more than a year after the Red Cross Ball, till she bumped into him as she was leaving Madam Shek's after her Chinese lesson. She learnt then he was also taking lessons and she had admired him for making the effort. She now remembered how catty Phoebe Knight had been at the ball and felt mischievous. Having dinner with him would irritate Phoebe no end. But aloud she said: "I'm not sure that's a very good idea. People might talk."

"Oh, come on! This is Bangkok. Who's to know? It's not as if we were having a clandestine affair. Only dinner. It may be my last supper. I might get blown up by a land mine tomorrow. Or shot. Would you deny a condemned man his final wish? Besides, I can take you to the best French restaurant east of Marseilles."

"In Bangkok? That I've got to experience!"

"Good. See you in the lobby at seven. You were on your way out. Can I give you a lift?"

"No, thanks. I was just going to walk down the street to look for presents. Women have to do such things, you know."

"Okay, see you later."

The moment Baxingdale disappeared Lucille regretted her decision. She remembered dropping her guard the evening of the ball. His self-assured presence, his deep baritone voice, had touched her. She had long associated that kind of voice with manliness. As a teenager she had fantasized over being serenaded, just like in the movies. After a few drinks she might get carried away again. She warned herself to be vigilant as she stepped outside the hotel.

The morning air was warm and close. She strolled in the direction of the Erawan Shrine. Located on a small plot at the corner of a busy intersection, it was dedicated to a local deity with four faces. She had been too embarrassed to tell Baxingdale where she was heading.

The deity commanded a big reputation among Hong Kong's society ladies. Many made frequent pilgrimages to Bangkok, claiming the deity could grant wishes if convinced of a person's sincerity. They talked about its powers in confidential whispers during shopping sprees and afternoon tea parties. They exchanged stories of how so-and-so had secured a late pregnancy or how a certain woman had got her husband's mistress to disappear after making offerings at the shrine.

Stories abounded about the deity's supernatural powers. Some said it had been born out of a golden egg from heaven and was an embodiment of all virtue, moral excellence, kindness and compassion. Others said it had been sired by a sacred dragon with seven claws and came into being from lotuses spewed from the dragon's mouth.

Lucille was half-sceptical about such tales. But then, religions were full of strange beliefs. Serenity had told her of great Buddhist masters imposing koans or nonsensical tasks upon their disciples, like hearing the sound of a one-handed clap or seeing their original faces before they were born. She did not know whether the deity figured in the Buddhist pantheon. Serenity undoubtedly would. But, if she had asked before coming to Bangkok, her mother-in-law would certainly guess what was in her heart.

On arrival at the shrine, Lucille found a small gathering of supplicants making offerings. The aroma of incense hung in the air. The golden deity with four faces was enthroned beneath a golden canopy decorated with mosaics in glittering reds, greens and yellows and enclosed within steel railings. Vendors hovered, offering sets of candles, joss sticks and garlands of flowers at fancy prices. Four sets were required because supplications were supposed to be made in front of each face, moving progressively to the left.

The moment Lucille arrived, vendors milled around her, importuning in high-pitched Thai voices. Lucille hesitated. This was absurd, she thought. How could she have used taking the sun in Phuket as an alibi for this silly venture? She could not be *that* desperate! How could a modern, educated woman like her seek divine intervention from some dubious god? Yet there remained at the back of her mind an irrational hope, as tenacious as the hopes of others for the winning numbers in a ten-million-to-one lottery draw.

The vendors continued to press around her. She shook her

head and smiled defensively. Gradually they peeled off in search of more promising customers, all except for a teenage girl with a harelip, who persisted with an awkward grin. In the end Lucille felt sorry for her and bought a set of offerings.

No harm done, she thought, as she followed the routine. She lit candles and joss sticks before each of the four faces and hung the garlands on the metal railings. She repeated her secret wish for freedom together with her son and bowed before each of the four faces, without entertaining any real hope of her wish being granted.

What was her wish anyway? Did freedom mean happiness? Did it mean being rid of her unloving husband? If so, that would involve leaving Hong Kong. Practical people associated with Xavier would cut her after the split and she would be left with no friends. And what about her son? She definitely would not leave without him and Xavier would never allow that. And Serenity. Could she abandon her after the kindnesses she had shown? All roads seemed to lead back to the same dead end.

When she returned to the hotel, she found a message from Baxingdale, suggesting casual clothes for the evening. She selected a white linen trouser suit with a halter top, which left her back and shoulders bare.

She turned up promptly in the lobby at seven, to find him already there, dressed in a black open-necked shirt and a pair of white trousers. His hand held a purple orchid.

"I'm glad you've dressed sensibly," Baxingdale said, proffering the orchid.

"Oh, you shouldn't have!" Lucille said. "It's gorgeous. Thank you very much."

"I'm sorry, I didn't mention that the restaurant has no air conditioning."

"I thought you said it was the best French restaurant east of Marseilles."

"I did. But 'best' doesn't mean most fancy or most modern."

"What's its name?"

"Hasn't got a name."

"You're pulling my leg!"

"A tempting prospect! But the restaurant really has no name. It's run by a Thai friend of mine, a linguist by the name of

Sunand, and most of the cooking is done by his wife, a Vietnamese. He used to be a language professor in one of the local universities but gave it up to work as an interpreter for the American military in Vietnam. The pay was better, you see. Then he saw what was going on and got sick of it. He came back here and opened a restaurant. He felt he had chosen the wrong side for the sake of money and that had stripped him of the moral authority to return to teaching. Come, I'll tell you the rest in the taxi."

During the ride Lucille learnt that the restaurant was located in a two-storeyed tenement in a depressing suburb. The top floor was used as a hostel for college girls of slender means studying in Bangkok. In return for free bed and board, Sunand expected them to work a certain number of hours each week waiting at table and serving as cleaners and dishwashers. It was his way of affording them the opportunity for practising English or French and gaining an insight into foreign behaviour. The restaurant was patronized mainly by academics, journalists, junior diplomats and staff from the United Nations Economic Commission for Asia and the Far East. Sunand and his wife lived in a bungalow in the compound in the rear.

When they arrived, Lucille found a deep, open-fronted establishment with about a dozen tables covered with plastic tablecloths in red and white checks. Most of the tables were already occupied. Overhead a number of electric fans whirled, wafting out smells of cooking onto the pavement.

"See the number on the building?" Baxingdale said, pointing to a narrow, six-inch-long metal plaque nailed above the centre of the wide entrance. "That's the house number. Regulars just call it 178."

A small, rotund man wearing a pair of black-rimmed glasses at once rushed forward to greet them. "Ah, my English friend, it is good to see you again," he said, in slightly stilted English. "What brings you to my poor country this time?"

"A secret mission," Baxingdale replied, hugging him like a long lost friend, at the same time waving to a couple of diners.

"Ah, another exposé!" Sunand said, in his excitable voice. "But bringing along such a charming lady? Can't be all work."

"Sunand, this is a friend from Hong Kong, Lucille Chu.

Chance placed us in the same hotel. I've told her this is the best French restaurant east of Marseilles. So don't make a liar out of me."

Sunand placed his palms together in a traditional Thai greeting. "My English friend is lavish with praises. My humble establishment is honoured and will do its utmost. Such a charming lady deserves the best table in the house, away from both the kitchen in the back and the pavement at the front, but close to a window with a capricious breeze."

On the way to their table, Baxingdale shook hands with a suave dark-skinned man. He did not effect introductions.

"Indonesian attaché. A genial rogue. Let me explain Sunand's regime. There's no menu. You can always get onion soup or a salad for starters. The daily dishes are written on the blackboard on the wall. There's only red or white house wine, both very good. That's it. No frills."

Lucille looked over at the blackboard. The choices were coq au vin, lapin provençale and bouillabaisse.

"I'll have the chicken and a glass of red wine, please. No starter," she said, when Sunand came to take their orders.

"Same for me."

"You seem quite at home here," Lucille said, after their drinks had been served.

"It's the itinerant life. One has to develop friendships and safe corners like commercial travellers do. I used to nip over here quite a lot when I was covering Vietnam."

"The customers are mostly foreigners. Don't the Thais like French food?"

"They do, but most are too poor to afford Sunand's fare, even at his modest prices. The rich prefer their meals in more sumptuous surroundings, with waitresses serving them on their knees."

They chatted like old friends during the meal. The coq au vin was excellent, as was the wine. Sunand came by occasionally to enquire if everything was to their liking. As the evening proceeded, the wine took its effect. They began telling each other about their childhoods and their families and their likes and dislikes.

"You know, I can't really believe I'm having dinner alone in a strange town with the wife of one of the most powerful tycoons in the Far East," Baxingdale said, after tartine and coffee had been served. "Do you remember when I bumped into you at Madam Shek's? I wanted to invite you for a cup of tea then but I didn't dare."

"Why not?"

"I didn't want anything bad to happen to you."

"How could anything bad happen to me through having a cup of tea with you?"

"I jinx women, I'm afraid. They get blown up or sent to labour camps for exchanging a few words with me."

"Oh dear, you sound as if you head an anti-feminist terror group! What of Phoebe Knight? Has anything bad happened to her?"

"She's had to settle for less than what she wanted."

"Don't we all?"

Lucille gazed into Baxingdale's grey eyes and saw for the first time how much sadness they contained. He appeared slightly lost and yet the eyes were so appealing that she wanted to comfort him. But she simply couldn't find the words. So she lapsed into silence.

"Hey, do you like jazz?" Baxingdale asked, suddenly.

"Sure!"

"Great! I'll take you to the greatest jazz spot west of New Orleans."

Lucille laughed. "In Bangkok again? Has this one got a name or also only a number?"

"This one's got a name. It's called the Blue Note."

Baxingdale settled the bill and, after much ceremonious leave-taking, hailed a taxi for Patpong, the night-life district.

The Blue Note was a dim-lit establishment, with tables packed close together and a long bar. There was a good crowd and at the bar a couple of unescorted Asian girls were dispensing bold, inviting looks. Otherwise the customers were civilized and cosmopolitan. A four-member Filipino combo was playing and half a dozen couples were dancing on a circular space measuring little more than six feet in diameter.

They found a table close to the band.

"Miguel!" Baxingdale called, waving to the stocky, grizzled

saxophonist and bandleader. The man smiled and began playing with added verve.

Baxingdale suggested neat brandy as the mixed drinks at the club were unreliable. Lucille agreed. When the music ended, Baxingdale excused himself and went up to the band to exchange slaps on the back with Miguel before shaking hands with each of the other musicians. Animated conversation followed. After much to-ing and fro-ing, Miguel handed Baxingdale his saxophone and picked up the microphone.

"Ladies and gentlemen," Miguel boomed. "We have a special treat tonight. An English friend, a distinguished writer, is going to play jazz for us. No! No! Don't make for the exits! The idea is a little strange, yes. The combination of an Englishman and jazz is — how do you say it? — a bit odd? But this Englishman knows his jazz. Please give him a big hand, ladies and gentlemen, my friend Sebastian Baxingdale."

Baxingdale bowed, Miguel picked up a clarinet and the augmented band began playing *Blues In The Night*.

Lucille gave herself over to the music. Baxingdale was good. As she listened to him nursing melancholy notes out of the saxophone, she felt she had been lured inside his world of displaced people, exiled musicians, professors lost to teaching, women consigned to labour camps, journalists bearing witness for the world. All had been uprooted, no longer belonging anywhere, driven by economic winds and political tides. Baxingdale was comfortable among such people because he, too, was a displaced person. He had told her earlier in the evening that he had lost his country because he no longer approved of what it was turning into.

They were two of a kind, she and Baxingdale. An accident of birth had made her American but she did not belong there. Neither did she truly belong in Hong Kong. Her home was there, her son was there and the Chinese roots she sought were there. But it was also full of commercial vulgarity and phoney snobbery.

Ah Yuen, too, was only American through accident of birth. He did not belong across the Pacific. Hong Kong was his real home. Between the gentle teachings of Serenity and the demanding pedagogy of Tutor Tsim, between the heroics of Bruce Lee and the eccentricities of the Evergreen Tea House, he was already putting down roots. To take him to America would turn him into part of the next generation of displaced persons. Yet, if she could not take him with her, then what was the point of freedom at all? A great part of herself would be dead.

Baxingdale's saxophone number finished to thunderous applause. He returned to the table, smiling broadly and sweating a little. "Hope I haven't made a complete ass of myself. It's been a long time since I played with Miguel and his boys. It felt really good."

"You *were* really good," Lucille said. "A man of many talents, I see. What got you into jazz? Not a particularly British thing, is it?"

"Jazz is more international and cross-cultural than most realize. Look at what's just been produced by the coming together of an Englishman and four Filipinos. Look at the people here, from all corners of the earth, trying to make sense of it. It's not just music. It's music, moods, colours, experiences, dreams, subversions, all absorbed and re-arranged, synthesized, perfected into a new reality, a fresh statement, a challenging point of view. It's marvellous. It's like encountering a new love in an unlikely place."

"Wow!" Lucille gasped.

They sipped their brandies and gave themselves over to the mood and the music. Suddenly, an incongruity crept across Lucille's mind. How could Sebastian be so carefree on the eve of risking his life for a horror story? Had he become so reconciled to the notion of death? Had he nothing he wanted to live for? A mixture of concern and pity welled inside her. She wanted to tell him to be careful, but that would sound banal.

Just then, the band began playing the same Nat King Cole ballad they had danced to at the Red Cross Ball.

"They're playing our song," Baxingdale said. "Shall we?"

Lucille hesitated. She knew, even before his hand touched her bare back, that she was about to find an unlikely love in an unlikely place.

Revelations

27

"You're early tonight," Lucille said, indifferently, when Xavier strode into their bedroom. "Mother's had another attack."

"No worse than usual, I hope?" Xavier said, as he undid his tie. He barely looked at his wife while changing out of his business suit.

"Didn't appear too serious. She seems to have something on her mind, though. I've put her to bed."

Xavier nodded and went into the bathroom. He took a quick shower and came out in silk pyjamas and dressing gown. "I'll look in. I'm early enough."

"That should make a change."

Xavier was annoyed by Lucille's jibe. Why couldn't she understand what he was trying to achieve? Why couldn't she be like other wives and occupy herself with shopping or mah jong or raising Ah Yuen? Why demand constant attention when he was already fully extended? He felt too tired for an argument.

He made for his mother's suite. The voice in answer to his knock sounded a trifle wan. It occurred to him suddenly that he had not ventured inside her bedroom since leaving for Princeton. Almost twenty years!

The room was unchanged from his boyhood, except for a set of bookshelves holding volumes displaced from his father's study. In his own mind the removal of those books was justified. Seeing them in his mother's room, however, struck him as a rebuke.

Apart from that, the two elegantly carved bedside tables were littered as usual. Recent additions included the miniature pine from his father's study and some bottles of enteric coated aspirin and nitrate pills. The absence of clock and radio underlined his mother's removal of the constraints of time and worldly affairs. Yet, on a stand in the alcove where he used to take meals, there rested an old black Bakelite telephone whose purpose he had never managed to figure out. He couldn't remember ever hearing it ring or seeing his mother use it.

His mother, dressed in white cotton pyjamas, was propped up against a stack of pillows. She was reading the *Lotus Sutra*, her tousled hair spread across her shoulders. That unfamiliar sight, together with her reading glasses, made her appear aged, in spite of her smooth and translucent skin. A thin camel-hair blanket protected the lower part of her body from the air conditioning.

He remembered being told that his mother's double bed, with its elaborately carved headboard, once had a canopy. That had been removed, as had its spring mattress, to leave only wooden boards covered by a thin rush mat. It must be damnably uncomfortable sleeping that way. Something to do with her ascetic leanings, he supposed.

"Mother, how are you? Lucille said you had an attack."

Serenity put down the scripture and peered over the top of her half-moon glasses. "Ah Seng, what a surprise. Nothing serious. Dr. Chow's pills really do work. Lucille's been fussing as if I were an invalid. What about you? You're seldom back so early. Something the matter?"

"A dinner was scrubbed. Plane bringing the guest of honour got delayed."

"His misfortune, my gain," Serenity said, fingering a string of wooden prayer beads.

"What brought on your attack? Have you been over-tiring yourself?"

"No. I only chased Ah Yuen around the garden a bit."

"You shouldn't have done that! He's no longer a toddler. He's almost twelve. How can you keep up with him? Dr. Chow warned that angina could be brought on by exertion. You should see a specialist, take some tests. Dr. Chow says you've refused. Why?"

"Dr. Chow worries too much. I don't want a stranger poking around my body at this stage in life."

"Dr. Chow's only a family doctor and you're getting on. You can't be too careful."

"Death is but a transition. It comes to us all. If my next existence beckons, I'm ready."

"No use rushing out to meet it, for heaven's sake! Why suffer if medical science can bring relief? If you don't trust local experts, go to the Stanford Medical Centre or Johns Hopkins.

Dr. Chow and Lucille can go along to make you feel more at home. We just want you to get better."

"I know precisely what'll make me better."

"What?"

"Seeing more of you and having more grandchildren running around. Lucille wants that too."

"Well, I don't!" Xavier sat down on the bed beside his mother. His body sagged. "I'm sorry, Mother. Please try to understand. What has Lucille produced except a sickly child? I can't stand any more like that. I'm away half the time, London, Zurich, New York, making deals, taking care of business. A man shouldn't have to come home and worry about sick children. He should be enjoying such time as he can devote to them. I never got much time from Father, even thought I wasn't sickly. I'm much busier than Father ever was. I can't bear a few more like Ah Yuen."

"Oh, Ah Seng, Ah Yuen suffers from ill health. There is no reason for other children to be the same. Besides, how much time does it take to lunch at the Evergreen with Ah Yuen once in a while? You say your father never gave you enough time, but did you not feel his love for you?"

Xavier laughed. "His love for me? He didn't love me. If he had he wouldn't have done his utmost to keep me out of Gold Star. About the only time we had some real conversations was during those few days in Taiwan."

"He was trying to protect you."

"How convenient! Well, I don't have time for sick children. Ah Yuen was an accident, if you must know."

"An accident! He's such a marvellous boy. You should treasure him and be proud of him."

"Mother, I've told you I haven't got time. I'm turning Gold Star into a world-class company."

"And that's more important than raising your own flesh and blood? If you think so, you're chasing an illusion. To climb high is to risk a big fall."

"No danger of that, Mother. I'm in total control."

Serenity clutched her chest and winced with pain. She gasped. The prayer beads fell from her hand as she reached vainly for her pills.

Xavier jumped to his feet, unscrewed the bottle of nitrate

pills and poured a number onto his palm. Serenity helped herself. He held the glass of water as she swallowed the pills. "I'll send for Dr. Chow," he said.

Serenity raised a hand to deter him. She fell back against the pillows, closed her eyes and breathed deeply for a while.

"Mother, you can't go on like this."

Serenity did not reply. She continued to breathe quietly. After a few moments she retrieved her prayer beads and offered a thin smile. "I'm all right," she said. "It passes quickly."

Xavier sat down again on the bed. After a moment of silence Serenity murmured: "You're rising in the world and that incites envy. There are uncomfortable things you should know."

"Can't be very important or juicy. Father's been dead eleven years and nobody's approached me for hush money yet."

Serenity sighed. A look of sadness entered her eyes. "I keep postponing this. Now it's time. Before I begin, I want you to remember, no matter what, that your father was a good man, one filled with human kindness. He might have appeared on top of the world to others, but inside he was greatly tormented."

"All right. Give me the inside dope. Maybe I can get to understand him better."

"Your father had no choice with his life. Your grandfather sent him here from Canton to start a branch of the family business, because he was the only one who knew English. The family required him to buy a shop building and a warehouse, both of which he found. The properties were registered in his name for convenience.

"In those days there were lots of private clubs in the Western District, not far from Hollywood Road where the shop was. Merchants used to congregate there, both for pleasure and for business contacts. Your father went, too. Those clubs fell out of fashion after the war, however, and now they have virtually disappeared.

"They were called clubs because the British made them register as such to disguise the fact that they were high-class houses of pleasure. Such places had long been part of Chinese life. There used to be celebrated ones in Yangchow and Soochow, staffed by state courtesans accomplished in music, literature and the arts. Scholars, merchants and officials frequented them.

"They apprenticed young girls bought from poor families. For most, life in those places was infinitely preferable to poverty at home. Before reaching a suitable age, they would be used for fetching tea, preparing wash basins for guests, and the like. If they displayed talents, these would be cultivated and they would be allowed to entertain customers with song, dance or conversation.

"Your father came across a sixteen-year-old girl at one of the clubs. She was known as a pei-pa girl because she played the mandolin and could sing. The girl was also talented in other ways. She could match couplets and hold her own in discussing calligraphy, painting and literature. Your father took an instant liking to her and soon spurned the working courtesans in favour of conversation with her."

"Sounds like something out of *True Romance*," Xavier said, smiling, listening to what he regarded as the inconsequential peccadilloes of any average businessman.

Serenity continued without heeding the remark. "The club owner saw at once that he had a love-smitten young man on the hook. He took full advantage. He hinted that the girl had reached sixteen and the honour of deflowering her would soon fall to the highest bidder. Your father was beside himself. He wanted to rescue the girl, to buy her freedom.

"By then, the girl had also developed an affection for your father. She had never met a man so scholarly and handsome. She fell hopelessly in love. She was, of course, not a virgin, having already been palmed off as one on half a dozen occasions. The girl tried to warn your father by dropping hints. But the prospects of freedom and of being with the man she loved proved too tempting for her to be more specific.

"The Sino-Japanese War was then intensifying. The Japanese had invaded South China and captured Canton. Your grandfather and his family fled to Szechuan. Contact was lost. Your father could neither explain the situation nor ask for money. When the club owner intimated that he was about to decide on offers, your father took matters into his own hands. He sold the shop building and paid what was demanded for the girl's freedom, thinking he could square things later."

Serenity paused and reached for her cup of tea.

As she sipped, Xavier said: "So Father lifted some family silver to blow on a bit of fluff. That sort of thing hardly merits a raised eyebrow nowadays. Every red-blooded young man goes around sowing wild oats at some stage."

Serenity heaved another sigh. "It took some time for your father to re-establish contact. Then catastrophe. Far from considering the deed an act of kindness, your grandfather berated your father for becoming a thief and an embezzler. To him, the Chu name had been sullied. He threw your father out and struck his name from family records. Family members were forbidden contact with him.

"Your father was devastated. Family ties had always been important to him. He found himself adrift in a strange town, with no means of support. He settled for odd jobs and took temporary shelter with the girl in the warehouse, but your grandfather soon sent agents to take possession. Your father and the girl found themselves on the streets. The world he had previously known suddenly ceased to exist. His family was gone, he was penniless and the clouds of war continued to gather."

"What happened to the girl? Did she dump him when she discovered he was broke?"

"She wanted to go back to her former life but your father would not hear of it. Then the girl got pregnant. They married and she bore him a son."

After the briefest of moments, Xavier cried: "No! Not you! You're not telling me you used to be a... ?"

"A courtesan?" Serenity answered blandly. "What can I say?"

"How can this be!" He rose from the bed and stared at his mother in disbelief. The control that earned admiration in boardrooms around the world deserted him. The images he had built up of his mother suddenly shattered and her face became too shameful to gaze upon. He felt soiled, betrayed.

Why had he been saddled with such a curse? The only two women he had ever loved had both turned out to be whores. What had he done to deserve such a fate? He stood in a daze. His thoughts went back to the time when he had caught his mother in tears hugging an old pei-pa. The tensions he had previously detected between his parents now found an explanation.

Serenity watched her son in silence, her fingers counting off the beads on her rosary.

"Who else knows about this?" Xavier demanded.

"What does it matter?"

"Of course it matters! I'll be at the mercy of everyone who knows." His voice turned shrill. "They'll have the power to destroy my reputation, can't you understand? I have to seal lips. Who are they?"

Serenity remained composed. "I don't know. Many of those connected with the club are now dead and gone. Some of the Evergreens know. Uncle Yue certainly knows, but he has treated me with consideration all along. That's why he and your father became such firm friends. Why should you be fearful or ashamed of the truth? I'm not. I was what I was. Now I'm another self. When your father was prominent, there was no gossip about our private lives. No one has approached you for hush money, as you've said. Why should anyone dig up the past now, unless someone feels grievously wronged in some way?"

Xavier reflected upon his mother's words and became calmer. "You're right, I suppose," he said. "But it's vicious out there. It's best to be careful. The press is always digging for dirt. Just look at the stories about the women in Father's life."

"There was never a shred of truth to any of them."

"Come on, Mother! Let's face up to it. Where there's smoke there has to be a little fire. Might as well tell me, now that I know something about your relationships. Might as well know about other scandals and infidelities so that I can be prepared."

Serenity shook her head, sighing again. "You've misunderstood badly. Stories of your father's involvement with actresses and singers were without foundation. Gold Star was investing in the entertainment business, financing films, concerts and cabaret acts. How could he have avoided mixing with such people? We loved each other as deeply as any two people could possibly love. We understood each other's needs, shared each other's pain. We spoke on the telephone every day and you stood at the heart of many of our discussions."

"Me again?"

"Yes. Soon after you were born, the Japanese occupied Hong Kong. Food became tightly rationed. There was never enough to eat. The Japs set up a rationing system that required hours of queuing for pathetic amounts of every necessity."

"Yes, Father told me."

"We had no money. We only had you. When an acquaintance proposed smuggling in food from China, your father joined in. The food he brought back kept us alive. During one expedition, their fishing boat was attacked by pirates. Your father and his companions fought them off. In the process your father killed one of the pirates."

"Father told me he just knocked some attackers into the sea."

"He might have knocked some into the sea as well, but he certainly killed one of them. He smashed the man's skull."

"He had a right to protect his property."

Serenity took another sip of water. "Between smuggler and pirate, who occupies the higher moral ground? Your father always considered himself a man of education, a moral and decent man. Killing someone troubled him, particularly when he felt no qualm or hesitation at the time. He confessed actual exhilaration.

"He brooded over this, became increasingly at war with himself. Couldn't resolve the darkness eating into him. Logic and the metaphysical systems he had studied were of no help. He didn't realize that a mind not free to perceive the illogical and the senseless is divided against itself. He had not yet learnt the need to rid himself of the intellectual biases befogging simple truths. It was... "

"You've just told me Father was an embezzler, a smuggler and a killer and that you used to work as... , I mean, in a house of pleasure," Xavier interrupted. "Spare me the religion, for heaven's sake! Just tell me straight what happened next."

"Ah Seng, if you want to hear the truth, you'll have to let me tell it my way," Serenity said, still fingering her prayer beads.

Xavier sat down on his mother's bed again and clasped his head in his hands. "All right. I'll try not to interrupt."

Serenity sighed once more. "I knew what was happening, but couldn't help feeling glad I had food to feed you. I tried to ease my own conscience by becoming a vegetarian and by passing some food to starving neighbours, like the family of Dr. Chow. The food saved them and he has felt beholden to us ever since."

Xavier tightened his grip on his head. So Dr. Chow knew as well. Thankfully, he was old and inoffensive and out of the business loop.

"Your father and his companions acquired a great many properties during the final year of the Japanese occupation," Serenity continued. "One of the first things your father did after the war was to repay your grandfather ten times over for the shop. But your grandfather was unforgiving. He refused the money. Just left it in the bank. Your father wrote to his brothers and sisters but none of them replied.

"When this house was built, a Meditation Room was provided for me. I tried to get your father to become a Buddhist, so that we could find our way out of our misery together, but he was too bound by logic and science, by the established values of his upbringing.

"The post-war recovery was a boon to your father and his friends. Virtually everything they touched turned into wealth. Their reputation grew. Gold Star became a household name. But what was the use of wealth? Deep inside he was utterly miserable."

As Xavier listened to his mother's calm and measured tone, he felt a growing apprehension. It was as if his mother's very calmness presaged another terrible revelation.

He heard her tell of the Communists' proclamation of a new government in China in October 1949, of their consolidation of power and their bloody campaigns to root out capitalists and other opponents. His grandfather, a landowner and a prominent supporter of the Kuomintang, was naturally targeted. His father was deeply concerned and the lack of news only made matters worse. It took some time for the full awfulness to filter through. It appeared the Communists, having discovered the money remitted to his grandfather, had accused him of being in league with imperialists. His grandfather denied the charge and disclaimed any knowledge of who might have remitted the money to him.

The Communists did not believe him and apparently made him kneel on broken glass to force a confession. He remained silent, however. After two days, the Communists brought out his wife and made her kneel beside him. She could not bear the pain. The grandfather put an arm around her, picked up a piece of glass and cut her throat. Then he did the same to himself.

Xavier raised his head in shock. "Why have you hidden this from me for so long?"

Serenity reached for Xavier's hand. Tears rolled down her cheeks. "We wanted to spare you. You were only a boy then."

Xavier allowed his mother to hold his hand. His spectacles had misted over and he removed them with his free hand to rub his eyes. The death of his grandparents was an abstraction. He had never known them. Yet he was being tarnished by the manner of their passing. What was the use of his parents' emphasis on the importance of the family when it was a source of so much embarrassment and shame? His grandfather took lives too, his grandmother's and his own. His own reputation was now being undermined. A total stranger could ruin him with a few carefully chosen words. The son of a killer and a whore. The grandson of a murderer and a suicide. Gossip would spread like wildfire. Competitors and even associates would snigger behind his back. Could he ever hold his head high again? It was intolerable! It was so utterly unfair!

He heard his mother speaking again.

"Your father was devastated. He felt personally responsible for the deaths of his parents. He came close to taking his own life. I warned him I would follow. That stayed his hand. The weight of guilt crushed him. I know, because I felt guilty too. The entire disaster could be traced back to me. If I had not fallen in love, if I had not hidden the fact I was damaged goods, if I had not married and brought you into the world, your father would not have been in such a mess. He might have escaped the Japanese occupation, rejoined his family and fled before the Communists came.

"I felt walled in, that it was all karma, inescapable. I began pondering about sin, retribution, atonement and redemption. I turned to Buddhism. Increasingly it came to me that I should atone, for sins I had committed knowingly or unknowingly, in this or in some other existence. By so doing I hoped your father might be spared. I tried to identify a penance to show my sincerity. I eventually settled upon a vow of chastity.

"I told your father I wanted to enter a nunnery. But there

was you. You needed a mother. Yet, if I did not go off somewhere, I couldn't fulfil my vow. I loved your father. If he so much as touched or embraced me, my resolve would melt. Love and passion would rule again and I would never find redemption. Your father was not a Buddhist but he understood. He was very clever, however. He said he wanted to suffer too. He argued that staying with him in the same house would make for a more severe penance."

As Xavier listened, he began to understand the relationship between his parents. Why could he not love like that? Fei-Fei was a vanished dream. As for Lucille, for all her physical attractiveness, he never really took to her. Perhaps deep down he held it against her for not producing a strong and worthy son.

His mother's voice, now sounding weary, cut into his reflections. "Your father had to contend with other deaths, too," she said. "Workmen died at Gold Star construction sites because contractors did not take proper safety precautions. An aged couple committed suicide because their grocery store had been driven out of business by a Gold Star supermarket. Such disasters added to your father's distress. He could hardly wait to quit commercial life.

"He discussed it with his closest friends, but they needed him to remain part of their group. Their earlier successes had caused too many people to invest in their enterprises. They had wider responsibilities. Disengagement was no easy task. They began, however, to channel some of their money into non-commercial projects, such as maintaining the Evergreen Tea House.

"Your father saw the dilemma of his friends. Nonetheless he began a gradual withdrawal. He assigned his Gold Star income to me, to spend on charities of my choice, and left your upbringing almost entirely in my hands. He hoped I could influence you away from the life he found himself trapped in. I tried my best but nothing I did could deflect you. When you began to work on Wall Street and even changed your name, we knew we had lost. Your father lost heart and began losing his will to live."

Xavier withdrew his hand sharply from his mother's and jumped up again. "Oh, no, you don't!" he cried. "You're not going to burden me with guilt! I'm not going to carry the can for Father's death."

"No one's blaming you. The coroner said it was an accident."

"That's *damned* clever! But it won't work! You knew all along it wasn't an accident, didn't you? What did he do? Did he telephone you in advance? Tell you to hand me his precious Piaget watch?"

Serenity bowed her head and made no reply. More tears rolled down her cheeks.

"If Father feels guilty over making too much money, that's his problem. I don't feel any guilt. I'm proud of what I've achieved. When I go around the world, I don't find any tycoon worked up because he's getting too rich."

"I'm sorry, Ah Seng. It seems I've failed both you and your father."

"Don't feel badly, Mother," Xavier said, with a bitter smile. "You did your best. It's just that I don't buy into that do-gooder stuff. Those who dream of an ideal world seem to forget that it is people like me who produce the money to sustain and feed the hungry millions. Without us, most of mankind would still be crawling around in the mud. We bring order, prosperity, opportunity, growth."

"Can you be so certain?"

"Yes, Mother. Goodnight. I'll get Dr. Chow to look in the morning."

Coup and countercoup

28

On September 9, 1976, Chairman Mao died.

For months the great and infallible leader of the Chinese Communist revolution had pondered his fate. Ten years before, he had presided over eight rallies at Tienanmen Square, each involving well over a million of his ecstatic Red Guards. The sunlight on his face, the shouted adulations, the roar of young voices swearing oaths of allegiance, had all been so intoxicating! They were his instruments, to use as he directed. With them, he could smash everything that had gone before and shape a new and more glorious China.

That had been his lifelong dream, a Communist utopia on a scale never attempted before. Ah, what a vision! No one, living or dead, could hold a candle to him when it came to such dreams. He alone was masterful enough, brave enough, determined enough, to brush aside sentimentality and the inhibitions of the past. China had to be driven to greatness through sheer human will, through the dumping of old thoughts, old culture, old customs and old habits. It had to leapfrog the whole capitalist stage in human development set out in Marxist theory, to go from a semi-feudal society straight into a full-blown socialist one. National transvaluation. A new, dynamic society of Nietzschean "supermen". The price might be high, but well worth paying. He had already sacrificed eight members of his family, including his first wife, to bring the revolution thus far. Had he not told Nehru he was prepared to see half the world's population perish in a nuclear holocaust if that could ensure the triumph of his brand of Communism?

Things had not gone exactly according to plan, however. His Red Guards had fire enough in their bellies and strength enough in their sinews. Within two years they had wrought unimaginable destruction to old institutions and caused the deaths of half a million diehards. Yet the new order failed to materialize. Why?

It could not be due to any defect in his conception. It could only be due to the bunglings of his disciples. Or perhaps to the stubbornness of old teachings and the sabotage of old unreliables like Chou En-lai.

Chou had never been a true revolutionary. Too diplomatic and too squeamish. He had allowed Chou to remain Premier because they had been through much together. But with every passing year it became more obvious that Chou could never amount to anything more than a nit-picking mandarin-administrator of the traditional mould. Chou had betrayed him, just like all the others, watering down the purity of his ideas. Well, Chou was gone now. Died in January. But so had the glory days of the Great Proletarian Cultural Revolution. They would never come back and he was too old to shake the world again.

What was as wrenching as that missed opportunity was the spontaneous outpouring of grief for Chou at the last Ching Ming Festival. Ordinary people flocked without official sanction in their thousands to Tienanmen Square, with their pathetic wreaths, silly poems and white silk flowers. Such obscene displays of emotion! It made him sick. Hurtful too. Nothing similar would mark his own passing. All he could look forward to was some bloodless state-sponsored ritual.

He felt cheated. He was a greater man than Chou, greater than all of them. He deserved his rightful place in history and in the collective consciousness of his people. But his standing had been eroded by the calumnies of enemies and the incompetence of his disciples. His wife and her hangers-on had been pathetic. Pity he had to rely on them. If they had done their jobs properly, no ungrateful peasant would have ever declared at the mourning for Chou that the dead Premier had placed a bowl of rice upon his table whereas Mao, the Great Helmsman of the nation, had only showed him beautiful paintings of banquets and feasts!

Perhaps the world was not yet ready for a seer of his calibre. To be surrounded by mediocrities was a tragedy. They were already squabbling over his mantle. What contemptible creatures! All talk and no delivery, occupying the toilet only to fart.

Well, if his people's vision of heaven extended no more than that of toads at the bottom of a well, if they cared only for paltry bowls of rice, then he would deliver them to Hua Kuo-feng.

Hua was as safe and unexciting a pair of hands as could be found anywhere. Hua could deliver rice, to be sure. Anointing him would be terribly pedestrian, however. The man had no charisma, no outward grace, just a great bulk with a shambling walk. No "superman" in the making there. Acquitted himself well enough though, running Hunan Province, and had not stepped out of line following a promotion to the Politburo in 1973. Had not done too badly either during his stint as Minister of Public Security. Deficiencies in experience were counterbalanced by an honest and thoughtful temperament. Hua should have enough good sense not to be over-awed by the Shanghai gang. That lot had had their opportunity and had made a mess of it. Now they would have to take their chances. Whether Hua himself would survive in the end was something else again.

Thus Cheng Ching imagined how Chairman Mao, racked by chronic constipation and failing health, might have reflected during his final few weeks. He engaged in such speculations to relieve the tension of waiting. With the death of the Chairman, the bickerings and manoeuvrings were coming to a head. Ideologues pitted against pragmatists, nationalists against internationalists, idealists against opportunists, conservatives against modernizers, radicals against revisionists, mortals against would-be supermen.

Cheng Ching was only a pawn in a complicated political game, a game with neither rules nor a clear knowledge of the other participants. That ignorance left him on edge. Yet, in a sense, he was glad. His fate had been consigned to the hands of others, absolving him from the horse-trading and shady dealings that had to be part of the contest. He would be no good at that. Perhaps he was not even good at being a Communist. Reconciling ends and means had always been troublesome for him.

Recently he had called on his adoptive father only to impart important information or to respond to a summons. He knew how preoccupied the General must be, so he contented himself with drawing inferences from developments gleaned through the General Office.

The eulogy delivered by Hua Kuo-feng on September 18 at

the commemoration of the Chairman's death had at first left him on tenterhooks. Hua had taken pains to warn against plotting. But to whom was the warning directed? In whose direction was Hua leaning? Hua's support was crucial. If the remarks were directed against his adoptive father and his group, then the situation was grim. Both of them might be rounded up at any moment.

The General had instructed him to keep a close eye on Director Wang. Wang's support was crucial, too, because he controlled Unit 8341 guarding the Chung Nan Hai complex. Wang had been closely identified with the Cultural Revolution, but the General said he had a hold over the burly Director and was trying to bring him on board.

After a week of taut nerves, Director Wang personally brought Cheng Ching some secret Party files and suggested he might care to study them. Cheng Ching knew then that the support of the Director had been secured. Because the Director had worked closely with Hua when the latter was Minister of Public Security, the auguries were good that Hua might be enlisted as well.

This was more or less confirmed on October 4, when Party organs controlled by Mao's widow and her Shanghai group printed an article attacking Hua as a rightist. The attack suggested two possibilities — either the Shanghai group judged itself strong enough to win power or they were trying to create chaos as the prelude to a coup.

From that time onwards, Cheng Ching went around as if some capricious alarm clock had been installed inside his brain. Every thought, rumour, clue, conjecture or fact could set it jangling. It would go off when he detected a slightly tighter cast to Director Wang's mouth or when he realized that half of the three-hundred-odd members of the Central Committee had risen to power during the Cultural Revolution. Such alarms would continue as he calculated the divisions among the twenty-five members of the Politburo and who had something to gain or lose by an alteration in the power structure.

His imaginary alarm clock was ringing overtime when Hua called an emergency meeting of the Politburo for the evening of October 5. As a member of the General Office, he was deeply involved in the preparations. The meeting could determine once and for all how power might be devolved.

A palpable air of tension developed in the General Office. Everybody knew matters were coming to a head. Senior cadres eyed one another, unsure where individual loyalties lay or how a realignment of power might affect each of them.

Discussions within the Politburo proved heated. Mao's widow attempted to use forged documents to prove that Chairman Mao had preferred her as his successor. She suggested that Hua should accordingly propose her as the new Chairman of the Party. Hua declined. The meeting broke up without a decision. It was agreed, however, that another meeting would be convened to resolve the issue.

The delay was torture for Cheng Ching. He struggled to concentrate on his work, as his internal alarm kept going off. Then Director Wang sent for him.

"I need you for a mission tonight," Director Wang said. "I want you to stay in the office till dinner time."

Cheng Ching nodded. His heart pounded as he made his way back to his own office. What could the mission be? To convey secret messages or to doctor Party files to disprove the claims of the Chairman's widow? Or had the Director switched allegiance again and the request was nothing but a ploy to arrest him after others had gone? Should he alert his adoptive father? Or would he be adding to the General's worries by scaremongering?

Then, when dinner time approached, Director Wang sent for him again. "I want you to go to the homes of Comrades Wang Hung-wen and Chang Chun-chiao," he said. "Tell them Comrade Hua wants an emergency meeting of the Standing Committee of the Politburo at 8pm, in the No.2 Conference Room in the Huairen Hall in Chung Nan Hai. It is to decide on whether a plenum of the Central Committee ought to be called.

"You're known to them both as a senior cadre in the General Office. Not unusual for urgent and confidential messages to be conveyed this way. They'll have no cause to question what you say. Nor is there a need for you to answer questions or say anything else. Just act naturally."

"Yes," Cheng Ching said. But the message did not seem to

make sense. The deaths of Chairman Mao, Premier Chau and Marshal Chu Teh had reduced the Standing Committee to just four members. Wang and Chang were leaders in the Shanghai faction. The remaining two members were Premier Hua and Marshal Yeh, a namesake of his adoptive father's. The Standing Committee would not be able to decide anything. At best a two-two split — unless someone had already sealed an underhanded deal.

Those calculations alarmed Cheng Ching again. "The Standing Committee'll have its job cut out," he remarked.

Director Wang scratched the side of his big, red nose and replied: "After you've delivered the messages, come back to the General Office. I shall be gone by then. Stay put and shortly after eight you should be receiving a telephone call. The caller will say: 'I can have supper with you tonight because my headache has gone and my stomach upset is better.' Or he will say he can't and give a variation of that statement, such as his headache being better but not the stomach upset. If there's a variation, remember the precise wording. In either event, telephone General Yeh at once and convey the message word for word. He'll know what's required."

He returned to the General Office and waited. At precisely five minutes past eight the telephone rang. The pre-determined words came over the line without alteration. He felt buoyed up and happy as he passed the news to General Yeh.

It appeared Wang and Chang had been arrested without fuss at the Huaiwen Hall. It was over in less than two minutes.

But what of the other leaders of the Shanghai gang? Anxious as he was, he could not ask over the telephone. He curbed his curiosity and set off home on his bicycle, pedalling down the Avenue of Eternal Peace. When he came to the portrait of Chairman Mao beaming down from Tienanmen, he felt renewed hope for the future of his country.

Cheng Ching learnt subsequently of the fate of Mao's widow from secret reports. She must have had a presentiment of disaster for she had been changing her place of sleep every night. It was the duty of Unit 8341 to know where she was at all times, however, so it was easy for Director Wang's special squad to pick her up at a residence near the Temple of the White Pagoda.

She yelled and screamed and rolled on the floor when arrested. When her female attendants realized what was taking place, they cursed her, spat on her and told her she deserved her fate. They accused her of watching pornographic Western films and reading decadent foreign magazines in the privacy of her home.

How undignified, Cheng Ching thought, when he read the reports. How unlike Chang Chi-hsin, the woman cadre shot in Liaoning the previous year. Chang Chi-hsin had demanded justice for General Peng and Chairman Liu Shao-chi and had paid with her life. Chairman Mao's nephew had ordered her vocal cords to be severed to prevent her shouting defiance while being led to the public execution ground. But she had remained uncowed to the end. How magnificently she had behaved compared with Chairman Mao's scheming wife!

Yao Wen-yuan, the fourth leader in the Gang of Four, was arrested at his home the same evening. During that night and the following day, thirty close associates of the Gang were taken into custody. They included the Minister of Culture and Mao's nephew.

The news of the Gang's downfall was greeted with jubilation throughout the country. Once the initial euphoria was over, however, Cheng Ching felt ambivalent. The leaders of the Gang of Four were under lock and key. General Yeh and his supporters had won the day. But oppressors and criminals still sat in the Politburo and corrupt careerists retained power in the administration. That spelt uncertainty. Scepticism and fear still pervaded Peking.

Something else troubled Cheng Ching. How could the fate of a thousand million people be determined by back-room deals stitched together by a handful of men? When would the democratic processes and the rule of law foreseen by Marx come into being?

There were also the pressing problems of poverty and hunger and social collapse. He remembered his father telling him of the abject poverty and sufferings of people he had encountered during the Long March. In Kweichow he had found people dressed only in loincloths, living in huts made of mud and lath. Their chief food was corn and bits of cabbage. The infant mortality rate was fifty per cent and life expectancy thirty years.

Half a century later, Cheng Ching discovered from reports in the General Office that the situation in some areas had remained largely unaltered. The only positive thing the Cultural Revolution had brought was to send millions of city youths into remote regions to taste the harsh realities of country life.

When he met General Yeh for dinner some days later, he gave voice to some of his reservations.

"Yes, we've wasted twenty-five years," the General said. "Be patient. The Great Wall wasn't built in a day. Problems have to be tackled systematically, one at a time. The political struggle is not yet over. There are many factions. The Gang of Four is but one. Some who are our allies now can become our enemies tomorrow. We must proceed cautiously and remain on guard. A revolution within a revolution takes a long time. Simply weeding out undesirables from the General Office will be no easy matter."

"People are dying of hunger. When will they be fed? There have been vast injustices. When will sufferers have their names cleared? And what of the thousands who have forfeited their lives simply for speaking the truth?"

"Be patient! Be patient! Food will be produced. Criminals will be punished. Those who have been wronged will be rehabilitated. That I promise you. But some things take time. Certainly much longer than I have. That's why people like you must continue with those tasks."

Cheng Ching felt depressed by the inconclusiveness of the coup. It had been two and a half years since his adoptive father had broached the subject of toppling the Maoists. That period since had been the most stressful of his life. Worse than Korea. In Korea, at least one knew who the enemies were. Here there were only shadows, intrigues and shifting alliances. Small wonder his father hid himself away in a godforsaken village.

He wished he could re-join his family. An uneventful life seemed suddenly attractive beyond words. He had done enough for his country and the Party. It was time to honour the promise made more than twenty-four years ago. He would speak to his adoptive father at the first opportunity.

Before he could do so, however, a letter came from Thirsty Hills on October 29 to report the passing of his father.

The puppet master

29

Cheng Ching stepped out of his air-conditioned office onto the private balcony. Immediately the heat enveloped him like a warm, damp towel. He had been in Hong Kong for two months but still found its humidity uncomfortable, although he was wearing little more than a white shirt and a pair of dark-blue Dacron trousers.

The humidity was not the only thing he found disagreeable. The city's cocky edifices of glass and concrete seemed to ignore the harmonies of nature. Their pointed spirals poked into the heavens while their oblique planes and angles formed narrow, sunless canyons, thick with shadows, as if designed for ambushes and dirty deeds.

As a good Communist, he was not overly preoccupied with the harmonies of nature. And yet, as a Chinese, how could he avoid an attachment to nature? It was in the blood. But he was not in this self-satisfied place to enjoy the pleasures of natural things. It was to discharge his patriotic duties. The wealth and materialism all around provided fertile ground for spying, corruption and the exploitation of human frailties. In the short time he had been in the post he had already developed an ambivalence towards the city and its inhabitants. The whole place seemed to reek of a money sickness. Even the very young were masked by precocious cunning.

From thirteen floors below, the noises of the city billowed up towards him, jarring, insistent and full of vulgar energy. From the moment he committed himself to his adoptive father's quest to rid China of the Gang of Four, he knew that success would bring him to this uncongenial place. It was, he supposed, less disagreeable than the place he might have ended up in if the coup had failed!

General Yeh had instructed him that his first task was to neutralize the remaining supporters of the Gang of Four in Hong Kong. Then he would have to ensure the continued generation of foreign exchange to support the Four Modernizations. To that latter end he would have to assume oversight over the vast complex of banks, newspapers, schools, trade unions, department stores, travel agencies, shipping lines, trading companies and other economic, cultural and artistic organisations controlled by the Party in Hong Kong.

Finally, there was the responsibility for security and intelligence matters, securing by fair means or foul information on the latest Western technology and weaponry. All in all a daunting undertaking! The prospect of presiding over inter-ministerial and inter-provincial jealousies was already disheartening him. The saving grace was that he was accountable only to the Secretary-General of the Party and to his adoptive father. General Yeh had by then assumed the positions of Deputy Chairman of the Military Affairs Commission and Chief of the General Staff of the People's Liberation Army.

To the world at large, he was a deputy manager in the foreign-exchange department of the Hong Kong branch of one of China's state banks. Only a couple of members of the Standing Committee of the Politburo had been appraised fully of the exact nature his job. In Hong Kong, only the Director of the New China News Agency, as de facto representative of the Chinese government and Chairman of the Hong Kong and Macau Work Committee, had been given an indication of his authority.

Cheng Ching continued to brood over those responsibilities on the balcony. With so many overlapping layers of authority, with so much jockeying for power, he was like a puppet master controlling too many strings. If he got them tangled the consequences could be catastrophic. How much more pleasant if he could lay them all down to return to Thirsty Hills. His mother could do with his help. And there was still the unfulfilled promise to his father to work for the village. When would he ever honour that?

Those thoughts made him turn abruptly to return to his office. He carefully locked the French windows behind him and reset the alarm.

His office was by no means the kind used by a lowly functionary. Its parquet flooring was partially covered by a thick, hand-woven Tientsin carpet and there was the rare luxury of an attached bathroom and toilet. A painting of misty mountains and gentle waterfalls hung on a wall and beneath it stretched a long sofa with his jacket carelessly thrown upon it. Next to the sofa was the door to the room. It was steel-lined and soundproof. Beyond it lay an ante-room attended by two young men of military bearing and two women private secretaries.

The most unusual feature in the room was a rare six-foot-tall Chubb safe embedded into the wall and equipped with both a combination lock and a key lock.

Cheng Ching went over to the safe and twirled the combination lock. He extracted from beneath his shirt a metal chain holding two keys and inserted the appropriate one.

The safe was divided into two compartments, by a pair of metal drawers set across the middle. Both the upper and the lower compartments contained files distinguished by jackets of different colours. He selected three and carried them back to his rosewood desk. Then he returned to the safe, pulled out one of the metal drawers and extracted two small code books. In the process two photographs fell to the floor.

He picked them up. One was of a fair-haired Westerner and a girl in a floral calico dress. The other showed himself and a beautiful girl, both in the uniform of the People's Liberation Army. He gazed at the latter photograph. He had had that taken with Ying twenty-four years ago, almost to the day, he thought wistfully.

How many twenty-four years were there in a lifetime? Ying was now married and out of reach. He was married too, to the Party and the nation. There was no point spending the next twenty-four years dreaming of what might have been. He replaced the photographs in the drawer and returned to his desk with the code books.

As he sat down he saw the Chinese painting with misty mountains confronting him. What was reality and what was illusion, he wondered. Were those mountains any less real than the three telephones with scramblers on his desk?

He smiled ironically to himself. A spymaster and overlord! One had to be some sort of crazy romantic to believe that killings and dirty deeds were essential to a better world!

Of the three telephones on his desk, one was red. It was his secure line to Peking. He was about to compose a coded message to his adoptive father when one of the black telephones rang. It was one of his secretaries informing him that the afternoon despatch box had arrived. He told her to bring it.

The secretary placed a black box on the desk and retreated.

Cheng Ching took the chain from around his neck and unlocked the box with the second key. Among the documents inside were copies of Internal Reference News and Reference Materials, two secret compilations regularly distributed to cadres of ministerial rank and above. His copies had been couriered from Peking. There was also a summary of the Q List interceptions from the previous day.

Cheng Ching quickly scanned the documents from Peking. After satisfying himself that none required immediate attention, he turned to the summary of the Q List interceptions.

The Q List was a document drawn up by the British Special Branch containing the names and addresses of people and organisations in Hong Kong whose mail would be intercepted. They might be drug traffickers, triad bosses, key members of Communist organisations, local personalities with dubious affiliations and lawyers, bankers and accountants involved in money laundering or other shady deeds. Sometimes several targets might be located at a single address. When the name for a particular target was unknown, only the address would appear in the Q List and all letters addressed there would be examined.

Interceptions, he had already learnt, were effected at the General Post Office. The list was regularly updated and made available to the Postmaster General on a personal basis. The Postmaster General saw to it that the Sorting Office placed all targeted correspondence in a special pigeonhole. During the night, workers specially trained by the Special Branch would open, photograph and re-seal designated letters, before returning them for normal delivery, albeit a day late.

The Special Branch had failed to realize, Cheng Ching reflected with satisfaction, that two of the postal workers assigned to the clandestine work belonged to one of his intelligence units. When they photographed letters for the Special Branch, they also made copies for the Motherland.

It would be normal for those on the Q List to have their telephones tapped as well. But his agents had not yet penetrated the relevant section of the Hong Kong Telephone Company.

What irritated Cheng Ching was his inability to discover what the letter Q stood for. He had gone over and over again all the English words he knew beginning with a Q. He had consulted the Oxford Dictionary and had eventually narrowed possibilities down to quarry, queer, questionable and quisling. But his inability to settle on a definitive answer bothered him like a recurring itch.

As he went through the day's interceptions, he noted with surprise that Chu Wing-seng's name had been added. How two-faced the British were! They would appoint a person to sit on their innermost council one day and rifle his mail the next. And all the while they would mouth their rubbish about the rule of law and the sanctity of the Royal Mail.

He wondered suddenly if the British knew their Q List arrangements had been compromised. If so, would they root out his agents or keep them on in order to feed through misleading information? He would have to establish the truth. In the meantime, information from that source had to be treated with circumspection.

But what of Chu Wing-seng? Why had the British targeted him? He had never met the man. There had been no inkling in Chu's dossier of any involvement in crime. Could it be political? Chu had no Party affiliations, though he had been cultivating a number of senior cadres in Peking and in Kwangtung Province. At the same time his corporation maintained an office in Taiwan. All indications pointed to Chu being more interested in profits than principles. He must order a fresh probe. Possibly he might raise the matter at the next meeting of the Hong Kong and Macau Work Committee.

Cheng Ching opened one of the files taken from the safe. It dealt with his bank's involvement with Chu Wing-seng and the Gold Star group. He flipped through it because he had been invited, along with other managers in the bank, to a cocktail party hosted by Chu Wing-seng that afternoon. He had to brief himself. But he found the information in the file well short of requirement.

Cheng Ching completed his coded message to General Yeh and saw to its despatch. He then put the files and the contents of the afternoon despatch box into the Chubb safe.

He stretched himself and had a quick wash in the bathroom. He then picked up his jacket from the sofa and headed for Chu's cocktail party.

The Work Committee

HONG KONG

JULY 1978

30

It was close to dinner time when Cheng Ching left his sanctum on the thirteenth floor. On the twelfth floor he picked up a bodyguard as he entered the lift. Another late meal, he thought, as he emerged from the lift. A car was waiting to speed him and his escort to a meeting of the Hong Kong and Macau Work Committee.

Cheng Ching inwardly cursed the British as he sank into the rear seat of the car. Hong Kong was Chinese territory. Its existence depended on China's goodwill. Yet the Chinese Communist Party was being forced to operate under false colours and to use a ridiculous alias, simply because the British had proscribed the Party under their Societies Ordinance back in 1949. They would pay for that arrogance one day.

Unfortunately, the time was not yet opportune. Too many things remained unsettled in China. General Yeh had indicated on the red telephone that morning that the new power structure still had to be stabilized. Hua Kuo-feng, Mao's successor, was under pressure from both leftists and rightists. The vast oil painting, hanging in the marbled foyer of Peking's main railway station, depicting Hua receiving his mandate from Mao, might soon have to be removed. How slippery was the grasp on power!

Cheng Ching reconciled himself to the tedium of secret meetings of the Work Committee held at ever-changing venues. The selected spot that evening was the office of an obscure trade union on the second floor of a crumbling tenement. Its location, in a narrow side street off Southorn Playground, was equally obscure.

As the car neared its destination, he marvelled at the teeming life in that rundown neighbourhood. It was a good location for a meeting. Any foreigner would become immediately conspicuous.

The car stopped at the mouth of the street, next to a shop selling herbal brews. Cheng Ching picked out two men in Hawaiian shirts at a table. They had glasses of some brown concoction and a radio phone in front of them and unnatural bulges beneath their shirts. The moment he alighted, one of them picked up the phone.

Cheng Ching followed the bodyguard on the short walk to the appointed building. The ground floor was occupied by an ironmonger's shop. The shop next door sold joss sticks and paper replicas of mansions, gold bullion, limousines and gorgeous gowns to be burnt as offerings to relatives in the afterlife. Both shops were shuttered, although lights within suggested continuing activity.

Sandwiched between the two shops was a narrow flight of creaky stairs. A sign over the entrance indicated that the stairs led to the office of the Amalgamated Union of Metal Workers. A young man in a Hawaiian shirt and a pair of dirty jeans loitered at the foot of the stairs. On the pavement outside the ironmonger's shop, two men who looked like coolies were playing Chinese chess under a street lamp. Several onlookers clustered around them.

The young man at the bottom of the stairs immediately stood aside for Cheng Ching to pass. Not a single word was exchanged. The bodyguard joined the spectators around the chess game.

Cheng Ching found eight men with sallow and impassive faces inside the room, including the Director of the Hong Kong branch of the New China News Agency. The Director was the de facto representative of the Chinese Government in Hong Kong and was formally the Chairman of the Work Committee.

The situation was ludicrous, Cheng Ching thought. It had arisen because of British refusal to countenance the establishment of a formal diplomatic mission in the colony. Another slight to be settled.

Cheng Ching had noted from the dossiers in the General Office that the Director was an old revolutionary, already past his prime. The post had been awarded as a sinecure prior to retirement.

The men were seated on cheap, metal folding chairs arranged around three battered but sturdy mah jong tables placed end to end. Each had in front of him some documents and a cup of tea. Teapots stood on the tables for replenishments. Three or four aluminium ashtrays were filled with cigarette butts.

Fluorescent tubes emitted a dingy, bilious light. The room

was dominated by a large photograph of Chairman Mao. Yellowing Venetian blinds had been lowered, cutting out any vagrant breeze. Two electric fans stirred the smoke-tainted air. It occurred to Cheng Ching that the setting was probably not dissimilar to that used by the founders of the Party in Shanghai decades before.

Although the appointed hour had not yet been reached, Cheng Ching nevertheless apologized as a matter of courtesy because he was the last to arrive. His brooding presence at the previous two meetings and the scar of battle on his cheek left little doubt where real power lay.

He studied the sombre men gathered around the makeshift conference table. Except for the Director, he did not know them well. They seemed joyless and etiolated, as if all the gayer hues of life had been drained away. How different they were to General Yeh, Old Tung, Mad Fan and his own father.

They lacked passion, Cheng Ching thought. They had become, like his erstwhile colleagues in the General Office, time-servers set in their ways and slaves to the prevailing Party line. The keen edge of daring had probably been blunted by the dizzying material abundance in Hong Kong. No doubt some were already surreptitiously trading in stocks and shares and making provision for their children's education overseas.

They had ceased to be revolutionaries. Agendas, discussion papers and minutes cushioned them as they did corporate executives. It was a security nightmare. Small wonder the British Special Branch and MI-5 so often obtained details of matters discussed. Perhaps Chairman Mao had a point when he spoke of the need for perpetual revolution. How could such passionless men be entrusted with noble assignments?

"We seem to be all here. Shall we begin?" the Director asked genially, after someone had poured Cheng Ching a cup of tea. The Director's voice sounded hoarse from too many cigarettes.

There was a quick shuffling of papers followed by general assent. People delivered reports on hardy perennials — poor recruitment among left-wing trade unions; fluctuations in hard-currency remittances; recent United Front efforts; gains or losses in market share for Chinese foodstuffs, cement and steel; and intelligence about Kuomintang activities.

Cheng Ching half-listened. He was more interested in assessing the speakers than hearing what they had to say. He knew from their dossiers they had all been activists in bygone struggles. Most held pedestrian jobs to disguise their clandestine lives. Two had served with the East River guerrillas during the Japanese occupation. One of them had done time in a British prison following the spill-over of the Great Proletarian Cultural Revolution.

Collectively, the men around the table could exercise more power than the British colonial government. On a command from Peking, they could make hot money turn tail, investment capital dry up, banks to suffer runs and the local currency to collapse. They could arrange for lives to be snuffed out and whole families to disappear. But, placed in charge of the city, none would know how to keep the wealth pouring out so magically.

Cheng Ching's ruminations were interrupted by a high-pitched, rather womanish voice. It was Comrade Tang, a plump, engaging man in middle age. His cover was that of a solicitor's clerk.

He talked long-windedly about the system for securing embargoed machinery for the Khmer Rouge, ordering consignments in the names of local sympathizers and paying for them through China Resources, a Chinese state company registered under the local Companies Ordinance. He anticipated that problems might arise if the Registrar of Companies started examining the records of China Resources.

As discussions proceeded on how best to overcome the problem, a voice suddenly demanded: "Why should we help the Khmer Rouge at all? They've been killing our compatriots in Cambodia." It was Comrade Fu, a lean man with a sharp, narrow face, resembling a ferret's. He was in charge of cultural and educational affairs.

Cheng Ching remembered that Fu had hardly spoken during the last two meetings. It was as if he had been lying in wait. He recalled from the dossiers that Fu had once been a leading light in the All-Circles Anti-Persecution Struggle Committee, set up during the 1967 confrontation. He had served a two-year sentence in Stanley Prison for injuring a police officer during a riot.

"There are larger issues at stake, Comrade Fu," the Director said. "There is much confusion in Cambodia. Lots of people are being killed. A revolution is not a tea party."

"Reports say the Khmer Rouge have massacred at least 100,000 Chinese during the last twelve months," Comrade Fu continued. "We should not be strengthening them. Attempts to achieve racial purity through massacres are contrary to Marxist principles."

"We can always count on Comrade Fu to offer us a fresh perspective on everyday problems," the Director said. "The Khmer Rouge are not just killing Chinese. They're killing their own people as well, not to mention the Islamic Chams and other minority tribes. But we have to deal with the Khmer Rouge because an enemy of an enemy is a friend."

"Comrade Fu has a point," Cheng Ching interposed, pleased to discover a comrade with fire in his belly. "Principles are important. Comrade Fu has proved his commitment to the anti-colonial and anti-imperialist struggle. His hunger strike in prison in support of a demand for the right to have the complete works of Chairman Mao available has been hailed in the *People's Daily*. He has rightfully emerged a hero.

"Our leadership, however, distinguishes between relationships involving states and those involving fraternal parties. These are again divided between those dealt with centrally and those left to local initiatives. In the case of machinery for Cambodia, that's a relationship for Peking to handle, since Cambodia ships tropical products directly to China in payment."

"Comrade Cheng has summarized the position well," the Director said, with alacrity. "I think we can leave it there."

"What about guns and ammunition in the vaults of the Bank of China?" Comrade Fu persisted. "That's a local matter."

The Director's jaw dropped. Others made a pretence of studying their papers or sipping their tea.

Cheng Ching glanced around the table but most avoided his eyes. The Director was bent over lighting a cigarette. Fu was obviously someone reckless enough to pursue awkward subjects, Cheng Ching noted. He wondered if the man could be bent to serve his secret purposes.

"Well, what about the arms?" he asked.

"State banks have more branches now," Comrade Fu said. "Shouldn't arms be more widely dispersed? In 1967 the *People's Daily* called upon the people to mount a courageous struggle to smash British rule. We went into the streets but we were not supplied with guns. We used home-made bombs. The struggle was a failure because some elements in the Party were too cautious, too faint-hearted, too fearful of the consequences. We could have taken this city, if we had had weapons."

"Well, what can we learn from the lessons of history?" Cheng Ching asked, as soothingly as he could. "Urban uprisings were a favourite with comrades in the Comintern, but they invariably failed in China and wasted many lives. Chairman Mao corrected that erroneous line. He reminded us that uprisings in China had to be peasant-based. That insight eventually led the Party to victory.

"In the case of Hong Kong, the line was set down by Comrade Chou En-lai decades ago. The British presence is a problem left over by history, to be addressed when the time is ripe. Though Comrade Chou has since gone to meet Marx, that position remains unaltered. The situation here is not favourable for armed struggle. We must not overreach ourselves, though it is correct not to allow socialist principles to be watered down by material considerations."

"Yes, we must concentrate on the Four Modernizations," the Director chipped in. "In a very short time, this city should fall to us like a ripe plum."

"But a poisonous one," Comrade Fu retorted. "This place is a breeding ground for reactionary prejudices and bourgeois corruptions. People are behaving more like petty capitalists with every passing day. It proved very difficult removing bourgeois influences from Shanghai after Liberation. Hong Kong will be much worse. We must lance the canker. We must not surrender to the black winds of economism. Though foreign earnings may appear as attractive as sets of cavity-free teeth, we must not allow them to subvert principles. Why keep arms if we never intend to use them?"

"Another problem left over by history," the Director said. "Our primary mission at present is to generate foreign earnings for the Motherland to modernize. I was not party to the decision to bring arms here. So far as I understand, the situation then was more fluid than it is now."

Cheng Ching, sensing that the discussion was drifting, intervened again. "There seem to be three issues. First, there is the historical fact of weapons having been stored in the vaults of the Bank of China. Second, whether weapons should have been distributed in 1967. And third, whether they should be more widely dispersed now. Does that cover it?"

A murmur of agreement arose from around the table.

"Good," Cheng Ching continued. "What has been done in the past is not a matter that concerns us. As to the non-distribution of weapons in 1967, the roots of those demonstrations must first be examined. Why did they occur? Were they spontaneous local outbreaks or had they been centrally planned? Who initiated them and who was responsible for their direction? Had they been authorized by the Party or had they been instigated by anti-Party adventurers? Why did they fail? Did the issue boil down to the availability or otherwise of weapons? Those are matters currently being investigated by both the Party and the State. We should await their conclusions.

"The third issue goes to the heart of Party policy. It implies a greater likelihood of using weapons, which in turn implies a policy of more robust opposition to British rule. Is there such a policy? The Director feels this place will fall in due time into our hands like a ripe plum. That seems to be the prevailing view. But if there is a significant desire for re-examining the issue, we can always refer the matter upwards."

Others around the table quickly caught the sense of Cheng Ching's remarks.

"We should guard against adventurism and deviations to the left," someone ventured.

"Banks in Hong Kong operate under licences, too, and are subject to inspection by the Commissioner of Banking," Comrade Tang's high-pitched tones took up the argument. "For reasons well understood by all, the Commissioner has desisted from examining certain vaults in the Bank of China. But that cannot be counted on to continue indefinitely. Banks now face growing competition and need more space for safe deposit boxes, customer counters, rooms for investment counselling, and so on.

Far from dispersing weapons, we should remove them."

A murmur of approval went round the table. Comrade Fu, finding himself isolated, retreated into a sullen silence. After the remaining business had been disposed of, Cheng Ching spoke again.

"I wonder if the comrades might assist me," he said. "I find my files woefully inadequate on local personalities. They lack depth. I recently attended a cocktail party given by Chu Wing-seng of the Gold Star group. He is reputed to be one of the wealthiest men in the Far East, decorated by the French and the British. His initiatives in China are well known. He has textile and toy factories in Kwangtung and a hotel in Shanghai and is spearheading a number of new projects elsewhere.

"But what is the extent of our involvement in those activities? Gold Star is an umbrella for many little-known companies registered in Liechtenstein, Montserrat and the Turks and Caicos. Some of our state banks have extended facilities to a number of them. The Motherland has been stung by fraudsters in the past. We don't want state funds lost through lax financing.

"My dossier does not say much about the man or his antecedents. How did his family acquire its wealth? Is Gold Star solid? Chu himself was educated in America, but what are his real sympathies? Has he Taiwan or CIA connections? He appears to be a member of many local and international organisations. There's one known as Phi Beta Kappa, another known as the Young Presidents Organization of America. I've no idea what they are. Can anyone elucidate?"

There was a general shaking of heads and blank looks around the table.

At last Comrade Sun, an elderly cadre in charge of United Front activities, responded. "My section is responsible for cultivating Chu Wing-seng, but we haven't met with much success. Chu's a bit of a cold fish. He claims his interests lie in business, not politics. I've dealt with him when he donated a wing to a university hospital in Canton, to be named after his father. Came up with the money all right. The initial approach was made by a Dr. Chow, a graduate of the university and physician to the Chu family.

"His father, Chu Tung-po, was also a man of some mystery.

Came to Hong Kong from Canton before the war to expand the family's crockery business. Pretty much a nonentity. But by the end of the Pacific War he had amassed vast holdings in land and buildings. That provided the basis for his business empire. No one's quite sure how he gained so much property. Perhaps he was a collaborator. In any event, he died in an accident at sea a while back."

"All this should have been in my files," Cheng Ching said. "It's obvious more exchange and co-ordination of information is required. Anything else?"

"The elder Chu had been helpful towards the Motherland at one time," Comrade Sun added. "He shipped in embargoed supplies during the Korean War. Of course, we paid him handsomely. His actions were surprising because his father was a staunch supporter of the Kuomintang. The whole family suffered during the rectification campaigns of the 1950s. Not exactly sure what happened. I believe his parents died then. Should be able to find out from the records of the Kwangtung Public Security Bureau. Apart from that, I can add little. Perhaps Comrade Tang knows something more. He works in the office of one of Chu Wing-seng's solicitors."

Comrade Tang took over the narrative. "I'm a clerk with Rand and Knight, one of a number of law firms retained by Chu. I haven't pick up much because the corporate structure of Gold Star is complex. Many firms are involved. I'll try to see what I can sniff out.

"One thing's certain, however. Chu is the darling of the garment industry. He found a way around European Economic Community rules governing textiles and quotas. EEC rules provide that any product that changes shape or utility in a particular place can be deemed to have been made there for certificate-of-origin purposes. Chu came up with the idea of manufacturing individual fronts, backs and sleeves of garments in China, where labour costs are lower, and shipping them to Hong Kong to be stitched together to form whole garments, qualifying them as Hong Kong products. He's ingenious at finding loopholes. Everyone's following his example now. People hail him as a wunderkind because of Hong Kong's lop-sided reliance on textile and garment exports."

"That illustrates the kind of poison that's being spread here!" Comrade Fu cried, vehemently. "In a socialist society, such actions would be classified as fraud. In this cesspool of capitalism they're praised and copied. The poison will soon contaminate the Motherland! What will happen to socialist honesty then? The leadership must address such problems, sooner rather than later."

Silence descended around the table.

After a moment, Cheng Ching said: "Ah, socialist honesty in a cesspool of capitalism! What an intriguing topic for Marxist-Leninist dialectics! As a newcomer, I should like to hear more about it. But such a discussion might be more fitting over a good meal and a large jar of wine. Would you do me that honour after our meeting, Comrade Fu?"

Comrade Fu looked nonplussed for a couple of seconds. "Delighted, Comrade Cheng," he said, hesitantly, and chuckles of relief broke out among the assembly.

The meeting began to disperse. By convention, the Director was the first to leave. The others followed, one by one or in pairs, at irregular intervals. Cheng Ching and Comrade Fu left together. After that, the chess-players under the street lamp and the onlookers also faded away.

Shifts in the wind

The enormous mirrored chamber in the World Trade Centre Building was filling up rapidly. The great and the mighty of the patriotic left came in dark well-tailored suits indistinguishable from those of corporate fellow-travellers and diplomats seeking friendship with China. They made their entrances and shook hands with the Director of the New China News Agency and his deputies, before blending smoothly into one of the existing clusters of guests. Good manners and personal insecurities dictated that arriving guests attached themselves to groups whose status more or less approximated their own. Women guests were conspicuous by their rarity.

One wall of the room was dominated by a large replica of the national emblem of the People's Republic of China — a garland encircling five stars shining above Peking's Gate of Heavenly Peace. The occasion for the party — the celebration of the twenty-ninth anniversary of the founding of the Communist republic — was made manifest by a red banner with gold characters hanging above the national emblem.

A workman was kneeling on a festooned dais beneath the decorations, engaged in last-minute checks on the unsightly bundle of cables connecting microphones and television lights. Press photographers and television cameramen hovered everywhere.

At each end of the room buffet tables, garnished with Chinese and Western hors-d'oeuvres, stood ready for consumption. Chinese dim sum and skewers of chicken and barbecued pork kept company with Parma ham, smoked salmon, miniature sausages, curry puffs and dainty vol-au-vents. White-gloved waiters in smart maroon jackets circulated with trays of drinks.

Sebastian Baxingdale stood with Derek Soames, the newly promoted Assistant Director of Information Services, to one side, against the wall opposite the dais. They made an unlikely couple, one tall, clean-cut and alert and the other resembling a bored and bulging burgher, with his nose tucked into a glass of rapidly vanishing beer. They appeared like pale foreign ghosts at a predominantly Chinese gathering.

Baxingdale listened to the chaos of dialects resounding around him. To his ear some greetings seemed pitched half an octave too high and the occasional outbursts of laughter seemed artificial in their mirth. He divined a strange mixture of exaltation, uncertainty and scepticism in the mood, perhaps even a touch of apprehension. The political and economic equations had shifted dramatically over the last couple of years. For many, the fall of the Gang of Four had fractured established allegiances and relationships. In the continuing power struggles, forging fresh links was both risky and difficult. A power-wielder one day might turn out to be a counter-revolutionary the next. Guilt by association was a contagious disease. But not to have contacts at all was to be left at the starting gates in the race for opportunity and wealth.

Only the previous month Baxingdale had noted the Ministry of Petroleum trumpeting about China's "magic weapon" of oil. Apparently the Victory Oilfield in Shantung had proved a great success, with revenues sufficient to finance 120 large-scale projects to be completed by 1985. The target list included iron and steel complexes, railways, power stations, harbours and coal mines. Sulphur-free oil had been discovered in Hepei Province and in the South China Sea. With such juicy possibilities, hesitation was fatal. He had little doubt that the stampede by international oil and money men towards the Ministry of Petroleum had already started.

At the same time, the political landscape in Hong Kong was shifting. British dominion suddenly appeared vulnerable and not to be taken for granted. The fact that for the first time in twenty-nine years a British Governor had deigned to attend a Chinese national-day celebration was a straw in the wind. What did it augur? A belated recognition of a reality that had always been there or a preparation for some pragmatic deal, in exchange for retaining a degree of British influence in the uncertain years ahead?

Baxingdale knew that an overt division of spoils would be unseemly. Powerful local and overseas Chinese interests were in the scrum. Among the contenders were members of the

Chinese National People's Congress and the Chinese People's Consultative Council and leading lights in the Chinese General Chamber of Commerce. But, not being a professional China watcher, he knew few of them by name or sight, only by reputation.

"Who do you know here?" he asked Soames, suddenly.

"Well, let's see," Soames said, emptying his glass of Tsingtao beer in one gulp. "A few of the drinking crowd at the Victoria Cricket Club, representatives of Jardine, Swire, the Hong Kong Bank, Standard Chartered, Coopers and Lybrand. Then there's the Indian High Commissioner and the other consular types... "

"No, I mean Chinese."

"Ah! That's a different matter. Fraternizing with the enemy's new to me, you know. Previously we couldn't get within spitting distance of these fellows without having to report to the Defence Secretary and the Special Branch. Now it's our duty to accept invitations. What a bore! Most of these chaps are unknown because they never troop up to Government House to sign the book and hence are never invited to our functions. Political winds are definitely shifting."

"What an Alice-in-Wonderland world we're in!" Baxingdale said, shaking his head. "We're supposed to rule this place. There are people here who run banks, department stores, trading companies and shipping lines, who control schools, trade unions and newspapers, who bring in meat, poultry, rice and vegetables, delicacies like sharks' fins and swallows' nests, herbal medicines from Hupei and coffins from Liuchow. They supply oil, steel rods, cement and heaven knows what else. They trade in our property, stock and bullion markets, and yet, after 136 years, they remain largely faceless and anonymous to us. Amazing!"

"You don't know the half of it. You ought to see how some of the idiots really behave inside the establishment! Enough to drive a man to drink." With that Soames exchanged his empty glass for a full one from a passing waiter.

"What about you personally, Derek? You've never told me who your sources are among these people, apart from the female ones who swear by the properties of Connoisseur cognac!"

"Hey, I've already told you most of the people here don't belong to the usual cocktail circuit. They don't even speak our lingo. It's not as if they're into bridge or bowls or cricket. They haven't even got around to serving civilized drinks like G & T. For hard information I rely on the likes of T. P. Chaps like him'll do a lot better now that relations are less frosty. Can't hold them back any more. If you go into it, you'll probably find half of them connected in some way, gone to school or done things together during their youth. Might even be related, for heaven's sake! We've had to second T. P. to escort the Guv around today, to interpret and make introductions."

"Where's T. P. now?"

"Downstairs I suppose, waiting for the Guv and the Political Advisor to turn up in the Crown car."

Soames had hardly finished speaking when the Governor appeared at the reception line. He was tall, dour and patrician and was followed by the Political Advisor from the Foreign Office, the City District Commissioner T. P. Choy and a bodyguard who peeled off at the door.

Baxingdale watched the exchange of handshakes and diplomatic courtesies. He had witnessed such performances ad nauseam. The Director accompanied the Governor into the room. Television cameras rolled and flash bulbs exploded. Microphones were shoved towards their faces to catch any stray comment. Without hearing them, Baxingdale knew their remarks could only be in banal diplomatic-speak.

A waiter appeared out of nowhere with drinks. Small talk was conducted with practised cordiality. The media lapped up the photo opportunities. Then, suitably equipped with libations, the Director and the Governor mounted the dais, like a pair of diplomatic marionettes, and toasted each other's countries to the accompaniment of more media attention.

The atmosphere gradually became more relaxed. The ice accumulated over twenty-nine years slowly melted. The principals wove their way through the assembled guests, stopping at intervals to chat. Waiters circulated with trays of hors-d'oeuvres.

"Go easy on what you write today, won't you?" Soames said, out of the blue. "The word from Whitehall is that your pieces are bordering on the subversive."

"How jolly! The feeling's mutual!" Baxingdale replied. "I

think those weasels have been subverting the good name of our country for centuries."

"Okay, I agree, but we're just tiny screws in some vast contraption. We're expected to keep our places. Otherwise the whole damned edifice comes crashing down. I'd better follow the Guv and keep an eye on him. Reggie Boy has given strict orders. If anything goes amiss he promised he'll have my balls for breakfast."

"You mean the Chief Secretary?"

"None other. Sir Reginald Beaufont Quinn, Knight Bachelor, Companion of the Order of St. Michael and St. George and all the rest of that bullshit. Don't forget what I've said. See you at Szeto's afterwards?"

"All right. I had better snag a few contacts too," Baxingdale said, as Soames took his leave. He spotted two men talking a short distance away. One was sharp-featured and the other had an impressive scar on his right cheek. He remembered the sharp-faced man as Fu, the riot leader who had made a splash during the 1967 disturbances and their aftermath. It would be interesting to discover whether his stint in a British gaol had affected his views on current political developments. He made his way towards the men.

"Nei ho! How are you?" Baxingdale offered, employing the honorific mode of Chinese taught by Madam Shek. "My humble surname is Baxingdale and I work for the *Daily Globe* in London. May I offer my good wishes on this auspicious day."

"My insignificant surname is Fu, a teacher. This is Mr. Cheng, recently arrived from China to take up an appointment at one of China's state banks. It is gratifying to meet a Westerner who has taken the trouble to learn our language."

They shook hands and exchanged toasts.

Baxingdale studied Cheng as he might an opponent in the boxing ring before a bout. From the other's firm handshake and erect carriage he surmised well-defined muscles beneath the inexpensive suit. If the man was a banking executive, he thought, then Sebastian Baxingdale was Mother Goose.

"I trust Mr. Cheng does not find the pace of life in Hong Kong uncongenial," Baxingdale said.

"To speak the truth, this person hasn't quite found his feet,"

Cheng Ching replied. "Many things remain bewildering. Mr. Fu has been kind enough to show me the ropes."

"That is not unusual for newcomers. I went through that phase myself. May I enquire which department Mr. Cheng supervises in his illustrious bank?"

Cheng Ching made a deprecating gesture. "Mr. Baxingdale flatters my lowly position. I do not have the privilege of supervising any department. My duties merely involve dealings in foreign currencies."

"Ah, those can be onerous should turbulence hit the foreign-exchange markets."

"One lives in hope of being spared such travails. In any case, major decisions rest with my superiors."

"I wonder if I might seek a favour from Mr. Cheng. I have long wanted to write an article on the foreign exchange earned by China from Hong Kong and its changing importance as China modernizes. As has been recently announced, China's oil production is coming on stream to finance the Four Modernizations. The dependence on hard currency from Hong Kong must therefore be reduced. Might Mr. Cheng be in a position to assist with some facts and figures?"

"Mr. Baxingdale flatters this humble person again. Customers come to me to negotiate letters of credit and other petty commercial instruments. I have no knowledge of the foreign-exchange requirements of my country. Even if I had, I would be without authority to release that information. You know how bureaucracies work. Everything is a state secret. In feudal times, even the condition of the stools of an emperor was regarded as a state secret!"

"I'm all for leaving the condition of stools with bureaucrats!" Baxingdale said, laughing. "Let's drink to that."

The other two joined the laughter and all three toasted one another once more.

From the confident way Cheng ridiculed bureaucrats, Baxingdale surmised he had to be a senior cadre and one unafraid of speaking his mind. Cheng would be a contact worth cultivating. The man might even make a stimulating companion for an evening at Szeto's Bar.

"If I may make Mr. Baxingdale a suggestion," Cheng Ching

said, cutting into Baxingdale's thoughts. "It may be more fruitful to approach the Bank of China. It has far greater authority than my modest institution. If I might have your card, I can pass on your request."

"Of course! How remiss of me!" Baxingdale passed copies of his visiting card to Cheng and Fu. He took theirs in return. "It would be a great convenience to be put in contact with the right section," he added.

"Mr. Baxingdale," Fu said. "Though we have only just met, our encounter is auspicious. Your illustrious name has been known to me for a decade. I have been much impressed by the even-handed way you have written about Hong Kong issues."

"Mr. Fu is too generous."

"You once wrote an article on the economic benefits derived by Britain from its possession of Hong Kong. Do you remember?"

"That was a long time ago."

"Yes, but I haven't forgotten it," Fu continued. "Some years later, following local suppression of the Diu Yu Toi demonstrations, you wrote again about the right of citizens to demonstrate peacefully. As a teacher, I am prevented by the provisions of the local Education Ordinance from teaching civic consciousness in the classroom. There is no regulation, however, against students reading articles in British newspapers. So for a number of years I've made your articles available to my students. I think your words have stimulated them and this humble person thanks Mr. Baxingdale for that."

"Good heavens! I had no idea of my own notoriety!" Baxingdale said. "I'm glad my scribblings have been of service. My countrymen have a saying — there are many ways of skinning a cat."

Cheng Ching laughed. "Mr. Baxingdale jests excessively, to suggest that the British lion has turned into a cat!"

Baxingdale reciprocated with laughter.

"May I suggest, Mr. Baxingdale, out of respect for your professional eminence, another topic for inquiry," Fu said. "Chinese leaders have spoken of the imperative of seeking truth from facts. That is a good approach. The conventional wisdom advanced by many Western writers is that the prosperity, full employment and minimal inflation in Hong Kong have been a function of wise British administration, of adhering to free-market policies, low taxation and the rule of law. But is that really so?"

Cheng Ching intervened. "I'm sure our honourable guest would not wish to delve into political matters on such an auspicious occasion."

Baxingdale sensed that Fu had been nursing a feeling of wounded chauvinism that Cheng was trying to deflect. "Oh, no," he interjected. "I'm all for seeking truth from facts. Since Mr. Fu has given this unworthy person great face by offering his valuable insights, the least I can do is to benefit from them."

"I mean no offence, Sir," Fu said. "Nor am I aiming at a quarrel. I merely wish to express a Chinese point of view. This humble person's feeling is that the main reasons for local prosperity have been China's forbearance and the natural diligence of Hong Kong people. The British are here under the terms of treaties not recognized by China. But, rather than quarrel over that, China has decided to leave that matter to one side. It has instead taken pains to supply Hong Kong with inexpensive food, water and a wide range of daily necessities. It could have supplied more commodities of benefit to the local people, but the British have imposed quotas on essentials, such as rice."

"Ah yes, that has been a contention among rice merchants for some time," Baxingdale said. "I do agree that rice quotas are rather silly in a supposedly free market."

"China also stationed security forces along the border to deter Chinese citizens from exercising their natural desire to visit parents, relatives and friends in territory temporarily occupied by others. Those are the factors that have made for stability, low inflation and prosperity in Hong Kong, do you not agree?"

By now Fu was in full flow and Baxingdale nodded his agreement.

"Westerners wave the so-called rule of law around like a flag to justify colonialism at the end of the twentieth century. It is in fact a fraud. Local authorities have consistently perverted the law for their own purposes, to enforce or ignore as they wish. There are examples all around. The function of law is to deliver justice. King Solomon of the Jews knew this well. So did our own legendary Judge Pao. Where is the justice in preventing schools from teaching students about their own culture and their own historical traditions? Where is the justice in beating and imprisoning young men and women for demonstrating peacefully against plots to violate the territorial integrity of their country?"

Fu's voice rose with indignation as he fired his rhetorical questions. "In spite of provocations, China has stayed its hand," he continued. "It has not called upon citizens to rise and strike down unjust laws. It has suffered it compatriots to endure injustices for the sake of maintaining social order. If China had acted otherwise, how long would prosperity and stability in Hong Kong have lasted?"

"Mr. Fu, your thesis raises interesting issues. I sincerely hope we can debate them at length one day, over a pot of tea."

"I should look forward to that, Mr. Baxingdale," Fu replied with a smile, apparently soothed by the genial response. "We have each other's number. I'm sure something can be arranged."

They shook hands and Baxingdale took his leave with a half-bow. As he moved away, he suddenly caught sight of Xavier Chu, the husband of Lucille, the purveyor of Connoisseur cognac and much else besides. The young tycoon was deep in conversation with a Mr. Yue, a shipping magnate Baxingdale knew well. Both were slowly edging in his direction. His heart skipped a beat. He was fearful of Mr. Yue hailing him and entangling him in conversation with Xavier Chu. He turned around abruptly and headed for the buffet table at the far end of the room, away from the approaching pair.

It was not guilt that was spurring his retreat. He felt no guilt, because of the way Xavier Chu had treated Lucille. It was just that his sense of honour rendered it abhorrent to shake the hand that Chu, out of habit, would thrust at him. He could not believe that someone as intelligent as Xavier did not suspect his wife of having an affair. If he suspected, he certainly had the power and means to exact revenge. Yet, over the years, nothing untoward had happened either to himself or to Lucille. Even if Xavier did not love his wife, such behaviour was puzzling. What game was he up to?

Baxingdale had wanted more than once to confront Xavier, to tell him face to face he was in love with his wife and to seek resolution to their mutual predicament. But Lucille had forbidden that. She had her principles and her reasons, though she would not explain them fully. He could not understand how she could endure all the uncertainties and anomalies in their lives, the furtiveness and the last-minute readjustments to fit in an assignation. In a tight little place like Hong Kong, how long could a scandal be avoided?

They loved each other too much to remain apart. He wanted them to live together openly, to end the torment once and for all. But that hope still seemed light years away. He wished he were living in a different age, when challenging a rival to pistols at dawn was the normal code of conduct for a gentleman. That would settle matters. If he should forfeit his life in the process he would have no regret.

There was also the issue of Lucille's son, Ah Yuen. The boy was interested in writing and literature and on that pretext Lucille had brought them together a couple of times at the Foreign Correspondents' Club. A nice, thoughtful boy. But how could he ever become a father to him?

As Baxingdale pondered the complications, he kept one eye on the exit and the other on the possible approach of Mr. Yue and Xavier Chu. He felt no desire to eat or drink. He simply wanted to talk, about anything. Soames's gonads being served up for breakfast would do. Or even diplomatic tangos, political deceits, the hopelessness of the human condition. Any topic would do so long as it took his mind off Lucille and the cul-de-sac they found themselves in.

He had an article to write on the shifting political landscape, but that was not required till much later that night. In the meantime, he just wanted his time occupied. Otherwise, he would go out of his mind thinking about Lucille.

As soon as he saw the Governor taking his leave, he too slipped out to head for Szeto's Bar. Until Soames or T. P. turned up, he could at least bend Szeto's ear at the long bar.

Doctor Chow

"Can't anything be done? The pain seems to be spreading to her left shoulder and arm. What about a bypass or something?" Xavier Chu asked, as he accompanied Dr. Chow down the sweeping staircase of the Chu mansion.

Dr. Chow was a gangling, loose-jointed man, several inches taller than Xavier. He carried a battered Gladstone bag of brown leather. Clad as he was in a Harris-tweed jacket and tie, he appeared over-dressed for a midnight house call. By contrast, Xavier was in a maroon dressing gown and beige shantung pyjamas.

"Probably too late, Mr. Chu," Dr. Chow said, with a touch of formality. It had not always been like that. He had attended Xavier as a child and during the days when he played bridge or mah jong with the elder Chu, he had addressed Xavier as "Little Seng". But the visits and games had stopped with the passing of the father. The son's absence in America and subsequent rise in the commercial world had distanced them.

"Why? We keep hearing about the great strides in medical science. Why can't something as simple as angina be fixed?"

"It can," the doctor replied. His face was etched with old age and fatigue. He had been asleep when the summons came. "But it does require the co-operation of the patient. I've been urging your mother to see a specialist for years. Angina is caused by a temporary inadequacy of blood to the heart muscles. In elderly people that might be due to hardening of the coronary arteries. Possibly blood clots as well. Picked up early enough, a simple bypass would do the trick. But your mother has consistently refused to see a specialist. I'm just a G.P. There's only so much I can do."

"I'm not blaming you, Doctor," Xavier said, drawing a deep breath. "I appreciate everything you've done. Really. For both my mother and my son. His asthma seems to be on the mend, I'm glad to say. I'm just annoyed that my mother's so mule-headed. Is a bypass utterly out of the question now?"

They reached the bottom of the stairs. The light from the crystal chandeliers lit up the doctor's tired features. "I'm sorry, Mr. Chu," Dr. Chow replied. "I've always regarded your family as personal friends, but I can't recommend surgery till your mother's been examined by experts. You know her situation better than I do. She had a severe case of influenza a couple of months ago and that may have caused some inflammation in her heart muscles. It would need sorting out before surgery. There's no immediate danger, but time's not on her side."

"Why can't we forget about muscular inflammations and bypasses and simply give her a new heart?"

Dr. Chow chuckled wryly. "At her age? You can't order a new heart as you would a new car or yacht, you know."

"Why not? It's all a matter of supply and demand, like everything else in the world. Price determines availability."

Dr. Chow shook his head and chuckled again. "Do you realize how long most people have to wait for transplants? The waiting lists are horrendous in every country in the world. In Hong Kong, we haven't even got around to organizing a waiting list. Nor donor cards either. You know what Chinese are like. Many of us believe in entering the next life with our body parts intact. We haven't yet convinced people of the value of donating organs to save others. Families often object, even if a person is willing.

"In such circumstances, where are we to get a heart? It cannot be just any old heart, but one that's compatible in blood and tissue types. There is something called human leukocyte antigens or HLA for short. It's virtually impossible to find two people with the same set of HLAs, except with identical twins. To prevent rejection, HLAs have to be as close as possible. Immunosuppressive therapy has to be used. People die randomly in traffic and other accidents. But before their organs can be used, the medical authorities have to be assured there's been no queue-jumping and that ethical standards have been fully complied with."

"Wait! I've an idea," Xavier said. "You don't have another house call, do you?"

"No, heaven forbid."

"Good. Let's go to my study. I'd like to bounce a few things off you. Care for a drink?"

"A cup of tea would be nice. Dragon's Well if you have it. Otherwise Jasmine."

"Fine!" Xavier said, leading the doctor into the study. "Take a seat while I rustle it up."

Left to himself, Dr. Chow was struck by how the study had changed since he was last in it with Xavier's father. Gone was the untidy accumulation of crates and boxes. Gone, too, the Chinese books. The bookcases were now filled with volumes on business and banking and handbooks and statistical digests.

The display cases were bereft of antiques. Those objects of art had once been favourite subjects of discussion between himself and the elder Chu. Now the shelves boasted photographs in sterling-silver frames and a collection of trophies. The largest picture was that of Xavier in morning coat and striped trousers at an investiture at Buckingham Palace. Others captured him receiving the Legion of Honour from the President of France, shaking hands with the President of the United States, enjoying the company of President Suharto of Indonesia and sharing a joke with President Marcos of the Philippines. Family photographs were not included in the display.

The starkest difference lay in the space between the display cases. The two scrolls of calligraphy by Teacher Tam had disappeared. He used to admire them for the sheer strength and beauty of the characters. They had been replaced by a dazzling collection of awards and honours, the most impressive of which were the ribbons and insignias of an Officer in the Most Excellent Order of the British Empire and of a Chevalier in the French Legion of Honour. Among the other exhibits were diplomas from Princeton and Harvard, a glittering steel plaque certifying membership in Phi Beta Kappa, and a framed letter bearing the red embossed seal of the Colony appointing Xavier to the Executive Council of Hong Kong.

The doctor's inspection of the exhibits was interrupted by Xavier returning with a Filipino maid. The girl was carrying a pot of tea, a Chinese teacup and a glass of Coke on a silver tray.

"Sorry I took so long," Xavier said, motioning the doctor to a seat across from his desk. "Maids are not what they used to be."

"I don't think I've been in this study since your father passed away," Dr. Chow remarked, warming his hands around the cup of tea. "Has changed a mite, hasn't it? Pity my visits are confined to ailments now. Not like the old days."

"We must try to change that," Xavier said, with an apologetic smile. "Sorry I don't play bridge or mah jong. But, if what I'm about to say works, we should be seeing a lot more of each other — and under much happier circumstances."

"I had been meaning to inform you, Mr. Chu, that you should start looking for another family doctor. I shall be retiring next year. I can recommend someone and work him in, if you wish. You can rest assured I won't leave your mother in the lurch."

"My dear Doctor, why think of retirement when the best is yet to come? You are still fit and able. You still have great contributions to make to the cause of medicine."

"Of course I shall finish off the hospital project in Canton. That is in honour of your father. I would never abandon that halfway. They're putting in some of the equipment now."

"That's small beer, Doctor. Let me tell you about my vision and the crucial part you can play. You're the key. I need your medical knowledge and your connections in Canton to get the show started."

Dr. Chow sipped his tea with a look of mild bewilderment. "What vision are you talking about?"

"Organ transplants, on demand!"

"That's impossible!"

"Nothing's impossible. Just think, Doctor, where is there an endless supply of fresh human organs? In China, of course! They execute thousands every year. The wonderful thing about Chinese law is that once a person has been convicted of a capital offence, all civil rights are lost. Convicts belong to the state, body and soul. After execution, families cannot even claim their corpses. Are you getting the drift?"

Dr. Chow appeared alternatively dazed and alarmed. He kept shaking his head.

"Hear me out," Xavier said. "All we need is a little tinkering around the edges and we'll have a world-beating transplant enterprise. It will set new standards in availability and efficiency. It's a simple matter of looking at things from a fresh angle. That's what entrepreneurship is about.

"Instead of waiting for someone to die before seeking out patients, you line up patients needing transplants first. You carry out in advance blood and tissue typing, liver-function tests, HLAs or what have you. Armed with a clear idea of compatibility, you can pick and choose compatible organs, which are healthy and disease-free. No hepatitis, no diabetes, no nothing. You execute the criminals only after patients have been matched and ready to go! Maximum efficiency in the use of scarce resources. Should be possible to do half a dozen transplants with one execution. Heart, liver, spleen, lungs, kidneys, blood, bone marrow, all stripped out together! One death to save many! It's marvellous."

"It's outrageous!" Dr. Chow gasped. "How can anyone sell such a scheme?"

"I can sell anything. It's all a matter of approach. The profit motive. Look at the objective factors. The Communists are executing a lot of people. They have to spend money just to dispose of the bodies. Now, if the authorities can be made to see a convict as an asset, capable of producing money and saving lives, they will sit up and take notice. Everybody can gain from it. *Everybody*!"

Dr. Chou shook his head and made as if he were about to speak.

But Xavier stopped him. "Look, the Communists have embarked upon what they call the Four Modernizations. They want to cut loose public-sector units and make them self-sufficient. Service organisations such as hospitals are bound to experience spending constraints. The general population is too poor to pay. There's insufficient income to pay staff, let alone improvements. The conventional solution is to withdraw services. It must come to that. Before long, hospitals in China will demand payment in advance before treating patients.

"What are the sick to do? Their families are too poor to pay. Lack of affordable medical attention will stir up dissatisfaction and unrest. I can offer a way out. Organ transplants can bring in big money. Not only that. Because of sheer numbers, China can soon be at the forefront of transplant technology. Modernization. Understand? There'll be scope for experimentation too, such as combining surgery with traditional techniques, like acupuncture. There are all kinds of possibilities."

"You can't deal with a human being, even a criminal, as if he were a bag of beans!"

"You can't be sentimental in business. It's all a matter of pitching the proposition in the right way. I know people in the Politburo. A few high-ups in the Ministry of Public Health and in Public Security Bureau as well. I know how their minds work. I can talk to them, gauge their reaction. I'm confident they'll give the nod. Once we get that we can work our way down the hierarchy, to the provincial and city levels.

"Now let's consider the issue from the other end of the chain — from the point of view of convicted criminals. They have nothing to lose and everything to gain by co-operating. If they don't co-operate, justice is swift and certain. Being selected as a suitable subject means they can live longer, months longer, perhaps even years. While submitting to tests they'll be treated well, given good food and cured of diseases. Foul-ups and administrative delays occur in every system. We just have to make them work in our favour. Convicts waiting to be matched will be no different from prisoners on Death Row in America. To encourage co-operation, a small grant might be made to families after execution."

"Stop! What you're suggesting is monstrous!" Dr. Chow said. "There'll be an international outcry. No self-respecting surgeon would take part in such a scheme."

"Come, now, Doctor. Let's not get carried away. There'll be an international outcry only if people are aware of how the organs are come by. We don't have to say anything about that, do we? Once the scheme is in place, it will become a state secret, the disclosure of which will be punishable under Chinese law. To all intents and purposes we're only setting up an institute to train Chinese doctors in organ transplants. It will have the most up-to-date equipment and use the latest techniques. Plus some Chinese innovations. Money is no object. We can say more organs are available simply because there are more Chinese dying. Our handling of donors is perhaps more systematic and efficient? We open the institute to patients from the rest of the world as a gesture of international goodwill. For a price, of course."

"Your proposal goes completely against Chinese values.

Doctors, in particular, are supposed to save lives, not take them."

"But doctors *will* be saving lives! And on a grand scale under my scheme. As individuals, doctors are no different from other people. They have their price. There was a report in the newspapers just the other day about doctors in China routinely severing the vocal cords of convicted traitors — without anaesthesia, mind you — to prevent them shouting defiance or protesting their innocence before being shot. That was what started me thinking about this. Those doctors were just trying to earn a living, carrying out jobs assigned them by government. Ethics don't come into it."

"I'm sorry. I'm too old for new projects. I wish I could help, but I cannot see what possible service I can perform. I'm not a surgeon."

"Ah, Doctor, you want to help. That's good. I knew I could count on you! Now we're talking turkey, as the Americans say. I wasn't intending for you to deal with patients. Your role would be to talk to the professors at your old university and to the doctors at the teaching hospital. You've already won their respect by getting them a new hospital wing, helping them to modernize after years of neglect. Now go and excite them with a bigger and grander vision — a whole new institute specializing in organ transplants. The only one in the world. It's real pioneering stuff. Will make all of them rich and famous."

Xavier leaned back, folded his arms and studied the effect of his words. He took a big gulp of Coke. "More tea?" he asked.

Dr. Chow shook his head. "This is beyond me," he said. "An institute for organ transplants. It would take years to come to fruition. I'm too old. I can't handle it."

"Just concentrate on the big idea. In talking to your contacts, let it drop that such a modern and cutting-edge institute might be a suitable monument to honour China's paramount ruler. Human beings have little vanities, you know. Who could possibly pour cold water on a project named after a nation's leader? I'll set up meetings in Peking while you make your contacts in Canton. Entertain your friends and colleagues royally. I'll pay.

"Before the project comes on stream, surgeons in Canton will have to start practising on local patients, perhaps for free. In business that's known as 'loss leaders'."

"How can you be sure of paying patients? In the West you can't advertise. There are also malpractice suits to worry about."

"Who has ever heard of anyone winning a law suit in a Chinese court against a Chinese state institution? I have a lawyer dealing with the external aspects. He used to work for the Director of Public Prosecutions. He knows how to tie up these things. To paraphrase an old saying, our successes will be hailed and talked about, our failures will be interred with the dead.

"There'll be a lot of spin-offs. I haven't even begun to tell you about them. Every one's a money-spinner. Just imagine, if someone from Beverly Hills or Palm Springs can afford to come to China for a transplant, isn't it reasonable to assume that his or her family will want to come as well? Family members have to live somewhere. Why not a luxury hotel complex right next to the institute? There are bridge tours, music tours, archaeological tours. Why not a medical tour? Don't worry, Doctor. I'll see to it you get a slice of the action."

Dr. Chow rose from his seat. "It's getting late, Mr. Chu. I'll think about what you've said. I don't want to keep your chauffeur up late."

"Forget about the chauffeur. He's glad for the overtime."

Xavier walked Dr. Chow to the front door. The Filipino maid who had brought in the drinks was waiting to open it.

"I'll talk to my mother again about the specialists," Xavier said. "Just look after her well in the meantime. I'm a man who knows how to show his gratitude."

Reverse osmosis

HONG KONG

MAY 1980

33

"It's a lie, a British plot!" The Director's bushy eyebrows bristled as he spat out the words at an impromptu meeting of the Hong Kong and Macau Work Committee. At the same time he waved a document in the air. "The normal line of communication is between their Political Advisor's Office and the New China News Agency. There has been no contact, none at all, unless they went directly to Peking or to the Kwangtung authorities. In either case, Peking or Canton would certainly have consulted me."

Cheng Ching allowed others to make the running after providing the report. His concern was to keep discussions focused. "I've checked with the Foreign Ministry and the Kwangtung authorities this morning," he announced. "They've had no approach."

"Then why are we being accused of refusing to supply Hong Kong with more water? Why are they using that to justify this reverse osmosis nonsense?" the Director demanded.

"They aim to turn us into a laughing stock," Comrade Fu said. "Whether scientifically feasible or not, the people of Hong Kong are not going to drink reconstituted shit! They'll blame China for bringing this upon them. It's a British ruse!"

The faces around the oval table displayed varying degrees of agitation.

"We first have to figure out what the British are up to," Cheng Ching cautioned. "Only then can we decide on a response."

The document before the meeting was a translation of a Land Development Policy Committee paper. It had been secured by an undercover agent in the Government Secretariat. It dealt with water supplies. The Committee, made up of senior British civil servants in the Secretariat and top officials in the Public Works Department, had recommended enhancing water supplies through a scientific process known as reverse osmosis. The process was a form of desalination and was reputedly capable of converting even raw sewage into drinking water. Effluent could also be disposed of in an environmentally friendly way. Plants had been constructed and were coming into use in the Middle East.

"Look how they've tried to blame us," the Director said, racing through the arguments in the translation. "Projections of population growth, increasing requirements for water, unreliable pattern of rainfall, limited catchment areas, the lack of suitable land for new reservoirs and the reluctance of China to sell more water. Note the final argument!

"Then the solution on a plate: reverse osmosis! Technical and town-planning experts have conveniently identified a site in Shatin, close to an existing sewage outlet into the sea. Consultants to study cost implications further. What we don't have are details of the discussions in the Land Development Policy Committee. What arguments led to its proposed recommendation to the Executive Council to engage consultants?"

The Director smoked furiously after highlighting sections of the purloined report. "How can they do this? We've been supplying water since 1960 and now this slander, accusing us of being unco-operative. If we don't act quickly, we could be facing a fait accompli. Very difficult to undo. Peking will blame us for messing things up, ruffling feathers. Even suspect some of us of stirring up trouble out of sympathy for the Gang of Four.

"Why have the British continued with their Cold War mentality? What have they got to fear from us? Isn't it enough that they've completed the High Island Reservoir and wasted money on that silly desalination plant at Lok On Pai? Why another expensive scheme when they can easily buy more water from us? Why seek confrontation and unnecessary expense instead of peaceful co-existence?"

"Because they'll be wasting somebody else's money," someone said. A murmur of assent went around the table.

"The Governor came to our National Day celebrations. When he returned from Peking he told people to put their hearts at ease. I thought that marked the start of a new relationship," the Director continued. "I had anticipated retiring on a happy note, with the issue of Hong Kong safely left to be settled — in the wise words of our departed Comrade Chou — when the time was ripe.

"Now there's this baseless accusation. Do we know how

quickly they intend putting the matter before the Executive Council? It can only lead to a row. We must stop it. Better a small row now than a big one later."

"No indication on timing yet," Cheng Ching said. He had, after two years, grown accustomed to the Director and other members of the Work Committee. They would frequently dig up past British wrongs to underline their own patriotic credentials. Circumstances had removed them from the cut and thrust of Chinese politics and left them in a place where promoting socialism was akin to a temperance league recruiting members inside a crowded bar.

"The British are two-faced," Comrade Fu said, screwing up his sharp features in disgust. "They're always cooking up mischief. They've probably got the measure of our troubles. Our coffers are empty, our economy in collapse. We've more than twenty million unemployed. Last year's war with Vietnam didn't help. There are political problems brewing all over the place. Hong Kong's the only bright spot. Earnings here are vital for getting the nation back on its feet. They want to slow us down, make us more pliable. They must be using this reverse osmosis as a lever for some concession. But what? Why pick on water as an excuse, after so many years of co-operation?"

"The British cannot be trusted," Comrade Sun declared, his lips quivering. "I've had direct family experiences. They were responsible for the deaths of two of my uncles before the last war. They trumped up charges to banish them, because they were Marxists. The moment my uncles crossed the border, they found the Kuomintang waiting. They were arrested, tortured, executed. The Brits had been hand in glove with the Kuomintang all along.

"They keep practising subterfuge and double dealing. We went to the trouble of making extra fuel oil available during the Opec crisis, but they still conspired with the Americans to deny us modern technology. I suspect this latest move is an attempt to squander Hong Kong's reserves, to benefit British companies and hold back China's recovery. They've long been known as a perfidious race."

So have we, Cheng Cheng thought, as he listened to the animated speculations and the tales disinterred from the bowels of history. The strings to his puppets were becoming tangled.

He had to perform upon too vast a stage, to manage too complicated a range of duties.

He had spoken to General Yeh that morning. The political situation in Peking remained unsettled. Following the reversal of the counter-revolutionary verdict on Chang Chi-hsin, the reformers felt strong enough to push through the rehabilitation of Chairman Liu Shao-chi. But horse-trading was still in progress. Director Wang and a number of Politburo members with Maoist sympathies were now under investigation for corruption and other misdeeds.

When he had been in Peking the previous month, his adoptive father told him the British had raised the question of the future of Hong Kong. What fools they were, his adoptive father had declared. If they wanted to run the place, they should have left well enough alone. Perhaps they wanted to pile on the pressure while China was weak. A miscalculation. The Politburo was hardening. There was no possibility of any agreement that reflected poorly on the nation's pride. It was doubtful if anyone would risk a decision of that magnitude until the power structure had stabilized. His adoptive father had instructed that, for security reasons, no whisper of the British probes was to be passed on to cadres in Hong Kong.

Cheng Ching waited for the cross-talking to subside. Then he said: "Just because the British have bested us in the past does not mean we should credit them with more imagination and cunning than they actually possess. This might be a simple case of corruption by an official or officials unknown. Someone might have slipped money under the table. That's not difficult to visualize."

"Let's flush them out then," the cadre in charge of media and public relations said. "The public would be with us if they knew the British planned to make them drink recycled sewage! We can expose the plot in our newspapers and make clear China's willingness to provide all the water required."

Cheng Ching shook his head. "Can't compromise my agent. The Brits'll realize I have a mole."

"We can get Chu Wing-seng to oppose the project in the Executive Council," Comrade Sun said. "He has been relying on us to get projects started in China. He has been seeking permission to bring in teams of Chinese doctors, for study tours and attachments to local hospitals. He's been talking of donating a new organ transplant institute to Canton, in addition to the hospital wing named after his father. Since we've been smoothing the way for him, he should do something for us in return."

"Not just doctors," the Director said. "I've had applications for visits by senior officials from the Public Security Bureau and the prison administration. Don't know what Chu's actually up to. The Canton authorities have been tight-lipped. But, so far as water is concerned, the question must be disposed of publicly, so that everybody knows the true position. Having it killed in the Executive Council will not do. If there's corruption, let's get some mileage out of it. Show up the British for what they are."

"Comrade Cheng is in charge of intelligence matters," Comrade Fu said. "Can't his people uncover the truth?"

"Not yet," Cheng Ching replied. "I have a suggestion. Let some independent source make the exposure. That would be more credible, making it more difficult for the local administration to brush it off."

"Anyone in mind?" the Director asked.

"The British journalist Baxingdale is a possibility. He has a reputation for not being in anyone's pocket. Leak the document to him. He should be astute enough to pick up the water point and start asking questions."

"Excellent. I second the proposal," Comrade Fu said. "I've had conversations with him. He's fair-minded."

"To play safe, I should speak to Chu nonetheless. We must prepare for contingencies," Comrade Sun added.

"Of course, but make it casual," the Director cautioned. "Chu's an important man, well in with certain quarters in Peking and Kwangtung. Don't want to rub him the wrong way."

The Director, concerned over his own position, decided that he should head a small working group on the issue.

"Comrade Sun, before you speak to Chu, we should have a word. I've some information that might prove useful," Cheng Ching said.

Comrade Sun nodded.

After further discussion about whether Peking should be appraised of the development now or later, the meeting ended.

Cheng Ching saw the participants off before heading back to his office. Two security guards were still on duty. Both secretaries had gone, however. Though the hour was late, there were things he wanted to mull over. He did not feel hungry. He told one of the guards to arrange meals for themselves and then disappeared into his office.

He turned off the security system for the French windows and went onto the balcony for a breath of air. The night was sultry and the hum of traffic incessant. Lighted windows grimaced at him. Fortune-hunters burning the midnight oil, he thought. No doubt working on ever more ingenious ways of turning shit into lucre! He shook his head and went back inside.

He unlocked the Chubb safe with one of the keys hanging round his neck and extracted a small stack of files. His adoptive father had involved him in a many-sided contest for the control of his country, to rescue it from chaos and injustice. The majority of those associated with his adoptive father now seemed to think capitalist practices were needed to revitalize the country.

The dogmas of the past were being watered down. Intellectuals punished during the Cultural Revolution were being rehabilitated. Properties confiscated from class enemies were being returned. State allocation of jobs had been discontinued. Price controls on a range of commodities had been lifted. Joint ventures with foreign and overseas Chinese entrepreneurs were being encouraged. All kinds of wheeler-dealers were jumping in with both feet. International carpetbaggers and global-marketeers were arriving by the day, offering export credits, soft loans, bribes, kick-backs. An agreement had already been signed with Japan for the joint exploration for oil in the sea around Diu Yu Toi. "Getting rich through labour" had become a fashionable slogan.

He sensed something deeply wrong. Foreign corporate buccaneers might be producing quicker economic results, but at the price of corruption, cynicism and a return of wide disparities in wealth. That type of free-for-all would not be good while the masses remained barely educated.

Something was already happening to himself in that new climate. Things he had done in recent years were weighing upon his conscience. He had helped to trap the leaders of the Gang of

Four with fake messages. He had employed bribery and corruption to secure modern arms for his country. He had instructed men to steal, and even to kill, to lay hands on foreign secrets. It was a slippery slope. Now he was about to pass to Comrade Sun information about the private lives of Chu Wing-seng's family members for the purposes of blackmail.

The alibi of a wider national interest was no longer convincing. A memory dislodged from the distant past no longer allowed him to be so easily appeased. He remembered his father pressing upon him the study of the Confucian classics, at a time before such studies became dangerous. Passages setting down the proper conduct for a superior man came back to him. Years of Hegelian dialectics and Mao Tse-tung Thought had not freed him completely from their moral hold.

Hong Kong might be an easy place to lose one's moral balance, but was there no depth to which he would not stoop in the name of his cause? Chu Wing-seng was not a particularly likeable person. His latest organ-transplant project in Canton reeked with the smell of corruption. Some of his business methods were ruthless, exploitative and bordered on sharp practice. But those were not sufficient reasons to use private information about his family against him. The fact that his mother had been an ex-courtesan and his wife an adulteress was nobody's business but their own. If someone had used Ying's willingness to serve as a mistress of Chairman Mao against her, he would have been outraged. A nation deserving of pride could not be built through such shameful and underhanded methods.

He needed a heart-to-heart talk with his adoptive father the next time he sent for him. His assignment in Hong Kong was troubling him. China was at the crossroads. A wrong turning could spell disaster. His father had taken the path of self-reliance at Thirsty Hills. His mother was continuing that journey. It was painfully slow but morally safe. Perhaps those who lived in poverty and hunger could not afford to wait. Even Chinese patience had its limits. The test for the current leaders must be to find ways of making up for a wasted generation without losing all moral standards. And he needed to hang on to his own.

Sweet sorrow

34

They lay limp and exhausted, as lovers do after the frenzy of love, soothed by the lulling purr of the air conditioner. Yellow strips of moonlight seeped through the shuttered windows, together with the distant ululations of hawkers, the click-click of mah jong tiles and snatches of Cantonese pop songs about unrequited love.

Lucille woke to those sounds, momentarily disoriented, until she realized she was in Seb's flat. A curtain of brown and white plastic beads divided the premises into a sitting room cum study and a makeshift bedroom.

How could a Westerner live so frugally and put up with the intrusion of so many Eastern sounds, she wondered. She enjoyed a surfeit of space in the Chu mansion, insulated by vast gardens and lawns. The sounds in the unfamiliar neighbourhood struck her as not altogether unpleasant, however. They carried a certain earthiness that reflected Chinese preoccupations with food, gambling and love.

As she attempted to identify the strands making up that medley, she realized she was lying on one of Seb's arms, with her face pressed against the curly hairs of his chest. He was still asleep.

Poor man, she thought, staying still so as not to wake him. At another time and in another place they would have been perfect for each other. Their temperaments melded like the black and white halves of the Taoist symbol for Yin and Yang. Though each had private hurts, a certain kind of fulfilment came when they were together. It was strange that she should have found it with a gweilo.

Perhaps that was what she had really been searching for all along, the love and attention of a good man. She had wrongly ascribed her former restlessness to some kind of cultural or racial inadequacy, due to the hostilities encountered during girlhood over the colour of her skin. It was that which had set her off on a long expedition to discover her roots. Her efforts had turned out to be enlightening. She had no regrets. But it had been the wrong remedy for the wrong ailment. Seb had provided the right one. In the process, however, he had created a different kind of restlessness.

Relocating to a city with an almost wholly Chinese population had opened up new vistas. Her smooth ivory skin no longer stood out. She had rid herself of her Toi Shan accent and had acquired the looks and habits of other Hong Kong society women. It was now people of other colours who were outsiders. Language and literature shut them off, ancient festivals and legends mystified them, and places such as the Evergreen Tea House offered them no welcome.

Living with Serenity and studying with Madam Shek had deepened her understanding of Chinese habits and attitudes. But the more she learnt the more she found herself slowly sealed within skein after skein of tradition. Her parents had previously impressed upon her the importance of family, relatives and clan, of links with ancestors long dead and generations yet unborn. Serenity and Madam Shek connected her further to the spiritual, intellectual and artistic heritage of an old civilization.

It was those spreading and deepening connections that engendered a new discomfort, a dissonance between her American pursuit of love and happiness and her Chinese concerns for social harmony, continuity and the greatest common good.

Seb was a decent man and she loved him. He could make her laugh and forget her troubles. He knew more about Chinese ways than she did. The orderly relationships espoused by Confucians, the quietism practised by Taoists, the Buddhist surrender of worldly attachments, were all familiar to him. In a different world, he would make an ideal mate. But he was still a gweilo. That was why whenever he hinted at marriage, she had been evasive. How could she explain the relationships within the Chu family and the unsettled values inside herself? She felt ridiculous rationalizing why she would agree to assignations only when Xavier was larger than life within the town.

Part of that peculiarity was born out of feminist pride, acquired at Berkeley. She resented being a trophy wife, putting on sweetness and charm for Xavier's business associates. She had done it nonetheless, for the sake of Ah Yuen and Serenity, to preserve harmony within the home and dignity before the servants.

But she also desired to live by her own rules. She wanted to make plain that misusing her came at a price. By being blatant about her affair she hoped to provoke her husband into a row, a divorce, a recognition of her as an autonomous human being. But he had responded to her absences with humiliating indifference.

During moments of anger she had really wanted to hurt him, to make him lose face by letting the world see him as a cuckold. But, on calmer reflection, what could that achieve and what did that make her? Consideration for Ah Yuen, for Serenity and for her own parents invariably stopped her.

She remembered that when she was a teenager her mother had demanded that she conform to Chinese notions of womanhood.

"You must marry your own kind," her mother had said. "Not one of those sweet-talking white boys. Stay away from them. Your father and I don't want to have half-breeds as grandchildren. Once you marry, you must stay loyal to your husband, no matter what. As the saying goes, if you marry a cockerel, you belong with the cockerel; if you marry a dog, you stick with the dog. That's our way."

Growing up in America had liberated her from her mother's strictures, but also left her confused and alienated. If she divorced Xavier, her parents would never understand. Exchanging a respectable Chinese tycoon for an impecunious gweilo journalist would make no sense to them. Romantic love hardly figured in their order of priorities. They might even disown her for heaping shame upon them, making them lose face among their Chinatown friends.

Serenity would understand, however, for she had spoken often about human desire being at the root of sorrow. Serenity had once handed her an old pei-pa, apparently charged with deep personal associations, and had asked her to destroy it on her behalf. She had carried it to the head gardener and watched its incineration together with the hedge clippings and lawn trimmings.

She could not understand the reason at that time. Now, in

retrospect, she realized her mother-in-law must have been trying to illustrate a point. But of what? How difficult it was to grasp messages delivered in such roundabout ways! Was it a Chinese habit she had not yet acquired? One thing was clear, however. She could not possibly repay Serenity's affection by walking out of the Chu family while her mother-in-law remained so unwell.

And what of Ah Yuen, the fruit of her own womb? She had nursed him from sickly infancy to rude health. But he had not grown into a happy young man. Bringing up a child was not as easy as she had once thought. She and Serenity had tried to teach him simple, decent values. Modesty, honesty, compassion, contentment, respect for knowledge, the unimportance of material possessions. Perhaps they had succeeded too well, for he was beginning to question the activities of his frequently absent father. Why was the family living in such luxury? Why was his father hell-bent on accumulating more wealth? Why was money mania gripping the entire city? Those interrogations came with distressing frequency and neither Serenity nor herself could provide simple, convincing answers.

The conflict between ideals and reality was already leading to tensions between Ah Yuen and his father. Sometimes arguments became so heated between the two that she or Serenity had to intervene. Xavier blamed the women of the house for filling his son's head with baleful ideas. In such circumstances, how could she risk inflicting further emotional damage on her son by revealing and explaining her relationship with Seb?

The only justification for marrying Seb would be to have the large family she had always wanted. But that might no longer be possible. She had hesitated too long. She was fast approaching forty and might not be able to conceive. Even if she had children, how would they fit in with Ah Yuen? They would be half-breeds, exposed to social disdain, regardless of whether they remained in Hong Kong or departed for some secluded village in Middle England. She could not in good conscience create another generation of misfits. And, if there were not to be more children, what was the point of marriage?

Deep down she knew she was irrevocably bound to Ah Yuen. She had somehow to ease for him the inevitable pains of growing up. She did not want him to suffer the kind of emotional dislocations she had gone through herself. If a sacrifice had to be made, it would have to be Seb. He was, after all, a man familiar with pain.

She had asked him once if it depressed him to be constantly detailing racial and political hatreds, wars and human disasters.

"I suppose someone has to tell the world that such horrors exist, in case anybody cares. Sometimes I get more sick of people not caring than of the madnesses themselves."

"There must be some people who care. Why not try a different medium, such as books?"

He had laughed. "Failed at that too and I've rejection slips to prove it. A man has to make a living. Sticking with what I'm doing is about my speed. Many years ago, an old friend, T. P. Choy, taught me two things about keeping sane. Recognize one's own limitations and accept the fact that human progress, if it takes place at all, comes at the pace of the slowest glacier. I'm resigned to both."

"You're not! I can't believe that! I've read some of your articles and I can tell you care. There's fire in your belly still. The world needs people who can see things as they are and yet can present a vision of what they could be. When I was in college, reading Simone de Beauvoir changed my outlook. You also have that kind of gift. You can make a difference, like Zola or Steinbeck."

"My dear girl, I've never aimed so high. A dyspeptic outpouring now and then — which readers of the *Globe* can safely ignore over their kippers or porridge —is about my speed."

Recognizing the depth of his unhappiness, her heart had gone out to him. He was like a latter-day Don Quixote, tilting against the forces championed by her husband. He could not possibly prevail, yet he kept trying. For such a man, marriage and family responsibilities would be millstones. She wondered if he had been using the cheapness of his quarters to justify to his employer the convenience of maintaining a base in Hong Kong, just to be close to her.

She ought to set him free. It had been the infrequency of their assignations and sheer good fortune that had prevented their liaison from becoming public knowledge. That situation could not be hidden forever. Yet, when she was in his arms or when they danced to the aching lyrics of a Nat King Cole ballad, the thought of giving him up was too excruciating to bear.

Sebastian stirred, interrupting Lucille's thoughts. Lucille leaned over and found his mouth. They kissed, not passionately but affectionately, like people long accustomed to each other. Sebastian semaphored with his liberated arm, provoking a creak of protest from the antiquated bedstead.

"Sorry, darling," Lucille said. "Did I put your arm to sleep?"

"What are a few pins and needles when I'm with you?" Sebastian replied, as he massaged his arm.

Lucille kissed him again, this time more lingeringly and passionately. She felt his big hands exploring her body, stirring her to renewed excitement. She shuddered. But, remembering the lateness of the hour, she pulled away.

"Please, darling. Don't get me hot and bothered. It's almost midnight. I ought to be going."

"Yes, I recognize the flavour of that kiss. It carries the taste of imminent abandonment."

"Leaving you is the last thing I want right now. But it *is* getting late. Xavier should be home." Lucille swung her legs onto the floor and switched on the bedside lamp.

"I wasn't referring to your leaving tonight, but your disappearance next week for most of the summer." Sebastian sat up and lit a cigarette. The brass bedstead creaked again in protest.

"Oh, darling, you know my routine. I've followed it for the last three years."

"I do know. That's the reason we get so little time together. Your trips, my trips, Xavier's trips. Your social obligations and my professional assignments. I'm amazed we ever get to meet at all."

Lucille heard an edge of resentment in his voice and saw how ridiculously big he appeared in the antiquated bed. She noticed too, for the first time, that some of the hairs on his chest were turning grey. Her heart melted.

"My son's an American," she said. "I've an obligation to take him there, to visit my parents and show him the country of his birth. I can't close off his options, regardless of what I may feel about America. When he's old enough, he'll have to choose whether to make his life here or over there, whether he feels more Chinese or American or just screwed-up like me."

"What'll it be this summer? You've already shown him the car-makers of Detroit and the dream-makers of Hollywood, the wheat belt and the Bible belt, New England and Basin Street."

"Universities," Lucille replied, rummaging for her underwear among the discarded clothes on the floor. "Particularly Princeton and Harvard, to see if he wants to follow in his father's footsteps. My goodness! My son going to university next year! I can hardly believe that!"

"Time catches up with all of us. For my money, you'll still be the best-looking mum of a university student anywhere in the world!" Sebastian grinned, as he watched Lucille pulling on her panties. Her breasts hung full and voluptuous above her slender waist. "And I love you," he added.

"I love you too. You know, I don't think I can stand it if Ah Yuen decides to study abroad. I hope he doesn't. It's hard to figure out what a teenager wants these days. I don't think he's very happy at the moment. He feels he's living a sham, disapproving of too much of what his father does, yet deriving his education and other benefits from him."

"What does he disapprove of exactly?"

"Quite a lot. He doesn't like his father blighting Chinese cities with billboards advertising consumer products. If there has to be brainwashing, he deems slogans like 'Hold High The Banner Of Socialist Equality!' and 'Down With Imperialism And Neo-Colonialism!' more elevating than 'Connoisseur Cognac Adds Zest To Your Life'. He objects to the hotels his father builds. Considers mass tourism a corrupting influence and, beyond its immediate injection of cash, an exploitation of poor countries. Despises his father, too, for being a British stooge, serving on the Hong Kong Executive Council to gain connections and commercial advantages. He thinks the British are up to no good. I'm worried he might just drop out or take to drugs like kids did back in the sixties."

"He could be right on more scores than one," Sebastian said, nodding, as he stubbed out what was left of his cigarette. "We British *are* up to no good. We've managed to hone hypocrisy into a sublime art. Whitehall and Westminster are preparing to ditch the people here, you realize? Makes me sick. I can't look my neighbours in the eye without feeling ashamed. It's just as well that you and Ah Yuen have American passports."

"Oh, darling, to be fair, few here ever expected anything from the British. If things went wrong, people here'll find a way out. They've always done that. They're not idealists like you or Ah Yuen. They know it's all about money and politics. It's a trade-off. They don't mind being exploited a bit as the price for keeping the Communists off their backs while they make their own fortunes. It's not your fault if Britain wants to trade the citizens of a colony for commercial benefits in their national interest."

"It's the way we're going about it that I find abhorrent. I can't escape my share of blame. Britain is the oldest parliamentary democracy in the world. In a democracy, when an electorate allows scoundrels into public office — through apathy or laziness or cynicism — then each member of that electorate must assume individual responsibility."

Lucille sat down on the bed and took one of Seb's hands. "Most people don't take such a strict view. Don't get so worked up. Save your anger for a book."

Sebastian gave a bitter laugh. "If I ever get around to writing one. This place deserves an honest one. But a book like that is beyond my talents. By the way, do you happen to know anything about this organ-transplant institute your husband's planning in Canton? I've heard some disturbing rumours. I've been trying to run them down, but no one is very forthcoming, particularly not your husband."

"Don't know a thing, except our family doctor is somehow involved. The last time Dr. Chow came up to treat Serenity, he didn't seem happy. Although Ah Yuen asked him about it, he avoided explaining. Would you like Dr. Chow's number?"

"Not a bad idea. I've got an odd feeling about that project. Something doesn't smell right."

Lucille rose to get the address book from her handbag and then read out the telephone number. She then extracted a comb and began tidying her hair. "You know, Ah Yuen's a lot like you," she said, patting her hair into place. "Always trying to right the wrongs of the world, to live according to ideals."

"Not destined to be as professionally unsuccessful, I hope! Pity I see so little of him. He's a bright lad. I like him enormously and wish we had a son of our own like him. My father passed away last year, as you know. If you keep refusing to allow me to make an honest woman of you, the Baxingdale genes are going to disappear from the face of the earth."

No, no, Lucille thought, dropping her comb and picking it up again. She knew what would come next. She knew she had to set Seb free. But she wasn't ready to let go. Stall, delay, prevaricate, she told herself.

She half-turned away from Seb and combed her hair furiously before a non-existent mirror. A warm sensation misted over her eyes.

"Seb, darling," she said, slowly and deliberately, averting her face. "I've been meaning to talk to you about our future. But now's not a good time. Why don't we each do some serious thinking during the summer and have a nice long chat when I get back?"

She turned and saw that Seb had caught the altered timbre in her voice and had understood what she was about.

"All right," Seb said, displaying a brave smile. A melancholy look entered his grey eyes. "Let's leave it till the end of summer. Just don't forget that I love you."

"I hate all these coming-togethers and damnable goodbyes!" Lucille cried suddenly, flinging her comb against the wall. She then picked up her handbag, rushed through the beaded curtain and headed for the door. The brown and white beads rattling noisily behind her and she heard Seb calling her name as she went out of the flat.

All of a sudden, as she scrambled down the narrow staircase, she realized she was shoeless. But she did not care. At the same time she heard a songstress on a radio somewhere crooning the lyrics of a popular Chinese tune.

"Beautiful flowers do not bloom for long;
Beautiful scenes do not last forever.
After our parting of this night,
When will we be together again?"

Those lyrics of sorrowful separation seared her heart. By the time she reached the street tears were running down her face.

Another stroll in the garden

35

Although Cheng Ching took the morning flight from Hong Kong, it was late afternoon before he arrived at Chung Nan Hai. His adoptive father's physical decline was more noticeable. Years of living on the political edge had taken their toll. His wife's death the previous year had not helped. The old man's hair had gone whiter and he now required the aid of a walking stick. A fresh note of urgency settled into his voice, as if conscious of time's headlong rush. His mind, however, remained sharp and lucid.

"Trust you've swept for bugs," Cheng Ching remarked, as he offered an arm on the way to the garden.

"Yes." The General took the arm. "Nothing found. Those shenanigans seem to have stopped once the Gang of Four got put away."

"No harm in being careful. Plenty of their supporters around, itching to worm their way back."

The spring air was fresh and clean. A hesitant sunset cast a soft and gentle light upon the garden. Here and there, in accordance with traditional arrangements, a solitary cypress or pine stood like a dignified sentinel guarding the re-creations of nature: a lotus pond, an austere rockery, a network of mossy, winding paths. Now and then magpies and ravens cut through the stillness with their cries. Peonies and chrysanthemums were unfolding in abundance.

"Erh Fu, why have you sent for me?" Cheng Ching asked as they began their walk.

"Several reasons," the General replied. "I want to know about Hong Kong and the British strategy at first hand. As I've told you, they've stirred up the issue of the New Territories lease. We've more pressing matters to attend to than that wretched sideshow. Can't understand why they can't follow the Portuguese example. Leave historical problems to be dealt with when the time is ripe. I suppose they're up to their old tricks, harrying when they judge their opponents weak."

Cheng Ching shook his head. "Not necessarily, Erh Fu. The British don't understand our ways. They're tripping over their own legalisms. The New Territories account for ninety-two percent of the colony. They've lease plots of it as Crown land for varying periods, up till the middle of 1997, raising very substantial revenue.

"The trouble is they're obsessed with legality, since the leases are based on one or the other of the unequal treaties. They have embellished their possession with Letters Patent, Orders in Council and heaven knows what else. Some key provisions expire in 1997. To their legalistic way of thinking, an end of those provisions mean an end to Crown leases, and ergo an end to significant revenue. Holders of existing leases cannot have them renewed or extended beyond 1997, leaving them with wasting assets. Banks, insurance companies and mortgage lenders in turn face problems.

"The big money boys have sunk a lot into Hong Kong, earning fabulous returns. Historically they've been doing a turn every four or five years. They naturally want such a satisfactory state of affairs to continue, with full legal coverage. That's why they've been pressuring the government to get an extended agreement."

"But 1997 has no significance from our point of view. We've always been prepared to let that date slip, if it suited our purpose. By the same token, we have made known that we scrupulously retained our right to take Hong Kong back anytime we wanted."

"I know, Erh Fu. The British recognize that they cannot hold the territory against our wishes. But they also figure we're not yet ready for a row. That's why they're playing upon what they consider their legal right under international law."

"What cheek! They weren't bothered by legal rights a hundred and fifty years ago when they squatted around peddling opium. If they want to keep making money in Hong Kong they should shut their mouths and take their chances. Aren't capitalists supposed to be risk-takers?"

"A fallacy, I fear," Cheng Ching said. "The bigger a corporation gets, the more cautious it becomes. At the first whiff of uncertainty, corporations make for the door, regardless of the ruin they may leave behind. They did that to Hong Kong in '67 and they'll do it again if things don't go their way. They want to have their golden goose and eat it as well."

"Well, now that that damned issue has been raised, we must deal with it. We've told them bluntly that Chinese sovereignty has to be admitted before talks, but they won't listen. Just had one of their ministers here, ostensibly to prepare for a state visit by Chairman Hua, but he kept neighing about Hong Kong in a disgustingly nasal way. By the by, for your ears only, we're trying to ease Hua out. He's been developing a fondness for the personality cult, like old Mao."

Cheng Ching sighed. "Can't our leaders ever shake off that emperor complex?"

"The Central Committee has recently decided to take back Hong Kong. Serve the Brits right for stoking the issue. A task force has been appointed to handle transitional issues. Recommendations will come before the Politburo soon. I need regular assessments from you. I don't want decisions taken based on old inflexibilities or false assumptions. I want my own thinking to be clear. Cadres in Hong Kong don't always report actual situations on the ground. Don't understand why they are reporting the masses there are in favour of continued British rule. Aren't the Chinese there patriotic? How can anyone prefer being ruled by foreigners rather than their own people?"

Cheng Ching bowed his head. "Some cadres have been in Hong Kong too long, grown accustomed to a bourgeois lifestyle. They've become like radishes, red only on the outside. Most Hong Kong people are emotionally divided. They're proud of being Chinese and don't like being bossed by foreigners. But on the other hand, they're afraid of change.

"The British have been very clever. They've given them more or less a free hand to make money, through a policy touted variously as 'free enterprise' or 'positive non-interventionism'. It's humbug, of course, but it suits local instincts.

"What they've done is to secure the semi-monopolistic position of the vested interests and then throw open the rest to a sort of dog-eat-dog competition. A lot of locals have done well, opening small factories, trading, speculating on stocks and shares, providing services of various kinds and paying bribes to get round rules and regulations. Many fear the end of such free-wheeling ways. They know it's easier to pull the wool over British eyes than over ours. To that extent the assessments of our cadres are correct. It's the devil they know rather than the devil they don't."

"How can we alter perception, before we go public with our intentions?"

"Very difficult question. The Politburo and the whole Party must understand that Hong Kong is not like China. We can't control information there. It's wide open. At the last count there are over seventy newspapers and 400 periodicals, not to mention two private television stations and three radio stations. They publish what they like. In the past, we've supplied some of them with material to expose the private lives of the Gang of Four. They can just as easily be turned against us."

"Can't we prevent that?"

Cheng Ching shook his head. "Impossible. People in Hong Kong have also always been free to come and go. Don't need exit visas. Same with money. Professionals are marketable all over the world. China desperately needs their talents. Frighten them and they'll leave in droves. A great many have left already. We must persuade those remaining to stay and those who have left to return."

"How?"

"Erh Fu, you must think me a genius who has all the answers."

"I do," the General said, smiling and squeezing Cheng Ching's arm affectionately.

"The people need reassurance that Chinese rule will not adversely affect their way of life. More talk of accumulating wealth not being a crime will go down well. Also the switching of emphasis from Marxist-Leninist and Mao Tse-tung Thought to 'socialism with market characteristics'."

The two paused in front of the rockery, made from eroded stones, grotesquely shaped, dredged from the bottom of Lake Tai. Such stones, moulded by sand and tide, had been in the lake for centuries. How many centuries, Cheng Ching wondered, would it take for his nation to arrive at a similar state of refinement.

"I came across a technological process known as reverse

osmosis," Cheng Ching said, when their stroll resumed. "It's for converting sewage into drinking water. We need something similar politically, to convert the five million citizens of Hong Kong into good patriotic Chinese.

"I've learnt a few tricks in Hong Kong. One of them concerns commercial advertising. When making an advertisement, the advertiser does not need to tell the truth, only to create an impression that what is being stated is true. The same principle can be applied to politics. For example, we can pledge to allow only Hong Kong people to run Hong Kong after the resumption of sovereignty. That will go down very well because only the British make the big decisions at the moment and there is much resentment about this locally.

"People will take that pledge to mean a commitment by the Central Government not to control local affairs. But that is not what the pledge means at all. Why? Because under British law, anyone who has lived in Hong Kong for seven years is considered a 'Hong Kong belonger'. We have thousands of agents and cadres living there, some for many years. They are all good and proper 'Hong Kong belongers', including several members of the Work Committee. We can send more, if necessary, before the resumption of sovereignty fifteen years down the road. We already have people in place to exercise control if the Party so desires. Should that eventuality arise, who can say we have broken any pledge?"

"I see! You are suggesting that we turn the old British legalistic game back against them!"

"Precisely. Britain will be forced to go along. It'll want to say what a marvellous job it has been doing to secure Hong Kong interests. It can hardly draw attention to the lack of substance in the pledge. It knows that its national interest lies in China itself and would be glad to disengage from responsibility for its troublesome trusteeship with a minimum of fuss.

"We have one further advantage in dealing with outsiders. The rest of the world isn't clear how we operate. They think Communist governments must be monolithic, with every pronouncement cast in stone. They don't appreciate our many levels of government and the ill-defined overlappings between the Party and the state. An announcement by one official does not imply that the contents have been handed down from on high. We can test an idea by using a sympathetic Hong Kong businessman or a mere city official. If the idea goes down well, a Provincial Governor or Minister might repeat it. We need not adopt any policy until it has been proven acceptable."

"Wonderful! Confusion for confusion's sake!" the General exclaimed with pleasure. "You are a genius! Assurances and mirages! That's undoubtedly the way to go. Tell them they can live as before under Chinese rule, betting themselves silly on horse racing and dancing throughout the night. One country, two systems. Ha! Brilliant!"

"There are, unfortunately, adverse effects for ourselves," Cheng Ching cautioned, rubbing the old scar on his cheek.

"You don't have to tell me that! I get cross when I see billboards around Peking advertising brandy and face creams where once they proclaimed good socialist ideals!"

"Whatever we allow for Hong Kong will create demand for similar treatment here, and I'm not referring just to consumer preferences. I'm fearful, Erh Fu, of a contagion from Hong Kong. Corruption and sharp practices are already evident. Crime, prostitution and drug-taking are rising. The level of education in our country is low. There's a lost generation out there. People are losing jobs under privatisation. Cadres have become corrupt, losing their revolutionary spirit and their socialist honesty. To open the country may be necessary, but pace and degree must be strictly controlled. Hong Kong-style wheeling and dealing is not to be recommended for us, even if we're advanced enough socially. It could make for great instability. Don't forget, we still have the triads to deal with. They're more sophisticated than our Public Security officials. We can't have them running riot. The old methods for handling them may no longer work."

The General nodded and sighed. "I understand. Don't mind telling you, the Central Discipline Inspection Commission has just produced a secret report about top cadres speculating, profiteering and misusing state funds. A few have been sucked unwittingly into triad connections. No one wants to cure one national sickness to succumb to another."

The two men had completed two slow circuits of the garden. When they came to a bench, Cheng Ching suggested resting a while. The sun had dissolved into little more than a splash of brightness on the distant horizon. Only the soughing of leaves breached the silence.

"What do you know about a Hong Kong man named Chu Wing-seng?" the General asked, after they had been seated.

"Quite a lot," Cheng Ching replied. "Have been investigating him, to determine his political orientations. Epitome of a Hong Kong tycoon, popular because he satisfies the greed of his investors but ruthless in pursuing his own goals. Useful man to have on your side but could be a formidable enemy. His methods are regarded by many as underhanded, but my people have not been able to pin anything criminal on him. Why do you ask?"

"He's been making a splash here. In very thick with a couple of members on the Central Committee. Taught them how to make quick money. Don't exactly know how. There's talk of insider trading and other activities I've never even heard of. Got some provincial leaders excited about starting a stock exchange in Shanghai. Building up quite a following.

"Rumour has it he's got a few Kwangtung cadres involved in an organ-transplant institute in Canton. Modernizing medical facilities, they called it. Talk of earning foreign exchange by selling organs from executed criminals to foreigners. Communists are supposed to be atheists and unsentimental, but that's going too far. Most people, even criminals, still want to enter the next world with their body parts intact. We can't strip bodies like abandoned cars. Public opinion will turn against us. We haven't gone through a revolution to sink to this!"

"I've heard those rumours," Cheng Ching said. "That's what I fear about allowing profits to dictate policy. Everybody who knows about that transplant project is tight-lipped. Chu's been bringing doctors to Hong Kong to study transplant techniques. On the face of it, everything seems above board. Prison personnel, too, ostensibly to set up research clinics using volunteers from the convict population. My people are still investigating."

"Can't always observe the niceties. Chu has money and money corrupts. Available evidence suggests Chu has already gone too far. We may have to deal with him sooner or later."

"He visits China often. Can't he be warned off?"

"Too many high connections," the General said. "We need all the support we can muster in the Central Committee. Don't know the extent of his influence either. He is already a destabilizing influence here. If the head of a serpent is severed, the rest will wither away. One day we may have to take drastic action."

Cheng Ching's throat tightened. Previously he had been an unquestioning believer in the cause. He had fought for it in Korea. Though doubts arose during the Cultural Revolution, he still subordinated himself to the collective wisdom of the Party. The harsh treatments meted out to many had been endorsed by the Central Committee. Likewise, the moves against the Gang of Four. But for a general and his adopted son to pronounce in secret the death of another man seemed wrong, no matter how high-minded the motive. That would be to return to the ways of the Gang of Four. It seemed almost laughable, in retrospect, that he should have been so concerned over disclosing details of Chu's private family affairs when he was now discussing Chu's possible elimination.

"You don't want me to finish my investigations first?" Cheng Ching asked.

"Yes, so long it does not drag on. Events are moving too fast. We can't afford to wait too long."

"You intend to have him dealt with in Hong Kong?"

"No, nor in China either. When the necessity arises he must be disposed of in circumstances so commonplace that no question would arise. Are there not mountain roads in Switzerland prone to accidents? Or perhaps a run-of-the-mill mugging in New York. You plan what's best."

Cheng Ching bowed his head. He might not be doing the actual deed. It wouldn't be the same as blasting the brains out of that frightened American boy in Korea. But so long as he served the Party, there would always be fresh enemies to dispose of, fresh calls to duty. He understood why men of principle often sought solitude away from the world. He longed to quit the pressures of power-politics to return to Thirsty Hills.

"I'll start the planning process. It'll be complicated," he said. "Chu's travelling plans are unpredictable and chaotic.

The General smiled approvingly. "There are two other

matters of importance I must discuss with you. You don't have to be told that politicians are chameleons. The Maoist of yesterday can become the dissident of today. Some well-meaning people in Hong Kong have been operating a pipeline to help dissidents out of the country. They think they are helping believers in democracy. The trouble is that they don't know enough about what's going on. We don't want supporters of the Gang of Four to escape justice. Instructions have gone out to Old Ironsides to tighten the net. You must do the same."

Cheng Ching nodded.

"You've done well," General Yeh continued. "You've got the Hong Kong operations in fine shape. Our armed forces have secured vital information and equipment. Soon it'll be time to bring you home.

"If all goes well, we should be replacing the Director in Hong Kong next year with a member of the Central Committee. The man we have in mind is currently Party Secretary of Kiangsu Province. A very good man. He should command enough standing in the Party to assume your functions as well as those of the Directorship. That'll make the chain of command less complicated in the run-up to 1997."

"I shall look forward to coming home! I've only seen my mother once since leaving for Hong Kong. It's about time I looked after her and kept my promise to my father. She's been struggling to carry on since his death."

"You can certainly return to Thirsty Hills for a spell. You deserve a holiday."

"Erh Fu, what do you mean 'for a spell'? I've done my fair share. I ought to go home and look after my mother."

"Stop this foolish talk. It's good to be a filial son, but even better to be a great patriot. You're meant for high office."

"No, Erh Fu, I don't seek high office. I just want to lead an ordinary life from now on."

"Because you don't seek high office that's why you must have it! Too many want it for the sake of fame or personal gain. People like you are rare. Your father did not misname you when he called you Cheng the Righteous. Can't you see?

"My time is short. What we seek to achieve will take generations. You must carry on after I'm gone. Inspire others to continue after you've gone. Otherwise, what would we have lived for?

"Here's what I've got planned for you. Return to Anhui, build up a power base. Without a provincial base, you won't get far at the centre. Get yourself known, gather supporters. Bring improvements there, just as your father has done. I'll use my influence to get you into the Central Committee. From there you can work your way into the Politburo. Then steer our country in the right direction. I'm counting on you."

Cheng Ching turned to look at his adoptive father. In the fading light, the General's white hair and sunken cheeks seemed to speak of weariness and old age. But defiance still shone in his eyes. The sight filled Cheng Ching with awe. He felt ashamed for wearying of the struggle, for wanting to hide away at Thirsty Hills. His adoptive father's face told him that the thirty years given to his country were not enough. He owed it to his father, to Ying, Old Tung, Mad Fan and countless others to carry on. Otherwise, how could their sacrifices be endowed with purpose? He had no choice.

"Erh Fu, we had better go inside," he said. "It's getting chilly out here."

More revelations

36

Serenity had been simulating sleep for the better part of an hour, but real sleep evaded her. One reason was the presence of Mrs. Yim, the night nurse, a fat, lumpy and over-solicitous widow, sitting under a dim reading lamp devouring one of her cheap romances. Another was all the legal rubbish Ah Seng had been pressing upon her in recent weeks — wills, probates, tax havens, estate duties, avoidance measures, trusts. She had been feeling something amiss for days. But was it *that* obvious that her present existence was heading towards a conclusion?

She had allowed him to have his way, perversely pleased he had been observant. She had no fear of passing into another existence. She had long been reconciled to it. She would have to endure many more before achieving Nirvana.

She hoped she had made the right arrangements for everyone, so far as she understood the mountain of legal documents. Modest bequests to Lucille and Ah Yuen; the house and its art treasures to the city as a museum upon Ah Yuen reaching the age of twenty-five; the rest into a charitable trust, with Lucille as trustee. The trust income would be devoted to educational charities and the initial upkeep of the museum. Ah Seng had wanted only a right of first refusal should Gold Star shares be sold. She was happy to oblige.

How people worried about death, Serenity thought. Why should so much attention be devoted to the useless physical shells that human beings carried around with them? About three months ago, she had slipped going to the toilet at night and had bumped her head on the edge of the washbasin. It was nothing serious but Ah Seng had insisted on hiring a night nurse to prevent similar accidents. It was true her limbs were not as reliable as before, but she was far from being an invalid. Her angina was only slightly worse and Dr. Chow had brought around young Dr. Lo to help look after her. The only thing she had against the new doctor was his excessive keenness to extract blood for tests. She loathed needles!

She had tried to dissuade Ah Seng from imposing Mrs. Yim. In the end, realizing it was his way of showing concern, she relented. Poor child, poor man. She pitied her son, as one who had learnt nothing of quietism and solitude. In solitude her spirit could roam, her mind could probe with its inner eye. To be placed under the surveillance of Mrs. Yim, particularly when her soul lay exposed and unguarded in sleep, was disconcerting.

Apart from Mrs. Yim's presence and Ah Seng's legal documents, her insomnia had another cause. A sense of unfinished business in respect of both Lucille and Ah Seng.

Lucille was as good a mother and as caring a daughter-in-law as any woman could hope for. But the poor girl was not at peace. To convince a woman brought up in America that existence was but a dream and that desire was the cause of all suffering required patience. She had tried to lead Lucille to the teachings of the Lord Buddha and to improve her Chinese by reciting the sutras. One evening, after recitations in the Meditation Room, Lucille had suddenly broken down and confessed that no love existed between Ah Seng and herself. She pleaded for Serenity's help in bringing up Ah Yuen, as if she were on the verge of running away and abandoning her marital home.

In order to comfort Lucille and to indicate that she understood her suffering, Serenity brought Lucille to her room and showed her the old pei-pa. She watched her fingering its smooth frame and its silent strings with bewilderment.

"This instrument once formed an important part of my existence," she said. "But it's now only a reminder of happenings of long ago. The seasons come and go, the moon waxes and wanes. Existence passes like a dream, like a breeze between bamboos. It is difficult to free oneself from worldly cravings. Perhaps we can help each other free ourselves."

With that, she instructed Lucille to destroy the instrument. Lucille had hesitated before accepting the instruction, but did not question it. From that moment an understanding grew between them. That had been more than six years ago, when she had sensed Lucille to be at her unhappiest. Now, particularly with Ah Yuen growing up, the girl had become more poised and self-assured.

Serenity turned on her bed. Through the gloom she could not detect the old black telephone that rang no more. It was all that remained from a long-lost era. Only the unfinished business with Ah Seng remained. All of a sudden it seemed to take on a fresh urgency. She sat up and reached for the bedside lamp.

Mrs. Yim rushed up, flesh quivering beneath her winter clothing. "Do you need medicine, ma'am, or help to go to the toilet?" she asked.

"Neither," Serenity said, switching on the light. "What time is it?"

"Almost quarter to midnight, ma'am."

"Please go and see if my son has returned."

"Yes, ma'am."

Mrs. Yim disappeared but was back within three minutes. "Not home yet, ma'am. Neither is young Mrs. Chu."

"Mrs. Yim, would you kindly go downstairs and wait for my son? Please tell him the moment he's back that I would like to see him, no matter how late it might be."

Mrs. Yim looked doubtful for a moment, before nodding and leaving the room.

Left to herself, Serenity savoured again the delight of solitude. She looked at the minature pine her husband had left and smiled. She had cared for it and it had remained more sturdy than herself. Small wonder the Chinese regarded the pine as a symbol of endurance.

You've done well, little plant, she thought. We've both endured. I've lived to see my grandson grow into manhood, to feel him developing attachments to notions dear to his grandfather. He has rewarded my efforts, choosing to study history and philosophy locally, just to be close to this old woman. That is joy beyond measure. My task is done. Soon, little plant, we can both pass into another existence.

Serenity gradually drifted in and out of sleep. Her next awareness was the scent of perfume, a gentle touch on her shoulder and Lucille's voice asking: "Mother, are you all right?"

She opened her eyes and found Lucille, in a turquoise evening gown, squatting next to the bed. Behind her stood Ah Seng in a dinner jacket, and a quaking Mrs. Yim.

"I'm fine," Serenity said, smiling. She raised herself from

her bed. Lucille shook out the pillows and placed them behind her.

"Had a good evening?" Serenity asked, after she had settled comfortably.

"It was only dinner at the Chief Secretary's up the road," Lucille replied, affection sparkling in her eyes. "The men went on and on, talking shop, arguing about negotiations with Peking."

"Mrs. Yim said you wanted to see me urgently," Xavier interposed. "Gave us quite a turn seeing her waiting at the door."

"Sorry. I had something I wanted to talk to you about."

"Couldn't it have waited? It's half past midnight."

"I'd rather talk now, if you don't mind."

Xavier undid his black tie and the collar button. "All right, Mother, what is it?"

Serenity hesitated and seemed to address the room at large. "I wonder if I might have a few moments alone with my son?"

Xavier frowned and shrugged.

"Goodnight, Mother," Lucille said, kissing Serenity on the cheek before leaving with Mrs. Yim.

"Won't you sit down?" Serenity said, picking up her prayer beads from the side table and moving to make room on the bed.

Xavier obeyed. The fumes of alcohol were on his breath, possibly those of Connoisseur cognac. He began massaging his neck. "Well, what is it you want to talk about, Mother?"

Serenity looked at her son as her fingers worked the prayer beads. Vitality was seeping out of him, she thought. Behind his spectacles his eyes no longer shone with aggressive brightness. Though his face appeared youthful still, the signs of middle age had crept into his deportment. "I want you to do me a favour after I'm gone," she said.

"Mother, you're going to be around for a good while yet. Why this unseemly haste? If you want something done, just say so."

"You promise?"

"Yes, Mother."

"Since your father passed away, I've been sending money to one of his former associates in Taiwan. His surname is Fung."

"You don't mean Buck-toothed Fung?"

"You mustn't be disrespectful. He's an elder. He used to play with you when you were a baby. You should refer to him as Uncle Fung."

"I met him when I was with Father in Taiwan. The man strikes me as a rogue. Father said he was a habitual gambler and not to be trusted with money. Why should you be sending him anything?"

"Rogue or not, gambler or not, we owe him our lives. He made it possible for your father to get food during the Japanese occupation. Otherwise you and I might well not be here today. I want you to continue to send him money for as long as he lives."

"Payments out of gratitude?"

Serenity sighed. "Possibly, but not exactly. He left Hong Kong after the war. Your father kept in contact but I never saw him again. After your father died, he wrote, offering condolences. He also said your father had been sending him money to tidy up some unfinished business in Taiwan. He asked if the remittances would continue. That was the first I had heard about remittances. I didn't know what they were for. Your father never mentioned anything. I checked with your father's secretary and Mrs. Leung confirmed that your father had been remitting money to a lawyer in Taipei each year, to be drawn on quarterly by Uncle Fung. The sum was not large. I figured your father must have his reasons for the payments, so I continued the practice. Didn't want to upset whatever arrangement that might be in place. Apparently started back in 1956."

"Good grief! You're telling me that Uncle Fung has been taking money from you and father for twenty-seven years? What in heaven's name for? It must be quite some tidying up!"

Serenity hesitated for a long moment. "At first I didn't ask. A couple of years later, when Uncle Fung asked for an increase, I did ask. According to him, it was to take care of something you did."

"Something I did?" Xavier shook his head and spread his hands, as if deeply aggrieved. "Told you that man's a rogue. I didn't do anything in Taiwan."

"Uncle Fung said differently. He claimed you became involved with a dancing girl and got her pregnant. He said your father had a hand in the arrangements and offered to pay for an abortion. But the girl wanted to keep the child. So your father got Uncle Fung to pass her money on a regular basis to support mother and son."

"Fei-Fei!" Xavier sprang up. "Why didn't you tell me? Why have you kept it from me for so long?"

"You mean there really was a girl and a child? I never bought Uncle Fung's story because I always take whatever he says with several grains of salt. He said it was just wild oats and perhaps the child wasn't even yours. He said a small sum would be enough to keep the girl quiet."

Xavier removed his glasses and rubbed his eyes. He looked suddenly pathetic in his dinner jacket, like a head waiter who had just been given the sack.

"Wild oats! Fei-Fei wasn't the kind of girl to demand money. I loved her. She was in fact the only woman I've ever loved. I offered to marry her but she rejected me. You don't know how much pain that caused me. You should have told me about the payments! You've made me miss my chance!" Xavier's voice broke and he began to sob.

Tears came to Serenity's eyes as she watched her son's heaving shoulders. He wasn't just an insensitive business machine after all! He could be hurt like everybody else. And over a boyhood love, of all things! But she remained sceptical over the details. She leaned forward with outspread arms, reaching for him. Xavier fell into them and she held him tight. His shoulders quivered and the years fell away. He became her little boy again, just like that day he found her crying over the now-destroyed pei-pa.

"Holy Buddha, how was I to know the girl meant anything to you?" Serenity said, stroking the back of Xavier's head. "You never mentioned you had got involved with a girl in Taiwan. There's nothing unusual about teenagers having flings with dancing girls."

"It wasn't like that. She was from a poor family, trying to support them."

"They usually are. I doubt if you really got her pregnant. Apparently she wanted only money and your father was generous. Such things happen."

Xavier disengaged himself and rummaged for a handkerchief to wipe his face. "I loved her and she rejected me. The way she cast everything I had offered aside really hurt, Mother. It was the same when Father rejected me. I swore no one would ever hurt me that way again."

"Your father didn't reject you, Ah Seng. He loved you. You have to believe that. You just misunderstood what he was about."

"Why didn't you tell me about the payments earlier?" Xavier asked. He replaced his spectacles and his voice had resumed its normal tone. His features, too, were once again under control.

"I didn't really believe what Uncle Fung said, didn't want to complicate your life. You were married, with a son. You were swamped, coping with Gold Star. There were riots and bombs in the streets at the time. No one knew what was going to happen next. It's not uncommon for dancing girls to take advantage of infatuated boys. You think your father and I would have abandoned a grandchild if we thought there was the remotest chance it could be yours? Your father was not that kind of person and neither am I. Your father must have been unconvinced by Uncle Fung's story. That's why he never said anything to me."

"Why must you always think that whatever Father does is right? He's mortal, you know. He can make mistakes. Look at where he's left this family. Why can't you back my instincts for once?"

"Whatever took place happened a long time ago. No one has made a fuss since. Let it be over and done with. Just continue to pay the small amount as a gesture of gratitude. Uncle Fung is a very old man now and he's had an unfortunate life."

"I have to know the truth. Where's Fei-Fei now?"

"I don't know. For that you'll have to ask Uncle Fung."

"If there's any truth to the story, I have to find Fei-Fei and make things right for her. I can't bear the thought of her having to beg for money from someone like Uncle Fung. If I have a son, I want to reclaim him."

"You already have a son. Ah Yuen."

Xavier snorted. "Ah Yuen! Can't talk to him. He's a strange boy, a teenager who prefers the company of old men like Uncle Yue. They lunch at the Evergreen from time to time. Did you know that? They yak about tea and porcelain and ancient voyages by Chinese mariners. It's weird, I tell you."

"Ah Yuen has a right to develop his own interests."

"His own interests! They're a joke! Fat lot of good they'll do in the world we're in. Can't he grasp the fact — can't any of you grasp the fact — that I'm the one making history, that I'm giving substance to the new philosophy of global capitalism? I've gone further than any man has ever dared to venture. Why doesn't he study that? What's the use of a son like him? He'll just let everything I've done go to pot."

Serenity's heart sank. "Ah Yuen's your own flesh and blood," she pleaded. "Let him lead his own life. He doesn't have to follow you. It seems he's not interested in business. You've said before that you couldn't afford time for children. One reaps what one sows. You *don't* have another child. Ah Yuen's all you've got. Both your father and I know what Uncle Fung is like. He'll make up anything to get money, turning fiction into fact. Don't let his words upset you and fill you with unhappiness. You'll just end up chasing shadows and ghosts. Leave the past alone, Ah Seng."

"No, I must find Fei-Fei. I must look after her now. Where can I reach that old rogue?"

"I don't know. I didn't deal with him direct, only with a lawyer in Taipei."

"Who's the lawyer, then, and how can I contact him?"

"Ah Seng, do you really have to go through with this? She was a dancing girl. You met her at an impressionable age a long, long time ago. You cannot imagine the ramifications that sort of life can bring. Even if you find her, she won't be the beautiful and innocent girl you once knew. She would be a middle-aged woman, possibly ugly, bloated, even diseased. You might be utterly horrified by what you find."

"I got over the horror of discovering what you used to be, Mother. Is my love less worthy than my father's? Now tell me, who's the lawyer?"

Serenity gasped and bowed her head. She clasped her prayer beads between her hands and her body shook. "I don't want you to suffer, Ah Seng," she said. "I won't tell you."

"How can I arrange payments if you won't tell me?"

"I've just made a remittance. Another's not due till next year. I'll tell you once you've calmed down."

Xavier stared at his mother. "I'll get the information from Mrs. Leung."

"You seem to have forgotten you discharged Mrs. Leung for refusing to tell you about your father's personal affairs."

Xavier rose from the bed again. "I'll find Fung," he said, evenly. "I have ways of getting information, with or without your help. It just takes a little longer without, that's all."

"Ah Seng," Serenity half-wailed, as she watched her son turning to leave. She wanted to deter him, to plead with him again to leave well enough alone. She opened her mouth to call but no sound came. She fell back against the pillows, trembling, and felt a rushing pain in her chest.

The Chief Secretary's dilemma
HONG KONG
SEPTEMBER 1984

37

The office of Sir Reginald Beaufont Quinn on the fifth floor of the Government Secretariat was spacious and anonymous. Virtually every item of furniture in the room, from the portrait of the Queen hanging behind the desk to the ungainly armchairs, was standard government issue. The exceptions were two panels of temple carvings, gilded and mounted, decorating the wall opposite his desk. Quinn had acquired them for a song in Cat Street when he first came to Hong Kong thirty years before, at a time when such objects excited colonizers with their novelty and workmanship.

The Chief Secretary studied the carvings wistfully. They would have to be taken down soon, to be shipped to his retirement cottage in darkest Surrey, together with his collection of bronze Buddha heads and Buddha hands picked up during official trips to Bangkok much earlier in his career. Those items, exquisitely crafted, would provide a point of reference for inquisitive neighbours, nailing his long association with a mystical East. They would also provide launching pads for entertaining tales to deflect curiosity about his early life in Britain. Even in front of his wife and children he disliked references back to his parents' haberdashery shop in Basildon. It was simply not a suitable ancestry for a knight of the realm.

Of course, such souvenirs also harboured risks. The more discerning might see them as desecrations, the destruction of foreign heritage and alien gods for the sake of money rather than culture. His own role in fostering tourism might be called into question, although he was proud of having had a hand in making tourism the second most important industry in Hong Kong.

One of the telephones on the desk rang and the Chief Secretary picked it up. It was Miss Pringle, his Personal Assistant, reporting that Mr. Xavier Chu had arrived.

Sir Reginald looked at his watch. It was five minutes before the appointed hour. He crinkled the corners of his hazel eyes and said: "In five minutes." He needed a moment to arrange a more sombre and sympathetic countenance. His visitor's mother had recently passed away.

Altering his appearance was not altogether an easy matter for Sir Reginald. He had no overtly attractive attributes and making himself likeable took a lot of practice in front of the mirror. His facial muscles were now so well conditioned that putting on a warm gaze and an attentive half-smile presented no problem. But putting on a mournful look was a different matter. In any event, his ruddy complexion, acquired through exhausting weekend walks with his wife along the Sai Kung Peninsula and in the Plover Cove Country Park, did not marry well with a doleful appearance.

Whilst preparing himself, Sir Reginald selected from an in-tray a "Top Secret" file and placed it in front of him. He was not sure what it contained because its crimson jacket was marked only with a Safe Care Registry number and the words "Top Secret" in black. But its contents did not matter. Its presence was enough to underline his involvement in great affairs of state.

A tap on the door heralded the entrance of a blonde woman, middle-aged and generous around the hips. "Mr. Chu is here, Sir," Miss Pringle announced.

Sir Reginald came round his desk to shake the visitor by the hand. "Can Miss Pringle get you tea or coffee?" he asked

"No, thanks. I shan't be long," Xavier replied.

Sir Reginald nodded and Miss Pringle retreated. He waved his guest into one of the armchairs and said in suitably lugubrious tones: "I'm very sorry about your mother, Xavier. Those long final months must have been very trying. Our deepest condolences."

"Thank you, Reggie. It was good of you and Brenda to come to the funeral. Thanks also for the floral tribute."

"If there's anything Brenda or I can do, please don't hesitate."

Sir Reginald restored his warm gaze and his half-smile. He liked Xavier Chu. The fellow was good-natured and respectful, in spite of being such a power in the commercial world. Sensitive to the proclivities of government, too. His wife, Lucille, was intriguing, a real stunner. They hosted the most delicious and sort-after Chinese dinners imaginable. But more than anything else, he liked Xavier because he made him feel superior. One needed the company of a diminutive man to feel like a giant at five-seven.

"There is something, actually," Xavier said. "I'd like leave of absence from Exco."

"But Exco's still in recess. You don't need leave."

"Yes, I know, but it'll resume in days and I need to get away. My mother's left me with some unfinished business."

"Of course, of course. I'm sure the Governor'll understand. How long do you want?"

"Not sure. Make it open-ended?"

"That's rather awkward. It has to be gazetted and so forth. The Governor won't like your being absent at a critical time like the present. Peking's being particularly intransigent. The Old Man relies a great deal on your advice, you know."

"Come on, Reggie. You don't have to flannel me. What's my advice worth? Nothing! Consulting Exco's just window dressing to calm the locals. You know it and I know it. If it hadn't been for the insistence of the Governor, Whitehall would have kept us in the dark till everything's been stitched up. Our not knowing anything makes for a less complicated life in Whitehall."

Sir Reginald was taken aback by his visitor's uncharacteristic candour. During all the years he had known Xavier, the man had always spoken in smooth, accommodating tones, like someone chasing a sale. The unexpected change threw him, but he maintained his half-smile.

"That's unfair, Xavier" he said, in a parody of light-heartedness. "You shouldn't be taken in by Peking-inspired leaks and mischievous articles. Journalists are always after sensational headlines. The Governor has always felt a strong sense of moral responsibility for the people of Hong Kong. You've got to remember that this is a colony, however, and we're just civil servants. We try our utmost to put the local case, but in the final analysis we have to take orders from London."

"The Governor *is* a fine man. But you have put your finger on it. Good intentions and moral responsibility don't count for much without power. Whitehall's calling the tune and it is concentrating on the British national interest. A few million lesser breeds half-way round the world, well, they're are just an inconvenience aren't they? Better to sweep them under the carpet.

"You remember the Foreign Secretary coming in April and telling Exco that Britain couldn't achieve continuing British administration under Chinese sovereignty? Some of those silly Exco appointees actually wept! They believed Britain had genuinely fought the good fight and lost. I never did. I knew all along it was a confidence trick, stitched up beforehand, possibly in a corner over canapés at one of the innumerable gatherings of international diplomats. I'm not without connections across the border, Reggie. Or elsewhere, for that matter. The Chinese told Mrs. Thatcher in no uncertain terms long ago that sovereignty was not negotiable and continuing British administration after 1997 was out of the question. I don't know why your Ministers fooled people into believing otherwise."

The Chief Secretary swallowed hard. In his heart he knew Whitehall had been economical with the truth and the local administration had been forced to play the accomplice. But 1997 was still thirteen years away. Anything could happen before then. One certainty was that he would be retired a year hence and guiding the colony through the transition would be somebody else's responsibility. He wetted his lips before attempting to salvage some self-esteem.

"Xavier, we've known each other a good long while. Surely you're not suggesting we've been deliberately selling the colony down the river? You must accept that we've tried our best. Just think of the number of trips Ministers have made to Peking and the diplomatic notes flying all over the place. The files on this are about a mile high. I've just been looking at another set of Priority telegrams between our Ambassador and the FCO."

The Chief Secretary gestured vaguely towards the Top Secret file on his desk.

"We can both see the shifting power equations, Reggie," Xavier replied, matter-of-factly and with an innocent smile. "We both realize China's going to be the big bonanza in the decades ahead. Britain wants to trade us for that. Can't blame Britain, but can't fault us for making our own arrangements either.

"Quite frankly, you guys bungled it from the start, sending MacLehose to talk about land leases in the New Territories. There's a Chinese way for dealing with such matters. You've got to know when heated words and sabre-rattling are for real and when they're just play-acting. The long-running row between the mainland and Taiwan is a case in point. In due time it'll be settled in a Chinese way. What if it takes a hundred years to arrive at? What is a hundred years, so long as there's money to be made in the interim? Your experts don't seem to know our mentality. That's why their initiatives blew up in their faces. And we're being made to pay the price."

"I'm sorry you feel that way, Xavier. Negotiations are still going on. There're still important things to play for. That's why we need your advice."

"Nobody needs *my* advice. It's all a done deal, so far as I'm concerned. I've got to attend to things left by my mother."

"All right. I'll clear things with the Governor. Where are you off to?"

"Taiwan."

"Xavier! You're joking! You can't go to Taiwan! We had an explicit understanding before you joined Exco that there would be no going to Taiwan. That's politically unacceptable. Good God, man, you're an important person in this part of the world. The local media are like bloodhounds. The moment they sniff where you've gone there'll be enormous headlines. Peking'll accuse us of playing the 'Two China' game. Local confidence will be dealt a blow more serious than when Jardines moved domicile to Bermuda. You must consider the bigger picture, the welfare of the community at large.

"Strictly between you and me, we're having enough problems as it is. We've just found out that Kwangtung Public Security have nabbed a Hong Kong social worker for smuggling dissidents out of China. Those bleeding hearts do get us into awful jams, you know. The Chinese have kept mum about the arrest so far, so we're not sure what they're up to."

"Social worker? What's the fellow's name?"

Sir Reginald rose and went to his desk. He extracted from his in-tray an orange-coloured file marked "Secret" and flipped through a few pages. Then he read out the transliteration of a Chinese name.

He heard a sharp intake of breath from his guest. And then a muttering which sounded like "Little Ho".

"I beg your pardon? You know the man?" the Chief Secretary asked, as he resumed his seat.

"Yes, we used to go to the same school. Belonged to the same Boy Scout troop."

"Well, he seems to have gone to the bad."

"Impossible! The man hasn't a devious bone in his body. He's a British subject. You'll make formal representations, of course. Get him consular access. Otherwise they might shoot him."

"Can't do that, I'm afraid. The intelligence is secret. Can't be compromised. In any event, Peking's position is clear. Every Chinese in China comes under its jurisdiction. We can't argue that issue at a critical time like this."

"As a British subject he's entitled to British protection."

"Not when he's in China, I'm afraid."

"Not even if he were Anglo-Saxon?"

"It is pointless speculating about theoretical situations. We must deal with actual circumstances. There's too much at stake at the moment. We can't risk upsetting Peking over the fate of one man who has apparently broken Chinese law."

Sir Reginald's voice was thick with hurt. The implication of racism got under his skin. His complexion had lost some of its ruddiness. His smile had vanished.

Xavier's face, too, seemed drained of expression. "Well, perhaps I can do things governments cannot," he said, evenly. "In any case, I have business in Taiwan."

The Chief Secretary saw eyes as hard as pebbles behind the spectacles of his visitor. He knew that whatever influence he might have had over that baby-faced man was gone. He was now the supplicant. "Can't that be done elsewhere?" he half-pleaded. "Bring the people here or to Japan. Do what you have to, but not in Taiwan."

"Sorry. It's got to be Taiwan. If being on Exco makes things difficult, I can resign. Then I'll be a completely private person."

"That's worse! How can you possibly be a completely private person, for heaven's sake?" the Chief Secretary cried, shaking his head distractedly. "You're the Chairman of Gold Star. You control a big chunk of the economy here, not to mention interests in other parts of the world. Resignation from Exco would suggest major policy differences between you and the government. Going to Taiwan might be taken to imply a pull-out of Gold Star from Hong Kong. Rumours would buzz like hornets. Please, Xavier, think it over. Find another way. Or at the very least postpone your trip till the deal with Peking has been done. We've been friends a long time and I've never asked for a favour. I'm asking now. Please don't do this on my watch."

"Well, there may be a way around the problem," Xavier said, pausing as if pondering a solution.

The silence lengthened and the Chief Secretary waited with bated breath.

"My mother used to give money to a number of Buddhist organisations," Xavier finally resumed. "One of them has a monastery in Japan, in Hokkaido. I can contact the abbot and see if I can go into retreat there, to mourn the passing of my mother, as it were. We could let it be known that I'm so grief-stricken that the length of my retreat is indefinite. I would also formally hand over the running of Gold Star to my deputy to make the story credible.

"I'll have to stay in the monastery for at least a few days, until the media pack gets tired of waiting around outside. So far as the world is concerned, I'm in retreat. Full stop. Neither you nor the Hong Kong government need be concerned with anything else that I might do. Would you be satisfied with that?"

"How can you pull that off without anyone finding out? You have to pass through immigration and customs to get out of Japan and the same again on entering Taiwan."

Xavier smiled. "Leave that to me."

The Chief Secretary rubbed his temples with both hands. "I don't know, Xavier. Sounds awfully risky. If anything goes wrong, London'll have my head, perhaps even my pension."

"It's important for me, Reggie. London doesn't have to know anything. So far as you're concerned, I'm just on leave to mourn my mother in a monastery in Hokkaido. No one can be responsible for anything else I might do. If I'm caught, you don't know a thing. Just blame me... for deviousness, treachery or whatever you like."

The Chief Secretary sucked in air through his clenched teeth. "It might just work. We'll have to co-ordinate press releases.

Once the Gazette Notification is out, the media will demand details. We must stick to the same story. Do you mind if I send somebody around from Government Information Services to tie things up with you?"

"By all means. Whom do you have in mind?"

"Do you know Derek Soames?"

"Certainly. Reputation for being an alcoholic."

"Exactly! Perfect camouflage. The media know Soames is seldom trusted with anything very sensitive. Got a loose tongue. If he handles Press queries about your leave, everybody will be off guard, figuring it to be something routine and innocuous. Of course, you must under no circumstances tell Soames anything about Taiwan or this social worker on the other side. Or your own people, for that matter. Not even Lucille. Everything must remain strictly between you, me and the walls in this room."

"Naturally."

The Chief Secretary heaved a sigh of relief. "Thanks, Xavier," he said. "You're a real friend."

"An official friend or a personal friend?"

"Both, of course," Sir Reginald replied, with a chuckle. He felt he had pulled a tricky chestnut out of the fire.

"Of course," Xavier said, smiling as he rose to leave.

The two men shook hands and Sir Reginald accompanied his guest towards the door. As they reached it, Xavier asked: "Reggie, since we're such good friends, official and otherwise, how come you never hinted to me that your Special Branch has been tapping my phones and opening my mail?"

"What! Tapping your phones, opening your mail? Really? How outrageous! I had no idea. Those intelligence types sometimes get out of control."

"That's strange. I have it on good authority that my name's on the Special Branch's Q List. I understand also that every name going onto that list has to be specifically approved by the Chief Secretary."

Sir Reginald's jaw dropped and his face went dead.

Xavier smiled again but his eyes remained stony. As he reached for the doorknob, he said: "Thanks for being such a pal."

Confronting the past

38

Personal matters were making a mess of his business life, Xavier Chu thought, as he tried to find his way along the side lanes spreading like rabbit warrens behind the main thoroughfares of Taipei. He had just spent ten tedious days in Japan, negotiating with intermediaries to rescue Little Ho from his predicament. He supposed it was a success of sorts. In consideration of money deposited into Swiss bank accounts and pulling strings to get children of some Communist cadres into institutions of higher learning in America, he had received an assurance that the death penalty would not be demanded. The only other concession was that Little Ho would not have to serve more than five years in prison. Now he had to turn his attention to locating Buck-toothed Fung and discovering the fate of Fei-Fei. It was a pity such tasks could not be delegated to any of his minions.

At last he found the right lane. The number given was a narrow, four-storied structure tucked away in a corner, abutting the back of a small shopping complex on one side and a dealer in mirrors and glass on the other. Across the lane there was a fruiterer and a seller of fresh tofu. The human traffic through the lane and the numerous motor scooters parked along its length suggested a lively working-class environment. At the rear of the shopping complex a leaking drainpipe sent a ribbon of green slime slithering down the wall onto an almost non-existent pavement, before trickling messily into a storm drain.

Badly designed and built on the cheap, Xavier surmised, with his property developer's eye. He moved towards the sturdy metal gate with a half-grille guarding the entrance. He studied the names alongside the cluster of bells next to the grille. After he found one on the first floor marked "Fung", he pressed it.

Presently, a woman's voice shouted from somewhere overhead, in Mandarin: "Who you looking for?"

It took Xavier a while to realize the voice was coming from a small balcony jutting from the first floor. He stepped backwards and, looking upwards, saw a tiny balcony encased with metal bars, like a cage. From there a white-haired woman peered at him suspiciously.

"I have present for Uncle Fung," Xavier replied, in halting Mandarin. He held up a carrier bag containing two bottles of Connoisseur cognac and smiled.

"Who are you?"

"The son of Chu Tung-po."

The head examined him up and down and then disappeared. After a while the metal gate to the building scraped open and the owner of the head of white hair stood before him. She was dressed in a blue cotton track suit much the worse for wear and a pair of rubber flip-flops.

"Please follow me. There's no lift."

The cramped hallway and staircase were badly in need of a fresh coat of paint. But otherwise the common areas were well-swept, indicating that the residents had not yet completely abandoned their care.

Xavier noted the matronly proportions of the old woman as he followed her up the stairs. Though her movements were slow, the provocative sway of her bottom reminded him of Fei-Fei's.

On the first floor, a metal grille similar to the one at the entrance stood ajar. Behind that was an opened wooden door. The old woman led Xavier into a small sitting room. The furnishings were sparse, with only a few relics from more prosperous times. Patches of mildew disfigured the walls. There were two chairs, set on either side of a nondescript wooden table. Although the window and the doorway to the balcony were open, there was an unpleasant odour.

Xavier placed his gift on the table. The old woman invited him to sit, poured him a cup of tea and then disappeared into another room. After a few moments, Buck-toothed Fung emerged in a wheelchair and propelled himself over the parquet flooring towards Xavier, stopping about ten feet away.

"Uncle Fung, you're ill!" Xavier said, jumping up from his seat in surprise and reverting to Cantonese.

"Not ill. Just crippled. Dead from the waist down," Buck-toothed Fung said. His lopsided eyes shone brightly in recognition.

"How did it happen?"

"Knocked down by a truck. Three years ago."

"I'm really sorry to hear that. Mother and I didn't know. Otherwise we would have asked after you long before now."

Xavier saw that Fung's arms and shoulders remained powerful though his hair had greyed considerably. His legs, however, had shrivelled, judging from the folds of his black cotton trousers. A plastic catheter bag half-filled with a yellowish liquid hung from a hook on the side of the wheelchair. A tube connected to the bag disappeared inside Fung's trousers, explaining the smell.

"I've brought you some cognac," Xavier said, smiling.

"You haven't changed much, only plumper. Want to challenge me at a fingers-guessing game again, I suppose?"

"Oh, no, I wouldn't dare! The cognac's intended for your enjoyment, at your leisure."

"I imagine you haven't gone in for fingers-guessing at all, have you? That's much too low-class for an important man like you. Hard to believe I used to bounce you on my knees."

"Mother often spoke kindly of you, of how you saved us during the Japanese occupation."

"Did she? She's dead now, more's the pity. Read it in the papers." Buck-toothed Fung sighed and a faraway look came into his eyes, as if his thoughts had wandered off to some distant realm. Then, suddenly, he added: "Your mother was the most beautiful girl I had ever met. And her music! Oh, so exquisite, so sad. I used to hide in a corner and listen to it whenever she played or practised. I pretended she was playing the pei-pa for me. I loved her, you know, more than life itself."

"You?"

"Is that so shocking? Do you think ugly people have no right to love?" Buck-toothed Fung propelled the wheelchair within two feet of Xavier with powerful twirls of his arms.

"Of course not, Uncle," Xavier cried, recoiling from both the hostile approach and the nauseating smell. "Your remark just caught me by surprise, that's all."

"I never told her, you know," Fung said. "I loved her from a distance, protected her at the club. I was the door-keeper, the bouncer, the tough guy with triad connections. The boss was a bastard, always trying to make as much money out of her as possible. I stopped him more than once, threatened to wring his bloody neck.

"Then your father came along. What chance had anyone against a gentleman like your father? He was so handsome and he was always bursting out with poetry and sweet talk. When he bought her freedom, I thought I would go mad. I didn't know whether I should be glad she was being rescued from the club or whether I ought to kill your father."

Fung paused and his eyes took on a distant look, as if he were re-living some situation from long ago.

"Then the war, and everyone was up against it," he continued after a while. "What's the use of poetry and book-learning in times like that? I knew your father couldn't cope, especially after you came along. I called round, got your father involved in smuggling food. It was to save your mother, really. But I guess you don't want to hear about that, now that you've become such a big shot. One thing I have to say about your father. He was a very decent man. He never let friends down. He was generous, too, because he could relate to human weaknesses."

Xavier felt increasingly ill at ease as he listened to the ugly creature ruminating about the past. He hadn't come to hear such awful secrets. Fung loved his mother! The notion of her being loved by such a monster was utterly revolting. Yet he had to humour him if he was to gain the information he wanted.

The encounter was not turning out as Xavier had expected. Fung's confession, his accident and his straitened circumstances had thrown Xavier off balance. He could no longer speak as if he were making a business proposition. He was not even certain how he ought to broach the subject.

"What brings you to Taiwan? Must be some big deal for you to risk relationships with the British to come here," Fung said.

"No, no deal at all. I'm on a purely private visit."

"Why have you searched out this old uncle, after... what?... thirty years?"

"Twenty-eight, Uncle."

"Ah, whatever." Fung gave a dismissive wave of his great paw. "I would invite you for a meal except I'm a prisoner. Can't negotiate the stairs in this damn wheelchair and Mama Mui hasn't the strength to manage. Her cooking isn't up to much either."

"Oh, that isn't necessary, Uncle. Please don't stand on ceremony. What I need is just a bit of information."

Fung's crooked eyes narrowed suspiciously. "Information?"

"Yes, about a girl I met when I last visited Taiwan."

"When was that?"

"1956."

"1956! You want information about a girl you met in '56? Why chase after such an old one if you want a bit of fun?" Fung's mouth twisted into a laugh and, lowering his voice, he added: "Can get you a sweetie, young and new. Still got a few connections. Just tell me what you like. Of course, girls are no good for me any more. Dead from the waist down. Nothing operates. All I've got is that old hag."

"I'm not after that kind of fun, Uncle. Just want to contact the girl you introduced to me, the girl who kept me company when my father was suddenly called away to Japan."

"That was a long time ago. I was always introducing girls to people in those days. Can't expect me to remember which is which."

"This one was special. She's supposed to have had a child, the one my parents kept sending you money for."

"Oh, *that* girl!" Fung shrugged and laughed feebly. "Can't say I remember very well. Only vaguely, you understand, not even her name. Memory's not what it used to be. Well, you've caught me out, haven't you? A man has needs. A decent drink, an adequate stake for a tussle with chance. Your old man was a soft touch. Come to think of it, I did do that girl a favour, as I recall. Got her away from the triads or something. Mama Mui might remember. We always used to work together. We were on to a good thing with your father. Why give it up? Look how I live now. Are you here to demand the money back?"

A chill came over Xavier. It was exactly as his mother had warned and as he himself had half-suspected. It had been a fraud all along. It was revolting to deal with such a creature. But something deep inside him rebelled against the death of hope. If there was no offspring, perhaps he could at least find Fei-Fei.

"Please don't worry about the money, Uncle Fung," Xavier said, reassuringly. "You can have more if you help me find the girl. Her name was Fei-Fei. She used to work at the Starlight

Rendezvous. Do you remember what happened, where she went? Have you any idea how I can reach her?"

"Ah, the Starlight Rendezvous!" A glimmer of recollection entered Fung's eyes. "Mama Mui!" he yelled.

The white-haired woman flip-flopped into the room in her rubber slippers. "What you yelling about now?" she demanded.

"This here gentleman wants to find a girl named Fei-Fei who used to work at the Starlight Rendezvous. You remember anything?"

"Fei-Fei?" Mama Mui said. "So many Fei-Fei's have passed through my hands. How am I expected to remember all of them? When was this? I haven't been involved in that business for more than ten years."

"I met her in July of 1956," Xavier said. "She was seventeen at the time and very beautiful."

"Good gracious!" Mama Mui exclaimed. "You come now to look for a girl you met in 1956? What for? Guilty conscience? You men are all the same. You take your pleasure and then disappear, not caring how much hurt you leave behind. Women have hearts, you know! You can go back to your wife or whatever you have. I'm not going to get involved in this."

"Mama Mui, don't be like that," Fung said, in a wheedling voice. "The gentleman said there'll be money in it if the girl can be found. It'll be good for the girl, too. Better late than never. What'd you say? Wasn't there trouble of some sort?"

Mama Mui sat down sulkily on the remaining chair in the room. After a while she said: "Where was the girl from?"

"From the north. I think she said she was from a fishing village near Su-Ao."

"What else?"

Xavier shook his head. "Don't know much else. We travelled together for a week, to Fa Lien and Sun Moon Lake. Uncle Fung arranged everything. I was told she got pregnant but I didn't learn about that until recently. The only other thing I recall is that I bought her a jade pendant, real Burmese jade, the shop told us. It was round, with a hole in the middle like the old symbol of heaven."

"What else about this girl do you remember?"

"She had a big mole on her left buttock," Xavier said.

"A mole on the buttock!" Mama Mui wailed, bursting into tears. "Oh, *that* Fei-Fei! Heaven forgive us!"

"What? What? What mole?" Fung interjected.

"You old fool! You should die the death of a thousand cuts! You brought terrible harm to Fei-Fei because of your greed! Fei-Fei reminded me of myself. I should have done more to protect her. I hate you! I should have left you to rot ages ago!"

Mama Mui wept uncontrollably.

Fung looked astonished. "Don't know what you're talking about," he said, weakly.

Xavier looked from one to the other. "Please tell me what happened, I beg you."

After Mama Mui had recovered a degree of calm, she told her story, punctuated by sobs.

"Yes, I remember Fei-Fei," she began. "That swine brought her to Taipei to train her as a dancing girl. I was managing girls at the Starlight Rendezvous at the time. Fei-Fei was good. She was very popular. A really sweet girl, gutsy too. From the moment I took her under my wing, I knew we had something in common. I too have a mole on my left buttock, you see. I grew to love her, like a godmother with a god-daughter or like elder and younger sisters. It would have been a good deal all round if the arrangement had lasted. But that rogue got into debt gambling and sold her to the triads."

Mama Mui interrupted her narrative with a fresh bout of sobbing.

"She got pregnant all right. She confided in me. She told me she had fallen for a rich young man who wanted to take her to Hong Kong. I know about love, I do. I too dreamt of it when I was young. I told Fei-Fei at once not to breathe a word about it. She also told me the young man had given her an expensive jade pendant and asked me to hide it for her. I did. If that villain had got his hands on it that would have been the end of it."

"What jade pendant?" Fung asked.

"Shut up!" Mama Mui glared Fung into silence before continuing: "The silly girl wanted to have the baby too, you see. I told her that would be impossible. The triads would never hear of it. It would spoil her appeal. How could anyone pass off a girl with stretch marks as a virgin?

"The whole thing did not have to happen if that sorry excuse for a man over there hadn't been so heartless and greedy. Your father gave him money to buy Fei-Fei's freedom. I urged him to pay the triads, to let Fei-Fei go. But he lost it gambling. When the triads ordered an abortion, Fei-Fei refused. They raped her and beat her. Not that beautiful face, of course. She came home with broken ribs and bruises all over. It broke my heart. But no one can walk away from triads. You have to settle with them, one way or another.

"Not satisfied with the harm he had done, that monster invented another story to get more money from your father. He did pay something to the triads, I have to admit. But he should have sent Fei-Fei for medical attention as well. Instead he spent what was left on more gambling."

Mama Mui was again overcome by tears.

"I paid for her freedom, didn't I? I was in trouble. I had no choice. What more do you expect? Let them kill me?" Fung shouted.

"Shut up, you good-for-nothing! May you rot in hell! You should have solved your own problems, not pass them on to others!"

Turning to Xavier, Mama Mui continued: "The triads left the poor girl black and blue. But she was not so much worried for herself as for her child. She begged me to sell her pendant and get her to a hospital, so that she wouldn't lose the child. I was afraid that once anyone knew about the pendant, the money would be taken and Fei-Fei would be no better off.

"Fei-Fei was in no fit state to travel, but I thought it best to get her away. I and some of the girls got together some money and one of them volunteered to take Fei-Fei back to Su-Ao. I told Fei-Fei it was better to sell the pendant when she got home and use the money to settle with the triads. That was the last I saw of her."

At the end of the account Xavier's eyes were red-rimmed behind his spectacles. He blinked hard to fight back the threat of tears. "Did she have the child?" he asked.

"Don't know. Lost touch after that," Mama Mui said. "None of us dared to contact her. The triads were always snooping around. We were in a terrible business. If the triads found out I had helped hide a jade pendant, they would have come after me for their cut. Perhaps after Fei-Fei too. I allowed our connections to slip. At the time I envied Fei-Fei her chance to break free because your father was still sending money regularly. I didn't know till long afterwards that the fiend over there had been spending it on himself."

"You spent that money too, you old bitch," Fung cried.

Xavier tried to imagine Fei-Fei's ordeal and looked at the half-man with hatred. If Fung had wealth and riches, he would know how to bring him down. But he had nothing worth taking any more.

Xavier's next instinct was to hammer him, to beat him to a pulp. He was already a cripple, carrying the stench of human decay. Still, he had those strong killer arms and grappling with him would be like catching hold of a poisonous snake at Pokfulam all over again, a risk to life and limb. He could only triumph in boardrooms and air-conditioned offices, with writs, eviction notices, repossessions and withdrawals of credit. Even if he could prevail, killing Fung would be doing him a favour. Turning to Mama Mui, he asked: "Where can I find Fei-Fei now?"

"Don't know. The girl who took her to Su-Ao might remember. But I doubt if she's still in the business. It has been a long time."

Xavier took a large bundle of banknotes out of his pocket and pushed it across the table to Mama Mui. "Please help me," he said. "It's important I find her."

"I don't need money to help you. Oh, poor Fei-Fei! She deserved better."

"Take it anyway. It might help the girl to remember."

"Can't promise anything. I'll make inquiries, but that will take time. Where can I reach you?"

"Not convenient to contact me. I'm not in a hotel and not using my own name. I'll call in a few days. Please do your best. Tell the woman who helped Fei-Fei to Su-Ao there'll be a reward for her too."

"You're going to be in Taiwan for some time then?"

"As long as it takes."

"Good. It might take weeks. Even months."

"What? Just to find someone who's been in the business here?"

Mama Mui shook her head. "You're obviously a stranger to our way of life. When a girl leaves the business, she wants a new life, family and children possibly. It would be normal for a girl to bury her past as deeply as she can. I'll have to do a lot of sniffing around to locate the one who helped Fei-Fei, if I can locate her at all. And even if I find her, there's no guarantee she'll help. She wouldn't want her past dug up again after all this time. It's a very long shot you're betting on."

Deep disappointment creased Xavier's youthful face. "Please do your best. It is an urgent matter. I'll stay in Taiwan as long as I can. But if I have to leave before you've made contact, I'll give you a Taiwan number to ring. Just tell whoever answers who you are and say you need to talk to me. Nothing else. Then I'll come right back."

Mama Mui nodded and Xavier rose to leave, with Mama Mui escorting him to the door.

"Wait!" Fung called after him. "What do you think I've been doing the last three years, stuck in this fucking chair? There are always things people wished they had not done or had done differently. I didn't do right by your father or Fei-Fei, but saying sorry doesn't alter anything. I'll tell you something for free, out of consideration for your father's friendship and the memory of your mother. We who live by our wits can see things others cannot. There is a darkness hovering around you. Beware. You're rich and famous. Just get on with your life and leave the past alone. Forget Fei-Fei. Go home and don't look back."

Xavier stared impassively into the eyes of the broken old man, baffled by his strange warning. What kind of darkness was the rogue talking about? His mother had died and that certainly left a hole in his life. But his businesses were thriving. Was Fung just fishing for pity or angling for more remittances? The brute was now a cripple and utterly dependent on Mama Mui. Was he afraid Mama Mui would abandon him if she got a generous reward for finding Fei-Fei? That would serve him right.

He looked at Fung without pity and left without another word.

Alarm bells

39

Lucille was sitting at her dressing table, one hand holding the telephone to her ear, the other fingering the string of prayer beads left by Serenity. When she was put through, she said: "Reggie, I've a problem. I need your help."

"Ah! A lady in distress." Sir Reginald Quinn's voice, warm and indulgent, came back over the line. "How may I be of service?"

"Did Xavier tell you anything about his movements when he asked for leave from Exco?"

"Nothing at all, except what's been in the newspapers. Entering a monastery to mourn the passing of his mother and all that. Can't quite remember when he left. Some time in October, wasn't it?"

"Yes. He didn't say how long he would be there, did he?"

"A respectable period, I should think. You mean he gave no indication? That's odd. Wasn't it once a Chinese tradition to mourn for a year upon the passing of a mother? Not that I expect that nowadays, of course."

"Xavier's not a traditionalist. I can't see him mourning for a month, let alone a year. But it has now been almost six weeks since anybody has heard from him."

"Really? The government certainly expects to have him back in harness before long."

"The Deputy Chairman at Gold Star rang this morning and asked if I'd heard from him. Of course, I haven't. Xavier's not the kind who rings home. He just does his thing. Comes back when he's good and ready. But he's never been absent this long without communicating with his office."

"Well, he's never mourned the death of a mother before, my dear. During the final months of his mother's illness, didn't he cancel his overseas trips? I'm not suggesting he intends to mourn for a year. It's just that death sometimes does strange things to people. Was his office expecting to hear from him during his retreat?"

"Well, yes and no. They say he normally keeps in touch during his travels. He's usually very hands-on. But this time nobody's heard from him since early November."

"Where was he when he last called?"

"In Japan."

"Well, there you are! That's the explanation. He's in retreat. Probably doesn't want to be disturbed. Can't his office reach him at the monastery?"

"The place has no phone. It's quite remote, deliberately cut off from the world to foster spiritual development. The regime's very strict too, I gather. Can't even send a telegram there."

"Ah, a situation calling for the return of cleft sticks." A chortle came from the other end of the line.

"Cleft sticks?"

"Sorry, my dear. Poor joke. Used to send messages across the bush in them during an earlier period of Empire. But, if the place has no phone and he called in November, that suggests he left the monastery at that time, at least temporarily. The question is: did he go back or did he go elsewhere? Did he want to be left undisturbed or has he started picking up on unfinished business?"

"Even if he were working on deals, he should be back by now. I think he might be missing."

"Missing? Surely not?" The Chief Secretary's voice rose in surprise. "What makes you say that?"

"He told his Deputy he would be back to attend the signing of the Sino-British Joint Declaration in Peking. That's due in a few days. That's not the kind of thing Xavier would want to be left out of. His Deputy doesn't know what to do."

"Oh dear! Could he be intending to fly direct from Japan? Or perhaps he might already be in China somewhere, immersed in one of his many projects."

"No one knows. His Deputy has rung a few likely cities, but no one has heard from him. Can't you get Interpol to check on his whereabouts?"

"Interpol deals with international crime. So far there's no evidence of any crime."

"But he might be missing."

"That's possible. But no one has reported him missing. A person can't walk into a police station in Hong Kong and report someone missing in Japan or Timbuktu. A report must be filed at the place where the person was last seen. That would be Japan. There's no hard evidence that Xavier's missing. Only a supposition, due to an absence of contact. There might be a simple explanation."

"What if a newspaper asks about Xavier?"

There was a long pause on the line before Sir Reginald spoke again.

"Lucille, I want you to stay calm and not to worry. Here's what I'm going to do. I'll send an urgent signal to the Embassy in Tokyo to run Xavier down. Or at least to establish his whereabouts. Please don't speak to anyone about Xavier, particularly the media. I'm sure he's not missing. Just temporarily out of contact. This is a very sensitive time. Can't have a lot of false alarms around. The Prime Minister's going to Peking to sign the Joint Declaration. Can't cast a cloud over that. I'm sure there's nothing to worry about. Are you at home at the moment?"

"Yes."

"Good. Please stay there. I'm sending someone from Government Information Services to see you. Derek Soames, the Deputy Director. Perhaps you know him. It would be helpful if the Deputy Chairman of Gold Star could be there as well. Would you and Gold Star mind the government handling media queries — if any — about Xavier? For the time being at least. Would that be a problem?"

"Not with me. I don't know anything. That's the problem."

"Thank you. It'll eliminate crossed wires."

"If Xavier can't make the signing ceremony, doesn't somebody have to be notified?"

"That's still a few days away. Leave that to Soames. He'll work something out with you."

"Will you let me know the moment you hear from Tokyo?"

"Of course, my dear. There's not a thing to worry about. Everything's under control."

Everything was *not* under control, Lucille thought as she put down the receiver. She had told the Chief Secretary less than half the truth. The fact of the matter was that the Deputy Chairman was worried about something else.

There had apparently been a fire at a plastic-toy factory in a

362

town not far from Canton. Seventeen women workers had lost their lives and dozens of others were injured. The cause of the fire was unknown, but apparently it occurred in the middle of . the night. The deaths were caused by the exits of the quarters for workers, located above the factory, being locked. The factory was a joint venture, the main partners being the town authorities and a well-known American manufacturer of toys. However, Gold Star, as the party putting together the original deal, also held a small minority stake. The Deputy Chairman urgently needed Xavier to handle the Chinese authorities, to get them to keep a lid on the tragedy to avoid adverse publicity.

But that was not the end to the tale of woe. Another disturbing telephone call, this time from the Chief Accountant of Gold Star, filled her with alarm. She recalled the conversation as she began counting off prayer beads furiously with the fingers of one hand. That activity, however, did not produce the calming effects it used to bring to Serenity.

The Chief Accountant apparently handled Xavier's more mundane personal finances, such as paying wages to the staff at the mansion, Ah Yuen's school fees and other outgoings. She had never dealt with such matters and had no inkling of what the maids, the cook or the chauffeur were paid, let alone the cost of utilities, insurance and other necessities.

Thinking about it now, she realized how much she had taken for granted. When she shopped, she merely used one of the credit cards given her by Xavier. She never had to reckon the cost. In addition, a not ungenerous sum appeared each month in her bank account to take care of incidentals such as facials, hairdressing, tuition fees for Madam Shek and the occasional present for her parents or brother.

The Chief Accountant's contact was her first real indication of the vast machinery supporting her orderly life. The man explained that there were insufficient funds in her husband's private account at Gold Star to cover either the end-of-the-year bonuses due the staff at the mansion or the annual insurance premium for the mansion and its contents.

"How's that usually handled?" she had asked, taken by surprise.

"What normally happens is that I pay from Mr. Chu's private

account," the Chief Accountant had replied. "Whenever funds run low, I prepare a transfer chit for Mr. Chu to sign. Funds are then replenished from one of Mr. Chu's bank accounts. But Mr. Chu hasn't been available to sign anything, so money cannot be transferred. I'm sorry to trouble you. I couldn't approach the Deputy Chairman or the Financial Director because this concerns Mr. Chu's private affairs and Mr. Chu's very strict about keeping details between just the two of us. If he finds out I have even spoken to you, he'll get very upset. Shall I inform the staff at the mansion that their bonuses will be deferred until Mr. Chu's return? As for the insurance premium, I can get that deferred because the bill is from a Gold Star subsidiary."

"No, no! Just tell me the amount needed and I'll send a cheque. I want everything to function normally. What about the daily provisions, groceries, wine and so on? Do you pay for those from Mr. Chu's private funds as well?"

"That depends, Mrs. Chu. Spirits and wine come from another Gold Star subsidiary. Much of the food and the daily delivery of flowers come from yet another. From time to time, Mr. Chu allocates costs, either to Gold Star's budget for official entertainment or to his personal account. There's no problem with those at the moment because Mr. Chu hasn't made allocations. After he has done so, I pay the personal expenditure on his behalf."

"Do you handle credit-card payments as well?"

"Yes, Mrs. Chu. The same system applies. All hotel bills and meals abroad go into corporate accounts. Mr. Chu then determines which other items should go into corporate accounts or his own."

"Thank you. I'm sure Mr. Chu will return soon. Should you run low again, please let me know. Now tell me what amount I ought to send."

She was taken aback by the figure suggested by the Chief Accountant. She had no idea outgoings were so enormous. She did not have much in the way of ready cash, except for Serenity's bequest. The amount now requested would just about wipe out her bank balance. Xavier was meticulous about everything. His failure to issue instructions or to make alternative arrangements worried her. It signalled some form of disaster.

What could have happened to him? He was unlikely to be still at the monastery. If he had met with a serious accident, she would have been informed by now. He was unlikely to have been kidnapped or held hostage. Japan was a very safe country, not given to such crimes. In any case, no ransom demand had arrived. Could he have gone off somewhere else? To China, America or Europe? Why the silence? The possibility that he might have run off with a woman she dismissed utterly. He simply wasn't that type. There was no romance in him. Or sexual drive either. So where had he disappeared to? She couldn't work things out.

If he did not turn up soon, she would have to dispose of valuables to plug the gap. The treasures around the mansion belonged to Serenity's trusts and could not be touched. She thought of the jade seal Xavier had given her in happier times. That could raise a few bucks, but nowhere near enough to ward off a further cash crisis. Besides, Xavier's name was engraved on it and that would start tongues wagging.

There appeared to be only her jewellery to fall back on. The indignity of using them as collateral for a bank loan or taking them to a pawnbroker loomed. She hadn't a clue how to set about doing either.

Suddenly, something else came back to her. Shortly before Xavier's departure for Japan, she had noticed while he was placing some documents into his briefcase that it was stacked with American banknotes. They were in hundred-dollar bills and she had no idea what the total value might come to. The sight had surprised her, for Xavier had the habit of using plastic whenever possible.

That incident now nagged her. She had not bothered to ask at the time, but what could he have been up to? It had to involve some transaction he did not want to be traceable. Was there a connection between that money and his lack of communication? She felt irritated by the mystery. Her thoughts flew immediately towards protecting Ah Yuen from whatever might be presaged by his father's disappearance, particularly so soon after the passing of his grandmother.

As trustee of Serenity's fortune, she had to protect the assets of the trusts as well. But how? The bulk was in Gold Star shares. The world of business was largely alien to her. She knew enough, however, to realize that rumours would circulate once Xavier's unexplained absence became public. The value of Gold Star shares might plunge. If something untoward had indeed happened, there was no telling where things might lead.

* * *

After Soames had called and a common response to possible Press queries had been worked out, Lucille telephoned Baxingdale to ask him to dine with her. She broke her own long-standing rule never to see him unless Xavier was in town. But it was an emergency and she needed someone to tell her troubles to. Seb was the only man she could trust.

Since they ceased being lovers almost a year ago, Lucille had met with Seb on only three occasions, each time at the tea lounge on the Mezzanine Floor of the Mandarin Oriental. She had selected that public and popular venue because she wanted both of them to be on their best behaviour and not be led into temptation. She loved him still but she also loved another — her son. She could not possibly risk causing Ah Yuen hurt at this stage of his life. The likelihood of bumping into friends and acquaintances at the Mandarin lounge was her assurance that neither Seb nor herself would lapse from sentimentality to loss of control. For dinner that evening she had chosen Jimmy's Kitchen, a popular but cozy restaurant in the heart of town, for the same reason.

"Xavier has disappeared and I don't know what to do," she blurted out, once they had been served aperitifs. She then unburdened herself of all she knew and all that the Chief Secretary had said.

"There's no need to get into a tizzy quite so soon," Baxingdale said calmly. "There are some days to go before the signing ceremony. Xavier will certainly want to be at that sort of a do. If he doesn't show, then it'll be time enough to start worrying. Since the Embassy in Tokyo is looking into his whereabouts, I would relax for now."

"How can I relax when I face the embarrassment of not being able to pay my bills?"

"Let's analyse the situation step by step, beginning with

what's obvious. Xavier couldn't have been kidnapped because no ransom has been demanded. Robbery and accidents can also be ruled out for the time being because no police authority has been in touch. That leaves the possibility that Xavier is in a situation where he has not been allowed to get in touch with anybody or where, by choice, he doesn't want to be in touch with anybody. The first is difficult to imagine. So it's more likely to be the second."

"Xavier has never overlooked the need to provide money for his family. Never. This is so unlike him."

Baxingdale shrugged his shoulders. "Maybe so. But sometimes people change. His mother's death and going into that monastery might have triggered a reappraisal of his own life. It happened to Saul on the road to Damascus. Perhaps he just wants time for reflection."

"He could just tell people that and keep paying family expenses."

"Perhaps he's at a place he doesn't want people to know about. People have secrets, you know."

"Where can that conceivably be? He travels the world all the time and relishes the limelight."

"With that pile of cash, he might be engaging in something shady or clandestine, like an arms deal in the Middle East or a political mission in Taiwan."

"Taiwan? He never goes there. Gold Star has a liaison office in Taiwan but he never calls there. Even dealings with that office are left to the Deputy Chairman. If he's there, I can ring the office and find out."

"I wouldn't do that if I were you. If your husband doesn't want to be found, the liaison office won't be in the know. In any case, I'm sure your Deputy Chairman must have tried already. A call from you will merely add fuel to rumours and draw attention to his absence."

"I just don't understand what all the mystery's about."

At that point an elderly waiter came to asked if they were ready to order. They did so.

After the waiter had left with their selections, Baxingdale said: "Look, there are more sides to your husband than any ordinary man can comprehend. When you add in political dimensions, there's no telling where that might lead."

"Why should he be involved in Taiwan politics? I though his main political interest was to cultivate leaders on the Chinese mainland."

"I'm only speculating, my dear girl, putting bits and pieces together. I don't know anything for sure. You must know there is a sizeable group of Kuomintang supporters in Hong Kong. The civil war between them and the Communists is not over. It is still being fought by political, economic and other means. The Taiwanese group here, though underdogs, are a committed and stubborn bunch, sustained by income from rackets of one kind or another, pretty much like the warring factions in Northern Ireland.

"What's in store for them after 1997? The British have so far tolerated them, after a fashion. But would the Communists be equally forbearing after 1997? Or would they face elimination one by one? They're not going to sit around waiting for that to happen while they still have bargaining strength. They can make this place ungovernable in the run-up to 1997, unless a deal is struck that takes account of their vital interests. Do you remember the rioting a few years back when some junior civil servant tried to tear down Nationalist flags in a resettlement estate?"

Baxingdale broke off his sombre exposition when an acquaintance passed by the table and they exchanged greetings. He then continued.

"Not unnaturally, all parties want a quiet life before 1997, not the least being the British. But the Brits can't afford to be in contact with the Taiwanese, lest they're accused of engaging in a two-China plot. What can be more convenient than using Xavier, a private individual, to broker a deal? Quinn hasn't given much away, of course. But don't you think it's strange that he should be so keen for the Government Information Service to control the flow of information concerning Xavier's movements?

"On the other hand, I may be barking completely up the wrong tree. It might be the Chinese or the Taiwanese who might be using Xavier for that purpose. He would in many respects be ideal, since he has access to some very senior leaders on both sides of the divide, not to mention good standing with the British and the Yanks."

"My goodness! How complicated you make life sound! If Xavier is steeped in such a political game, it's small wonder he has forgotten about providing his family with money. What am I supposed to do in the meantime? I don't even know where I'm supposed to fit in Gold Star, now that I'm the trustee of both his mother's wealth and his son's inheritance. Doesn't a trustee have obligations under the law? How am I to discharge my obligations? Everything's in a mess. It's completely maddening."

Baxingdale nodded and sighed. "I'm sorry I'm no help on that score. You had better consult a lawyer, but then you don't have money for one, do you? Why not have a quiet word with Christopher to see what he advises. In the meantime, I'll use the few contacts I have in Taiwan to see whether I can come up with something. I would go to investigate myself except I'm due to leave for Peking the day after tomorrow, to set up coverage for the signing. But chin up. I'm sure things will sort themselves out."

"Thanks, Seb, for saving me from going to pieces! I'll wait for news from the Embassy or wherever. I can't imagine how I can ever manage without having you to lean on once in a while."

"You don't have to imagine anything. You have the means to eliminate that dreaded possibility, you know, regardless of whether Xavier is lost or found," Baxingdale said, with an ironical smile.

Just then the elderly waiter came with their dinner.

Friendly advice

40

Despite Seb's reassuring remarks over dinner, Lucille had remained restless in bed that night. She had always associated politics with activities that were sinister and underhanded, like the Kennedy assassination and Watergate. She was not surprised to hear that Xavier might be involved. What irritated her is that he should turn her life upside down because of that. She had somehow to stem the haemorrhage of her own funds to avoid a scandal. Even if that meant swallowing her pride to cadge legal advice from Christopher Knight, it had to be done.

There was a certain over-smoothness in Seb's old friend that she did not like. Moreover, she knew that his spiteful wife was not above making wounding remarks behind her back. But beggars couldn't be choosers.

The following day she turned up at the wood-panelled establishment of Rand and Knight. Christopher Knight did not keep her waiting. He came to reception looking prosperous and over-fed, in a three-piece pin-striped suit, and greeted her with warm commercial friendliness.

"Lucille! How are you? Just the woman I want to talk to," he said, taking her hand and ushering her into an easy chair in his office. "I've been trying to reach Xavier. How long's he going to remain in Japan? When's he coming back? One newspaper speculated this morning that he might miss the signing ceremony in Peking. That's not so, I hope. We don't want people reading the wrong message into his absence."

"Wrong message?"

"Well, you know how stories go around. Some people will attempt to tar us with that bad fire at a toy factory in Kwangtung. Hell, we've only a very small stake and no management responsibility. But we do have involvement in a lot of other factories and any tightening of fire and factory regulations will affect our investments."

"You don't need Xavier around to spell out the facts of the case, do you?"

"Of course, not. But he has a unique way of calming nerves."

"Well, I don't know when my husband's due back. Can't possibly keep up with his movements."

"Damn! Trying to reach him's a devil of a job. There's apparently no phone, no telex, no nothing in that monastery. No sense of urgency either. Thing's have popped up and I need instructions fairly smartly."

"Have you tried a cleft stick?" Lucille said, smiling innocently.

"What?"

"That was what Sir Reginald suggested."

"That old windbag! Thank God he's heading for retirement. Has he been trying to reach Xavier too?"

"Yes. I believe it's some Exco business."

"Did the old bird find him?"

"No."

"Damn! I'm quite stuck now. The comrades in Canton seem to be back-pedalling over the organ-transplant institute. They don't always play by our rules, you know. I need to know how to respond. Well, I suppose a few years from now we'll all be playing by their rules, so we might as well get used to them."

A slender Chinese secretary entered the room with two cups of tea. She set them down on a small table between the two chairs.

"Thank you," Knight said. "No calls please."

The girl nodded, smiled at Lucille and left the room.

"Now, where were we?" Knight said, appearing distracted for a moment. "Ah, yes. Sorry, I've been going on about my worries when you've come for legal advice. Shoot."

"Well, there are two or three things I'm confused about that I would like to get straight. First of all, you drew up my mother-in-law's will and trust deeds. There's a provision about donating the mansion and its contents to the city as a museum when my son reaches the age of twenty-five. Is it possible to make that donation earlier?"

"Earlier? Why would you want to do that? The mansion's a fine old place. Must be super to live in. Why give it up before you need to? Is that what Xavier wants?"

Lucille smiled innocently again. "I haven't discussed the matter with him yet. But Gold Star Construction has just completed a block of luxury flats at Pokfulam. The penthouse is gorgeous. With my mother-in-law gone and my son at university, the mansion's too big, particularly when Xavier's away half the time. The penthouse will be more convenient for where my son's studying."

"I see what you mean. Pity just the same, such a fine old place. Things are never quite as simple as they may appear. You'll have to go to court. Variation of trust and all that sort of thing. Besides, you'll have to get the government to accept the gift before the appointed time. As I recall, Xavier cleared the original bequest on the basis that he would personally guarantee its running costs for the first five years, in case of a shortfall in trust income. If government takes over the facility earlier, I imagine it will require a similar guarantee."

"Good gracious! Have things got to be so complicated, even when one is trying to give away a fortune?"

"Afraid so. Otherwise how can we poor solicitors earn an honest meal?"

"My heart bleeds for you. Is this variation of trust the kind of stuff you normally handle?"

"Yes, if someone gives me a retainer to do so. However, speaking as a friend, can't this wait till Xavier's back? If he likes the idea he can talk to the government more easily than I can about bringing forward the handover date."

"I thought you told me once that solicitors do not have friends, only clients or opponents."

Christopher Knight gave an easy laugh and laced his stubby fingers over his comfortable paunch. "Has to be an exception to everything. Since I'm not charging my hourly rate for this interview, I can only regard you as a friend."

"Thanks," Lucille said, with a supercilious arching of her eyebrow. "I suppose it does make sense to wait till Xavier's back. But what about my position as trustee? The trusts control a large chunk of Gold Star shares. Shouldn't I be sitting on the board to look after the assets?"

"Whoa! Whoa! You're now talking about playing with the big boys. Have you discussed this with Xavier? I'm not sure I'm the right chap to advise you. My position's a bit tricky. Possible conflict of interest, you know."

"Chris, for heaven's sake stop talking like a lawyer and start explaining things to me as a friend. I don't know the first thing about Gold Star except that it produces a lot of money for my husband."

"All right. Let's start with basics. Rand and Knight is not directly involved with the Main Board of Gold Star. We've only been retained by nineteen subsidiaries in the group, mainly those involved in venture-capital projects. A few of them are also publicly listed companies in their own right. Now and then we handle bits of private work for the Chu family. Got that?

"Now, Gold Star is essentially a holding company, with its own set of legal advisers. Its shares feature as one of the components in the Hang Seng Index. So everything it does attracts a lot of attention. It has under its umbrella more than a hundred subsidiaries. They also have their own sets of legal advisers. So has Xavier in his personal capacity. Your husband is a firm believer in divide and rule. As Chief Executive, he has never allowed anyone to know more than he deems prudent or necessary. Talk in the coffee shops says that even his Deputy feels left out. You're following all this?"

"After a fashion."

"Good. Now, control over most subsidiaries flows essentially from a commanding stake in the main corporation. Xavier has absolute control because he and his late mother together owned more than fifty-one percent of Gold Star. Old Mrs. Chu never took any interest in the business and left it to Xavier to exercise her voting rights. But now you're the trustee and your question about a seat on the Main Board suggests you're thinking of voting separately from Xavier."

"I wasn't thinking of voting for or against anything. I just want to clarify my responsibilities as trustee. I had no idea Gold Star is supporting the entire Hong Kong legal profession!"

Christopher Knight smiled unctuously, unlaced his fingers and rubbed his palms together as if they itched. "Come on, Lucille, don't forget we're friends. Something's going on. When the wife of the Chairman of a corporation like Gold Star starts asking about a seat on the Main Board, something's afoot. As Mrs. Xavier Chu you may never be in want, even if the heavens should fall. But most people are not as fortunate. They have to rely on friends to pass them a good tip once in a while."

Lucille was taken aback. "I don't know of anything going on! I'm just trying to find out my legal responsibilities as a trustee."

Knight leaned forward and lowered his voice. "That won't wash, Lucille. There have been sharp fluctuations in the price of Gold Star shares over the last couple of days. Again this morning. No doubt part of that is due to the factory fire and talk of Xavier missing the signing ceremony. Then you come in here fluttering your innocent eyes and asking about a seat on the Main Board. I've been around this place long enough to pick up the scent when something's cooking."

"Chris, you're completely mistaken," Lucille said. Her mind raced. She had wanted an indication of how best to protect Serenity's legacy. But, in approaching Chris for legal advice, she had found herself credited with information about price fluctuations she knew nothing about. What a corporate minefield she had stepped into! She wanted to leave. But she was afraid an abrupt departure might confirm Chris's speculations and lead to more rumours and market volatility.

"Come on, Lucille, you can tell me what's going on. Xavier's not going to miss something as big as the signing ceremony unless he's onto something even bigger. I'm your friend. You can tell me about it. Whatever's afoot must affect the value of Gold Star shares. It can't do any harm to take me into your confidence before plans become public."

"Isn't that privileged information? I thought it was improper to use insider information."

"But not illegal. At least, not yet."

Lucille saw a rapacious glint in Christopher Knight's eyes. It occurred to her suddenly that the rumour mill could be exploited to support the price of Gold Star shares. Circumstances had left her stranded in an unfriendly world and she had to come to terms with it. She saw her primary duty as protecting Serenity's legacy and, indirectly, protecting Ah Yuen's future as well.

So she said: "Well, Chris, if you promise to keep this absolutely to yourself, Xavier did mention an American conglomerate offering a huge premium to buy into Gold Star. Or at least, into a number of its operations. With Xavier away,

I'm not sure what the state of play is. Do the movements in share prices imply there has already been a leak?"

"Can you see now, Lucille, why it's important to have friends? They can scratch you in places you cannot otherwise reach. Gold Star shares will rocket once the news is out! You want me to deal for you on the q.t.?"

"No, thanks. My only concern is stability in income for the charitable trusts I'm responsible for."

"Well, it's money for jam."

"Don't go wild, Chris. I don't have all the details. Don't go hocking Phoebe's jewellery on this," Lucille said with a smile, as she stood up to leave.

Christopher Knight grinned. "Incidentally," he said, "you're entitled to a seat on the Main Board. That's a bit of free legal advice. From a friend."

As Lucille left the building, her legs felt weak. What had she done? Had she already learnt the first lesson in survival in the commercial jungles of Hong Kong?

Bill of sale

41

There he was, larger than life, Sebastian Baxingdale thought, as he spotted Xavier Chu among the thousand or so dignitaries crowding the reception room in the Great Hall of the People. Xavier had not met some uncertain fate, as both Lucille and Hong Kong officialdom had feared. He had turned up after all, like the proverbial bad penny, for the diplomatic highlight of the year.

Baxingdale studied the tycoon's switched-on smile and his eager pumping of hands and felt annoyed by his re-appearance. If the man had vanished without trace, a future of some sort might yet have been possible for Lucille and himself. Lucille's beautiful face floated momentarily before his mind's eye and caused his heart to ache. What now? It seemed their relationship had to remain in cruel limbo.

The music from a military band flooding across the room, sounding anything but uplifting to Baxingdale. He eyed again the assembled guests and media representatives waiting for the much touted signing of the Joint Declaration on the future of Hong Kong by the Prime Ministers of Britain and China. But the appointed hour had long passed and there remained no sign of either. Many guests were fidgeting, the more geriatric wilting. Most belonged to the Chinese Communist establishment and were dressed in Mao jackets or ill-fitting Western suits. The British contingent consisted mainly of Westminster has-beens and left-leaning types categorized by their hosts as "old British friends". Attendees from Hong Kong, numbering about a hundred, stood out anomalously, in their immaculately tailored suits and designer accoutrements.

Baxingdale recognized among the Hong Kong guests several leaders of the colony's commercial, industrial and financial sectors. Some had risen from humble beginnings to reach the heights of wealth and influence. They had all accumulated enough of both to call it a day, to slip into pampered retirement in some safe and salubrious retreat. Yet here they were, in spite of the ideological gulf separating them from the mainland leadership. Were they present to pay homage to their future masters, lured by the opportunities held out by "Socialism with market characteristics"? Or were they simply anxious to play their part in the modernization of their country?

The motives of his own countrymen were clearer. He recalled the non-attributable briefing for British journalists at the Embassy the previous day. The briefing officer was of a type he knew well, sporting sandy hair, pale watery eyes and a short, supercilious nose. The stamp of cleverness, honed at some ancient university and seasoned with dry sherry and vintage port, adorned him like a badge.

"Ladies and gentlemen," the spokesman had said in a well-oiled voice. "You've all studied the Joint Declaration. It's a unique document, a triumph of pragmatism. It will have the force of a treaty once registered with the United Nations. The agreement is imperfect. Let's make no bones about that. But don't forget that the Chinese hold most of the cards. It does represent the best that's achievable. The stark alternative, as the Foreign Secretary has taken pains to point out, is no agreement at all. That would leave the people of Hong Kong without protection, completely at the mercy of the Communists.

"Some of you have been critical. But we do not live in the best of all possible worlds. The primary job of our government is to look after the British national interest. We must keep in mind the big picture and not pile on gloom and doom. This is not Armageddon. Thirteen years still remain before the transfer of sovereignty and, as someone once observed, a week is a long time in politics.

"Drawing a line under Hong Kong will open up a whole new relationship with China, translatable into jobs, trade and prosperity for our nation. China has a population of over a billion — and rising. We in the West have recognized it as the great market of the coming century. It'll need telecommunications, railways, mass transit, dams, bridges, power stations, sewage-disposal systems, oil-drilling equipment, machine tools, everything you can think of. At the consumer level, just imagine what it would mean if only half the Chinese smoked a packet of cigarettes a day, drank a pint of lager, sipped a dram of whisky, ate a patty of beef or consumed a bottle of bitter lemon."

"Sounds like ministerial wet dreams," an irreverent spark had interjected, provoking raucous laughter.

The briefing officer smiled indulgently and moved on to the need to stem the brain drain of professionals from Hong Kong and to preserve British investments in China and the colony.

"What about our responsibility for British subjects of Chinese race?" Baxingdale asked, when the meeting was opened for questions. "The Liberal Democrats have suggested that all British subjects from Hong Kong should be given right of abode in Britain if they want it. What is the government's position?"

"The government's responsibility is to look after the British national interest," the spokesman replied. "It is no use speculating on proposals from people with no responsibility for government. Hong Kong is part of China and, after 1997, Hong Kong citizens will be reuniting with their own kith and kin."

Other questions in a similar vein received equally evasive answers.

Madness was a minority of one, Baxingdale reflected, remembering the briefing. To him, the whole saga of dealing with the Chinese had been littered with miscalculations, bungles and ineptitudes. The MacLehose initiative, the Craddock memorandum, the ill-fated Thatcher visit of 1982, the drawn-out negotiations to settle a mere agenda and the inevitable surrenders in 1984. Whitehall and Westminster were simply too obsessed with rigid legalisms to accommodate the Chinese fluidities of face, fudge and deliberate absent-mindedness.

Baxingdale's thoughts were interrupted by a gathering murmur, followed by an outburst of clapping. He saw the two Prime Ministers leading in their delegations. Shutters clicked and cameras whirred. He noted a shiny spot on the tip of Margaret Thatcher's nose and detected a slight variation in her gait. Designer shoes squeezing toes, he supposed. Serves her right.

The Chinese Premier, Zhao Ziyang, on the other hand, was bespectacled, urbane and garbed in a suit of the best British worsted. He gave an impression of being less self-satisfied than he might have a right to be.

The two delegations trailed their leaders like camp followers, in strict order of protocol. The leaders stood at pre-arranged places behind a long table, offering smiles and their best sides to the exploding flash bulbs. A few scratches on heavy bond paper and the deal was done. Bill of sale duly signed. The signatories displayed their teeth and applause followed.

Champagne corks popped and libations flowed. Media representatives quickly homed in on selected dignitaries. Greetings were shouted, handshakes exchanged, toasts drunk and awkward smiles erupted on Eastern faces. Two septuagenarian comrades, mistaking Baxingdale for an "old British friend", shook his hand with vigour and toasted him with mao tai. Conversation bubbled around the chamber.

The obligatory group photographs followed. As the delegations lined up, Baxingdale sighed. Why should his country suffer to have its humiliation recorded for posterity? Britain had just agreed to delivering several million freedom-loving human beings, together with children yet unborn, to Communist sovereignty on the stroke of midnight on the 30th of June 1997. What could be more dishonourable than that? The shedding of the imperial past was to the good, but the manner of his country's disengagement left a nasty taste in his mouth.

Baxingdale watched Mrs. Thatcher conversing with a short, rotund, chain-smoking old man who looked like an Oriental version of James Cagney. He was dressed in a Mao jacket buttoned up to the neck and seemed to be responding with no emotion to whatever the British Prime Minister might be saying.

Baxingdale regarded the old man with admiration. That man had been the real architect of the Joint Declaration and personified a reawakened China. He had put the Iron Lady of Europe in her place two years ago and he dominated her still. How could any Western politician deal with an old fox like that? In the West, to be on the losing side of a political argument meant only a few years in petulant opposition. In China it meant the forfeiture of freedom and, possibly, of life itself. That bred a different kind of politician. The only official position held by the old man was that of Chairman of the Central Advisory Commission of the Chinese Communist Party. Yet he was the Paramount Ruler of almost a quarter of the world's population. He had arranged the nebulous catchphrases thrown as lifelines to the detested British.

"One country two systems."

"Fifty years without change."

"Hong Hong people running Hong Kong."

"Socialism with market characteristics."

Masterly! The man had coined those phrases to suit his own agenda. Yet, without them, Britain could never have bamboozled a sceptical Hong Kong public into believing that, behind closed doors, its emissaries were extracting significant concessions from Peking on the territory's behalf.

An attendant passed with a tray. Baxingdale took a beer. He felt conspicuous and out of place. He gravitated towards some of the Hong Kong representatives he knew and was soon greeted by a shipping magnate named Yue. He was on friendly terms with the magnate, whom he had once interviewed about the development of Chinese merchant fleets. Mr. Yue was a heavy, thickset man in his seventies, with bushy eyebrows and a large, flat nose, and was commonly regarded as one of the Evergreens associated with the father of Xavier Chu.

Mr. Yue greeted Baxingdale warmly, offering his right hand and raising a glass with his left. They drank a toast.

"Dis is histollic occasion," Mr. Yue said, heartily. "Abbyone can now move fawwad."

"I take it you endorse the contents of the Joint Declaration?" Baxingdale responded.

"You asking me as Chinese, as Blittish subject, as shipping man, as Hong Kong lessident or as glandfada?"

Baxingdale, reminded of the older man's limited English, at once switched to Chinese. "Is your opinion necessarily different in each case?"

"Of course," Mr. Yue readily responded in Chinese as well. "Man lives at many levels, each with own dimensions."

"Well, let's hear all of them!"

"Ah, Mr. Baxingdale, this is hardly the time and place. But, to show I'm not jesting, let me say this: as a Chinese I'm proud of this agreement. It settles the return of a lost piece of the Motherland. No Chinese can quarrel with that.

"As a British subject, I feel rather let down. If someone pays protection money and finds in time of need that he has no protection at all, how do you think he will feel?

"As a shipping man, I'm optimistic. More business, more

cargo. More cheap cement, steel and building materials coming from China, more Hong Kong products going out. I profit both ways.

"Peking now talks of adapting socialism to the Chinese situation." Mr. Yue lowered his voice and added: "Who knows, a dose of Hong Kong capitalism may produce better results than a generation of socialism. In time to come, Hong Kong moneymen may take over China instead of the other way around! That's a thought, isn't it?"

Baxingdale laughed and Mr. Yue joined him.

Mr. Yue was about to continue when a Chinese functionary came up to him. The newcomer was from the Hong Kong and Macau Office of the State Council, bearing information about seating arrangements for the banquet to follow. Mr. Yue effected introductions and pleasantries were exchanged.

Baxingdale, seeing little prospect of returning to the subject of the earlier conversation, bowed and excused himself. "I've got to earn my keep, rustle up a few useable quotes before everybody scatters for the banquet. We must continue our topic when we're back in Hong Kong."

"Please give me the honour of inviting you to lunch," Mr. Yue said, reciprocating the bow.

"That would be delightful. Thank you."

"I shall take you to a traditional Chinese tea house not frequented by Westerners. It serves excellent meals. I'll telephone you when I get back next week."

Baxingdale wove his way to the margins of the hall. He could not help marvelling at a man like Mr. Yue. He possessed that certain Eastern mellowness and charm often found in Chinese of the older generation. By every account the man had started as a struggling fisherman, with little more than a seaworthy boat and an abundance of courage. He had prospered enormously under British rule. Yet he was now warming to a regime dedicated to the destruction of capitalism. What did that suggest about the Chinese character? That it placed nation and race before financial gain? Or that ideology was but a means to an end? Or sheer optimism that pragmatism would win through in the end? An answer remained elusive.

A waiter came by and offered Baxingdale another drink. He

declined. Instead he lit a cigarette and took out a notebook to jot down some of his thoughts.

The diplomatic charade was winding down. His Chinese liaison officer had previously told him that journalists would be dining with their minders in a special section of the banqueting hall. The thought of sitting through another two hours of anodyne chitchat was more than he could bear. The vast chamber, abuzz with small talk, suddenly seemed claustrophobic. And there was always the possible embarrassment of coming face to face with Xavier Chu. When attendants began ushering guests towards the banqueting area, he manoeuvred towards an exit.

Outside, snow was falling from a sombre evening sky. The heavy snowfall served to cover some of the ugliness of the squat, rhetorical monuments in Tienanmen Square. Cutting winds from the Gobi threw up flurries.

Baxingdale turned up the collar of his overcoat and went down the very steps upon which Margaret Thatcher had stumbled two years earlier. In retrospect, that stumble had been a dismal augury of things to come. At least, many Hong Kong inhabitants took it as such and planned their futures accordingly.

Baxingdale strode across Tienanmen Square in the direction of the Gate of Heavenly Peace. In the distance, the giant portrait of Chairman Mao beamed down. As he approached it, he saw what appeared to be a familiar figure standing before the portrait in the swirling snow. Something about the silhouette suggested it might be Cheng Ching. He had not seen the man for more than a year, ever since Cheng got transferred back to Peking, and he was keen to find out what he was up to.

Cheng had been one of the truly powerful men during his time in Hong Kong. He was also one of the most uninhibited and likeable Communists Baxingdale had ever met. His influence upon the negotiations with the British must have been crucial. He not only knew Hong Kong inside out, but had got the measure of every British weakness. Yet it was odd that he did not surface during the negotiations. Nor was he present at the signing ceremony. Surely such an important and talented man could not have fallen from grace?

Baxingdale's heart skipped a beat at the thought. It intensified his desire to renew his acquaintance. He yelled out Cheng's name as he quickened his step. The wind, however, snatched his voice away. He put his head down against the snow flurries and trotted towards the silhouette.

By the time he got within recognisable distance, however, the man had disappeared among the heavy human traffic along the Avenue of Eternal Peace.

Fallout

42

Baxingdale sat gloomily and alone in a corner of Szeto's Bar. His thinning hair and worn Harris Tweed jacket lent him an academic air. He had a pint of lager in front of him but was in no mood for solitary drinking. He was hoping that Soames, Choy or some of the other regulars would turn up soon. Conversation would take his mind off his experiences of that afternoon. But it was a Wednesday and evening horse racing at Happy Valley had drained the place of regulars.

Two waiters were idling near the entrance, waiting for the late-night trade to pick up, while Szeto, the owner, stood behind the long bar whetting a throwing knife.

The knife was Szeto's trade mark, one of a set of six. He always carried one while working, in a sheath strapped around his waist. Its keen edge was excellent for slicing lemons and limes. It appeared suitable for more deadly purposes, too, and Szeto's dexterity with it often led customers to speculate what his occupation might have been prior to bar-tending. But Szeto had a charming way of deflecting enquiries. He would merely admit, with an indulgent smile, that he had tried his hand at many occupations.

Baxingdale had got no nearer to pinning Szeto down than anybody else, despite years of patronage and conversation. But on this particular evening, Baxingdale was not concerned with Szeto's past. His mind dwelled rather on the future of his old university friend, Christopher Knight.

He had visited Knight in remand prison that afternoon, after learning of his arrest from newspapers. His friend was being held on embezzlement charges, pending trial.

"How the hell did you get yourself into such a mess?" Baxingdale had asked.

"A mo-mo-momentary lapse," Knight had replied, more cheerfully than Baxingdale had expected. But the lawyer had clearly lost weight and the dullness in his eyes revealed an obvious despair.

Baxingdale had been surprised also by the recurrence of a stammer in his friend's speech.

As Knight's story unfolded, Baxingdale learned that his friend had picked up information on a pending take-over of Gold Star by an American conglomerate. The source appeared to have been Lucille of all people!

Lucille would be about the last person to know anything about Xavier's intentions for Gold Star, Baxingdale thought. It had to be a miscommunication. But Knight had not elaborated and he did not want to probe too deeply lest his own relationship with Lucille slipped out.

Knight had apparently acquired his misinformation at a time when Gold Star shares were falling over fears of the company's responsibilities for deaths and injuries in a fire in a Kwangtung toy factory. The establishment was partially owned by Gold Star. The disaster resulted in increased provision for contingent liabilities in the company's Chinese joint ventures. When Xavier issued a profits warning on that account, share prices started falling further.

Knight, armed with the mistaken information about a take-over, thought the timing opportune for making a fortune. He began acquiring Gold Star shares through a private off-shore company.

Then two simultaneous announcements unsettled the market further. The first was that the Chu mansion would be handed over to the city earlier than anticipated, to be converted into a public museum. The second was that Lucille would be given a seat on the Main Board. The moves were interpreted by some as evidence of a split within the family, with Xavier Chu no longer commanding the decisive voice. Share prices fell further, but Knight kept buying.

When margin calls eventually came too thick and fast, Knight first pledged his home and then Phoebe's jewellery to stay in the game. When that still proved insufficient, he began "borrowing" money belonging to clients. By then he had started to panic. He could not understand why an announcement about the take-over was being withheld. He did not dare broach the subject with Xavier for fear his secret acquisition of Gold Star shares would be discovered. In order to stem further falls, he leaked the prospect of a take-over to a few shady speculators. His contacts thought he had inside information by virtue of his legal position and started buying. A take-over buzz went around the market. Prices leapt.

But, ironically, it was that very rise in the share price that led to Knight's downfall. The Stock Exchange questioned the sudden volatility and asked for an explanation. Xavier Chu responded by saying that he saw no reason for the erratic movements and added that rumours in the marketplace about a take-over of Gold Star by an American corporate giant were completely without foundation. The share price collapsed again and Knight did not manage to get out in time. His misappropriations came to light.

"Couldn't anyone have helped you?"

"Who? From th-th-those who had lost fortunes because of my tip? From that ba-ba-bastard Harry Rand who had been enriching himself on my efforts for years? He re-re-refused to stand by me. Xavier wo-wo-won't touch me with a ten-foot pole. He thinks I've been playing games behind his back. If either had been willing to cut some slack, th-th-things might have blown over. Now I have to face the music."

"What about bail?"

"What with?"

"Jesus Christ, you're a lawyer! You must have known the risks you were taking!"

"It's this aw-aw-awful place, Seb, wh-wh-where wealth, power, status, all seemed to be there for the taking. You see pe-pe-people less worthy than yourself growing fat. Tycoons only get their wrists slapped for insider trading. Xavier makes piles as-as-asset-stripping and exploiting le-le-legal loopholes. And you begin to think: 'Wh-wh-why not me?' I thought I had found a way to satisfy Phoebe and the children. Wa-wa-wanted them to be proud of me. The pu-pu-punt just went horribly wrong."

"I'm so sorry. Anything I can do?"

"Wha-wha-what can you do? The evidence's overwhelming. I'll just ple-ple-plead guilty to get it over with. I wo-wo-won't be allowed to practice for a good long while even after I get out. Tha-tha-that's not a good position to be in when you're approaching sixty. Phoebe's gon-gon-gone off with the children.

She's bitter about my lo-lo-losing her jewellery and our home. Wants a divorce."

"God, I wish things had turned out differently, Chris. Phoebe always had expensive tastes. You've known that all along."

"Yes, but mo-mo-moths always fly towards the flame, don't they? Bo-bo-both of us seem to have allowed our lives to slip by without m-m-much to show for it. You should find yourself a good woman to share what's left."

"I'm not sure that'll work. I've been a bachelor too long."

"A man has time to th-th-think in here. Give it a shot. I'm finished, but there's still hope for you. Yo-yo-you used to say that to die at a time of one's own cho-cho-choosing was the greatest gift bestowed by the gods. There could be something in that."

"I didn't say that. I was merely repeating what the Greeks used to believe. Don't do anything crazy. Look after yourself. You've a clean record. The court is bound to take that into account."

Knight nodded. "Thanks for coming. You don't know wh-wh-what a friendly face means at a time like this."

Baxingdale leaned back in his chair, trying to shake his mind free of the afternoon's interview. What a role reversal! There had been a time when he had contemplated suicide and Chris had tried to cheer him. He wished he could do something in return. But that was the story of his life. Always too impotent and powerless to make the slightest difference.

"Find yourself a good woman," Chris had said. He had found one. The trouble was she was someone's wife and somebody else's mother and also trustee to a vast fortune left by a generous old lady. How could she lay down all those entanglements? And for what? To spend time with an ageing hack at the end of a precarious career? The equation simply didn't make sense.

That reality was brought home to him the previous week, when Mr. Yue invited him for lunch at the Evergreen Tea House. The place turned out to be the very same tea house that had refused him entry years before, during his army service. It seemed to have retained an arcane air of exclusivity and as he was taking in the atmosphere, the food and the conversation with his host, who should have turned up but Xavier, Lucille and their son!

He had never taken Xavier for a family man or one who would frequent an establishment as unfashionable as a tea house. Yet there he was, with his entire family, and with a reserved booth to boot! When the newcomers came forward to greet Mr. Yue and himself, he had felt an excruciating sense of embarrassment. He was barely able to meet Lucille's eyes and when he took Xavier's outstretched hand he couldn't help wondering if the man knew he was the one who had cuckolded him.

Perhaps there was something in that old saw about the path of true love never running smooth. The possibility of humiliation was always there. Cruel separation, too, awaited the most committed lovers. Romeo and Juliet, Aberlard and Heloise, the Cowherd and Weaving Maiden of Chinese mythology. To be in the same city as Lucille, breathing the same air, and yet needing to keep his distance, was a torment. He doubted if he could endure it much longer without going out of his mind.

Baxingdale allowed his mind to recall other memories of Lucille. After a long while he shook his head, unable to go on. He took a swallow from his glass and just then saw Derek Soames striding into the bar.

The hour was late but Soames was still dressed in a suit and tie, which suggested he had come straight from the office. His florid features showed the stress of too many unaccustomed responsibilities.

Soames ordered a beer from Szeto at the long bar and brought it to the table before sitting down. "Why so glum?" he asked, after first quenching his thirst.

"Been to see Chris Knight," Baxingdale replied.

"Oh, sorry about that. Damned stupid thing to do for a man of his experience. Hell of a way to end a career. Got a clean record, I understand. Might be a plus. Don't suppose you're in the mood for more bad news, are you?"

"There's never a good time for bad news is there? What's up?"

"I've just sat in on a meeting between Reggie Boy and the visiting proprietor of your newspaper. Reggie Boy stitched you up good and proper, the swine! He told the noble Lord you were letting the side down by constantly harping on the negatives.

Doesn't take a genius to see he's angling for you to be replaced."

Baxingdale shrugged. "It doesn't matter, old chap," he said. "It has been on the cards for quite a while. My present contract runs out in three months and every sign is that I wouldn't get another. If I had wanted one, I would have tempered my words. Instead I insisted on showing the great British public how its honour was being tarnished. Not that anyone cares very much or takes much notice. Perhaps it's just me, feeling guilty that my country is selling people here down the river."

"You don't represent your country."

"Maybe not. But in a democracy I'm partly responsible for putting those rascals in."

"Quinn suspects me of feeding you information, too. I think he had me in on the meeting just to make that point. If he had his way, I would be on the next plane out, except that I know where some of the bodies are buried. I'll be sixty next year and the chance of getting another contract is about zero. Ah, I don't give a damn any more. I'd just as soon round up a few of my girls and open up our own topless bar. Reckon I'd make a damned sight more than spinning for the government disinformation service."

"Only if you don't drink up the profits first!"

Soames made a rude gesture and the two friends drank in silence for a while. Presently, T. P. Choy entered the bar.

"Why so glum?" Choy asked, upon joining the pair. The remark caused both Baxingdale and Soames to burst out simultaneously in laughter. "What's the joke?" the newcomer persisted.

"That's exactly what I said when I came in," Soames explained. He then went on to detail the dismal happenings.

"Well, they say that misery loves company," Choy said. "So I might as well tell my own tale of woe. I've just heard that an old friend of mine, a social worker, has been sentenced to five years in China for helping to spirit dissidents out of the country."

"Oh, gosh! That's terrible," Baxingdale commiserated.

"It's usually the death penalty, so my friend's lucky. There has always been something of a Boy Scout about him. Helping others came as second nature. Too bad nobody can help him."

"He's a British subject, isn't he?" Soames asked.

Choy nodded.

"Can't diplomatic pressure be brought to bear?"

"Not for a British subject of Chinese race getting into trouble in China. The Chinese are then left to deal with him as if he were a Chinese citizen."

"Sounds damned racist to me," Baxingdale said. "Is there such a provision under dual nationality laws?"

"Don't know about nationality laws. It's certainly practical politics. Britain wants to keep Peking sweet during the transition."

"This isn't right. What about the British commitment to human rights?"

"You ask Whitehall that."

"If nobody intervened, how did your friend get off so lightly?"

"I've no idea. It's a complete mystery. He must have a fairy godfather somewhere."

"I suppose if I wrote about it I would be accused of letting the side down again."

"Indubitably," Soames declared. "But think of how it would get Reggie Boy's goat!"

It occurred to Baxingdale suddenly how little wisdom and justice obtained in the world. Everything seemed to be rotting away beneath ever-increasing layers of hypocrisy — freedom, civil liberties, human rights, democracy, peace, the rule of law, the public good, the national interest, growth, progress, world security. All were just words. At bottom, strings were being pulled by money and power, and against those corrupting forces few decent individuals could prevail. People such as Christopher would stumble and others would be made sacrificial lambs. But the struggle had to continue until human beings started living for something larger than themselves and their puny spans on earth. Otherwise there was no hope.

His companions had fallen silent, as if they too had become preoccupied with thought. But it was a warm and companionable silence, the kind they had been accustomed to sharing before.

At last, Choy spoke. "Has either of you seen today's *People's Daily*?"

Baxingdale shook his head and Soames said: "You seem to

forget, my dear fellow, I have to rely on translated summaries of the Chinese press and they don't appear till the following day."

"Sorry. Forgot you're an illiterate gweilo! There's an item in today's issue that should interest both of you. It's about Cheng Ching."

"What's happened to him? He hasn't ended in gaol as well, has he?" Baxingdale asked, apprehensively.

"No, quite the reverse. He's been elevated to the Central Committee of the Chinese Communist Party and simultaneously appointed Party Secretary for Anhui Province."

"No joking! Always thought he would go places. He must have done the Party some service to gain such rapid promotion."

"What do you imagine he has been doing in Hong Kong these last few years?" Soames asked. "You're the one who has been having little tête-à-têtes with him. You ought to know. Special Branch seems to have diddly squat on him, except for his membership in the Work Committee. I'll bet my favourite whore he's played a major role in nutting out Chinese tactics during the negotiations."

"He's certainly been studying us. Knows our weaknesses through and through," Choy agreed. "Can't imagine the old commissars in Peking dreaming up on their own slogans such as 'Horse racing as before, dance as much as you want.' That's the stuff for calming local nerves. Madison Avenue couldn't have done it better."

"But he didn't show up at the signing ceremony," Baxingdale said. "That struck me as odd. I thought I spotted him afterwards, outside the Gate of Heavenly Peace. But the person I saw got away before I could reach him. So I'm not absolutely sure it was him. I'm glad he's got where he has in any case."

"He wasn't a run-of-the-mill Commie, was he? He's a few cuts smarter than most of them."

"Yes, he's what people might call a thinking man's Commie. When we had our chats he reminded me of those old socialists that chaps like us used to believe in and admire."

"And who disappointed us after getting into power."

Baxingdale sighed. "Politics is a desperate old game. I would give Cheng Ching the benefit of the doubt. He seems more selfless than most and he might turn out better than most."

"Only if he can resist the age-old temptation to enrich his nearest and dearest."

"So far as I can make out, the only living relative he has is a mother, who apparently still rears pigs for some godforsaken village in Anhui. By all accounts she's a true daughter of the Revolution who refuses to be pampered by her son."

"Then let's drink to true daughters of the Revolution everywhere and long may they remain so," Soames said.

"I'll second that," Choy said. "If Cheng Ching turns out as selfless as you think, it should augur well for China."

The three men emptied their glasses and ordered a fresh round.

Life and death in Su-Ao

43

The Pine and Bamboo Tea House was a working-class establishment and Xavier Chu entered it like a tourist who had strayed off the beaten track. He noted at once that it was not in the same league as the Evergreen. No porcelain paintings of famous tea drinkers or framed quotations extolling the virtues of tea hung from the walls. Its tables were of unvarnished pine and its stools uninviting. Two large earthenware tubs with stalks of listless bamboo offered an excuse for its name.

Xavier eyed the customers enquiringly. He had on a charcoal-grey Cashmere overcoat to guard against the sharp winter chill and his stylish clothes drew curious looks. He took a piece of paper from his pocket to check the name and address given by Mama Mui. Both were correct. At last his mission was drawing to a close. The need to make another clandestine trip to Taiwan was a bother. But at least he would soon discover what had befallen Fei-Fei and his son.

An aged waiter with a shaven head and fingering a discoloured dish rag approached. He ushered Xavier to a table and asked his preference in tea.

"Whatever's convenient," Xavier replied, settling himself onto one of the stools. It was indeed as uncomfortable as he had imagined.

The waiter shrugged, disconcerted by the unorthodox reply. He disappeared, to return quickly with a teapot in one hand and a large brass kettle of boiling water in the other. He placed the teapot on the table, lifted its lid and poured boiling water into the pot from a considerable height. Not a drop was spilt. He then filled an earthenware bowl with hot water, took a handleless tea cup from a stack, sloshed the cup in the water and placed it before Xavier.

"Does the gentleman wish to order food?" the waiter asked.

"Not just yet."

The waiter shrugged again and took his brass kettle on his rounds of other tables.

Xavier stared at the wet cup. He could not bring himself to pour a cup of tea let alone to drink it.

Presently three men in worn cotton-padded suits entered the tea house. The first thing Xavier noticed was their height, several inches taller than himself. Then the similarity in their tough, rough-hewn faces. It marked them as siblings. They had an air of primitive dignity. Their complexions suggested constant exposure to the elements. It was difficult to determine their ages, however. Fei-Fei had informed him that she was the eldest, so he calculated they must all be younger than himself. Yet they looked older. They headed straight for his table.

Xavier stood up and smiled on their approach. "You gentlemen are... ?"

"Is it the case you are Mr. Chu?" one of the men asked in Mandarin, with a strong trace of local dialect. "We are the younger brothers of Fei-Fei. I'm Kee, that's Tsai and that's Kun. We received a message you wanted to contact our family. May we enquire the reason?"

"Please be seated and partake in some tea," Xavier responded, in his own halting Mandarin.

The men took the three remaining seats at the oblong table. They brought with them the smells of the sea and of honest toil. Xavier tried to do the honours by rinsing cups in the bowl as the waiter had done. But the hot water scalded his fingers. His guests looked on with indifference. He filled the rinsed cups, including his own, with a dark liquid from the teapot. "Please, take some tea" he said, and lifted the cup to his lips. The tea tasted strong and acrid. He did not know its name and disliked its flavour but swallowed some nonetheless.

The three men did likewise. The hands holding the teacups were strong and callused.

"Would you care for something to eat?" Xavier asked.

"There's no need for ceremony," Kee replied.

The shape of Kee's eyes reminded Xavier of Fei-Fei's, but they were frosty and unfriendly. He had little experience dealing with such dullards. They seemed unimpressed by either his status or his wealth. He had tried to prepare for the meeting but could not think of a convincing explanation for wanting to contact Fei-Fei or her family.

"Is Fei-Fei well?" he asked, unsure how to get things started.

"She no longer lives in our village," Kee replied. "She has retreated to the mountains." He was apparently the eldest of the three and it fell to him to be the spokesman.

"She's married, I suppose?"

"No, she never married."

"What a surprise! She was such a beautiful girl."

"She told us someone promised to marry her and take her to America. But no one turned up."

The statement flustered Xavier. He reddened slightly. "I'm sorry," he said. "I'm supposed to be the man she was waiting for. I should have come a long time ago. But there was a misunderstanding. I thought she did not care for me. So I went to study in America. We lost touch. I didn't have her address. It has taken me a long time to re-establish contact."

"She said a certain Uncle Fung undertook to get a message to you."

"I didn't get any. If I had, I would have come right away."

The three brothers looked at one another, as if weighing the veracity of the explanation.

"How did you meet our elder sister? At the hotel where she worked or elsewhere?" Kee asked, after a pause.

So the family was unaware of Fei-Fei's activities at the Starlight Rendezvous, Xavier thought. His mission was now more difficult. He would have to tread warily. "Yes," he said. "I met her at the hotel restaurant. Please take me to her."

"You the one who got her in the family way, then abandoned her? According to the friend who brought her home, ruffians beat her for refusing an abortion. Was that your doing? You afraid she might lay claim to your family fortune, sully your family name? It's wrong to take advantage of an innocent girl. We're an honourable family."

"I have never for a moment doubted the honourable standing of your family. Neither did I send anyone to beat her. That was the last thing I would do. I love her. All this has been a terrible misunderstanding."

"Why seek to see her after twenty-eight years? Haven't you done harm enough?" Kee's voice was as chilly as the winter weather.

"Please let me see her. I mean her no harm. I'm here to make amends. I'll explain everything in front of her."

"Too much time has passed. Our elder sister is at peace with her son. Leave them be."

The waiter turned up to replenish the teapot. "You gentlemen care for some food?" he asked.

"Not now, not now!" Xavier snapped, waving him away. "Can't you see we're busy? We'll order later."

The waiter made a wry face and moved on.

"Please! You don't understand. I love Fei-Fei. I've always loved her," Xavier said, beseechingly, in a low voice. "I'm very rich. I'll make it up to her and to your entire family. I'll put things right. Anything you want. Just take me to her."

Kee shook his head, in a gesture of finality.

Xavier looked appealingly to the other two. "I can make all of you rich if you would only allow me to see Fei-Fei," he said.

"Perhaps we should allow him to meet Elder Sister," Kun said. He was the youngest of the three and was speaking for the first time.

Kee held up a hand immediately to silence him.

"Now, there's the voice of a practical man!" Xavier said, with an ingratiating smile. "There's something in it for everybody. What harm can be done by allowing me to see her? It'll clear up old misunderstandings."

"You really want to see our elder sister?" Kee asked, after a weighty pause.

"Yes, certainly. I've been longing to see her for years."

"The journey is long. At least half an hour by car just to get to the bottom of the mountain. Then a long, steep climb. You sure you're up to it?"

"Yes."

Kee nodded and the four men rose from the table as one. Xavier left a generous sum on the table. He felt a sense of accomplishment. He had surmounted the first hurdle. Though he was dwarfed by the three men, he felt in command, like Alexander or Napoleon at the start of a campaign.

Outside, Kee hailed a taxi and gave directions. It dropped them at the bottom of a flight of uneven granite steps where a big sign indicated they led to the Temple of the Goddess of

Mercy. The steps were about twelve feet wide and four feet deep. The human traffic was heavy. Those proceeding upwards were laden with incense, joss sticks and offerings, while those coming down wore expressions of having unburdened themselves. Kee led the way. The others followed in ragged procession.

It took more than three hundred steps to reach the temple. Xavier was already sweating and out of breath. He unbuttoned his overcoat to reveal a blue blazer and grey hopsack trousers beneath. The fragrance of incense and the sound of chanting to the beat of wooden clappers filled the air. In the temple courtyard, fortune-tellers and palm-readers were conducting a roaring trade. Worshippers and supplicants were rattling fortune sticks and tossing hexagram tokens out of tortoise shells. Along the edges of the courtyard there were stone benches and at the far end a small pavilion. A number of elderly women sat enjoying the fresh air.

"This is our elder sister's favourite temple," Kee said. "The easy part of the journey is over. From here on there are no more steps, only a winding path. Do you wish to catch your breath?"

Xavier shook his head. He could do with a rest. His throat was parched. He wished he had drunk more tea, foul-tasting though it had been. But he had no wish to display physical weakness before the three brothers.

The path beyond the temple was narrower and paved with gravel. Human traffic was replaced by flies and insects. The path branched off here and there to woodsmen's shacks or allotments for flowers or vegetables. Twenty minutes later it narrowed further and became plain trodden earth. Rugged woodland, with oak, cedar, cypress and fern, loomed on either side. Signs of human habitation petered out. The party was reduced to proceeding in single file, with Kee in the lead and the other two brothers making up the rear.

After a while Xavier slowed to a stop and drew several deep breaths. Insects brushing against his sweating face annoyed him. He took off his Cashmere overcoat and found that it had picked up bits of twigs and bramble. He no longer felt in control. He extracted a monogrammed handkerchief from his pocket, removed his spectacles and wiped his face. The pale blue shirt beneath his blazer was already stained with sweat.

"Whatever made Fei-Fei come to live in such a remote place?" he asked.

"For solitude," Kee replied.

The brothers waited patiently, unbothered and expressionless. Xavier felt a twinge of unease, but there was no alternative to resuming the journey.

After another twenty minutes, the group came across a young man sitting on a boulder by the side of the path. He was a good-looking fellow in his twenties, muscular and tanned. He stood up on the group's approach.

"Preparations ready for our guest?" Kee asked.

"Yes," the young man replied, gazing at Xavier.

For a fleeting moment, Xavier imagined the man might be the son of Fei-Fei. "He's... ?

"My eldest son," Kee said. "He's alerted Elder Sister you might be coming."

Xavier nodded and the group continued along the path, leaving Kee's son behind. "How much farther?" Xavier asked, after another ten minutes.

"Not far," Kee replied, without turning round.

About a hundred yards on, Kee stopped. "We can go through here," he said, indicating a barely discernible track leading off the path. "It's a short cut."

Xavier hesitated. The track appeared to rise more steeply than the path and was even more encumbered by undergrowth. His leg muscles were twitching from fatigue and he felt fried by the sun in spite of a stiff breeze. But he could think of no face-saving way to ask for a rest or even to call the whole thing off. So he struggled after Kee, step by agonizing step, scuffing his earth-caked Bally shoes. Sweat poured down. His collar turned damp and tightened. His overcoat seemed like a burden, hampering his progress. He was also losing track of time. It seemed the closer he got to his destination the slower time seemed to drag. Kun was following more closely on his heels than previously. He resented the man's nearness and his rough scent of toil.

After what seemed like an eternity of effort, he found himself in a small clearing. The scene from that vantage point was breathtaking. The sea stretched into infinity. The lush green hills in the foreground reached out on either side to embrace a bay. A waterfall bubbled down a hillside in the middle distance. Far below, the yellow roof of the Temple of the Goddess of Mercy poked out of the surrounding greenery.

Xavier doubled over, his hands pressed against his knees, sucking in great gulps of air. He was just about all in and didn't care that his overcoat was trailing the ground. But his trained developer's eye noted the site's potential for holiday villas and profitable building. He took off his blazer as well and wiped his face again. He immediately felt the cold wind on his sweat-soaked shirt and shivered.

"Much farther to go?" he panted.

"Almost there," Kee said.

After a while Xavier saw he was at the corner of a clearing. A small mound of earth, half-hidden by shrubs, was marked by a tiny headstone engraved simply with the characters: "A mother and child." At the foot of the mound lay fresh joss sticks, candles, paper offerings and a box of matches. The remnants of previous offerings were also visible. He was taken aback. It was obviously an illegal burial site. "What's the meaning of this?" he demanded. "I've come to see Fei-Fei."

"There rests my Elder Sister. Her child too," Kee said. "Don't you want to pay your respects?"

Xavier's head spun. He felt shattered. The bundle of clothes fell from his hands. He had spent weeks on secret arrangements, bypassing government regulations and controls. He had rekindled memories of love and hope. He had dreamt of another son and a more splendid life. All that to end with a mound of earth on an unfamiliar hill? No, he could not accept that without proof. It had to be some kind of trick.

"You mean she's dead?" he cried. "When? How? You've tricked me!"

"No. Our beloved elder sister lies there. She was badly injured when she came home. The doctor thought the child she was carrying might be injured too. He wanted her to abort, to be on the safe side. But she refused. She was convinced the father would come and she wanted a child to show him. She suffered terribly while waiting. In the end both she and the child died.

"Before she passed on, she said she wanted to be buried here.

We had been here once, during an outing, when we were children. She loved the spot and the view. Burial here is not allowed. But we buried her just the same."

Xavier looked from the mound to the impassive faces of the three brothers. The account rang true. He could visualize Fei-Fei behaving that way. The pain of that double loss was more excruciating than any he had ever experienced. But, though his private hopes had been crushed, his business instincts had not. They now took control.

"Look," he said. "Let's approach the situation rationally, one issue at a time. If Fei-Fei is dead, then that loss is as much mine as yours. If she likes it here, I'll buy the whole hill. I'll build a mausoleum in her honour."

"You haven't paid your respects," Kee interrupted, pulling Xavier up short.

Xavier wasn't sure what he ought to do. He seldom accompanied his mother to the tomb of his father during Ching Ming Festival. He had little idea of the proper procedure. He also felt ridiculous in his shirt sleeves, sweating and dishevelled. Eventually he squatted before the mound, lit candles and joss sticks and planted them where the burnt- out stalks were. He bowed his head three times before the mound and was about to rise when Kee said: "You said you would explain everything before my Elder Sister. Now's the time. How did you get her into such a situation? Who was responsible for hurting her?"

Xavier rose slowly and turned to face Kee. He realized he was not in a position to explain anything. The truth was irrational, bizarre, unlikely to be acceptable to the brothers. It would only fuel their fury. The truth was that she was a whore, controlled by triads, plying her trade at the Starlight Rendezvous. He had embarked on this mad quest because there had been the possibility of a child who might be his. He could not entrust Gold Star to sickly Ah Yuen. That boy was simply unfit to conquer and rule. But how to explain all that to three stupid fishermen?

The only solution was to buy them off. Blood might be thicker than water but money was thicker than blood. He had established that as an empirical truth, again and again during the course of his rise in the world. Had he not crossed a few palms a short while back to save Little Ho from execution? With that in mind he went over to his blazer and extracted from one of its inside pockets two thick wads of American banknotes. They were damp with his own sweat. He took them to Kee and held them out.

"Look," he said, in a businesslike tone. "I have brought this money for your family. If it's not enough, I can get more. I don't want bad blood between us because of Fei-Fei. She was dear to all of us. Quarrelling isn't going to bring her back."

Kee stood with arms folded across his chest, staring dully at Xavier. "You should not have come," he said.

Xavier went from one brother to the next, holding out the American dollars and urging them to take them, but they remained as silent and as unresponsive as Kee. Their eyes appeared cold and reptilian. Or perhaps like the eyes of dead fish. He came back in front of Kee and set the banknotes on the ground. Every man had a price, he thought, and I will buy you silly clowns yet.

"All right," he said, addressing no one in particular. "You're smarter guys than I had figured. You want more? I'll give you more. Just state how much you want. I'll write a letter and one of you can take it to a bank in Taipei to get the money. I'll stay with you till the money's safely in your hands. Then we'll call it quits. No police, no nothing. No need for violence. All right?"

None of the three responded.

The thought dawned on Xavier then that the brothers wanted more than money. They seemed to be poised around him, cold, menacing, lethal. He needed to mollify them. He noticed his father's magnificent Piaget watch with the black dial on his wrist and he immediately unstrapped it and held it up to Kee. The gold casing glittered in the sunlight.

"Look," Xavier said. "This is an heirloom from my father. It's quite rare. It's worth a small fortune. Take it as a goodwill present from me. Just name whatever sum you want. Violence won't bring Fei-Fei back. Nothing can change the past."

Kee remained unmoved. Xavier took a couple of steps towards Tsai and proffered the watch again. Tsai, who had barely uttered a word till then, suddenly exploded.

"You think you can buy everything with money, you miserable piece of turd?" he shouted. With a brush of the hand

Tsai sent the watch flying into the undergrowth. "You said you wanted to spend the rest of your days with my Elder Sister. I'm going to grant your wish!"

Xavier recoiled several steps, stumbling first across his discarded clothes and then trampling upon the lighted candles and joss sticks before the small mound.

That mishap seemed to infuriate the brothers. Kun walked towards him menacingly. Xavier was unable to retreat. His legs could no longer move.

Kun unbuttoned his padded jacket and took from around his neck a pendant. He held it out towards Xavier.

Xavier recognized at once the jade pendant with the hole in the middle he had given Fei-Fei.

"You're soft and stunted, without a touch of manliness about you," Kun said, his mouth twisted into a sneer. "I don't know what my Elder Sister ever saw in you. You're unworthy of her. Yet she thought only of you. On her deathbed she made me promise to return this should you ever come. She was concerned you might need this bi for your soul to ascend to heaven. But there'll be no heaven for you. Only the lowest level of hell! I've worn this pendant for twenty-eight years to keep alive my hatred for the man who brought ruin and death to my sister. Now at last you're here. I can see your pathetic face. Take it! I've discharged my promise."

Xavier shook his head. Tears poured down his face.

"Pathetic!" Kun said, placing the pendant on top of Fei-Fei's grave before he edged inexorably towards Xavier. His brothers also closed in.

A confusion of images rushed through Xavier's head. They were of his mother and Fei-Fei. His mother hugging a baby in the rain, leading him to school by the hand, crying over an old pei-pa, clutching her chest in pain. Then Fei-Fei in the throes of love, her moans, her cries, and finally with a dead child.

"No! No!" he cried. Then a dark patch spread quickly down from the crotch of his grey hopsack trousers.

Farewell

The hour was late. Diners at both of the main restaurants at the Victoria Cricket Club had dribbled away. Even in the more popular of the two, only a table of three remained. Those stragglers consisted of Derek Soames and his guests, Sebastian Baxingdale and T. P. Choy.

Soames had been drinking copiously since the start of their meal but he still felt stone sober and out of sorts. His companions had drunk less but were mellowing into a touching melancholy. Perhaps the two cups of coffee after dinner had taken away the effects of the wine, Soames thought. Damned silly. He wanted to be drunk tonight of all nights, to be forgetful and irresponsible. But it was not happening.

He saw the anticipatory glances of the waiters and knew it was time to leave. They were into their third snifter of Connoisseur cognac and the last two inches of their Cuban cigars. But he did not want the evening to end. After all, it was a farewell dinner for a friend he might never see again.

He and Baxingdale had become chums in spite of their differences in temperament and upbringing. What first drew him to the journalist was the fellow's sense of justice and distaste for cant. He had seen at once that those qualities marked him as another potential outsider among the colony's expatriates. It did not take long for them to strike up a friendship, to become fellow conspirators in exposing cock-ups and social prejudices in the colonial system.

His friend's departure would rob his own life of much colour and purpose, he reflected gloomily. He hoped they had done some good during the last eighteen years. Things would never be the same again.

"When are you actually flying out?" he asked gruffly, jolted into speech. His voice sounded over-loud in the echoing emptiness of the room.

"Monday," Baxingdale replied, tapping ash off from what remains of his Davidoff.

"Couldn't you stay?" Choy chipped in. His voice was coloured with resignation.

"Not without a job. And who would employ a Jeremiah at a time like this?"

"Didn't you tell me Mr. Yue, the shipping tycoon, had been hinting at his need for someone to help with English documents? That's his way of offering a job, you know."

"Yes, but I'll be no good at dealing with flags of convenience or piracy in the Straits of Malacca. Wouldn't be earning my keep and it wouldn't be fair on Mr. Yue. Writing's the only thing I know."

"Intend to work for another newspaper then?"

"No, not immediately. Might try writing a book first, until my money runs out."

"A book? You never told us you were planning a book."

"I wasn't planning anything. The idea just surfaced in me."

"What'll it be about?"

"Hong Kong."

"That figures, but in what form? Personal reminiscences, a social and political analysis of colonial rule, a novel or what?"

"Don't rightly know yet. So many extraordinary things have happened to me here. I'm not sure whether I should recount them factually, polemically, philosophically or through fiction."

"Forget the philosophical approach. It's self-defeating," Soames pronounced. "Everything here's a metaphysical contradiction. Just write about the shenanigans of the rich and powerful. Pick up the current gossip and embellish the details. Everyone has skeletons in the cupboard — the heads of princely hongs, High Court judges, bankers, diplomats, senior bureaucrats, venerable local families and even your left-wing contacts. That is what will tickle the public fancy."

"Much of that stuff would be libellous."

"So what? Dirt sells. It'll make you a million. Worry about the libel suits afterwards. Dare the rascals to sue. They would only lose more face."

"If that's such a good idea, why don't you do it and make the lolly yourself?"

"Beyond me, old boy. After twenty years of churning out government handouts my prose has gone stiffer than a wooden spoon. Besides, given my own peccadilloes, it wouldn't be sporting for a pot to call the kettle black."

"Don't be put off, Seb," Choy said, leaning closer to Baxingdale in a gesture of solidarity. "A good book about Hong Kong is long overdue. This place deserves one and you can do it justice. But why not write it here, where everything has happened? The flat you've got can't be too expensive. I can find you a cheaper one, if you like, on one of the outlying islands."

"Thanks, but what money I have is likely to go further living in an English garret. Besides, I need a bit of distance. I need to see this place more objectively than I can now."

"I shall miss you," Choy said, dispiritedly. "I shall always be grateful for your intervention which allowed my godson to get away with a suspended sentence. He's been teaching for the last ten years in Canada, did I tell you? No Englishman has ever fought our corner as tenaciously as you have."

Baxingdale waved self-deprecatingly with the hand holding his cigar.

"Hey! What about me?" Soames snapped, in deliberately quarrelsome tones. He had picked up an altered timbre in Choy's voice and was fearful of the evening descending into sentimentality. "I'm an Englishman too. Half the stuff Seb churns out are based on leaks from us. Don't give him all the credit. We put our backsides on the line too every time we spill the beans to him!"

"So what do you want?" Baxingdale asked, surprised by the outburst. "You want every leak acknowledged in print?"

"No!" Soames declared, sitting up haughtily. "We want justice. We want recognition for all the times we've saved those uppity colonial arseholes from themselves. We want to know why we've been denied gongs for services above and beyond the call of duty."

"Yes, yes! And nothing less than the Garter would do," Choy agreed.

The exchange brought a lighter mood to the table and the three friends emptied their glasses in a series of high-spirited toasts. Soames then signalled for replenishments, much to the dismay of the weary restaurant staff.

After fresh pegs of Connoisseur cognac had been poured,

Baxingdale said, reflectively: "You know, I'm going to miss this place like the devil. It's amazing how it has thrived, in spite of so many political and economic storms. To a large measure the credit rests with us British, but not in any sense that our Westminster's tribes would understand. British ineptitudes and misconceptions are so bloody marvellous, when you come to think about them. They leave our mandarins with the illusion they're in charge, while allowing locals to go about their business in their own way.

"Take our blind faith in the law. We think that simply passing a law will alter society and human behaviour. It must be a great source of amusement to locals. We've banned the Communist Party for donkey's years, yet there's hardly a Chinese who doesn't believe that the Communists have already penetrated every segment of our society. We've enacted labour legislation to conform to the highest standards of the I.L.O., but all I've got to do is to go out onto my balcony to see every provision ignored. It's all a tremendous joke!"

"The girls in Wanchai are grateful beyond words for our ineptitudes," Soames said. "If our administration were halfway competent, most of them would be in the Po Leung Kuk and their families would be starving. And pimps would lose their commissions, Yankee sailors their recreation and drinking establishments their customers."

"Profits from tourism would go down, mortgage payments would be in arrears, property prices would drop and the stock prices would fall," Choy chipped in.

Baxingdale entered the spirit of things. "There would be bankruptcies and foreclosures. Banks would find their deposit base squeezed, their liquidity ratios breached and the velocity of money slowing to a crawl!"

"And those moneybags allegedly representing our community in the innermost councils of government would be up in arms because their profits are disappearing and their investments are turning shaky!"

The friends were by now laughing boisterously and emptying their snifters with extravagant toasts. Soames signalled for another round and the maitre d' and a waiter approached with an air of disapproval.

"Please get me the bill also," Soames said soothingly, when he saw their downcast faces. Then, as if by way of an excuse, he clapped a hand on Baxingdale's shoulder and said: "My friend is going to leave us for good. We have to give him a proper send-off."

"Of course, Sir," the maitre d' said, appeased. "Please take your time."

After the attendants had retreated, Soames said: "Speaking of moneybags, do you know Xavier's gone walkabout again, as the Aussies would say?"

"Really?" Choy said. "Saw nothing in the Gazette."

"It wasn't gazetted, thanks to another stroke of genius by our Chief Secretary."

"I heard something last night," Baxingdale confessed, "when I rang Lucille to say goodbye. She said Quinn had been ringing her to find out where Xavier's gone. What's going on?"

"Did she say where her husband is?"

"No, she doesn't know. Xavier seldom tells her about his movements. She thought he might have gone to China to sort out problems connected with his organ-transplant project."

"Well, the inside story is that towards the end of last month Xavier asked to be excused from the next Exco meeting. Reggie Boy took it upon himself to agree and to mention his absence at the meeting, thinking that the gazetting palaver was unnecessary for just one meeting. But Xavier has now been absent for three meetings and has neither written nor telephoned. The Governor is less than pleased and there's growing pressure from other Exco members for an explanation and for an announcement to be made. The trouble is that nobody seems to know where Xavier is. An announcement under such circumstances might spark another fiasco on the stock and financial markets. Reggie Boy wants me to prepare for a salvage operation, just in case."

"Good grief! Not again!"

"His so-called disappearance could be calculated," Choy observed, blandly.

"I first met that bugger thirty years ago, when I was still in the university and he was only in high school. I detected a ruthless and calculating streak in him then and nothing he has done since has suggested he has changed his stripes. With the signing of the Joint Declaration, the colonial administration must become increasingly a lame duck. If he were to lead a movement to distance local bigwigs from the Brits, it might earn him kudos with our future masters. Temporary market chaos wouldn't matter to him. It would be just a bit of added theatre to underline his importance and his steadying effect on the market. They would also provide him a further opportunity to fish in troubled waters."

Baxingdale shook his head in dismay. "Quite honestly, I'm sick of his scheming. I'll be glad never to clap eyes on him again."

"Well, don't be disheartened so quickly. I've only put forward one theory. There could be another equally plausible one."

"What do you mean?"

"I've been tracking the propaganda war between the Nationalists and the Communists in their newspapers. Following recent pronouncements from Peking about cracking down on corruption, a report appeared in the KMT alleging that a number of senior cadres in Canton have been arrested in a clean-up operation. There has, of course, been no confirmation from Peking.

"But for every cadre who is corrupt there first has to be a corrupter who is equally guilty. Suppose that in the course of his activities in China Xavier has crossed the wrong palms or backed the wrong faction. That's well within the realms of possibility in the present shifting political climate. He has to be pulling strings to bring teams of doctors and public security officials here for training attachments. Suppose he's been nabbed in the corruption crack-down and is now being used as a proxy in some wider power struggle. Suppose he's being held incommunicado somewhere and... "

"Holy Moses!" Soames exclaimed. "There'll be fun and games all right! Reggie Boy'll have a lot of mealy-mouthing to do."

"You're right! The ramifications can be shattering," Baxingdale said. "If Xavier's in trouble, I would hate to think of what might happen to the stock market. He won't be just another Chinese social worker the Brits can wash their hands of."

"Certainly not!" Soames cried. "I can already visualize the fizz coming out of Reggie Boy's retirement party! The night's still young. Let's explore Choy's theory further at Szeto's."

"Why not?" Choy said. "Drinks on me."

Author's note

LONDON, 2003

In order to lend flavour and authenticity to the novel, I have blended fact with fiction. In doing so I have tried to reflect the day-to-day hardships, aspirations, resentments, intrigues and cross-purposes colouring the decades following the end of the Pacific War.

A novel, naturally, has to have characters. I have created a range of fictional figures; some I have placed in public offices that actually existed at the relevant times. An example would be the Director of the New China News Agency in Chapters 30, 31 and 33, who bears no resemblance to the actual Director at the time. The same is true of the Chief Secretary of Hong Kong in Chapters 37 and 39, whose physical features, mannerisms and intellectual outlook are totally at odds with those of the actual Chief Secretary of the time.

I wish to state categorically and unambiguously that all characters, except for historical personages such as Chairman Mao or Sir Murray MacLehose, are entirely figments of my imagination. None of them is based on any individual, living or dead.

I have also on occasion found it convenient to place events outside the actual time of their occurrence. I hope those with an intimate knowledge of Hong Kong would not quarrel with such liberties.

For example, I suggest in Chapters 29 and 37 that as late as 1984 the British Special Branch was targeting certain individuals and organisations whose names appeared on the "Q List" of those suspected of dangerous political or criminal activities. Their mail was opened and photocopied during the night at the General Post Office, prior to delivery. In fact, the practice ended at the General Post Office in 1982.

Again, in Chapters 30 and 33, I give accounts of meetings of the then underground Communist Hong Kong and Macau Work Committee. Though the Work Committee actually existed, those particular meetings and their participants are entirely fictional. The meeting described in Chapter 33 was purportedly held to discuss a proposal by the colonial administration to construct a plant to produce potable water from sewage through a process known as reverse osmosis. Such a proposal was actually mooted, but it was in 1979 rather than 1980.

At the time, such plants were coming on stream in the Arabian Peninsula and a high-powered government committee considered a similar plant for Hong Kong. So far as I am aware, no detail of that project has ever reached the public domain. Since I played a minor role in that curious affair, it might be in the public interest for me to add a small historical footnote.

In 1979, I was — in my capacity as Secretary for Economic Services — the only Chinese member of an internal Secretariat group known as the Land Development Policy Committee, chaired by the Secretary for the Environment.

At one meeting, a proposal was tabled for constructing a plant at Shatin. It was argued that the consumption of water in Hong Kong was increasing at such a rate that additional supplies had to be assured for the future. The operating cost of an earlier plant to convert seawater into potable water had proved too expensive. The reverse osmosis proposal represented a fresh attempt to increase supplies.

I had reservations from the start. I pointed out that regardless of the scientific merits of the process, the people of Hong Kong would baulk at drinking reconstituted sewage unless all other alternatives had been exhausted. I asked about the possibility of simply buying more water from the Chinese under an existing agreement. A pipeline was already in operation and it was only a matter of getting the Chinese to sell more water. I was told that the Chinese had been approached but had refused to increase supplies. The answer puzzled me. Since responsibility for dealing with the Chinese rested elsewhere, I accepted what I had been told.

A few days after the LDPC meeting I was invited to a small dinner party at the Hong Kong Chinese General Chamber of Commerce. There were no more than about half a dozen guests and I was seated next to Mr. Ki Fung, the then Deputy Director of the New China News Agency in Hong Kong. After a few drinks I could not resist asking Mr. Ki why China was being so unhelpful over supplying more water to Hong Kong.

Mr. Ki reacted with bewilderment and asked what I was talking about. I then told him about the proposal to construct a reverse osmosis plant at Shatin being justified on the grounds that China had refused to make more water available.

Mr. Ki expressed amazement. He assured me that no request for additional water had been received and added that if such a request were to be made, it would be dealt with very sympathetically.

When I returned to my office the next morning, I wrote a confidential minute to the Governor, Sir Murray MacLehose, later Lord MacLehose, recording my conversation with Mr. Ki. The minute was routed via the then Political Advisor, Dr. David Wilson, later Governor and now Lord Wilson. I received no reply or acknowledgement from either. What did happen, however, was that the reverse osmosis project was dropped and a fresh agreement was reached with the Chinese over increasing water supplies.

Politics is a funny old game. I fear I have never fully understood how it ought to be played. Over the years I have occasionally wondered what might have happened if chance had not led me to a dinner party and convivial company had not spurred me into an unauthorized initiative in international diplomacy. Would Hong Kong be saddled today with an expensive plant that it has happily done without ever since?

As a former Hong Kong civil servant, I should like to add one final observation. Nowadays it has become fashionable in certain quarters to denigrate Chinese officers who had served the British Crown and to dismiss them as "puppets" or "running dogs". It should be remembered that during colonial rule the official British position was that, pending a political settlement, the territory would be run in trust for the benefit of the local inhabitants. Reality might at times have fallen short of that commitment but many Chinese served the British Crown on that basis and discharged their duties in that light, so far as circumstances permitted.

David T. K. Wong
London, 2003